Shades of Aether

GAIL B WILLIAMS

Published by HanWill Publishing

This is a work of fiction. Names, descriptions, entities, and incidents included in this collection are the product of the author's imagination. Any resemblance to actual persons, events, and entities is entirely coincidental.

Cover Art by Deranged Doctor Design

ISBN 978-0-9573439-2-4

To the dreamers and believers

Chapter 1

Maker clenched his hands at his side. He had been about to knock the door of number seven, his neighbour's door, but Edwards, Professor Richards' gentleman's gentleman, had pulled the door open before he could take the two steps from pavement to porch.

"Lord Fotheringham."

This time it was Maker's jaw that clenched. He wasn't impressed by his own aristocracy and sometimes, like now, being reminded he was the fifth Earl of Umbria was more weight than he wanted to carry. But saying so was just wasted breath.

Edwards stepped back. Not breaking his stride, Maker stepped in and the man closed the door before melting away. Not that Maker cared, his attention was caught by the young woman who was side on to him, by the consol table on the left of the wide hallway. She was dressed in a black gown with purple stripes, the skirt held wide by a hooped petticoat. He could see from where he stood that the gown's hem was fraying, some of the ribbons were loose and a seam or two were giving way. She wore the most disgusting brooch he had ever had the misfortune to see, boxy with thin brass tubing, oversized and utterly out of place, it weighed so much it was pulling at the fabric of her dress, like an anvil on a bed of daisies. Her pale skin was rainbow-coloured from the ever-moving aetheric light over which she was lowering some kind of lampshade. As the shade covered the light source, the light became a steady blue-white. The girl smiled, apparently pleased with the result.

"How?" The word escaped him in his surprise. Aetheric light was readily available, but the colour tones made it less popular than gaslight. The colour problem was why gas pervaded and no solution had been found - until now, apparently.

"Prismatic glass," the girl explained as she faced him. "I'm not convinced it will make aetheric lighting more economical than gas, or safer, but at least the single colour makes it more bearable." Her direct gaze travelled from his eyes to his tie pin and back.

"Amethyst."

Maker forced his gaze to stay on the young lady's eyes as he offered her the stiff respect of a small bow. He didn't need to check the jewel nestled in his perfectly tied cravat to know what stone it was. "Emerald," he corrected.

"No. My sister is Emerald. Your tie pin is emerald, as are your eyes, but I am Amethyst." There was an amused twinkle in her expression that belied the plain nature of her features as she reached for and donned the simple black gentleman's top hat that rested beside the lamp. "But I believe you were looking for Professor Richards, he's in his study."

The young lady raised a gloved hand in the general direction of the room before offering an elegant curtsey and sweeping out of the Belgravia mansion.

Unsure how to categorise the encounter, or understand why his heart was beating quite so quickly, Maker watched the lady's departure.

"Interesting girl, that one."

Too interesting. Maker controlled his features and turned towards the study. His friend and mentor was at the door, the crooked smile the old man wore suggesting a number of things best not considered.

"Indeed." Maker offered another bow in greeting, thinking that a top hat was as peculiar a finish for a female as that ugly brooch.

"Oh relax, boy," the older man said, "no need for such formality between friends. Come in, come in."

The leather soles of Maker's boots clipped across the black and white marble of the foyer as he followed his friend, the note of his footfalls changing as he entered the study. Most of the wood panelling of the room had been hidden by bookshelves. Professor Richards had been an avid reader from the moment he learned how to do it, and an academic life had done nothing to decrease that pleasure. He lived for books. The shelves were full and the two desks in the room were covered with books that lay open, note pads and loose sheets covered in the old man's now shaky handwriting were spread over, between, beneath and around, some had even fallen to the floor.

Maker's hands curled into tight fists behind his back; the mess made his skin crawl. How could any man work in such disarray? His own inclination was to a tidiness some called obsessive, others perverse; he considered it natural and useful. He knew where everything was and could quickly find whatever he wanted or needed. It was one of the few things about him of which his father approved.

"So, to what do I owe the pleasure of this unexpected visit?"

"Message." With the word, Maker produced a small vellum envelope. It had arrived at his door only two hours previously and he had responded precisely at the time on the invitation.

The Professor momentarily clenched, then casually reached out and took back the short note he had sent his friend. "Of course." He flicked the note to his left; Maker blinked at the accuracy of it landing in the fire. "Now let's forget about that, shall we?"

Marker watched white blacken and curl. It wasn't a roaring fire, but it was enough. So the Professor was hiding something. He turned back to the older man to try to decipher what it was.

Richards had returned to his desk chair; the clattering told Maker that the Professor had again not concerned himself with his own sense of being or the physical world. He had obviously missed the chair seat and had to readjust, focus to sit safely. Maker took one step towards the desk, the professor was almost hidden by the mound of books, his half-moon glasses perched precariously on his forehead; almost as precariously as the gas lamp on the corner. Maker knew it was only his height that allowed him to see the man at all. The wire rims before his wide eyes, and the sharp nose they rested on, made the Professor look like a myopic hawk.

As Maker concentrated on the Professor, his glance must have been too sharp; for a moment, the Professor flinched beneath it. They both turned to the study door at the unexpected light knock.

Amethyst came into the room as she spoke. "Sorry, Professor, I forgot the bag." Following her gaze and direction, Maker saw a battered brown leather bag. Something vaguely square but oddly lumpy. The construction was perhaps eighteen by twelve inches. The leather was being pushed out of shape, age had softened the material and it was forgiving of the strange lumps and bumps beneath.

"Of course, my dear." The Professor stood as she picked up the bag.

It made an odd clunking sound. Metal on metal. Tools striking together?

"Miss Amethyst Forester." The Professor raised a hand to her before sweeping it in Maker's direction. "Lord Fotheringham."

She offered Maker another curtsey, and he responded with a bow.

"Pleasure to make your acquaintance, Lord Fotheringham."

Before Maker could respond, there was another knock at the door, then Edwards stepped in.

"Professor, there's a gentleman here to see you. Mr Brown."

Maker noticed how Richards paled at the name, but the old man quickly rallied. Brown walked in without invitation. He glanced at Maker and Amethyst, then turned a neutral expression on Richards. Maker knew a poker face when he saw one and this one would have lost money at every gentleman's club in the City, if it had ever been admitted in the first place. He also knew Richards well enough to see the increased tension in his friend.

"Were you not," Richards said, turning to Maker, "about to take our friend to the exhibition?"

"Exhibition?"

Maker was a little surprised that the rough demand was Mr Brown's and not his own.

"Paintings," Amethyst said with a smile. She also stepped forward, walking between Brown and Richards as she reached for Maker's arm, appearing to nestle her hand in the crook of his arm, when in fact she was grabbing hold to guide him out. "The Royal Academy," she explained, "just opened a new exhibition, I've been looking forward to it immensely."

One look at Richards' ostensibly convivial face, the feel of Amethyst's tight grip, and Maker knew he needed to comply. For now. As he left the room and the building and strolled, oh so casually along the road, he decided he would wait no longer for an explanation.

"Paintings?"

"Yes."

Neither of them looked at the other as they walked.

"We," Amethyst told him quietly, "are to paint a picture of friends carelessly walking away from another friend's home, to appear as if all is well and normal and nothing strange or sinister is going on."

"Indeed?"

"Yes."

Maker felt the muscles in his jaw clamping. *Women are infuriating.*

"Explain," he demanded under his breath as they strolled across the wide road, careful to avoid the still steaming gift a passing horse had left behind.

She made no response until she had led him into the leafy shade of Belgravia Square Gardens. Only once they were along the path, shielded by the trees from the road, did she stop and turn to face him. "I can't really, I don't exactly know."

But she looked worried. Scrutinising her face, Maker could see Amethyst wasn't trying to hide anything.

"Explain."

Her brows rose at the imperious demand. Maker

had been told he was too short with people, but it was simply his manner, no offence was intended.

"What I mean, sir," she said, her tone frosty, "is that I know something is unsettling Professor Richards, but I know not what. Good day, sir."

If the tone hadn't stated so loudly that he'd upset her, the curt dismissal would have. Her corset clearly wasn't the only thing keeping her spine ramrod straight. As she walked, the thing in her bag clanked again; it was clearly quite heavy. Forcing his jaw to unclench, he moved after the young brunette.

"Miss-" He cut himself off, she had only given him her Christian name but it was too familiar to use that on so short an acquaintance. He couldn't remember what Richards had called her.

She turned to face him. Challenging him. Clearly, her silence would prove equally unforthcoming. A few minutes of knowing her and already he was primed to grind his teeth.

"Lord Fotheringham, was there something you wanted or may I be on my way?"

He was a good foot taller than her, but Maker got the distinct impression she was looking down her nose at him. Not that the nose was overly pretty, nor especially little. She was still looking down it.

"Heading?"

Her brows lowered, his curt tone not impressing her.

"Kew."

Now his brows rose; Kew Gardens was more than seven, possibly eight miles away. It was a minimum two hour walk. She shifted the bag again.

"Sir, I have a long walk ahead, if you've no

purpose-"

He saw movement on the road, just what he didn't need. "Hack."

"I beg your pardon!"

Amethyst looked insulted. He reached for her bag but she pulled her arm back and away, out of his reach.

"Cab."

"I can't afford a cab."

"I can," he grated. Unfortunately, Miss Forester wasn't easily moved; she resisted.

"Maker?"

The imperious call came from behind and his spine stiffened with ice. It was too late to avoid a confrontation now. Dragging in a deep breath, he drew himself up to his full six feet two inch height, then turned to the woman who had called his name. Lady Fotheringham. His *wife*. He tried not to sneer that thought, even in his head. Controlling the thought controlled his expression.

The tall cool blonde was delicate of feature, and fashionable of dress. Her hat always matched her gown, her bag was small and delicate. She was not impressed by the woman at his side, a fact made clear by the way her glacial look pored over Amethyst. Maker didn't move, but his instincts were on alert, his body tense, defence mode fully engaged. He faced the blonde, devoid of expression.

"Well?" Lady Fotheringham demanded.

The imperious tone was no surprise to Maker, but he got the distinct impression that Amethyst was bristling. Maker turned slightly.

"Miss Forester." He noted her slightly raised brows that he had finally remembered her name. "My wife."

Amethyst offered a slight inclination of the head. "Honour to meet you, Lady Fotheringham."

Violet did not look impressed; instead she scowled at her husband. "You have a position at Parliament, a debate you need to attend. You don't have time to-" Her frosty blue eyes raked over Amethyst again. "-waste."

He had not forgotten about the debate. What he had forgotten was that he had told Violet he had to be there two hours before he actually did, just to have more time out of the house.

"Well, I have no wish to hold anyone up."

Amethyst's tone was even, but he could see the hardness in her eyes. Violet had wished to insult and she clearly had.

"It was interesting to meet you." This time Amethyst offered a less than perfect curtsey before turning away.

"Let's hope we don't have to repeat the experience."

Violet's stage whisper was meant to carry and the trip in her step told him Amethyst heard it too.

Maker turned to his wife. "Inside." Taking her by the arm, he spurred her towards their house. He stopped listening to her complaints two steps on.

Chapter 2

Amethyst knew she shouldn't be shocked that Lord Fotheringham was married, particularly not to a woman who matched him for looks, breeding and elegance. Though she was surprised that he was married to a woman who appeared to outstrip him completely in coldness. She was amazed that was even possible. The pair of them were as perfect as carved white marble.

As quick as her anger had been to rise, it dissipated. She was beyond Belgravia Square, but there were still miles to go and her arm was already aching from carrying the bag. Unsure what was even in it, or why the Professor had wanted her to take it home, she shifted the weight to the other hand. That didn't help much, it just meant that she ended up leaning slightly in the opposite direction. Which, in a tightly laced corset, was still not comfortable. It was a long walk home; she knew from experience it would take her over two hours, and carrying this load would only increase that. As the man said, she should have taken a cab. As she'd said, she couldn't afford it. She trudged on.

"Miss!"

Amethyst kept going, her mind ticking off things she had to do when she got home.

"Miss!"

Someone really should answer the man. If she was lucky, her sisters would have done a lot of the chores, but she'd still have to put her mind to finishing the overskirt for Sapphire's new gown.

A vice clamped her arm.

Instinctively she turned, swinging the heavy bag. It

hit with a satisfying thud and the man near doubled over, grunting in pain. The grip around her arm, if anything, got tighter. Pulling away didn't work, so she hefted the bag to swing again, and her glare met cold emerald eyes. She froze.

"Lord Fotheringham!" Oh dear Lord, she'd just hit a peer of the realm. Her face washed with the shame of it. "I'm so sorry. You shouldn't have grabbed me without warning. What are you doing here?"

"Cab."

Amethyst looked at the small cab. The unmarked black vehicle was two-wheeled and originally designed to be horse-drawn, but the horse this time was of the aetheric persuasion; the driver still sat in the elevated rear seat, but the reins were gone, replaced by levers. Brightly polished brass pipes eased like octopus arms around the cab to the large black-painted engine that seemed to sparkle with the intensity of the energy it harnessed. On either side, the axle ran wide to allow the turning of the wheels the engine drove to move the cab along. Where she expected to see an exhaust flue was a wide, oblong profile pipe, roughly two by four inches, that ran back down under the cab to the rear, where it split in two before the driver's seat, allowing steam to rise behind the man. She looked back to Fotheringham; he was standing tall again, but his lips were a straight thin line. He looked like he was regretting his actions already.

This made no sense. She frowned up at him. "But I'm heading for Kew, aren't you for Westminster?"

"In."

The word was cold and uncompromising. Her feet were already sore and the bag weighed heavily. As did his gaze. His hold, which was already guiding her towards the cab, was equally unyielding. Since it seemed she had little choice, she acquiesced.

His grip loosened as she reached for the cab. She took an awkward moment to try to work out how she was going to hold the door frame, the bag and lift her petticoats not to step on them and trip like an idiot. She was a hand short. Suddenly the burden of the bag was lifted from her. She turned her head to nod her thanks to her companion and stepped up, sliding along the bench seat to sit at the far side and pulling her skirts in to make room for him. He passed up the bag once she was settled, and she pulled it to her side, to give him room to step in. As soon as he was seated, the cab gave a small lurch and they were off.

Joining the flow of traffic was easy and matching the pace of the other cabs gave the engine no trouble. Amethyst didn't travel by cab often, and never before in one with an aetheric engine, so she allowed herself a moment to enjoy the pleasure.

"It's surprisingly warm in here."

"Pipes."

She frowned and turned to her companion. "Sorry Lord Fortheringham, did you say something?"

Now he turned fully to her and she had the distinct impression he was scrutinising her as one might scrutinise samples under a microscope. "Pipes." He pointed to the brass entwined around the cab.

She looked at the exhaust. Of course. The pipes that ran from the driver to the engine would transfer power and steam and therefore heat. By wrapping the pipes around the cab, the occupant was cocooned in warmth. Amethyst suspected the cabbie was better off too, if to a lesser extent, still being exposed to the elements.

She looked around her and realised that their route had not changed. "We're still heading west."

"Indeed."

The tone told her nothing, so she turned to the man beside her. He looked resolutely ahead.

Even his profile belongs to a Greek God.

Amethyst pushed the thought away.

"Westminster is to the East."

"True."

She tried to hold back the rising tide of irritation. "Then why are we heading west?"

He looked at her and one brow raised. It was both enquiry and dare.

A slight frown bobbed on and off her forehead. "Why are you taking me home first? Don't you have a debate to attend?"

"Later."

"How much later?"

"Two hours." He drew a breath as if irritated that she'd forced him to say more than one word at a time. "Contents?" He pointed one long figure at the bag at her foot.

She shrugged. "Uncertain." Two could play the one word game.

For a moment she returned his gaze with a haughty one of her own. But his lack of reaction, then that one brow raise was her undoing.

"I don't exactly know what's in the bag," she relented. "Professor Richards asked me to take it home with me. For a few days. He said he'd let me know when he wanted it back."

"Odd."

"The Professor is." She smiled. "Hadn't you noticed?"

His eyes moved momentarily from her eyes to her mouth. An odd new sensation tightened her belly. She noted a muscle twitch by the side of his mouth that just might have been a smile. Of course he had noticed the Professor's eccentricities, they were hard to miss.

She dreaded to think what he'd seen when looking at her. Her dress had once been of the good quality, but she'd had it so long that the wear was becoming obvious. She should consider new ribbons, a little wider this time to cover the old and hide the separating seams. Thankfully, her black ankle boots were hidden by the fraying hem of her gown, but they were well worn, the soles so thin they offered little protection. Both shoes and hem were dusty from the streets. She wore no jewellery, only the brooch the Professor had insisted she take from him this morning, insisted she wear at all times. Rather gaudy and large for her tastes, this lord was bound to see it at as cheap and nasty, like her, probably.

Glumly, she looked down to her hands. No rings. A number of tiny scars from her tinkering. Nails bitten to the quick. She tugged the cuffs of her dress down and crossed her hands to best cover their ugliness. Being beside her was a huge step down for a peer. Clasping her fingers tighter, she took a breath and turned to her neighbour.

"Lord Fotheringham-"

"Maker."

That cut her off, whatever she was going to say flew out of her mind. "Sorry?"

His jaw clenched as he looked at her. "Maker."

"Your friends call you Maker?"

"Yes."

A nervous laugh escaped her. He really doesn't like using more than one word at a time. "So what should I call you?"

As far as she could tell he didn't move a muscle, but she got the distinct impression of chastisement.

"Very well then, Maker, I'm worried about the Professor, have you noticed anything?"

He was considering. She considered him. He was an intelligent man, in all probability he'd noticed many things. It was hard to ignore the fact that the Professor had been tense, jittery, paranoid, and totally evasive when challenged.

"No."

She looked at him askew. She would not be so easily diverted, but perhaps now was not the time.

"Why are you taking me so far out of your way?"

His look was neutral and unmoved.

Her brow tightened as she considered him. "You told your wife that you had to be at Parliament earlier than you really do. You're wasting time by taking me to Kew when you could be heading to Westminster, I'm sure you have fellows there you could spend time with. So either it's a really boring debate or you're really keen not to spend time with your wife." Something she could understand, she wasn't keen on the idea of ever spending time again with his wife.

Looking him in the eye, she tried to read his reaction, but his face was a blank mask, no more readable than if he were carved of stone.

"You know, it's your life, your choice. Thank you for the lift home."

Settling back in the cab, Amethyst considered where the warmest parts of the seat were. Her hands, as usual, were cold. She put one on the rolled wood at the edge of the cab, feeling the heat from the pipe beneath the curve. Her other hand moved to the padded seat. The thick leather was warm from the exhaust beneath. Her hand moved forward and back, her palm running over the warming material, her skirt rustling as she moved the fabric.

Warmth clapped over the top of her hand, freezing it in place and boiling her blood in an instant. She snapped to look - Maker's hand was clamped over hers: No blemishes on his hand. She realised in the close confines of the cab, her little finger had been running along his thigh. She looked up into those cold emerald eyes.

"My- my-" She swallowed the inexplicable lump in her throat. "My hand was cold."

"Is."

He turned his face forward, watching the road, but his hand remained over hers, warming her. Pulling her bottom lip between her teeth, Amethyst looked out the other way, trying not to react. She didn't want to seem like some kind of gauche bumpkin, but she wasn't sure what she should do. She decided if it was acceptable to a lord, it was acceptable to her.

The miles flashed by and all too soon the edge of Kew Gardens appeared. The warming presence eased from her hand and she turned to find Maker looking at her, that enquiring eyebrow up.

She frowned.

"Address?"

"Oh!" Of course, stupid of her not to think of it. She

turned to the small flap that allowed communication with the driver.

"Seventeen Lawn Crescent."

"Yes, ma'am."

It was a couple of streets back from the greenery of the garden, but they were soon stopping in front of her home. The three storey brick building was only a few years old, built when the railway arrived at the end of the 1860s. The family were the only ones to have ever lived there. It had never before felt like something she should be embarrassed by, but Maker's blank expression suggested that it was less than acceptable to him. Given his peerage, it probably was, but it was her home and he wasn't going to make her ashamed of it.

Maker stepped out first, and reached back to take the heavy bag and offer his hand to help her from the cab. She wasn't sure why she was suddenly reluctant to touch him again. But she pushed forward and took that hand. The connection felt like the time she'd stupidly put her fingers on both ends of an aetheric power source - yet this was much more pleasurable. And her hair wasn't about to burn or crackle.

"Thank you," she breathed as she took the bag. Behind Maker, she spotted her father looking out of the window of his study. All things considered, she didn't want Maker meeting her father, there would be far too many questions to answer as it was.

She curtseyed to Maker again, thanked him more thoroughly, took the bag and stepped to go around him, pausing only to say, "Good luck with your debate."

Even as she left him, Amethyst bit her lip. She wasn't sure if the sensation in her stomach meant she never wanted to see him again, or was desperate to do so, soon.

Chapter 3

Looking at the heavens, Maker was grateful for a clear blue sky where a few high clouds scudded with only the occasional disturbance from the handful of intercity airships that ran on a Sunday and docked in Hyde Park. As ever, there were rows of people around the docking pylons, the simple nature of their dress revealing their lower social status. He so envied them.

He would love to have been the kind of child who had been allowed to stand in the park gawping for hours at the technological marvel that brought people from Birmingham and Newcastle, Glasgow and Edinburgh, all the way to London and in less time than the train. He found his father's and grandfather's stories of days-long carriage rides and stays in coaching inns really rather quaint.

As a child, his boundaries had been restricted by his mother, now his life was restricted by his wife. He didn't enjoy riding with his back to the direction of travel, but Violet would not travel that way and her constant complaining when forced to do so was too much to be borne on such a beautiful day. So he let her have what she wanted to keep her happy, to keep her quiet. A part of him knew this was a fool's errand, but it was simply safer this way.

The fresh air and open view offered by the Barouche was as welcome as the panorama, though being *viewed* was more the reason that the open-topped carriage had been called for today. He looked across at his wife, her bored smile beneath her perfectly set curls, the silk hat, the latest fashion of course. Even after fifteen years of marriage, he could still accept that she was the most perfect looking woman. Delicate, evenly balanced features; perfectly smooth alabaster skin; long elegant fingers; graceful aristocratic posture; naturally slim frame. She was as perfect as a picture.

As was the girl next to her. A petite redhead, easily impressed and controlled. She offered him a small, almost apologetic smile, a small nod was his only response. They both knew where they stood.

He took a deep breath and let it out carefully. A mouse was better than a clawing cat. His eyes slid back to Violet. She was smiling at others like them, those out to enjoy a ride in Hyde Park. The brilliance of her smile would notch up when she caught the eye of someone of wealth or influence. She must have felt his look, as when she turned his way the smile remained on her lips, though her eyes were cold. "Your hat isn't straight."

His hand rose, tipped the brim slightly to the left. Now it didn't feel comfortable, but it was nothing he couldn't deal with.

"Will you be seeing the Professor this afternoon?"

He glanced from his wife to her friend. At least she had the good grace to look away. "Hopefully."

"And this evening? You'll be at the club?"

He hadn't planned on it. "Apparently."

She turned away in supposed innocence, turning to confide in the redhead. "All gentlemen enjoy time away at their clubs," she said softly. "Still, it gives us ladies relief from their demands."

Demands, he fumed, clamping his jaw and looking back to the airship pylons. He hadn't demanded anything of her in years. The mere thought made him shudder.

"Oh look."

It was the sneer in her voice more than the words that made him turn.

"It's the latest piece for the menagerie." Violet didn't smile, she was looking very hard at the subject of her scorn.

He twisted and saw any number of people. Were it not for the unusual sight of a woman in a top hat, he would never have known who Violet meant. Miss Forester was walking in the same direction they were travelling. The dress she wore was the same black striped with deep purple as last Monday. The only difference he could see today was that she had added a purple silk bow to the top hat. She had a surprisingly long stride, something he'd noticed last week; he hadn't needed to modify his own step to hers when they had left the Professor's house.

As they drew closer, Violet instructed their driver to draw up beside the lady.

"I am sure Lord Fotheringham would like to speak with his newest little friend."

Only Violet could manage to say something so considerate with such venom. Without a word, the driver complied.

Amethyst. Society would dictate he think of her only as Miss Forester, yet somehow he couldn't. Her initial invitation had been to call her by her first name and that was how he would always think of her. Whatever Society might say, whatever he might say.

Amethyst was walking at the side of the sand-covered track, minding her own business. Naturally, she knew when the carriage came to her side, matching her speed. She looked up and he saw her eyes were shaded by round purple glasses. Her brows rose as she focused on him.

"Lord Fotheringham."

"Miss Forester." Etiquette dictated that he at least incline his head towards her, but to do so now would cause his own hat to fall and that would never do.

He watched Amethyst turn to look at his wife. She smiled, but Maker had the feeling she wasn't that happy; she stopped to offer a small curtsey. "Lady Fotheringham."

"Miss Forester. How lovely to see you again."

There was little he distrusted more than his wife being congenial to another woman. His surprise was covered by the carriage coming to a halt and knocking his damn hat. The way Violet's eyes flicked to him, he automatically righted the brim.

"Err-" Amethyst glanced at him, her look uncertain, but there was no way he could help her as she turned back to Violet, "-and you. Fine day, is it not?"

"Indeed, and do you go somewhere special this fine day?"

Maker suspected the pause was while Amethyst considered lying. "To see a good friend." Miss Forester smiled. "But don't let me keep you from yours." This time she inclined her head towards the redhead.

"Would the friend you mention be Professor Richards by any chance?"

This time Maker saw the forced stretch of Amethyst's smile. "Indeed."

"Then may we offer you a ride?"

This time it was Maker's turn to look hard at his wife. Scowling wouldn't work, so he didn't bother. He let the weight of his gaze alone bear the message.

Violet's eyes flicked to his; she understood, but she wasn't to be dissuaded.

"I wouldn't want to intrude."

"Oh it wouldn't be an intrusion, we were just heading home and my dear Maker," - who didn't like the way her eyes glittered like shards of ice when they touched on his - "is intending to see the Professor this afternoon, you may as well go together."

He could see that Amethyst was about to find some other objection, but experience had taught him that compliance was the best option. He stood and opened the carriage door, jumping to the ground to pull down the steps for Miss Forester.

"In," he said as he straightened.

Her eyes narrowed, her lips compressed, but before she could do or say anything, he took hold of her upper arm and guided her into the carriage. She shook him off and for a moment he feared she would make a scene. Not that he wasn't used to women who made a scene, but he never enjoyed them. Thankfully, she reached down to hold the material of her skirts clear as she stepped up. The hoop of her skirt made things awkward, but when was fashion ever about practicality? Once she was settled, he stepped up behind her and sat in the only place left, beside her. He crossed his hands with a deceptively casual air. Glancing across, he saw that Miss Forester's hands were tightly gripped in her own lap. Was she too thinking of what should not have happened in the cab?

"Miss Forester."

Maker tensed as Violet spoke.

"Since my husband seems to have forgotten his manners, allow me to introduce my dear friend, Lady

Timpson. Maria, this is Miss Forester, a friend of a friend."

Violet couldn't have made her disdain much more obvious, yet both ladies managed the cordial greeting good manners required.

"A crinoline," Lady Timpson said, looking at the skirt. "So last season."

Maker could feel Amethyst bristling, but she said nothing. Good. Then she turned to Violet as the carriage began to move.

"Thank you for the ride."

Her words were as tight and grim as his wife's returning smile.

"Interesting brooch," Violet observed. Her look to Timpson was skewed, and the other lady elegantly 'hid' a snigger behind her hand.

As horrified as he was that Amethyst still wore that hideous thing, it was unfair of Violet to pick up on it.

"It was a gift," Amethyst stated flatly.

Maker held his tongue as his wife and her friend discussed fashion, for the greater part excluding Amethyst. Thankfully the younger woman didn't seem concerned. Then something caught her eye. For a moment, her glance switched to him.

"Do you know what that is?"

He looked across to what held her attention. There on the edge of the park was a podium on which a man stood with what had to be an aetheric engine and a plush chair, but it was difficult to see what the machine was for. The man on the podium was clearly the salesman, something of a jack-o-lantern, tall and slim in a terrible red suit that reached neither his wrists nor his ankles. He was too far away to be heard, but a small crowd was gathering. As they watched, the man drew a lady from the audience.

"No," Maker absently answered the question as the lady was helped into the chair.

Their route was veering slightly away from the spectacle and Amethyst had leant towards him to get a better view. The scent of warm lavender came with her. It wasn't a scent Maker would have associated with attraction, but that was what hit him. He glanced at her; she was completely absorbed in watching the lady in the chair. He could see the pulse in her neck, her skin was smooth, unblemished and slightly golden, obviously from the amount of walking she did. Some hair had escaped her bun and a tendril curled wantonly from behind her ear to flatter the line of her neck. Her eyes glittered with intelligence and curiosity. Her unpainted lips were slightly parted. He wanted to –

Swallowing, he moved his eye back to the engine. The lady settled, the salesman returned to the engine, said something to the crowd, then pushed a lever. The lady jumped, a laugh, nervous and uncertain rose from the gathering, then the lady settled back more calmly, and as they watched, there were vibrations and a distinct calming from the lady.

The carriage moved on and the spectacle was behind them. For a moment Amethyst looked over the back of the carriage, but she quickly turned, realising the social faux pas.

"What do you think that was?" she asked Maker.

He wanted to say it was an aberration, but even looking at her now he still wanted to kiss her. He hadn't wanted to kiss any woman this much since the first time he'd seen Violet. He'd assumed her reticence was maidenly coquettishness. His glance touched no more than Lady Timpson's hem. He knew better now.

"Do you know Morgan Flischer at all?"

Maker looked at his wife, doing his best to maintain a neutral expression, for all the censure his instincts put on the moment.

"Erm, no," Amethyst said, suddenly realising that lady Fotheringham was addressing her. "I haven't had the pleasure of that introduction."

Lady Timpson giggled behind her hand and looked to Violet, who smiled as if she'd just won a point. Maker's glance went to Amethyst's curious and suddenly wary look. He'd help her if he could, but experience told him he'd pay later and from what he'd seen of Amethyst so far, she was perfectly capable of defending herself. His hip was still bruised.

"Morgan Flischer," said Violet, using her most condescending tone, ice hard, "is milliner to the Queen herself."

"Good for him."

Maker sucked the air from his own mouth to keep from reacting, for all he wanted to cheer. Violet looked affronted.

"We were in the shop just yesterday," Lady Timpson advised. "Princess Beatrice herself was there."

"How nice," Amethyst returned.

Maker tried not to be proud of Amethyst as she faced the other two ladies so evenly.

"The Princess is such a sweet girl," Lady Timpson said most wistfully.

"Indeed," Violet agreed, her look to Amethyst somewhat less sweet. "Of course we have the good fortune of introductions to High Society."

"Indeed you have." Amethyst smiled easily in return.

Maker suddenly worried about the amusement he saw in her eyes.

"But then I've had the good fortune of an education and vivid imagination, I'll never be bored and rarely lonely. I've no need to rely on family, friends or a fortuitous marriage to survive in the world. Probably just as well, really."

And that easily, she robbed Violet of her barb. Violet's response was to go quiet. Violet going quiet was usually a precursor to trouble. That Amethyst turned to Maker was equally portentous. He prayed she wouldn't speak, wouldn't ask him anything, but that, it seemed, was a wish too far.

"How went your debate?"

There was no need to ask which debate she referred to and no way to ignore that Violet's flat-lipped look promised payment would be exacted later. He took the risk of meeting Amethyst's gaze for barely a moment as he answered.

"Well." Chin up, he turned his head away, choosing to gaze out of the side of the carriage and take no further part in the conversation as they moved through the streets towards Belgravia. Not that there *was* any further discussion. Hearing no more, he risked a sideways glance. Apparently all three women had taken their lead from him and were watching the passing urban landscape to avoid social intercourse.

Maker felt the strain in every muscle of his back as the carriage finally turned into Belgravia Square and drew to a gentle halt before number 30. Usually he would allow the driver to step down and open the carriage door, but now he moved immediately to the side and opened the door, jumped to the path, lowered the steps and offered his hand for Violet to step out. She took the offered assistance for propriety's sake, and he gritted his teeth as her nails dug through his kid leather glove. Her look was withering, but he held himself upright through it, untouched. His next offer was to Lady Timpson, who because of her shorter stature, needed a little more assistance to take the last step. Before he had time to turn back, Amethyst was already springing back from a light jump from the carriage.

"Well, thank you for saving me the walk." She smiled easily towards Violet.

Maker found himself tensing, waiting for the barb.

"I appreciate the consideration. Now, I'll leave you to get on with your day in peace, Lady Fotheringham." She offered a small curtsey. "Lady Timpson." Her farewell was more of a head bob. "Lord Fotheringham."

Apparently he didn't warrant even that minimal acknowledgement and she turned away, heading across the Square.

"Well!"

Maker felt every nerve stretch at Violet's sour word.

"What a terribly uncouth child."

"Beats downright rude." Maker's long stride was carrying him across the road before Violet's temper could explode. All he was doing was delaying the reaction, but she could sit and stew for a few hours. It was his habit to visit Professor Richards on Sunday after their taking of the air, and now was as good a time as any. Perhaps by some miracle, the ministrations of the diminutive Lady Timpson would soothe the savagery of his wife's tongue, but he had learned not to hope for too much.

Under the cool shade of the trees in the Square, Maker felt he could breathe again; his shoulders were the first parts of him to relax. He could see Amethyst in front of him. For a split second he considered calling her name, but that could carry to Violet, a prospect not worth considering. Still, they were both destined for the same place. As Amethyst reached the central flower beds, he was surprised to see her stop. For a moment she stilled, then knelt towards the bush there, a dog rose of sweet pink bloom and sweeter aroma. She was gently stroking a single bloom.

"I do love the simplicity of a dog rose," she said as he stopped at her side. "I am surprised to find them here though."

For the first time in a long time, Maker felt he was free to use more than a single word, but for the first time ever he didn't trust himself to speak at all. Instead, all he could do was reach out and take the bloom from the bush and place its short stem into her hair, at the side of the bun beneath her hat.

"Thank you."

She laughed. "Shouldn't I be saying that?"

For a moment she looked up and he felt that gut-wrenching urge again.

"Besides, what have you to thank me for? It was all I could do not to insult your wife and guest. As it is I fear I was rude." She sighed. "But I did promise the Professor I'd visit today, so…"

He raised a hand for her to proceed and she did. It was unusual and surprisingly relaxing to walk alone with a woman who would neither condemn nor praise him, who wanted nothing from him, possibly not even his company.

At number seven, Edwards opened the door before they could knock and allowed them in. He offered to take Maker's hat.

"I'm afraid Professor Richards isn't down yet, sir."

It wasn't unusual for the Professor to work late into the night and then sleep through the day. Maker nodded.

"Thank you, Edwards." Amethyst smiled as she removed her own hat and passed it across. "If you could arrange tea to be served in the study, I'm sure we can amuse ourselves for a while as you rouse the Professor."

Edwards answered with a small obedient bow and Maker followed the young woman as she thanked the butler and headed towards the study.

Her stop was so sudden he was unable to avoid stepping on her hem and bumping into her. The sound was small, but he distinctly heard a seam rip.

"He looks... erm."

"Yes." Maker fully understood her inability to articulate a reaction to the slumped form of the Professor in his desk chair.

"Dead."

Chapter 4

"He didn't just die!"

Amethyst paced the floor and railed at the uniformed officer who listened politely, but she wasn't stupid and she wasn't blind. There wasn't much room for pacing. Even in here, the Professor had crammed the floor space with bits and pieces of anything and everything. There were more heaps of books, the furniture was tight about the fireplace to allow for the stacks behind. Still the need for movement was too great, she had to pace, so she did the best she could.

It didn't take the keen eye of a hawk to see that the young constable was looking for support from the other men in the room. Maker had taken on statue-form again; cold, distant and emotionless. He stood rigid and upright by the fireplace, his hands clasped behind his back. His face blank. Edwards stood by the door, another frozen statue of a man. Why wouldn't they support her statements? Surely they knew she was telling the truth.

She turned to glare at the young uniformed officer as a knock at the front door was heard. Edwards moved out of the room.

The officer swallowed, his prominent Adam's apple bobbing in a way Amethyst was not in the mood to find comical.

"The, er, Professor was, well, an older gentleman."

Amethyst scowled. "He was only fifty-nine and in perfect health."

"Apparently not."

Amethyst turned to the doorway and saw a

gentleman entering. He was taller than her, but not as tall as Maker. Slim as a whippet, he still looked strong. Under his bowler hat was grey hair and a serious face, with a serious moustache. His starched collar was high and white, a black tie was neatly tied and disappeared under his waistcoat and matched jacket in slate grey. Just to check, she glanced at his shoes. Yes, highly polished black boots.

"Inspector Jenson." The young officer sounded relieved.

The Inspector nodded to the man. "Constable MacReady, can you bring me up to date on this matter?"

"Professor Richards, the owner of the house, was found dead in his study. The young lady here-"

Amethyst gritted her teeth and narrowed her eyes at the way he said that, as if being female made her less rational than her male counterparts. Who were still being suspiciously quiet.

"-suggests that it was not, as the doctor states, natural causes."

"Because," the Inspector said, "he was only fifty-nine and in perfect health?"

Since the Inspector had turned his attention to her, Amethyst concentrated on him.

"Can you advise me who you are," he asked, "and what your connection to the dead man was?"

"I'm Amethyst Forester, a friend of the Professor's. Edwards is, was, his gentleman's gentleman. And Mr Stony Silent over there is Mr Benjamin Maker, Lord Fotheringham. Apparently he has an earldom somewhere in the north. He also lives on the opposite site of the Square and has been a friend of the

Professor's for some years."

"When you say you were his friend?" The Inspector left the question there.

Amethyst took a breath, her fists balling at her sides. "When I say I was his friend, I mean I was his friend. I met him in a library four years ago. I attended one of his lectures, and got ejected for not being a student. So he came looking for me and taught me in his own time."

"What did he teach you?"

"Engineering." She crossed her arms and glared at him. "Who taught you chauvinism?"

She realised the mistake of that by the way his chin went up and his eyes narrowed. She'd insulted him, which she'd meant to, but that wasn't the way to get him on side and she needed to get at least one of these men to believe her.

"I know the Professor and I know he wasn't sick. He didn't just die, someone killed him."

The Inspector didn't say anything, just watched her.

"You don't believe me, do you?"

The Inspector took his time to consider, drew in a breath and then he spoke. "Prove it."

Amethyst pulled in her own deep breath and tried not to be too insulted. It was best to try to be reasonable, and start from the beginning.

"I noticed that the Professor was acting oddly a few weeks ago. Well, more oddly than normal. He's always been a bit strange. He'd been tense, jumpy. He sent out invitations that he then denied. It's all been out of character."

The Inspector had maintained eye contact throughout her rationalising. Now he looked to

Edwards and then Maker. "Can either of you confirm this assessment?"

"Completely."

Amethyst was so surprised at Maker's confirmation, she had to turn to look at him. He was implacable as ever. She caught Edwards' eye, and shot him a questioning look. However, the Inspector was more commanding of Edwards' attention.

"I'd have to agree, Inspector. The Professor has never been the most conventional of men, and he can be a little absent-minded, but of late there has been increased tension, he's become more secretive."

"I see." The Inspector turned back to Amethyst. "Does the Professor have any next of kin?"

"No."

While entirely accurate, Maker's response was hardly answering the question.

"Not anymore," Amethyst offered. "He had a sister, and she a husband and a couple of children, but they died on an Atlantic crossing that went down." Something Maker would have known since he'd known the Professor when it had happened, though she hadn't.

The Inspector was watching her, every inch of him was serious. She hoped he was taking her seriously.

"Over how long a time has this change come about?"

Amethyst frowned. "I noticed the first hints about three, maybe four months ago."

The Inspector turned to Maker.

"It first came to my attention only two months ago, but Miss Forester is here more often than I am."

Amethyst turned to Edwards. "You're here more than any of us, Edwards, what would you say?"

She hadn't meant to make the man uncomfortable, but clearly she had.

"I, er," Edwards stammered. "It's not my place to say."

"Mr Edwards," the Inspector said carefully, "you will probably have the most intimate knowledge of the Professor of anyone here, and if Miss Forester is correct in her assertions, than your knowledge of the man could be crucial in telling us what happened."

"It started about seven months ago. Small things. Not that they ever became big things, but they became more frequent, and thereby more noticeable."

"Did anything else change around the same time, something which may indicate the source of the tension?"

Edwards stared straight ahead, not looking at anything or anyone, retaining the perfect composure of a discreet servant. "I'm not aware of anything, Inspector, but I'm his butler, he didn't have much of a social life, and most of what he talked about - his experimentations - made no sense to me."

The Inspector considered, then turned back to Amethyst. "I understand your position thus far, but a qualified doctor has indicated a natural death. I have to accept his word."

"Autopsy."

She didn't turn to look at Maker, but she privately thanked him. "Exactly, you have to take his word after a thorough examination of the body, what he did here was rather cursory. If you order an autopsy, he'll have to look closer."

"I agree."

Amethyst felt some of the tension flow out of her.

"But I need a reason to order an autopsy."

"Of course." Amethyst stepped forward and drew the Inspector out of the room with her, leading him to the study. She went as far as the precluded steps she'd taken when Maker had been behind her. "This is where Lord Fotheringham and I got to when we found the Professor. Take note of the lamp."

It was a heavy brass oil lamp. It had fallen on the floor, the glass had broken. Thankfully it hadn't been lit when it fell, but it had spread a dark oily stain across the middle to the edge of the well-worn carpet. The rest of the study was its usual messy accumulation of books and papers, though in truth there were more on the floor than normal, but there were reasons for that.

"This-" She went over to the desk and stood behind it. "-is where the Professor was sitting. He was slumped forward, arms out ahead of him, it initially looked as though his falling forward had pushed most of these books onto the floor." She swept her hand over the edge of the desk. "Now the lamp is usually here." She placed her hand on the top corner of the desk. "What would be the left hand side when the Professor was sitting here."

The Inspector was looking between the lamp and the desk. Was he seeing what she was seeing? Now the Inspector moved over to the desk. Standing behind the desk, the Inspector looked again at where the lamp was. He looked to his side and pointed to the chair.

"The Professor was using that chair?"

She nodded. "Though of course it was pulled in tight to the desk." She hadn't thought of that before. "Which is odd."

"Why?"

"Take a look around you." Her hands spread wide

to encompass the whole room. "The Professor was exact only in his experimentation, not his personal habits. Sometimes I would see him sit on a chair and barely make the edge of it. He rarely sat square in any seat." She started looking around; suddenly she was seeing things her shocked mind hadn't taken into account before. "The books."

The Inspector looked around. "There are a lot of them."

"Exactly. And a lot of them are heavy in and of their own right. The Professor had them stacked along the edges of the desk. Almost like my brother and I when we were children making a fort. Sometimes when he was at his desk I couldn't see him for the books. While a bad stack can be easily toppled, it takes some pushing to shift a correctly balanced stack. Yet, when we found the Professor they were all as you see them now, on the floor."

Without a response, the Inspector pulled the chair across behind the desk, and sat down.

"Miss Forester, would you mind placing the lamp back on the desk."

Happily and quietly, she did so.

"And you say his hands were ahead of him?"

Again she nodded.

Putting his hands in front of him, the Inspector slumped on the desk. He picked up his head and frowned at where his elbows were in relation to the lamp and the desk edges.

"There were books here?"

"Yes. Those." She pointed to a stack on the floor to the side of the desk.

The Inspector's frown told her he was thinking

things through. When he reached out, she stepped out of the way and he pushed the lamp off the edge of the table. It clattered loudly. Then he stepped up and looked where it had landed. It barely made it onto the edge of the carpet, at least two feet from where it had been found.

He was seeing it too now, she was sure of it. Finally he looked at her.

"I'll order an autopsy."

Chapter 5

Maker walked to the front of the church directly behind the coffin. It felt odd to walk alone, Amethyst had done as much as him, if not more, to arrange this funeral and memorial, but as an unrelated female, she had no position and no place at a funeral.

He sat alone on the front pew, well aware the congregation was large and gathering behind him. What surprised him was that a few moments later, a thin Scot who looked more dour than the undertaker came to sit on his left. Maker recognised Professor Brookmyre, a colleague of Richards'. For a moment he wondered if Brookmyre was here to mourn the passing of Professor Richards or just his own career, which seemed to have been built on taking credit for Richards' brilliance and mis-publishing Richards' papers under his own name. Richards hadn't been bothered enough about glory to slap Brookmyre down, but the Scot wouldn't have had a career without Richards, and just about everyone who mattered knew it. Still, even Richards noted that Brookmyre's real talent was teaching and there were few enough talented teachers around for Maker not to want to see one lost.

More surprising was the arrival on his right of another mourner; Maker had to control his shock. Less than half the age of the man on his left, Bobbie Davenport had, surprisingly, chosen an almost identical outfit. Though not officially a student of Richards', Maker had sat in on a lot of meaty discussions between Bobbie and Richards. He looked across and though he said nothing, he hoped his look was sufficient warning.

Amethyst wasn't here because women weren't allowed at funerals, so to sit beside one, even one indistinguishable as such by dint of dressing as a man, put Maker in a very difficult position. Maker knew she was there as much as to support him as say goodbye to the Professor, and trying to eject her would only make a shameful scene. All he could hope was that nothing gave away the fact that she was a woman.

Her odd look, briefly raised eyebrows and an obvious shift of her eyes towards the back of the church questioned him. Not wanting to be too obvious, he turned back to the altar, forced himself to count slowly to twenty, before he turned around. There, sitting very much alone, and clearly causing some discontent among the male mourners, was Amethyst.

"Disgraceful," said a Scottish voice.

Maker shifted his focus to Brookmyre, who had also turned to look.

"A woman at a funeral, so disrespectful."

Knowing that this was anything but disrespect, the dismissive attitude made Maker's temperature rise, his muscles contract. The urge to slap a man down had rarely been so hard for him to control. But he was trapped by the convention that women simply didn't attend funerals. Sitting fully forward, he glanced at Bobbie. Her presence was not helpful. So he turned to the altar, to the beautiful stained glass, the image of Jesus and prayed for the grace he so desperately needed.

Since the vicar had actually known the Professor, the service was personal and touching. Maker struggled to hold back the tears several times, he saw eye wipes to his right and some sniffing and uncomfortable coughing came from behind him, suggesting other men were similarly struggling. For all his eccentricities, Professor Richards had been a well-liked and well-respected man.

When the time came to follow the coffin from the church to the grave, Maker found Professor Brookmyre at his side. It wasn't the man's place, but pointing that out and making a fuss wasn't really the thing to do either. Besides, this might just be an opportunity. Maker scanned the attendees as they processed out. He didn't see who he was looking for.

"No Brown," he ventured at last.

Brookmyre shrugged. "Why would he come? He and Richards were hardly friends."

Maker held himself rigid. "No?"

"No." Brookmyre glanced around, Maker didn't have to, he knew Bobbie had kept a respectful distance, and the others had amassed behind her. "Rivals if anything. Having been a great proponent of aetheric power, of course Mr Brown came to the University to seek Richards out. But from almost their first meeting, they were at one another's throats. Mr Brown was prepared to spend good money for research, but Richards wouldn't take it. I offered of course, Mr Brown's needs weren't extensive and the University needs connections with business to survive."

"Why?"

"Well, someone has to pay for our research."

Sometimes it seemed to Maker that everything came down to money. Could it really be the root of all evil? "I meant, why were they arguing?"

"Richards thought the direction of the research was distasteful."

"What was it?"

But they were at the graveside, and the vicar was preparing to speak again.

*   *   *

Maker returned home directly from Professor Richards' funeral. Professor Brookmyre had left quickly and Maker hadn't been able to speak with him again. Amethyst had, as custom dictated, stayed away from the burial itself; even Bobbie had backed away from that moment, though he knew not why or exactly when. Though Maker was sure he had seen Amethyst waiting on the edge of the cemetery, taking the long way in as the congregation left.

The wake was being held at the University, but Maker had an appointment across the road with the Professor's solicitor, Mr Courtney. He had come home only to see Violet, check if her earlier fit of the vapours had past.

The drawing room was richly decorated, with all the latest papers, fine examples of taxidermy under glass domes, large oil paintings on the wall, the latest of Violet herself dominating the room. The furniture was upholstered in deep red silk, the windows all but hidden behind velvet drapes with heavy tassels and thick sub-curtains of Nottingham lace to soften the daylight. The day was bright and crisp outside, but in here it was dull and oppressive. As he stepped inside and closed the door, Maker heard the rustle of fabric. When he straightened and turned, he found Violet on her feet, her skirt hem caught up, the fabric creased from being knelt on. Lady Timpson half hidden beside her, still sitting on the long couch, brushing down her skirts. For a moment, he looked at his porcelain perfect wife. Both women were slightly out of breath. At least Lady Timpson had the good grace to look away with burning cheeks at being found as they had.

"Maker."

At least Violet's voice was neutral, her activities keeping her in some measure happy at least. That was good.

"Why are you here?"

He wanted to point out it was his home and he had as much right to be here as anyone, but he hadn't come looking for an argument.

"I thought you had some... thing," she waved her hand dismissively with the word, "to attend."

"Funeral." What had he come home looking for? Whatever it was, clearly he wouldn't be getting it from his wife.

"Yes, well." Again her gestures dismissed the facts. "I was entertaining my guest. Were you planning on joining us?"

The way Lady Timpson looked up, the darkness of her eye was the most invitation he'd received in many a year, but her sort didn't interest him. He wasn't much into sharing intimacy.

"Will reading," he said, turning back to the door.

"Uh, the will. I suppose you should go, he might actually have left you something. Might make his odious company worth something."

Maker's hand clenched around the doorknob, twisted. If only it had been Violet's neck.

"When are you likely to be back?"

For a moment he turned back and regarded his wife.

"Dinner?"

"Ah." Violet looked momentarily abashed, but he recognised that for the falsehood it was. "I thought you were dining at your club tonight."

He'd made no such plans, but he had been home the last four evenings consecutively and this was Violet's way of telling him she'd had enough of his presence. "Indeed." He offered her and her guest a small bow and left.

The walk across the Square offered some refreshment, the air to breathe at least. Typically, his knock was pre-empted by Edwards, who advised that Miss Forester was in the drawing room.

Maker was surprised that Amethyst rose when he entered. Pale and drawn, she was dressed in deepest black with a collar of impressive English beadwork. He was pleased that she had accepted the gown he'd sent to replace the one he had inadvertently ripped. Mercifully, her note of thanks had reached him before Violet. She still wore that hideous brooch. Now there was a loyalty he did not understand.

Amethyst offered a watery smile and held out her hands to him. It would be easy, automatic even, to go to her, but years of being censured for his actions stopped him actually taking the offered comfort. Amethyst appeared momentarily offended, then looked away. When she rallied, head held erect, she was strained but controlled.

"How fare you, Lord Fotheringham?"

"Maker." Looking at her, he wished he could express his sympathies, return the comfort he derived from simply being in the presence of a woman who understood his own grief.

"Then how fare you, Mr Maker?"

He would have told her to drop the mister had she not moved to reach for him, his own stiffness driving her back.

"Please." She looked away. "Take a seat."

She sat, and he had the distinct impression that he had hurt her feelings.

"Sorry." He shouldn't care for her feelings, yet he found he did. There was sufficient room on the couch beside her, yet Maker moved to the wing chair beside the unlit fire. It was safer.

"Shall I call Edwards to bring tea?" she said at last, apparently to fill the chasm of silence between them.

He merely shook his head, uncertain he could speak without begging her to come to him.

"Mr Courtney is due any minute."

He nodded. He was as aware as she of the arrangements.

"Do you know why he asked me to attend this afternoon?"

Maker shook his head. It was logical that she was one of the Professor's beneficiaries; why else would she be asked to attend the reading of his will? As she looked at him, her eyes seemed to glitter, tiny tears on her lashes reflecting the light from the wide open window, only the thinnest of sheers here. Her grief was apparent and real. She, like him, had been a true friend of the Professor, and like him, she felt the loss most keenly. Now she looked away, using her ungloved fingers to gently wipe away the tears she couldn't hold back.

The ache in Maker's innards ground harder. Here was a woman who shared and understood his pain, one who needed comfort as much as he did. He would hold her as tight as she was holding her hands in her lap. But he had a marital duty he would not betray.

Chapter 6

Amethyst felt stunned.

Half this house, all its contents and all Professor Richards' fortune.

"Wh- wh-" She struggled to find the words.

She felt like a fraud. Maker was sitting beside her. Edwards and Mrs Shaw, the cook sat behind; they had each been granted the sum of one hundred pounds and very pleased with the gift they were. It wasn't life-changing, but it reflected their employer's esteem. She struggled to understand why Professor Richards would leave her anything, let alone almost everything. The other half of the house had gone to Maker, as the Professor's closest friend and favourite student, even if he had apparently never actually studied under the Professor at university.

"Why would he leave anything to me?"

Mr Courtney looked over his glasses at her, and she felt ever more idiotic for having to ask. "It was his choice; all I can tell you is that the Professor was very clear." He closed the papers in front of him and returned them to his folio. "Now, my business is concluded." He stood as he spoke. "If you have any further need of me, here is my card."

Numbly, Amethyst took the proffered oblong of card and continued to stare into mid-air. Vaguely aware of others leaving, she roused herself to see Mr Courtney into the hall, where Edwards took care of his needs, and under Maker's quiet guidance, she moved back into the drawing room.

Somehow the emerald paint, the white woodwork,

the light, the brilliance of the day streaming through the windows, felt like a betrayal to the loss she felt. She sank quietly to the couch and looked into the set fire. How could this have happened?

"Amethyst?"

On hearing the repeat of her name, Amethyst finally looked up to see Maker standing over her. She would like to think he looked concerned, but he was as ever, expressionless.

"Why would he leave anything to me?"

She searched his eyes looking for a clue, looking for anything to prove he was human. He must have cared about Professor Richards, he'd been a real tower of strength when they'd realised that the Professor had no one to arrange his funeral. She had offered to do it, it wasn't the sort of thing one left to the servants, but Maker had been with her every step of the way. Of course it helped that they had quickly found a letter detailing the Professor's wishes for his funeral and wake.

She looked at Maker. She'd seen carved marble with more emotion.

"What does one do with half a mansion in Belgravia?"

"Reside."

She frowned at him. His one word habit was starting to annoy her. "I'm being serious. I mean we both now own this house. Together. I can see that being a problem."

For a moment his brow flickered; it may have been a frown. "Why?"

"Well you and I have different interests, different lives. We might want to do different things with it. You already have a house, for all I know you might want to sell this house to someone?"

"You?"

For a moment she was shocked, then she laughed. "The only money I have is what Professor Richards left me. If I use it all to buy the house, what will I live on?" She looked at him again. "Do you want to buy me out?"

For a moment he seemed to consider it, then he shook his head.

"This is my chance for independence. Best chance... possibly only chance. My prospects for a good marriage are slim at best, if not non-existent." She paused and frowned. "Though I suppose with a Belgravia house and a small fortune, those prospects might just have improved." This time she sighed and sat back. "But who wants a marriage on those terms?"

Maker declined to answer and she needed to concentrate on more immediate matters.

"Do we both sell to someone else?"

"No."

Well that was emphatic. "Then what?"

"Reside."

"In which half?"

"All."

She searched his face looking for some clue as to what was going on behind those clear emerald eyes. "You think I should live here?" A small nod agreed. "That is I suppose what the Professor wanted."

"Precisely."

"Do I pay you rent?"

"No."

"Seems a little unfair on you."

His shrug was nonchalant.

"Will you keep a room here?"

Before he could answer, a light knock was heard at the door, and Edwards stepped in.

"Forgive me sir, madam." He bowed slightly. "I was wondering if you have any direction for myself or Mrs Shaw?"

Amethyst looked from Edwards to Maker. There was no dealing with this in a single word.

"I do." She took a deep breath as she stood. "I will be moving in, living here on a permanent basis. I hope you and Mrs Shaw will agree to stay on in my employ. The master bedroom will be made up in permanent preparedness for Lord Fotheringham should he or his guests ever have need of a bolt hole and I will take the lady's suite. I'll spend tonight at my parents' home, and move in tomorrow, if you think Mrs Shaw can have the room ready?"

Edwards assured her everything would be done as requested. When he was gone, Amethyst sighed, hung her head and allowed her body to slacken.

"Amethyst?"

He'd moved closer. She could feel his body heat. A human so close. It was foolish but she needed the contact, the contact she craved but never received. She turned and leaned into him.

"I'm not sure I can do this," she said, her words half muffled by his cravat. "It's so different from my family home. From my experience."

He said nothing, just stood there. She was presuming too much. Unable to look up at him, she pulled back, her head hung as she wiped away the tears burning in her eyes.

"I'm sorry, I just miss the Professor so much."

Before she could turn away, his hand came to her chin, tipping her head to look at him. "Never apologise." His thumb was gentle as it wiped away one big tear.

Chapter 7

After two nights in the House of Lords and a day spent in consideration of Violet's nerves, Maker stepped into number seven and felt the weight melt from his shoulders. This house felt like a haven, the one place he could be himself. All the internal doors were open and some windows must be too. Fresh air inside. Closing his eyes, he breathed deep and risked allowing himself to relax.

He opened his eyes at the sound of something thudding to the floor and an imprecation that really shouldn't come from a young lady. Apparently, he had relaxed too soon. He walked into the study to see Amethyst halfway up a ladder against the bookshelves, three books in her arm, another that she was scowling down at on the floor. Her cheeks were coloured, as if she'd been rubbing them. A single glance told him that the study was tidier now that he had ever seen it. Amethyst had been hard at work.

"Maker."

There was a smile on her face and in her voice as she greeted him. Something in his gut cramped. It had been a long time since anyone had seemed so pleased to see him.

"Would you mind passing that up to me? Save me climbing down to come back up."

Not trusting himself to speak, he simply walked across and bent to pick up the book. When he straightened, he had to force himself not to react as her fingers brushed against his in the exchange. Her smile and thanks threw his equilibrium off; especially when he noticed the tiny droplets of tears in her eyes. Even as she turned and put the books back in order, his reactions were hard to control. Her hair was in a loose bun at the nape of her neck, she wore a tired grey gown, featureless and unflattering, the type he'd expect to see on a stern governess, not the lady of the house. That hideous brooch did nothing to set off the look. The dress bore several dust streaks; she'd clearly been working like a servant. On the surface, there was so little that should attract him about this woman, he had no idea why he was so enchanted with her. He was also rather concerned about her.

"Amethyst?"

The book on its way to the shelf stopped. "Don't."

"Ame-"

"Please don't."

The book went back with the other in her arm. Taking an unsteady breath, he watched her gather herself before she looked back down at him.

"I'm sorry, Maker. I have had something of a trying morning."

She returned her attention to the bookcase, clearly she didn't want to talk about it, and he could respect that. However, she had been thrown into a new situation and she was struggling. There might be something he could help with. "Why?"

Her sigh was an eloquent expression of exasperation, but also a touch of relief. When she looked down there was a softness in her eyes, and appreciation of offered friendship.

"I went to visit my parents and ended up having a huge argument with my father."

When she didn't immediately go on, then the pause

started to stretch, he had to prompt her. "About?"

Her eyes had drifted away, as if she was expecting condemnation. "How un-ladylike I am. What an appalling example-"

She looked away and heavenward.

"Specifics?"

"How shameful it is that I live alone without a companion or chaperone."

"Ah." He had been thinking of that himself.

Her brows descended in quite the scowl. "Don't you 'ah' me. I'll say the same to you, Lord Fotheringham, as I said to my father. I am doing nothing wrong. And it's my life, I shall live it as I see fit."

That was only some truth in that rebellion, and while he admired rebellion, especially youthful rebellion, she had a whole lifetime before her that could be marred by single a wrong step at this stage.

"Society."

Her look was sharp, but under the rebellion he saw understanding dawn. She wasn't a foolish woman, or she didn't strike him as such, she would come around, hopefully without too much trouble. Twisting back towards the bookcase, he watched as she calmed herself and concentrated on the task at hand. A tiny smile of triumph as she placed the last book was especially enchanting. And something of a relief. He really had no right to this swelling of pride.

"Would you mind helping me with something?" she asked as she came down the ladder, stopping on the ground to look up at him.

She was awaiting a response. Of course his response was taboo. He offered a small shrug.

A frown fluttered over her brow and then she

smiled. "As you like, I'll take the lack of a refusal as an acceptance." She moved over to a large box which was pushed towards the edge of the room. "Can you help me lift this up and put it in there?"

It didn't seem like a big request, until he reached down and tried to lift the thing on his own. She was smirking as she gently nudged him to one end and took up the other herself. As they raised the box, Maker knew he could have lifted it alone if he had known how heavy it was to start with, but he wouldn't insult her by refusing her help; instead he walked backwards toward the lab.

"Bench?"

"Please." Her voice was strained, it was a very heavy box.

"Under?" There was just about enough room.

"On top. Put it under and I'll never pick it up alone."

He doubted she'd ever do that anyway. This was CAMM and he knew that even without the box, it was too heavy for Amethyst. He took the strain and eased the weight onto the bench.

"Thank you," she said as they pushed it securely into place and took a much needed breath. "There's something else I'd like you to take a look at if you wouldn't mind?"

Standing this close to her, the fetching flush the exertion had brought to her cheeks made him think of far too many things he'd like to take a look at. But that was forbidden. Not knowing what to say, he nodded just once.

She moved over the desk, which was still covered with open books and papers. "This," she said, placing her hand on one of the ledgers, "is the Professor's personal expenses ledger. He was surprisingly careful about recording every penny he spent. There are detailed accounts of the costs attributed to each experiment he did." She pointed to more loose leaf papers. "And here," she added, indicating one particular column, "he uses a reference system to show the connection. When he begins a new generation of experiment, he gives it an additional suffix."

Looking over her shoulder, Maker could easily see the logic she was referring to.

"So?"

She turned the page. The left hand page was complete to the last row, but the right was empty. Then he noticed them. The small fragments of torn paper in the pressured centre of the ledger. "Missing."

"Torn out," Amethyst agreed. "From what I can tell, these four experiments are missing."

This time she brought across a small square of paper in a different hand, more blocky and clear to read. Her handwriting, he recognised it from her thank you letter. Each had the same prefix, and four suffixes. Four generations of the same experiment.

"I can't find a thing with these references."

He looked pointedly across the room to the second desk, which was still piled with books and papers.

"Well, I was never going to get the whole room tidied in one day," Amethyst admitted with a wry smile and enchanting blush. "But everything I've picked up from over there was much older, two years old at least. These references only appear in the last nine months."

This was the Professor's study, but he conducted his experiments in the rear extension of the house.

"Laboratory?"

"I've looked. Plenty of actual experiments and notebooks, but nothing relating to these numbers."

That was strange. Maker took the square of paper from her hand and studied the numbers. AE59-1 through to AE59-4. He knew enough of the Professor's seemingly chaotic systems to know that AE related to aetheric experiments. But he had no idea what this fifty-ninth trial might be. He tried to recall if anything had happened nine months ago which indicated any particular interest. Nothing sprang to mind.

He looked at Amethyst. "Diaries?"

Her headshake was small. "Don't think the Professor kept any diary other than his ledgers and notebooks, but if he did, I haven't found any. The only room I've not checked is the master bedroom."

"Why?"

She didn't turn away in time to hide her scarlet blush. "That's your room now. I can't go poking about in there."

It was an odd thought, that there might actually be a room where his secrets would stay his. He ignored the knock at the front door, knowing that Edwards would deal with it. At home, though Violet might never share his bed, she thought nothing of invading his privacy. He knew she went through his pockets as often as she went through his pocketbook. She might not want him, but she would make damn sure no other woman got him. Not that he wanted any other woman. He focused again on Amethyst. *Until now. Don't even think it! Think about the problem at hand.*

To keep himself from the woman at hand, he moved away, towards the double glass door that led to the laboratory.

"Thoughts?"

"Would it kill you to use more than one word at a time?"

He turned, gave her the most imperious look he could muster.

Her lips compressed, but he thought he detected a smile in her eyes. "I don't-"

Her words were cut off by Violet's commanding tones.

"Well that can go, to start with."

Whatever Amethyst 'didn't' was lost under her frown and sudden departure for the hallway.

"Nothing from this house is going anywhere."

Trailing in her wake, Maker saw two men in brown overcoats reaching for the hall stand. Edwards was standing at the edges of the hall looking pale and annoyed. Violet was in front of them, Amethyst, her back to Maker, was facing the taller woman, her spine ramrod straight and her fists bunched behind her back. As plain as Amethyst was in her dull grey, Violet was vibrant in cream edged with gold. Violet looked positively pleased with herself, while Amethyst was quaking with anger.

"This is my house and I will do what I like with these hideous pieces." Violet's lace glove was flicked towards the hall stand. The only thing she was right about was that it was a particularly hideous piece. Ebonised carvings of something that might have been meant to be elephants but simply looked like some misshapen lump of... something Maker didn't want to define.

"This house is not yours."

It sounded as though Amethyst was trying to control her voice through clenched teeth.

"It's my husband's," Violet stated. "Which makes it mine."

"Wrong-"

"Amethyst," Maker warned as he stepped past her. "Violet."

"We are selling this house."

It was a declaration Violet had made several times since she'd discovered the terms of the Professor's will. One he had repeatedly told her she was wrong about. Now he looked at the two tradesmen behind his wife.

"Gentlemen," he said. "Leave."

"Stay," Violet countermanded.

The two looked at each other.

"Go." Maker didn't raise his voice, but his own anger was reaching Biblical proportions. "Now."

"They're staying to do the job I've hired them to do."

"Edwards." Now Amethyst's voice was calmer, dangerously so. "Go fetch the police, it appears a robbery is about to be committed."

"Robbery?"

Everyone was instantly quiet – and tense – at the imperious Scottish accent which projected through the open front door. Even Violet's eyes were wide with shock, her posture ever more upright, like a rabbit looking down the barrel of a gun and too afraid to see who might pull the trigger. As Maker leant one way to see past Violet, he was aware that Amethyst tipped in the opposite direction. He was also aware of the growing smiles and interest of the two removal men.

Half expecting to see a Highland warrior, complete

with kilt, claymore and woad, what he saw was a surprise. Even the wide brim of her bonnet was unlikely to touch five feet. She was a grey-haired lady, frail in all but voice apparently, bedecked in full mourning, looking over wire-rim half-moon glasses and leaning on a silver-topped ebony cane.

"Great-Aunt Flora!"

Great-Aunt Flora stepped into the hallway like a grand battleship steaming up the Thames.

"You." She jabbed one of the men in the chest with the bottom of her cane. "And you." The other was served with a not so light tap on the arm. "Out."

Grumbling, but showing signs of intelligence by their obedience, the two men left, Flora stepping forward out of their way and beside Violet. Edwards obligingly closed the door.

"H-"

Violet showed some sense, at least, in stopping at the rise of that cane. The sinking of his stomach assured Maker that Great-Aunt Flora could be very judicious, and a little too accurate with that cane when she wanted to. The formidable if tiny package turned to Amethyst.

"Now, Amethyst, dear." This time the tone was a gentle lilt of the highlands, deceptively calm and tranquil. "Is this or is this not your house?"

"Y-"

"Half."

Violet was treated to three pointed looks.

Amethyst was the one who took a calming breath. "Great-Aunt Flora, may I intro-"

"No." The formidable warrior was back. "Answer the question, girl, before I expire of old age before your very eyes."

"I own *half* the house." Amethyst focused on Violet with all the heat Maker had hoped had dissipated. "But *all* the contents. Professor Richards was very specific in that." Her attention returned to Flora. "Lord Fotheringham owns the other half."

Flora looked from Amethyst to Maker. "That tall streak of silence is, I suppose, this Fotheringham?"

Maker felt his brows rise: apparently this was where Amethyst had learned her disinterest in titles.

"He is, Aunty. Be nice."

The steely gaze turned icily on Amethyst. "I am eighty-eight years old, young lady. I have outlived three husbands, four children and even two grandchildren. I will not waste my time on being nice when there are faster ways to live. Who might this slip be?"

The cane tilted towards Violet.

"Lady Fotheringham."

Flora was not actually about to do anything very fast, but no one dared break the stony silence as she slowly swung her head towards Violet. "If you can afford a title, you should have no need to steal my niece's furniture."

"I was not!"

"Violet." Maker could see this was an argument Violet would not win, but he wasn't sure how much of a fight there would be before she backed down. The less the better from his point of view.

Violet scowled back, her pout and stamped foot impressing no-one. "Why are you being so difficult about this?"

"Obviously because you're being so stupid," came the sniffed Scottish answer.

Schooling himself not to react, Maker tensed

against his own desire to scream at the lot of them.

"How dare you?!" Violet's voice had risen an octave.

"Och," Flora said. "Are you sure she's a lady? Sounds more like a fishwife."

Now Violet turned to her husband, pointing at Amethyst, probably as the softer target than the old lady. "Are you going to let some hornswoggler talk to me like that?"

Apparently, he wasn't going to have much choice. Amethyst was snapping and there was nothing he could do to stop her. After Violet's insult, he wasn't even sure he wanted to.

"I have not cheated anyone out of anything. You have no right to remove anything from this house and if you try, I will call the police and have you arrested as a common thief."

Violet's reaction was more in response to being called common than the accusation of being a thief. "Then I suggest you move your contents out of this house, as I am having decorators come in to prepare it for sale."

"Like hell-"

"Stop!"

Maker's bellow was so uncharacteristic that both women quieted and focused on him. Only Flora, with her one brow cocked over those wire rims, looked vaguely impressed. The two younger women focused their not inconsiderable ire upon him. Keeping these women in the same place was not going to resolve this issue, so he stepped forward, took Violet's arm and headed out, Edwards obligingly opening the door. Violent wouldn't go without a parting shot, calling back.

"We'll sell it out from under you!"

"Never!" he hissed in his wife's ear.

Chapter 8

Maker carefully opened and closed his own front door. It might be against the fashion, but making the servants wait up for him after late debates when they were up with the dawn the next morning seemed wrong to him. So he carried his own key to let himself in, and let them all get the sleep they needed. His foot was on the first stair when he heard the moans of pleasure coming from the floor above. A glance to the hall stand told him that Lady Timpson was still here. There was also another hat, a bowler. He never wore a bowler, and nor did any man of close enough acquaintance to claim overnight accommodation in his home. He looked up the stair. Of course, he had every right to storm up there and put a stop to the activities causing all those groans. But frankly, he didn't want to. The very idea of what he'd see when he reached Violet's room made his stomach turn.

Instead, he turned the rest of himself around. This house had ceased to feel like home years ago, so he walked out of it. He walked across the Square. For a moment he stood on the doorstep. He didn't have a key for number seven to hand, but movement of light within the hall caught his attention. He knocked lightly.

The small squeal was matched by a shift of the light. He'd surprised someone. He heard movement, the chain on the door being slid into place. Then the door opened a crack.

"Maker."

The name echoed her relief even as Amethyst closed the door, removed the chain and pulled the door open again. It seemed she had disappeared, but she was simply keeping behind the door, which she closed as soon as he was safely inside. Her hair was in a loose plait that extended to her bottom. Not that he could see her bottom under the copious folds of her dressing gown. He'd like to. *Stop thinking of her bottom.*

When she turned, she looked pale. The light from the aetheric lamp was a constant shift over features that looked strained and a little frightened.

"Did you knock a few minutes ago?" she asked. "I'm sorry, I wasn't sure I heard anything the first time. My apologies for keeping you waiting. How many times did you knock?"

"Once."

Her eyes widened and she looked both confused and frightened. A bang towards the back of the house made them both turn. Leaving his hat on the stand, Maker took up the lamp and headed through to the study, and from there to the laboratory. A window was open and the shutter was banging. He placed the lamp on the sill and shut the window before securing the flapping half of the shutter.

"That must be what I heard," Amethyst said. "I was afraid someone had broken in. I was sure that I'd locked up tight though." For a moment, she simply scowled at the window. Then she turned to him. "Would you like a nightcap? I think I need a little something to calm my nerves." Her laugh was small and delicate, but strained. She didn't wait for an answer, simply leading the way back to the heart of the house. He took up the lamp and followed her.

In the drawing room, she moved to the sideboard, turned two of the lead glass tumblers the right way up and selected a decanter. He would have picked the brandy, but she took up the whiskey. Her hand shook slightly as she poured a finger depth of the amber liquid into each glass. Her head was hung as she turned and passed one to him, never meeting his eye as she walked around the wide couch to sit. He placed the lamp on the table behind the couch and moved to stand before the fireplace, where the embers still glowed. When he faced her, Amethyst was sitting primly, a mass of pale cotton in a very demure nightgown beneath the many layers of lace of the dressing gown. The shifting aetheric light behind her danced a rainbow through her hair, the reds lighting a fire against the auburn. He realised now that that dressing gown was about twenty years out of fashion, almost as old as the young lady herself. The wide lace trim was tattered, he could see that it had come adrift from the cotton in a few places. Amethyst really should treat herself to a new wardrobe now she could afford to, but he had yet to see her spend a single penny upon herself.

"What happened with your Great-Aunt Flora?"

Her eyes rolled. "I seem to have gained a house guest. "She's upstairs in the guest bedroom. Snoring loudly."

"Good."

Now she was frowning at him. "How is that good? She's one of the reasons I'm still awake."

"Chaperone."

That cheeky smile was back again. "And do I need one?"

She did. She really did. Right here, right now. "Yes." He took a swing of the whiskey.

Watching her too closely was a mistake, but he did.

And under the attempt at humour, she looked pale, sad. Stressed. He wanted to go to her, but, chaperone notwithstanding, that was forbidden. She was straining for normality when she looked up at him. She sipped the whiskey, her eye catching his as she moved. Her swallow looked false, she was clearly stressed.

"How was your debate?"

Violet never asked him such questions; if he tried to talk about his work, she simply brushed him aside. "Good."

Now Amethyst looked at him as if she was expecting more, but he had no idea what to say.

"Do you sit in the Lords or the Commons?"

"Lords." Though he felt a little odd about doing so, he had considered running for election, but Violet had screeched that it was a vulgar suggestion and why take the risk when he knew he had a place in the Lords. It was vaguely logical and he acted in the manner most likely to keep the peace at home.

"What were you debating tonight?"

Surprisingly, she actually seemed interested in what he did. Or perhaps she was interested in diverting herself from the strain inside.

"Aetheric concessions."

She smiled up at him. "Congratulations, two whole words together. Is there any danger of an actual sentence?"

Years of practice kept him from returning her smile. He was very much afraid that if he softened towards Amethyst he would soften too far and right now the idea of – *Don't.*

"Isn't that debate about giving concessions to the aetheric industry on tax and government subsidies?

Something about the support of an infant and growing industry?"

He nodded, impressed by her knowledge, starting to recognise the slightly squinted eyes as her thinking expression.

"If I remember rightly, isn't there some opposition as, should it be passed into law, it would unduly prejudice the similarly infant and growing electrical industry?"

Again he controlled his smile, though he was rather impressed that she was familiar with the bill and its implications. "Indeed."

"And are you for or against?"

"Against." *Definitely.*

She nodded as she looked at him. An odd sense of pride picked up within him. He didn't need to think about his answer, he'd spent hours looking at the figures and projections each way. He was convinced that while aetheric power was extremely useful, it was risky, more so than electrical power, especially when the aetheric supporters were talking about a grid to carry power throughout the nation. He was concerned how so much power, from a substance still not fully understood, could put so much at such great risk. Electricity, he supposed, was just as much of a risk, but that was the point - just as much, while the bill called for huge subsidies for aetheric power over electricity. Meanwhile, there was already direct evidence of people dying from domestic aetheric equipment.

"And was it a lively debate?"

She was pushing him to be more verbose than was his custom with a woman, but he could counter that push.

"Yes."

Her laugh was a small huff as she sipped her whiskey again. "Must have been interesting at least. One word at a time."

He realised she was teasing him, he could see it in her eyes. He realised he liked being teased. He liked a lot about her. He liked a woman who spoke her mind and had a mind worth speaking.

"I'd like to hear you in the Lords some time. I've heard there's a viewing gallery. Is it possible that I could watch your next debate? Would you take me to listen next time you're sitting in the Lords?"

Schooling himself not to be too flattered or pleased in her interest, he offered a simple "Yes" in response.

For a moment she smiled and thanked him. But the smile slipped away from her face as she bowed her head, looking into the now empty glass. She was hiding her face from him, he was sure of it. Something was wrong, and more than just a disturbed night's sleep. Given all that had happened recently, he supposed it was to be expected. But he also knew he should at least try to reassure her. He simply didn't know how.

"I'm sorry about what happened today."

Could she read his mind?

"I shouldn't have spoken to your wife that way."

No she shouldn't have, and he had the bruises to prove it.

"If you really want to sell…"

"No."

"I can get out of the house in a day."

Clearly she wasn't actually listening to him. "No."

"I mean it's not like I've much to take. Most of my stuff is still at home."

"No." Why did no woman listen to him?

"You might even sell the house easier fully furnished, whatever Lady Fotheringham might say about the hideous hall stand."

"I said no, damn it!"

She reared at his roar. Her eyes wide, her mouth slightly open in surprise. For a moment they were frozen that way, then she looked away. Stood up. Turned this way and that before leaning over the couch to place her glass on the table beside the lamp.

"Ame-"

"Good night, Lord Fortheringham."

Chapter 9

"Are you actually going to sit there and read the paper over breakfast?"

Maker didn't even move his eyes from the print. His remaining breakfast was triangle of toast and a hot coffee, the fuller plate having been removed already. "Customarily."

"Well it's a custom you can change as soon as you like." Even Amethyst realised she sounded like a snappy wife, but she reasoned Maker should be used to that. Besides, she still wasn't sure how she felt about being shouted at by him last night. "I am astonished that Lady Violet allows such disrespect."

This time she at least got a look. A challenging look.

"Oh, I suppose as a married woman and lady of the house, she is bought breakfast in bed."

"Indeed," Maker agreed and went back to reading.

"Doesn't make it any less disrespectful to me."

Judging by the breath he took, she wasn't impressing him much. But this was her home, if he wanted to eat alone he could break fast in his own home.

"If you must read, you could at least share the headlines."

"Tsar visit."

Amethyst frowned. She wasn't aware of any state visit but then, why would she be? "The Russian Tsar is in London now?"

"Two weeks."

Her frown didn't lessen. "Does that mean he's here

for two weeks or he will be here in two weeks?"

"Latter."

"Two words at a time too taxing for you?"

He rustled the paper and sighed as he turned it over.

This, Amethyst decided, was worse than when he'd started giving her financial and investment advice, and she was forced to ask twenty questions when a simple starting explanation from him would have saved them both a lot of time and effort.

"So Tsar Nicholas-"

"Alexander."

"- the Third -"

"Second."

This time she was the one who had to take the calming breath. "So Tsar Alexander the Second is coming to London on a state visit in two weeks time?"

"Indeed."

The light thud, shuffle, taffeta rustle announced Great-Aunt Flora was approaching for breakfast. This would be the first time that she had joined them for breakfast. As chaperones went, Amethyst found her wonderfully lax in her duties. *This will be interesting.*

"Maker, are you familiar with the concept of immovable object, unstoppable force?"

He eyed here curiously around the edge of the paper. "Yes."

The smile spread wide across her face. She turned her head to see Flora enter. It never ceased to amaze her that Flora could be hobbling on that stick one second and wielding it with the deadly accuracy of a quarterstaff the next - and the old lady never fell. "Good morning, Great-Aunt Flora."

"Morning, dearies. I'll have a full cooked breakfast,

and tea," the old lady told Edwards as he held the chair for her. Flora sat with exaggerated care in the seat opposite Amethyst, Maker between them at the head of the table.

Amethyst turned back to Maker, or more accurately to his paper. She wondered how long that would last. "So the Tsar. Isn't he the Queen's grandson?"

"Great."

She frowned over the paper at him. "Is that some idiosyncratic way of complaining about my talking?"

She watched muscles move in his jaw. Was he clenching his teeth or controlling a smile?

"Great grandson."

"Any particular reason he's coming over?"

"Flightpaths."

She looked across the table, only able to see part of the old lady. That part wasn't looking terribly happy.

"Are you feeling quite well, Great-Aunt Flora, you look a little peaky."

Whap!

They all jumped and the newspaper became a crumpled heap under the ebony slash of a certain cane.

Maker looked straight ahead of him, rather shocked.

"Much better now I can see you properly, deary. A great improvement, don't you agree, Lord Fotheringham?"

"Apparently." Maker sighed as Flora removed her cane and he reached for his coffee over the crumpled mess.

Amethyst's fork had stopped half way to her mouth, but after the sudden stillness, she placed the cutlery neatly on her plate, then moved her own side plate to Maker's side, reached out to place the shards of his side plate and discarded toast on it, before brushing crumbs from her fingers.

Taking a breath as Flora delicately reached for the remaining piece of toast in the rack, Amethyst tried to pretend all was normal as she looked at Maker. "What do you mean? Flightpath? And don't say the path of a flight."

This time she was pretty sure the muscle twitch was a controlled smile.

"London-Moscow."

Her brows raised. "Direct flights? Well, I suppose it's no different to London-New York direct."

"Closer."

He was sipping his coffee again and she was still hungry so she dug into her breakfast. She had just taken another mouthful when Edwards interrupted, serving a full cooked breakfast to Flora as he spoke.

"There's a Mrs Doherty to see you, Miss, she's in the drawing room."

"Thank you, Edwards."

Maker lent back as Edwards removed the ruined paper. "I know none."

"I do." Amethyst swallowed what she could of her breakfast, washing the rest down with a large glass of fresh squeezed orange juice. She stood, leaving her chair out as she moved to the hallway. She wasn't surprised to see a large perambulator in the corner.

Rushing down the hall, she stepped into the drawing room to see Mrs Doherty sitting on her sofa, a four year-old little girl sitting very primly to one side and a baby boy in blue on the other side.

"Sapphire!"

"Aunty Am!" Prim went out of the window as the

little girl jumped off the couch and flung herself at Amethyst, who easily swept her up into a big hug.

"Hello Miss Summer," Amethyst laughed, carrying the small girl with her as she moved into the drawing room and bent over to kiss her eldest sister's cheek, fondly wiggling the nose of the little boy Sapphire held. "And how is Master Winter?"

"He's a very good little boy," Sapphire said as Amethyst sank to the floor, Summer sitting with her.

"Can I look around?"

Amethyst didn't think Summer would sit still for very long, she never did. "Of course, but I suggest you start with that cupboard in the corner." Amethyst pointed to the cupboard in the far corner where, in hope that she would get a visit from her sister and niece, she had stored a number of small games, toys and children's books. Summer rushed over and gave a small cheer.

"Please may I play with these, please?"

Smiling broadly, Amethyst looked over at her niece, knowing that lots of children would never even have asked. "Of course you can, sweetheart." As she heard Summer pulling out toys, she turned up to look at her sister. "Thank you for coming to see me. I was hoping that Mother and Father might have; they were invited."

"Well, I think they might feel a little intimidated. Belgravia Square is rather out of reach for most of us."

"But I'm not. And you're here. Even Great-Aunt Flora is here."

Sapphire looked at her, wide-eyed. "You're joking!"

"No, she arrived a couple of days ago. Installed herself in a spare room and even now is taking breakfast with a rather shocked Lord Fotheringham."

"Oh dear," Sapphire said. "He didn't try reading the newspaper at the breakfast table, did he?"

As she nodded, Amethyst and Sapphire began to giggle.

"Do you have any crockery left?"

"A little." But the laughter had already left her. "Why won't Mother and Father visit?"

"You know what they're like, completely imprisoned by convention."

"Not that imprisoned," Amethyst argued. "Or we wouldn't be a jewel-box of siblings."

"Yes but-"

Amethyst wasn't entirely surprised Sapphire cut herself off. "You know, one day you are going to have to tell me what happened."

"Perhaps. But not today. My point is, they can't stand the idea that the neighbours might say something less than pleasant about us."

"Which only gives the neighbours more to gossip about." Amethyst was well aware that she was the source of more than one incidence of that gossip. She glanced at the door. Maker was out there somewhere, and all that was going on would just create more gossip. "Here," she said as she knelt up, "can I have a cuddle then?"

Sapphire sat forward and placed the baby into her outstretched arms. Sinking back down, Amethyst pulled her hair from the twist at the back of her head and used the loose ends to tickle the baby's cheek. The baby giggled and one small hand took a firm grip on the lock of hair. Suddenly Summer was at her side, holding out a rattle she'd found for the baby, shaking it in front on the baby's face, making Winter gurgle. Amethyst smiled.

A cough drew her attention to the door and she looked up to see Maker in the doorway. Her smile didn't dim at all as she looked up at him.

"Hello, Maker. May I introduce my sister, Sapphire Doherty? Sapphire, this is Lord Fotheringham, Earl of Umbria."

Sapphire offered him a nod in greeting, and he bowed with all the grace and respect he would offer a great lady.

"And this is Summer." The little girl stood very properly and offered a curtsey. Amethyst was incredibly pleased to see Maker offer her a bow too. "And this little bundle is Winter." She looked from the baby to the man and just for a moment wished that she was holding his baby. She had to say something, so that idea didn't completely distract her. "Are you leaving?"

"Indeed."

"Well, I'm sorry you can't stay a while. Oh, and thank you for last night."

She heard Sapphire's squeak and turned to her with a chastising look.

"Maker very kindly, and bravely, helped me out when I thought someone had broken into the house."

"Oh my word! Is everything well?"

"Everything is fine," Amethyst said. "I think it was just my overactive imagination."

"Probably the rafter rattling from all the snoring." Flora appeared at Maker's size. Amethyst considered him wise to graciously step aside for Flora. It at least saved him from being knocked across the hallway.

As her own smile froze, from the corner of her eye, Amethyst could see Summer struggling to control her laughter. They both had enough experience of Great-Aunt Flora to know where the snoring came from. She looked up to see Maker looking dead ahead, no eye contact, no chance to share a stolen moment of mutual amusement. *Just as well, probably.*

With a small cough of adjustment, Sapphire focused on Maker. "I hope that my sister didn't take up too much of your time, but thank you for taking good care of her."

Finally Maker looked at her. "Anytime."

Amethyst smiled her thanks and tried not to feel that reaction in her gut. She shouldn't be pleased just because he was in the room. She also knew her sister was adept at reading her, she just hoped that Sapphire wouldn't say anything in front of Maker. She knew how much his pride mattered to him, and she wasn't exactly looking to throw hers away. She focused on Maker.

"Just remember to ask first."

Frowning at Flora, Amethyst felt she had to remind her great-aunt of one simple fact. "Maker, you should feel free to visit anytime."

Flora grunted then tipped her head under that demure white lace cap to pin Maker with her look. "Feel it, but don't do it."

"Great-Aunt Flora, he owns half the house."

"We'll call that the outside half shall we?"

"Flora!"

"Well, I hope I'll see you again soon."

Amethyst was relieved as usual by Sapphire's saving diplomacy. This time, Maker offered her a bow before turning sharply on his heel and heading for the door.

"Well, he's gorgeous," Sapphire admired as soon as

Maker was out of sight.

"He's also married," Amethyst pointed out.

"Shame."

Amethyst felt her jaw slacken at Flora's comment. She was also uncomfortably aware of how Flora had actually watched Maker all the way out, a very appraising look on her face. Then the old woman moved into the room.

"Don't look at me like that, young lady," she said as she sat rather grandly in one of the wingback chairs. "If I were twenty years younger…"

"Only twenty?" Thankfully, Amethyst was saved from a lashing as Edwards arrived with a silver tray. He placed it on an occasional table, and Amethyst saw the silver tea service, the finest of their china and a plate of small cakes which she wondered if you even needed to open your mouth to eat. She also wondered who had requested it, or if it was something about which Edwards had made an assumption. If he had, it was an assumption she was grateful for. "Thank you, Edwards."

As the man bowed and left, Sapphire stood.

"I'll be mother, shall I?"

Watching how her sister was smiling, as if laughing at a private joke, Amethyst wondered what was so amusing.

"In about six months again, probably," Flora announced, then pinned a slack-jawed Amethyst with a look. "And don't you think I didn't hear your comment, young lady."

With the broadest smile, Sapphire placed one cup and saucer close to Flora, another near Amethyst before she sat back with her own.

"Well," Sapphire said. "There might be another bun in the oven."

"Sapphire, that's…" Amethyst didn't know what to say. "Wonderful." Winter pulled her hair. She looked down and then back up at her sister. "And really quick."

Sapphire offered a shrug. "What can I say? Adam and I enjoy -"

"Yes, thank you!" Amethyst cut her off. "I've heard how much you enjoy the private delights of the marital bed." So much so, she often wondered why Sapphire didn't keep the delights private.

"You wait until you know those delights, I'm sure your man Maker-"

"Would never betray his wife," Amethyst added quickly.

Flora nearly masked her comment with the teacup. "Now that really is a shame."

Chapter 10

Two days later, Maker found Amethyst sitting in the drawing room. Her book was open and she was reading; there clearly wasn't much left to read. As he stepped in, she looked up and offered a small smile in greeting before returning to her book. Such quiet acceptance was welcome after the frosty accusations of home. The accusations, he supposed, were of his own making. He knew how to handle his wife, he'd been a fool to forget that in absent-minded daydreaming of Amethyst smiling for him. It was necessary to correct himself; she smiled *at* him, not for him.

He moved to his usual seat by the fire, unlit at this moment. Yet after what he'd seen outside, he couldn't settle, so he stood up. For a moment he paced towards the window, but looking out only reminded him of what he'd seen while walking across the Square. He paced instead to the hearth and stood looking at Amethyst.

He could tell she was aware of his movements.

She turned the page. "Two paragraphs," she said.

It seemed only a moment later when she let out a groan, closed the book and put it on the seat beside her. She looked up at him.

"Flora?"

"Afternoon nap."

He listened.

"Don't." She smiled. Then waited while he looked uncomfortable again. "You clearly have something you want to say or ask, but I'll need something of a clue before I can satisfy your curiosity."

For a moment his jaw tightened before he could say

the name. "Silvestri."

"Ah," she said. "You saw that, did you?"

Indeed he had. As he'd stepped into the Square, he'd seen Amethyst walking on the far side towards home. As she'd approached the nearest exit point, she had been met by Mrs Silvestri and her daughter. They had clearly snubbed Amethyst, something he hadn't been able to hear had passed between them. Mrs Silvestri had been polite to him, but the usual stopping to chat which he couldn't abide was forgone. He didn't miss it, but noted it as unusual. He nodded.

"Hmm. You were in soon enough after me, so I did wonder." She looked out to the window, perhaps looking for more to say.

"Amme?"

She stilled at the use of her shortened name, but she didn't object. He watched as she took a breath and swallowed. "Because of my friendship with Professor Richards, I've spent rather a lot of time in Belgravia Square over the last four years. I had actually seen you a few times but only ever at a distance. But since the Silvestris live next door, Miss Silvestri and I, being of a similar age, were able to get to know one another across the garden fence as it were. A couple of years ago, we were quite friendly. Her parents were polite, nothing overly welcoming, but nothing to object to either. I mean I always knew they thought me below their station, but it was never overt or hurtful." She turned back to face him. She was trying not to look hurt, but she wasn't completely successful. "Then Gabriella was sent off to the Sorbonne and hasn't been allowed to speak to me since. What you saw was Mrs Silvestri making sure she never does."

"How?"

Amethyst reared at the question. Apparently now wasn't the time for single words, but now was also too late to realise that.

"It doesn't matter how. It only matters that it is what it is. Besides, you saw what happened because you were coming over here, was there a reason for that or did you just want to check over the house?"

"I don't check over the house."

Now her brows rose and she smiled. "Oh, more than one word - I must have touched a nerve there. So why did you come over?"

She was goading him again. He shouldn't like it and he mustn't fall for it.

"Be ready at seven," he said and turned to walk out.

"What for?" The question followed him, then he heard her standing and rushing after him. "Maker?"

As he turned to pick up his hat, he looked back at her. "Debate."

"I'm not debating it with you."

He raised his brows at her.

"I just want to know what to be ready - oh."

He didn't release his smile until he was out of the house. Amethyst blushed beautifully.

* * *

It was nearly ten o'clock. Amethyst stood with Great-Aunt Flora outside the House of Lords Chamber in an imposing room that was far taller than any she'd ever been in before. Except perhaps some of the cathedrals. She was still struggling to believe that she was here. She had never dared set foot into Parliament before.

And wondered if she would ever be able to come again; Flora had dropped off during the session and one particularly resonant snore had even stopped one Lord mid-sentence. Maker had been so good to them though, asked one of the liveried attendants to show them where everything was, and collect them when the debate was done. Now they were waiting for Maker to finish talking to another of the Lords.

The man he was with was short, shorter than Amethyst, perhaps only five feet tall. His back was obviously bent and he leaned heavily on the ebony cane he held, only the head differentiating it from the one Flora held, a horse head instead of a thistle. His beard was black as coal and his suit obviously tailored specifically for him, perfectly elegant and respectable. The man himself had spoken particularly well, he obviously had an accent, but it was schooled into refined tones. His speech had been in respect of a warrant to grant permission for a new sewerage works in the East End of London, but even while staying on topic, it had become clear that, like Maker, he was against the Aetheric Concession Bill, as he pointed out the dangers of a gas-releasing sewage works near a suggested factory for aetheric power cells. The resultant blast could level the area and then some.

Finally, Maker glanced up and saw her, as he and his companion stepped towards her and Flora. They moved closer to the men. Maker made the introductions, the other man being Lord Haversham.

"A pleasure to meet you, Lord Haversham. I thought you spoke particularly well tonight."

He took her hand and kissed it, bowed over it. For a moment, Amethyst felt like a real lady. But reality soon cut across that. Flora's dread looked dared him to be anything less than courteous. "Aye, well lass, there's sum'thin's as has to be said."

She blinked at him. His northern tones were much stronger now, less refined then those he'd used in the Chamber. He also wasn't giving her hand back, so she had to pull, gently, away.

"Some things yes, but there was an awful lot of waffle to start with."

"Filibuster," Maker said.

Now she looked curiously at Maker, who didn't look inclined to say more.

"He means that waffle was in fact filibuster," Lord Haversham supplied. "Ye see, each debate 'as a limited time in the Lords, otherwise we could be there all night on inconsequentials. So if someone wants to hold up a bill, they can gain the floor and talk nonsense for as long as they can, and use up all the time. It's called filibuster."

"Ah, I see."

"Thankfully it was cut short tonight."

"It usually goes on longer?"

"What stopped it?"

Amethyst's eyes went wide; she struggled to divert Flora but couldn't think of a thing to say.

"Heckling."

"Humph," Flora grumbled. "When my dear Henry sat in the Lords, he wasn't so easily distracted."

Feeling the weight of Maker's curious gaze on her, Amethyst felt she had to explain. "Flora's late husband."

"It was some unusual heckling from the gallery."

In their private exchange, Maker and Amethyst had

forgotten to warn Haversham from speaking.

"I didn't hear a thing."

"No? Well." Now Amethyst turned to Maker. "You were incredibly eloquent in there. Full sentences, coherent arguments with logical progression, a clear and concise opposition. Had I closed my eyes, I would hardly have credited it was actually you speaking."

"Perhaps you did," Flora leaned closer to say. "Perhaps it was you snoring."

Maker didn't respond. Haversham however laughed openly. Amethyst liked his laugh, but didn't like what he was going to make of the exchange.

"You know I think I have heard you speak more tonight than the entirety of our acquaintance so far. I do hope to hear you speak so more often."

Haversham laughed. "Oh, our friend's loquacious enough when the company is male, Miss Forester. I think our dear Lord Fotheringham is afraid of women."

For once, surprise was as clear on Maker's face as Amethyst suspected it was on hers. Flora's task was eloquent. Maker masked his surprise much quicker. Amethyst turned to him.

"Afraid of women?" She couldn't imagine Maker afraid of anything. "Why do you say that?"

"Well he speaks, as you say, articulately enough in the Lords, and at the club when he sees a need. Yet put him in the company of women, and it's back to one word at a time."

Somehow, she very much doubted that this was the true source of Maker's reluctant speech. "Well now I know he can speak so powerfully, I hope to hear him speak more freely in the future."

There was a small harrumph from the man himself,

but she and Haversham just smiled at the lack of reaction.

"Well I must be away, the future second Lady Haversham to woo."

Again he took Amethyst's hand and bowed over it as he kissed her knuckle. His eyes were sparkling with unplaced laughter as he looked her up and down. "Unless you might be partial to a little wooing?"

"Haversham."

The warning note in Maker's voice sent an odd shiver to Amethyst's core, but she just smiled at the short lord.

Flora's cane on the man's foot was much more effective.

"Try me again when you're looking for the third future Lady Haversham, I might be amenable then."

"I'll remember that, lovely lady."

"Don't." This time there was a thwack against the calf.

"My dear Lady Gordon, I do believe you attended the same school of cane management as my mother. It is a pleasure to have met you and been reminded of the dear woman." He offered a nod of farewell, then made his limping way away.

"What a charming wee fellow."

Amethyst looked to Flora then Maker, who seemed equally shocked by the statement.

Flora turned to Maker, the end of the cane went perilously close to his nose; Amethyst admired the fact that he didn't even flinch. "Keep the wee letch away from my niece." The thump was followed by the shuffle, but not by Maker or Amethyst. A few steps forward, the Flora called over her shoulder, "Are ye young 'uns not coming?"

Grinning broadly, Amethyst took the proffered arm and began the walk out at Maker's side.

"Stop," he grumbled as they paced slowly behind the black-clad lady.

She looked at him; since he showed no sign of pausing his walk, she didn't either. "Stop what?"

He glanced at her. "That."

It was impossible to be sure, his look had been so swift, but she had the feeling he had looked at her mouth. "What? Smiling?" No, she was in too good a mood. And judging by the dark look she got, it was irritating Maker, which just made her smile wider. "Does it bother you, Lord Fotheringham, that a woman can actually be happy in your company?" As she spoke, she wrapped her hands more intimately around his arm. "Or have I frightened you into silence?"

He kept his face deliberately forward. His eyes were narrowed and his lips compressed, but his arm had crocked to keep her more securely by his side. He didn't object so much as he'd like her to think.

"So, your friend Lord Haversham seems like an entertaining fellow."

"Hmm."

"Have you known him long?"

"Decades."

She looked up and thought Maker didn't look old enough to have known anyone that long. On the other hand, she believed he was in his thirties. "School acquaintance?"

"Indeed."

They were outside now and Maker paused only to look down the courtyard to see where his coach was.

When he saw it, he directed the ladies along the path and helped her into the closed body. The coachman had lowered the net curtains, they would be able to see out, but no one would be able to see them inside.

She swallowed the thought of what she might do with such privacy; she knew that it was just a ridiculous flight of fancy. Her hands were already cold in the chill of the night air. Rubbing them together, she looked to Maker. He had only to step inside. His gaze lingered on her hands. She froze. Was he too remembering their first cab ride together? The way his hand had been so warm over hers? Oh, the man was such temptation.

A not so discrete cough reminded both of Flora's presence. Maker graciously helped the smaller woman into the carriage. He saw that Flora was also sedated well, then looked again at Amethyst.

Suddenly, the cab door closed.

Clearly she didn't tempt him.

"Deliver the ladies safely home," she heard him call up to the coachman. "I've work to complete, I'll get a cab back when I'm ready."

Amethyst slumped and folded her arms in frustration. Had she really upset him that much? What had she done wrong?

Chapter 11

Amethyst went inside the house; unlike Flora who had actually snored herself awake at one point, she was far from tired. She should go to bed, it was late, yet she was too full of - something. Watching Maker speak so well had stirred her blood, she completely agreed with his point of view, but he formulated the argument so much more cogently than she would ever have been able to. Then he had dropped her, as though her presence shamed him. Even after the ride home, she didn't understand that. Perhaps she should ask him. She knew she wouldn't, there was too great a chance that she'd hear some things she didn't like.

"Don't set your cap too soon, young lady."

Amethyst stopped and looked up at Flora as she stood a few steps up and admonished her. She sighed.

"Great-Aunt Flora, I am not setting my cap at anyone."

"Good." Flora added a decisive nod to the word. "That Lord Haversham is not the man for you."

Amethyst watched Flora head up the stairs, unable to believe what she had just heard. She had a choice, she could go to bed and wrestle with her fears for the night, or she could try to do something useful. That might even take her mind off her worries. With a sigh, she headed to the study; there were so many things still to tidy up. Those experiments were still missing, perhaps more research might tell her what they were all about.

Not wanting to risk another lamp being knocked from the desk, Amethyst had placed a small table beside the chair on the door side of the fire. The broken oil lamp had been replaced by an aetheric lamp, the one that had her shade on. She flicked the switch on the base and for a moment a rainbow danced before colours coalesced into a white light that filled the room.

She had managed to clear most of the Professor's desk, so she sat there and wished some answers would come to her. Ledgers were ready for checking and she looked at them, but her concentration was shot, like a blunderbuss discharged at her soul. Maker's voice, his turn of phrase in the debate kept coming back to her. So different from his usual one word at a time conversation.

Was Lord Haversham right? Was Maker afraid of women? No, she couldn't believe that. She could believe him being *careful* around women. She was rapidly learning to be careful around his wife.

Shaking her head, she tried to drive thoughts of Maker out of her mind and focus on the ledger. It was starting to work when she heard the movement of the front door. The door closed, got locked. There was a pause - she suspected Maker was taking off his hat. Then those careful, precise steps. Obviously he'd seen the light and was coming towards the study. He stopped just inside the door, behind the occasional table that held the lamp.

"Hello again," she said when he said nothing.

Her greeting was a small nod.

For a few seconds she met his gaze and said nothing more. When she realised he wasn't about to start a conversation, she looked back down and tried to focus on the ledger. Knowing she wasn't actually reading a word of it, she hoped it appeared otherwise to Maker.

The minutes, or possibly seconds, stretched like hours, and when her nerves couldn't take much more, she looked up. Maker was still by the table; he seemed to be studying the lampshade. Her shade.

"Lord Fotheringham?"

On the second repeat of his name he turned to face her, his eyebrows up in mute query. Often, his brows said more than his lips.

"You seem rather lost in your contemplations there, my lord. Or do you simply admire my lampshade? It is rather an improvement over a naked aetheric light, don't you agree?"

"Yes."

"Works just as well over gaslight, though that I find is more golden then white light."

Maker had taken to staring at the shade again.

"There, you've drifted away again. May I ask your thoughts?"

His eyes slid back to the shade and one long finger tapped the glass. "Patent."

"Pending."

When he turned to look at her, he was frowning, clearly confused by her return. She smiled at his misunderstanding; it was nice to have the shoe on the other foot for a change.

"Firstly, thank you for the vote of confidence in suggesting that my shade should be patented. And secondly, you're a little late. When the Professor first saw the design and we discussed the formula for the glass-"

"Formula?"

Her smile broadened. "Yes, you see that's not standard opaline glass, it's my special formula, I call it

Prismatic Glass. But the Professor was so impressed with the design, he suggested that I patent not only the glass manufacturing formula, but also the shade design. He even assisted me with the patent applications. And suggested a few manufacturers I might trust to licence the product to. So you see, it has already been patented."

"Pending."

"No." She smiled at him again. "Sorry, that was my little joke. Not funny, but then, most of my jokes aren't. I actually already have the patents and the Professor had completed most of the negotiations for the licensing, though I have to admit that has rather stalled since his death." She sighed and sat back. "Though it's my idea and my design, they don't seem to want to deal with me directly. In fact they rather treat me as an idiot."

"Fools."

She looked back up at him and smiled. "Indeed. Perhaps they are not the company I should deal with. In fact, they aren't," she decided. "I'll find another partner company to work with. I must write to them forthwith and withdraw from the negotiations. They have plenty of unsigned documentation, but nothing on my actual formula or design." She felt like a weight had been lifted and put aside the journal she had been going through, to search for paper and pen in the drawers. As she did so, the mantel clock struck the hour. A glance told her it was two in the morning.

"Tomorrow."

She frowned up at Maker's word to find he had come closer and was holding out his hand towards her. She wasn't sure what he meant, but he looked meaningfully at the vellum in her hand.

"Later today," she agreed. She could write the letter later.

"Of course."

She put the paper down and rose. Now she was on her feet, the offer of his hand was gone. It was just as well, the temptation had been too tempting. The things Sapphire had told her about rattled around her mind, called to her. The idea of giving Maker her hand and letting him lead her to bed was far too great to consider. Now she'd thought of it, the image wouldn't leave her mind as she followed him, now carrying the lamp and her shade, out of the room, into the foyer and up the stairs to the bedrooms. She must get control of herself.

Chapter 12

He should not have accompanied Amethyst to her room. He should have just handed her the lamp and let her go on alone. The idea of kissing her goodnight was too clear in his mind, the thought of doing more than just kissing her was torment. Sweet torture. Now he paced his room alone, hating himself. He would never sleep tonight.

Usually, he was exhausted by an evening in the Lords, but tonight he felt invigorated. Tonight he had known she was watching with interest and when he'd found her afterwards, her greeting smile was manna from Heaven. He had experienced nothing like it.

Fool.

Indeed he was the worst kind of fool, a married man drooling over a woman twelve years his junior. He remembered when he had first met Violet. The house party had been his mother's idea, and a number of young nobles, male and female, had been invited, along with chaperones. Chaperones who, it turned out, were far too easy to distract and evade.

Violet had arrived fashionably late, her chaperone obviously frazzled, something he now understood. But Violet herself had been a revelation, the most beautiful creature his seventeen year-old eyes had ever seen. He had been upstairs, watching over the banister. His mother had greeted Violet, who had been all courtesy and good breeding. She'd moved with grace and subtle invitation. As she'd stood in the hall, the open door had allowed light to bound off the white marble floor, so when she looked around, complimenting his mother on the beauty and proportion of the house, the sun had set her golden hair alight like a halo. Then those clear blue eyes had turned to him. She was an angel and he'd been instantly in her thrall. Over the next three days he had fallen completely for the girl, and when she'd invited him to her room, he'd been too young and too besotted to refuse. The trap had snapped over him moments later. Her chaperone, the one Violet had assured him would be asleep for hours, had come to check on her charge and found them kissing. From that moment on, there had been no choice. It was a fairly chaste kiss now he remembered it. Not that he'd known at the time, back then he'd had no experience.

He looked around the bedroom, and this was the first night since then that he had felt free of the woman. He stood and moved over to the bed. He should at least try to get some sleep.

Sighing, he started removing his shirt. The fine cotton was half over his head when he heard it. A distinct sound from below. Throwing the shirt on the bed, he headed from the room.

With careful steps, and straining to hear, he descended the stairs. There was no sign or sound of movement or intrusion, but he had to check. The front door was locked, the dining room and drawing room - empty. The study empty and the laboratory - ah. One of the shutters hadn't been closed properly.

"Is that-"

Maker jumped, Amethyst's words cutting off as he turned to the surprising voice.

"Is that what was making the noise?"

He froze with his hand on the shutter, concentrating on it when all that filled his head were the very thoughts that had kept him from sleeping. "Bed."

"Well you don't have to be quite so snippy."

Stuck still holding the shutter closed, Maker looked after Amethyst's retreating back. He hadn't meant to snap, he wasn't angry at her, only at the temptation she represented.

Thankfully, he made it to his room without seeing Amethyst again. He made it to his bed too. Where he spent most of the night tossing and turning. When he did doze, his dreams were fever-pitch and full of a forbidden fancy. The image of kissing her. No chaste, light touch this time. But warm, forbidden and wanted, welcomed. Her taste. Her smell. Her arms around his. Their clothes falling away as they fell on a bed...

Before dawn, he blinked his eyes open. It had not been the restful night he'd been hoping for. He scraped one hand over his face, feeling the scratch of his beard. He needed sleep. Dragging a pillow over his head, he sighed and forced his eyes to close, the weight of the pillow and his arm pinning him down.

When he woke again, the windows were open, the curtains wide, though the window net made the light softer than the harshness of day. Even so, he could tell it was later than he should be sleeping in. Still tired, he threw off the bedclothes and stood. He was surprised to see his clothes had been laid out. Not the clothes he had been wearing last night, but fresh clean clothes. The ones he had been wearing were no longer on the floor where he'd thrown them.

He pulled the bell call, then moved to the adjoining bathroom where a plumbed-in bath and basin awaited him. Opening the tap, pouring warm water in the basin, Maker scratched at his jaw. He wasn't clean shaven because fashion expected it; he was clean shaven because he hated the way beard growth itched. He splashed water on his face, leaning to let the water drip into the basin as he lathered up the shaving soap. He was beginning to apply the soap to his chin when he heard the door of his bedroom open.

The man appeared at the bathroom door. Although as formally dressed in a black suit, this man was not Edwards. Younger and broader than Amethyst's butler, this was Blanchard, Maker's valet.

"You rang, milord?"

"Clothes?"

"I thought your lordship would appreciate fresh clothes after a long night in the Lords."

As Maker unsnapped the razor blade from its mother of pearl handle, he was grateful Blanchard didn't offer to do it for him. There was something about the act of shaving that he wasn't ready to share with anyone. The idea of someone else putting a knife at his throat was something he had reason to avoid.

"I brought across a day suit sir, I wasn't sure of your plans."

"None," he murmured as the blade stroked down his chin.

"Miss Forester has gone out for the day."

Maker stilled. "Mood?"

"I could not comment."

Maker turned to fix the man with a hard glare. Blanchard considered the matter.

"I did not see her myself, but I believe 'not happy' would cover it."

Maker returned to his shaving. He'd have to make it up to Amethyst somehow. Jewellery usually worked with Violet. But Amethyst wasn't Violet, and wore very little jewellery. Was that choice or cost? He wasn't sure. He'd think of something.

After dressing, he went to the dining room for breakfast. He tried to concentrate on the paper, but it wasn't working. Then the thud-shuffle of the approaching storm told him to put the printed material to the side. He would have to read it at the club.

"Good morning, Lady Gordon."

Flora pinned him with a glare and then looked pointedly around. "These surroundings are hardly formal enough for that, Lord Fotheringham. Now Maker, you will need to find a more agreeable manner of addressing me."

"Great-Aunt Flora?"

She arched her brow at him. "Would you have my niece feel insulted that you use more words to address me than you do to answer her?"

Maker felt trapped between the swords of Society and the mantrap of propriety. "Flora?"

"In private, that will do. Now my wee lad, Amethyst is my favourite niece. Reminds me of myself at her age."

"Redoubtable."

"And I hope long to remain so. Now, are you aware of how insulting you were to my favourite girl?"

"Unintended."

"Unintended or not, you must make amends."

Maker considered the words the echo of his own feelings. How could he apologise to Amethyst? What was he really apologising *for*? He didn't know the answer to that, but years of marriage had taught him that when a woman was annoyed with him, he should apologise, preferably with a gift in his hand.

"Thank you, Flora, I will think on your words." Taking up his paper, he offered a bow and - was stopped from leaving by the bar of her cane.

"Think from a distance, Maker. Act from as far."

He walked to Parliament, but lack of concentration soon drove him away. He walked the length of Bond Street and most of Oxford Street. There were plenty of things he could have bought, but in the end he saw the only thing he thought would mean something to Amethyst. At least he hoped so. Yet even as he was making the arrangements, he heard a man complaining about the time

Parliament.

"I mean for God's sake, take these aetheric inventors. They are completely hobbled by the costs, yet what are Parliament doing? The Lords in particular? They're holding up a bill that would help innovation, help make this country great. The Lords are nothing but an unelected leech on society; they do no good at all."

Handing over a note of the address, he was assured of a speedy delivery and left. But the comment stayed with him.

Two hours later, Maker sat in the coffee house with friends and looked around at his fellow men. Dressed in suits and hats, the clientele were a mixed bunch. They kept the female waiting staff busy. As a hereditary peer, it was his responsibility to sit in the House of Lords and do his best for the men and women of his country, his county. But there were times when he wondered if there was any point. He knew at least that the county was covered, cared for as well, probably better than he could care for it. Vegetables would be grown, bread would be baked, animals butchered. A loud laugh came from the opposite corner, a man he did not know was taking the liberty of squeezing the waitress. She looked less happy, but was quickly let go to get away. The squeezer and his companions were laughing. Without Parliament, men would still find women, there would be births and deaths, life would go on. And all the time his life felt frozen, worthless as a corpse.

"Have we lost you completely?"

Maker blinked back from his thoughts to his two companions. Haversham and Bobbie. Two less likely friends there never were. He was surprised and pleased that both were friends of his. It was this kind of situation that kept him from the depths of darkness that shadowed his heart. He was not free to live as he wished, but there was nothing to stop him picking his friends. Even Violet's nerves couldn't dictate his friendships; he wouldn't let them.

"Sorry?"

The pair laughed gently at him. It wasn't something he was comfortable with, but it was less uncomfortable than his thoughts.

"Do you think that the Lords are an unelected leech on society who just hold back progress?"

The pair blinked at him, then looked to each other. Haversham was about to smile when Bobbie said, "I think he's serious."

They turned back to look at him.

"No." Bobbie was emphatic, and as the only non-peer at the table, Maker valued the response. "Yes, you're unelected, but that's where your value lies. You aren't in it for the money; you might get paid for what you do, but only expenses. Members of the Commons get a salary regardless, and they've always got a motive. We've resolved most of the rotten borough issues, but there is plenty of corruption, power plays and manoeuvring to get to the top. Lobbying is hardly a new thing, and money talks. Politicians can be bought, the Lords act as buffer against that, they can afford to take a longer term view."

"I hope to God we do some good," Haversham said. "Otherwise my life would be nothing but gaiety, debauchery and booze. Which reminds me, I have to be off." Haversham stood and tapped his hat on his head. "The delightful little Miss Brightmoor won't wait forever and who knows, she could be my forever-one. And if not, maybe I'll move on to your delectable Miss Forester."

Maker tamped down the instant urge to punch. Haversham was merely baiting him. As the hunchback left, the two remaining friends smiled and saw him off. In the wake of his departure, Maker was unsure where to pick up the conversation.

"You are uncommonly quiet today," Bobbie said with soft seriousness, "even for you."

He looked at his friend. Bobbie Davenport dressed like a man, she even thought like a man, logical, irreverent, funny. She could out-think a lot of men. Out-drink a fair few - he remembered a number of hangovers as proof. For all he knew had happened to her, Bobbie still seemed so young to him. "Were you happy in your marriage?"

The surprise of the question was reflected in raised brows. But serious consideration soon replaced the look.

"I was content. It was what I was brought up to

expect, what I was expected to do."

That idea amused Maker, for all he didn't show it. "And you've done nothing expected since."

Bobbie's smile broadened. "Wonderful, isn't it? But my marriage is old news, can we not talk of current affairs?"

"Weren't we?"

"I was referring to what Haversham was saying, his looking for his forever-one."

"Non-existent."

Bobbie grinned. "For him, probably. He is rather mercurial in his loves and passions."

Now Maker was curious. "You?"

Bobbie laughed at that. "No, and nor am I liable to. I meant you."

Maker tried to find the words to express how impossible that idea was.

"I know your situation. I also know there are any number of women who would happily throw themselves upon your good graces and dismiss their own reputations in the process. You have the option of finding comfort elsewhere. Rumour has it you already do, and right across the street."

He felt his emotions tighten at the discussion. He was well aware of the possibilities and the rumours were an annoyance he wasn't sure how to shake, but there was an obligation he could never, ever be rid of. "A promise is a promise," he said. "I made a vow."

"So did she."

"Makes no difference. Besides, what you suggest seems so hollow. What woman would accept such a place? Who'd be a mistress rather than a wife?"

"One who truly loved you."

He couldn't but be tempted by the idea, by the images that came too easily to mind - but it was impossible. Preposterous. "I could not love a woman who thought so little off herself that she would accept such a compromise."

Bobbie looked inordinately saddened. "Well, I still hope you find your forever-one sometime."

"I hope not." Maker took the last of his coffee and returned the cup to the saucer. "I have a wife."

"More's the pity. No." Bobbie stopped him with a raised hand. "We each know where the other stands on that issue. But what of this Miss Forester? Is she as delectable as Haversham suggests?"

Maker sprung to his feet. "Good day."

"I hope-" Bobbie stopped him before he ran off. "-that I get to meet her one day."

Realising his foolishness in running away, Maker took a moment to recover. "So do I. Now, good day."

At home, after an excruciating meeting with his wife, Maker retired to his room. A few heartbeats later, Blanchard arrived and passed him a note.

You shouldn't have. There was no need. I love it. Thank you. So much. A.

Maker wasn't sure if his gut melted or froze. Whatever it was, he liked it. More than he should.

Chapter 13

Looking down at the dress, Amethyst knew it was the best one she had, but that it would never be good enough for present company. Thankfully, the sleeves were large and roomy, so she'd managed to hide the brooch, she didn't want to think about what this group would say if they saw that.

Amethyst felt totally out of place in a room that should feel just like home, since it was an exact duplicate of her own formal dining room. Of course, unlike her room, this one was richly furnished and full of the rich, the powerful and the worthy. Friends of Lord and Lady Fotheringham, and no one she knew.

She'd originally been placed closer to the head of the table, closer to Maker, where she might have been able to speak with him. But with Flora having declined the invitation at a late hour, the seating had to be rearranged. Maker himself had asked her to swap with another lady, claiming that he had business to discuss with the woman. But Amethyst had been watching, Maker was listening more than speaking, she didn't see any particular attention being given to the woman.

Without conversation to pull her attention, she considered all that Maker had done for her. He'd spent a lot of his time helping her through the legalities of the inheritance, helping her work out what she could do with her money, advising her in any way she asked when she turned to him with questions; when she could find the right questions - ones he could answer with his customarily short responses. She had found herself enjoying calculating the best way to ask him a question, and she found herself turning to him more and more. She'd never had much of a confidante before, and though she was a long way from telling him her intimate secrets, at least he was someone who was there for her. She hadn't had that in a very long time. He had been very good to her. Too good, probably. Tonight was his attempt to introduce her to more of Society now that her mourning period was officially over.

Lady Violet sat at the opposite end of the table from her husband and held court. A couple of times their eyes had met and she read the other woman's feelings clearly in that blue gaze. The lady was full of pride for her part in Society, the attention she could command, and the importance of those of whom she had the ear - and she didn't want Amethyst anywhere near that.

So Amethyst sat in the middle of the table with people either side of her, both of whom had their spines twisted away from her. The man across the table wasn't talking to anyone either, but when he looked at her, he'd sneered and made her feel like some kind of worthless rag on the road.

"That's unique."

The softly spoken words from her side surprised Amethyst and she turned to find the blond man to her left had turned to her. He had been sitting beside her through the first three courses, but with his back turned and his attention monopolised by the older lady on his other side.

For a moment, Amethyst wasn't at all sure what he was talking about. Then she realised she was playing with her pendant, a slim gold oblong containing six square-cut gems. She smiled.

"Actually Mr Sanderson, there are three more

identical pendants and two matching tie pins, so not unique at all."

His blue eyes sparkled in the swirling lights of the aetheric candelabras. "That sounds like there is a story behind it. I like a good story."

She liked the way his voice rose and fell as he spoke, there was a musical quality that made whatever he said worth listening to.

"The story is in fact right before your eyes." She held the pendant out and for once she was sure a man's eyes were focused on the pendant and nothing else. "To start from the top, these stones are Sapphire, Jasper, Jade, Amethyst, Emerald and Ruby."

The man considered a moment, then looked back up at her. "The names of your brothers and sisters?"

Her smile and the heat in her belly spread like warm treacle. "Exactly. Though it came about a little by accident. My eldest sister was supposed to be called Louisa, but my father bought my mother a sapphire pendant as a gift for giving him a daughter, and my mother loved it so much, she suggested they change the baby's name. When the rest of us came along, they followed the pattern."

"So the flow of the gems is the flow of your ages," he surmised. "Sapphire the eldest down to Ruby the youngest?"

She nodded.

"And you're just below the middle, fourth."

"Actually I'm equally in the exact middle. Jade and I are twins."

"Oh, so there's another just like you at home?"

She smiled. "Not quite. We're dizygotic. Jade was my twin brother."

"Was?"

Had she said was? That was unfortunate. This was the part she hated. She had to swallow before she could speak again. "He's no longer with us." And that was as much as she was prepared to say. "What of you, Mr Sanderson, are you from a large family?"

"The family is large, but not my part of it. I'm an only son. There are plenty of times when I was a child and I'd have family visits when I wished I'd had at least one brother or sister at home."

Amethyst remembered the exactly opposite feelings. "There were certainly times when I was a child that I wished I was the only one, but we all want what we can't have, I suppose."

He smiled at her. "Only because we can't have it. If we had it, would we want it?"

"The grass is always greener on the other side, you mean?" She sighed and glanced at the elegance of the table settings, the beauty of twin candelabras which gave the only light in the room. "I have wondered for years what it would be like to attend fine dinners given by great lords and ladies." She kept her voice low. "I'm sorry to say the dream was more inviting than the reality. I fit in better in my own head."

"You fit in perfectly."

She acknowledged his compliment with a dip of her head. "I'm more a freak on display, but I can live with that." She didn't like where this was heading, so she turned the conversation. "Though I cannot help but admire and enjoy the elegance of the setting. I find myself particularly drawn to these candelabra. The glass is so clean and crisp, yet it throws the light gently and casts us all in the magical beauty of the aetheric lights it frames so beautifully."

"Thank you."

That surprised her, but he was concentrating on the lamps now.

"Aetheric light does have a particular draw on the eye." His voice was soft, she doubted it would carry to any ear but hers. "Almost hypnotic."

"Hmm." But she was caught by what he had said. "Why did you thank me for complimenting the lamps, they're not yours."

His smile was spreading as he turned back to her. "Oh, but you see, they are. Lord and Lady Fotheringham may own them, but I made them. I actually designed these particular candelabra."

She must have looked as surprised as she felt, given what he said next.

"William Sanderson Glass Manufacturers? Please don't break my heart and tell me you've never heard of the family business."

She coloured and apologised. Of course she'd heard of them, they were well known and their glass sought after in many respects. Suddenly Maker's rearrangement of the seating became more acceptable.

"That's why I'm in London, meeting with some other designers, looking for new lines," he explained. "I'm always open to new ideas."

"And have you found any?"

His face fell a little. "Nothing that will set the world alight, but a couple of usable designs."

She rolled her eyes and was rewarded with a private smile. "Well, I have a design or two you might be interested in."

"How so?"

"Mr Sanderson?"

Amethyst jumped at Lady Violet's tone.

"What is it that you and Miss Forester find so absorbing a topic?"

"Glass manufacturing," Sanderson returned with an even tone as he turned to their host. "Miss Forester was just telling me she has some designs I might be interested in."

Though he threw the attention back on her, for once Amethyst didn't feel uncomfortable, because she knew she had something worth talking about. Lady Violet and the other guests were looking at her, so she pulled in a breath, trying to ignore the fact that Maker was standing and moving away from the table.

"I've found a way to make glass that turns this moving, coloured aetheric light into a steady white light."

"Impossible," the man across from her snorted.

Maker was behind her now, dipping into a sideboard. The footman had started collecting their plates.

"Not at all," she returned. "It took a long time to find the right combination of chemicals to add to the glass to make it work, but I found a way."

Suddenly Maker was leaning over her and placing a small aetheric lamp on the table. As he moved away, she felt duty bound to say something. Say *anything* not to notice how he deliciously smelled of fresh soap and being him.

"The glass itself is the complicated part of the process, getting the compounds in at the right time and right temperature was so difficult to master." She glanced at the man beside her. "Well, for me at least."

His smile encouraged her to go on as Maker placed a small round box at her side. She recognised it as one of the boxes she was keeping her samples in. "Once I realised that I had the glass right, I had to start looking at how to use the -" She looked in the box and stopped. Looking up, she saw Maker was sitting again at the head of the table. "This is what you picked for a demonstration? The worst thing I ever made?" She shrugged and looked to Sanderson. "You'll have to ignore the physical design, this was essentially my first attempt to make prismatic glass."

She reached into the box and pulled out the shade. It was a badly put-together rough cube, the glass was clearly lumpy and badly poured. She wasn't at all surprised to hear a number of sniggers from around the table, but she didn't care as she reached out and placed the shade directly over the aetheric lamp. The effect on the light and the gathering was instant. As the light turned white, the guests went quiet.

For a moment she glanced at Violet, whose utter silence was as cold as the look in her eyes. Any joy that Amethyst might have felt in the moment shrivelled.

"That's incredible."

It was the tone as much as the words that turned Amethyst back to Sanderson. Suddenly he was asking questions, tripping over himself to get them asked. Questions she had answers for. Not that she had time to give them.

"Ladies, why don't we remove to the drawing room?"

There wasn't really any choice, so with a small smile to Sanderson and Maker, she followed the other ladies from the room. She wasn't at all surprised when the miracle of her achievement was swiftly snuffed out as a topic of conversation.

Amethyst was surprised when Lady Timpson came to sit beside her.

"Still in the crinolines, then."

Amethyst looked down: solid purple satin with white collar and cuffs. It was her favourite dress, one of her best, but it couldn't hold a candle to the next worst in the room. Unlike her companions, she wasn't wearing a single diamond, and not one of these ladies had stopped at a single diamond.

"It's very brave not to bow to the whims of fashion."

At that point, Amethyst started to switch off. As other ladies began to join in the sniping, Amethyst felt herself wash hot and cold. She really wanted to snap back, there was plenty she could throw back at Lady Timpson at least, but she was a guest of Maker's and she couldn't afford to say or do anything that might reflect badly upon him. These women were verbally destroying what little self-confidence she had. She could feel the tears start to prick behind her eyes. If she didn't get out of here soon, she was going to shame herself.

She was just plucking up the courage to leave when the door opened and Maker led the rest of the men in. The tone in the air changed instantly, the sharpened hate she'd felt pointed at her drifted away, though it far from disappeared. Her eyes met Maker's; she wondered what he saw that made his look turn questioning. Blinking away the swell of need she suddenly felt, she looked away, grateful when Mr Sanderson appeared and made directly for her.

More of his initial questions came out and she was ready with answers. It was such a relief to finally be able to talk on a subject she understood. He wanted to know about her recipe, the cost implications, the designs she had. She was careful not to give him too many exact details; until there were contracts on the table, she wasn't going to give much away - she'd learned her lesson there.

Before she knew it, the clock was chiming one in the morning and the party was beginning to break up. When he discovered that she lived across the Square and was planning to walk home, Sanderson insisted on accompanying her. She tried to dissuade him, but there was little point and continuing resistance would look petulant. Instead, she smiled and accepted, and they left together. A fact that Maker seemed unreactive to as he returned her shade to her. She wasn't sure what reaction she wanted, but something would have been nice.

"Of course, I really need some proof of what you say."

"I have a laboratory set up at home," she said as they stepped across the road. "If you want to visit, I can show you on a small scale how I make the glass and let you see the improved shade designs I've come up with."

"Would two tomorrow afternoon be convenient for you?"

At her door, she turned and smiled at him. "Actually," she said, remembering the mess still in the laboratory and the amount of work she'd need to do to clean it up, "I'm busy tomorrow. The day after?"

Sanderson took her hand and smiled. "I'll look forward to it."

"As will I."

The kiss on the hand made her stomach churn in the most delicious way before he tipped his hat to her and left.

Chapter 14

Standing in the drawing room, surveying the results of her work, Amethyst finally felt like she had a room she could breathe in. No more clutter, so the furniture could be moved back, allowing her easier access to the windows, which were better for a thorough cleaning, not to mention improved by being open to let light and air in.

Last night, she'd been disturbed again by the sound of someone moving in the house below her, but Edwards swore that at the time - 1 a.m. - he had been asleep. She on the other hand had had to come down and investigate, only to find everything locked up. And even knowing that, she hadn't been able to shake the feeling that she wasn't alone when she should be. She simply had to get used to the noises of the house and the household; that was all. *Stop reading gothic romances before you go to bed.* Not that that name seemed to fit; there was little romantic about ghosts and ghouls. Still, in the light of day, everything looked different, brighter.

Sitting up, she looked at the book. No, not that romantic, even if Maker had presented it to her. *Especially since Maker presented it!* He was hardly likely to have a romantic interest in her. He was married and she was nothing special. He had simply guessed her taste correctly; he was after all a very intelligent man. And she had things to get on with to stop her thinking about him. She stood to go about her day.

The study, laboratory and the bedrooms all needed

work. In fact of the four bedrooms, excluding servants' quarters, which Edwards assured her needed no work, only two were useable. The master bedroom, which she had had cleared of the Professor's personal effects to allow Maker to use the room, and the largest guest room, which she'd selected for her own use. She and Edwards had moved enough clutter to give her sufficient access, but they'd run out of room in which to put things, so half the room was still piled with crates of her belongings. With this room cleared, at least she had somewhere she could sit and relax without being taunted by mess.

With a contented sigh, she sat down. The contentment lasted all of a few seconds. She should be doing something.

No, I'm going to have five minutes.

Since she had a habit of leaving doors open there was no knock to herald Edwards' arrival, he simply appeared in the doorway.

"A Mr Forester to see you, Miss."

She thanked the butler and wondered if her father or eldest brother was visiting. She was only slightly disappointed to see her father. Jasper's ever ready approval would have been most welcome.

Standing to greet her father, she offered and received a kiss on each cheek.

"Father, it's lovely of you to visit. Would you like any refreshment?"

He stood, looking rather nervous. "No. Nothing. Thank you."

"That will be all," she told Edwards.

As he left, Edwards pointedly looked to the door. Amethyst lightly shook her head and it was left open.

"Please, sit down," she said as she sat, only to look up and see her father still standing.

His expression was all too clear. He was not in the least happy with her. It was a look she was used to, he'd been disapproving of her choices since she'd been old enough to make them. She made her choices for her reasons and she wasn't likely to change them. This was not going to go well.

"So what can I do for you, Father?"

"Move back home."

Amethyst's brows rose, her jaw slackened. Her father was rarely so blunt and when he was, it was a sure sign of significant anger. Annoyance she'd understand, but what had he to be angry at her for? She pushed down her own irritation. She was a woman of independent means now; she needed to act like it.

"And why would I do that?"

"To stop people…" He paused, glancing at the open window and door. "Talking." This last was whispered as if it were some foul imprecation.

"No one's ever going to stop people talking," Amethyst pointed out. "The attempt usually backfires quite spectacularly. But I suppose you have a specific topic you want them to be stopped from talking about. What is it you want me to stop people saying?"

"That you're…" He actually looked away from her, shuffling his feet and turning his hat in his hands by the brim.

His obvious discomfort told her more than his words what he thought people were saying. She could do the polite thing and finish his sentence for him with some appropriate euphemism, but if he was going to make such accusations, he could damn well make them.

"That I am what?" She noticed the edge to her tone even if he didn't.

"A-" An abrupt start was tempered again to a whisper. "A *kept woman.*"

"The only person keeping me, is me."

"That's not how it looks. And I won't have it. Now pack your things and get back home."

"She is home."

It was uncertain if Amethyst or her father were more surprised by Flora's voice or appearance. The only explanation she could come up with for not hearing the thump-shuffle of her Great-Aunt's arrival was the pounding in her ears. Amethyst's blood was definitely up to hear the way her father spoke.

"Great-Aunt Flora." His surprise was evident. "I didn't know you were here."

"You do now." The thump-shuffle moved into the room.

Mr Forester looked back to his daughter. "Move home now and this can all be hushed up as a misunderstanding. If you stay… well…" Movement of his head didn't help elucidate. "I was never overly comfortable with your relationship with Professor Richards, I had hoped that he would redeem your reputation by making you an offer of marriage. But now it seems you were just his…"

Every muscle in her body had tightened. Professor Richards making her an offer of marriage was preposterous. He'd been nearly three times her age! No, this was not a problem with Professor Richards, or her, this was society's problem, and she wasn't going to let it browbeat her, not any more. She didn't let Great-Aunt Flora boss her around for all the older woman tried, she couldn't bend now to her father. She waited until Flora had taken what had become her regular seat by the fire.

"I was Professor Richards' student," Amethyst spoke carefully. "That is all."

"And what did he teach you?" The tone was more scathing than the words. "What did you learn that you now share with a married man?"

She gripped her hands together so as not to reach out and throttle him. "What's that supposed to mean?"

"Do I need to actually spell it out?"

Her back ramrod straight, Amethyst met his anger with equal defiance. She ignored the sound of the front door opening, not caring that Maker would hear every word they now said.

"Yes, Alan," Flora insisted. "You do."

His mouth compressed as he scowled between the two women, he chose to finish his glare on Amethyst. "People are saying that you're, well you're Lord Fotheringham's mistress. A kept woman. A slut!"

"I see." She felt the rage boiling inside her and tried to keep it inside.

"Despite my living here as a chaperone? What do you say?"

The hat was going around in his hands non-stop now. "What am I supposed to think? I'm sorry Great-Aunt Flora, but I didn't even know you were here. So clearly no one else does either. She suddenly moved out of home with hardly a word, nor any notice, into a house worth five times my own with no visible means of support but a man who spends nights here when his wife sleeps alone across the road! I will not have a daughter of mine branded a whore!" He turned back to

Amethyst properly. "Now pack your bags and get home."

The house felt deadly silent in the wake of his shout, yet all Amethyst could hear was the pounding of her own blood. The fact that Maker was standing in the doorway behind her father and unseen by the older man just made her anger colder. Obviously Maker had heard what her father had said, despite the unreadable mask of his features.

"No."

Mr Forester was clearly shocked by the response. "Do you dare defy me? You get home now girl, or I swear I will disown you."

"Now, Alan-"

"Flora, be quiet." No one had ever spoken to Flora that way and Amethyst struggled to believe that she had.

"Sorry, Flora, but this is my battle." The red mist had parted and Amethyst saw her father for what he was. A narrow little man who could see no further than his own nose. The changing of the world was nothing to him. He saw no need to change himself or the way he treated his family. His view of the world was so set, his determination so implacable that she had no doubt at all he would disown her if she did not comply. But since half of her had already travelled that route, there was no stopping now.

"You must, and no doubt will, do as you see fit." Even to her ears it was coldly spoken. "I am both surprised and disappointed in you, Father. To see things the way you do, you clearly know nothing of me, something I have long suspected. You not only don't listen to me, you don't give a damn either."

"I-"

"You will be quiet and listen." Amethyst sprung to her feet, surprising her father into silence. "You have had your say, now I will have mine. On Tuesday sixteenth, I came home from Professor Richards' funeral and will reading and at dinner I told you and the rest of the family that I was surprised to have been named Professor Richards' heir. I inherited his money, his belongings and half this house. If you didn't listen because all you care about are your more compliant children, that's your fault, your problem. I am not a kept woman. I am no man's whore. I am a single woman of independent means. Lord Fotheringham is kindly helping me to adjust to my new station in life – as an heiress. He is instructing me in the ways of a society of which we Foresters have only ever been on the periphery. He is assisting me to understand stocks and shares, so I can make better investment decisions to ensure that my fortune remains mine. He is supporting me through the loss of my closest friend.

"There are four bedrooms in this house, half of which belong to Lord Fotheringham as the house ownership was split equally between the two of us. If he were of a mind to use any or all of the rooms to sleep in, that is a choice he has the right to make. But let me be entirely clear – there is one bedroom he does not set foot in, and that is mine."

She was far from running out of steam, but she had to put an end to this before she or her father said something irrevocable.

"I am, despite your filthy accusations, still intact. Untouched. And I expect to remain so until either my wedding day or my dying day, whichever comes sooner. Now you have said quite enough, so I suggest you go away to consider your position. Mine will not change."

His features tightened and hardened. Narrow eyes shot poniards of anger. His hat was jammed back on his head, he turned on his heel, then stopped, surprised to find himself facing a taller, younger man.

"Lord Fotheringham, may I present Mr Alan Forester, my father. Father, this is Lord Fotheringham."

Horror filled her when Maker offered the respect of a small bow, but her father just stiffened.

"You should know my daughter's worth better."

Standing straight, Maker met her father's anger with quiet self-assurance. "I do. Why don't you?"

*　　*　　*

Maker stood and listened to the front door reverberate in Mr Forester's wake. That the man called his honour into question was nothing to Maker, but that he should know his own daughter so little he'd accuse her of being a whore and see Amethyst herself so upset – that strung every fibre of Maker's being as tight as piano wire. Yet here and now was not the time or place to call the man out.

"Well, that was fun."

Amethyst couldn't believe Flora had said that. She watched in disbelief as the older woman stood.

"I'll leave you two to talk."

It was hardly the job of a chaperone to leave a man and young maid together, but Maker was rapidly coming to appreciate Flora Gordon's unconventional approach to life. He nodded his thanks to the older woman and turned back to Amethyst. She looked angrier than he'd seen any woman before, even Violet, and her tempers could be quite explosive. Amethyst's whole posture was tight, her arms were straight at her sides, her hands fisted, knuckles white.

"Do you think the whole neighbourhood heard that?"

Her words were soft but heavy with hard implication.

"Unimportant."

He walked over to stand before her. Would that he could reach out and pull her into his arms. Only the curtains were open and anyone on the street would see. He wouldn't risk that, for Violet's sake.

"I'm sorry you've been accused so unjustly."

She turned and paced away, paced to the window, which she closed. And all the time he was trapped by convention into immobility.

"I can't believe people would even think such a thing. I mean, no man would look at me when he could have Lady Violet. It's an entirely ridiculous notion."

Unless you know Violet. Again, convention caged him, held back the disagreement he felt wholeheartedly. If Amethyst had the vaguest notion of what he was feeling, what he wanted to do, she'd run back to her parents in a flash, and rightly so. Perhaps he should encourage that. No. He didn't want her to go. It was pure selfishness on his part, but he wanted her close, even if she was off limits.

What worried him now was her pacing, her hands were wringing and she was looking anywhere but at him.

"You're not the type of man to throw over your

wife anyway. You're far too honourable."

There were times he wished he wasn't. Like now.

"I'm sorry."

Her voice was cracking, but before he had time to tell her not to apologise, she had fled the room. Fast footsteps ran up the stairs.

With a sigh, he realised that he had lost the opportunity to comfort her. He could hardly go up to her now. Not in her room. Not only was it not the done thing for a married man to step into the bedchamber of a maid, it was also far too much temptation.

Of course, what he had walked in on was a worry. He should have considered her reputation, yet somehow feeling so comfortable in Amethyst's presence had lulled him into a false sense of security. He had forgotten that the outside world would have an opinion. It always did.

Looking out of the front window, all he could see was the tree-lined square, but he knew that directly across the way was his home. The home he shared with his wife. What would Society say if it knew what went on inside those walls? Perhaps it already knew, perhaps people whispered behind his back. He probably deserved that. But Amethyst didn't. She'd done nothing wrong. He should leave. He should stay away.

"Sir?"

He turned to see Edwards at the door.

"Will you be dining with us this evening, sir?"

It would be best if he didn't. However much he wanted to. He filled his lungs and reached for a calm he wasn't feeling. "No."

Chapter 15

"Mr Sanderson!" Amethyst looked up at her visitor. She wasn't sure if she was pleased or disappointed that it wasn't Maker. He'd gone yesterday and hadn't been back, she didn't even know what he'd come over for, he must have had a reason. But Maker wasn't here and she wasn't going to waste her time thinking of him. Instead, she turned to the mantel clock. "Lord, I had not noticed the time." It was two o'clock, exactly when she had agreed Mr Sanderson could visit her as it was Flora's nap hour.

She closed the ledger she was looking through, and stood. Suddenly the serviceable grey dress she wore was too drab and shameful to be wearing. She had intended to change, to look better to greet her new friend, but time had had other ideas. He smiled, they exchanged pleasantries then quickly got to business. Amethyst liked that this man listened to her, he actually kept his attention on her, watched what she was saying. He treated her as an equal, he didn't try to fob her off with any platitudes, it was an unusual experience. He even took notes, things he said he'd have put in the contract.

Then he asked to see her latest design. She moved to the desk, switched on the lamp and moved behind the desk to retrieve the shade she had put away the night before to be able to produce it only when required. Now as she fixed the shade, she looked up at Sanderson. He was turned slightly towards the fire as he wrote again in his notebook.

"Where did you say the factory is?"

She waited, then looked up when there was no response. "Mr Sanderson?" He continued making notes as if she weren't there. "Mr Sanderson!"

He looked up and smiled, as if it were the first time she'd called.

"Ahh!" he said, putting his notebook away and coming towards her.

She couldn't help it, she was still frowning at him, at his odd responses. His face suddenly fell.

"Oh dear," he said. "Were you talking to me while I was sitting over there?"

"Yes."

He flushed like a schoolgirl. "I'm sorry. I should have explained. There was an accident, I'm almost completely deaf. I can't hear much with the right ear, no hearing at all in my left ear."

Which had been the one nearest her when she'd been talking.

"I can hear a conversation if I strain, but mostly I lip read. That's why I had to be so rude as to turn my back on you at the Fotheringhams' dinner. I feel a bit too young to be putting a trumpet to my ear all the time."

A small giggle escaped her at the image.

"I was struggling to read the woman's lips around the food she was cramming into her mouth, so I had to get my good ear as close to her as I could. My apologies about that too."

"You're forgiven." She smiled at him, and enjoyed his smile in return. "What happened? The accident?"

He shrugged. "An explosion at the factory. I was lucky, it burst my eardrums, and I got trapped under some falling masonry, but I survived, two of the men didn't."

"I'm sorry. That must have been very frightening."

Sanderson looked away, his mouth a grim line. He cleared his throat and concentrated on the shade. Amethyst realised she'd overstepped the mark.

"Sorry, I shouldn't have asked. What I did ask while you were over there however, was where is your factory?"

"Swansea."

That surprised her. She blinked. "Swansea?"

"There's a lot of really good stained glass makers there, it makes sense to be close, when we have a commission that needs their skills, we can get an artist who can fit in with the timescale. Now this," he murmured, turning his attention to her shining white shade, "is a thing of beauty."

As they talked, she listened to his suggestions on how the joints could have been better, and was careful not to give away any of her tricks or the ingredients of her formula. They weren't under contract yet.

"Ah yes," he said, "contracts. I'll speak with a solicitor this afternoon. Hopefully, we can have contracts drafted by tomorrow."

That was quick, but welcome.

They had spent so long, gone over so much, that by the time they were finished, it was only right to ask him if he would like to stay to dinner.

"I'd like that a lot. If I won't be inconveniencing you?"

She smiled. "Me, no. Can't necessarily say the same for Shaw - my housekeeper and cook." It only took a moment to find out, in fact, Flora had dinner plans outside of the house so there was no inconvenience at all and it was settled: Sanderson was staying for dinner.

Over the dinner table, Amethyst found that she enjoyed quiet dinners for two, though this time she had asked Edwards to make sure he remained in the room at all times. Given what people were saying about her and Maker, she didn't want similar rumours spreading about her and Sanderson, for his sake as well as her own. Though in fairness this might not help all that much; the testimony of a butler would be questioned, but it was too late to worry now. At home with her parents, dinner was either silent to the point of pain, or so boisterous it could get painful in the opposite direction. At times she missed the boisterousness, the buzz of conversation. She had been considering visiting her family, seeing her younger sisters, but after her father's visit, she wasn't sure she'd be welcomed.

As they talked, she found herself liking Sanderson more. He was easy company and a flattering conversationalist. What she disliked about the evening was something entirely about herself. She couldn't stop comparing him to another dinner companion. She had to stop it, it wasn't fair. Yet for all that it was a very pleasant night, she was rather relieved when Sanderson left. It was only as she was going to bed that she realised she still didn't know his first name.

Chapter 16

The contracts arrived midmorning and Amethyst gave them her full attention. So much so, she unwittingly skipped lunch and had to send apologies to Mrs Shaw for allowing good food to go cold.

She was pleased with what Sanderson was offering. Yes, she was chained in for a minimum of five years, but that made sense, the rewards for such loyalty were a lot more generous than what the Gibson Brothers had been offering her. She was a lot happier to sign this contract.

The sound of Edwards running up the stairs surprised her, then the front door opened before the poor butler could possibly have reached it. There was only one person that could be and she wasn't ready to face him.

Maker had kept away for the three days since that shameful visit from her father. She dreaded to think what Maker must think of her after that. He'd defended her honour as well as his own, but he said so little compared to which his absence was deafening. If Lady Fotheringham has heard - She shuddered.

Thankfully, she'd finished reading the contract, but she kept it open and kept her head bowed over it to maintain the illusion she was busy. She heard a small exchange, the men's voices too low to make out individual words. Then two sets of footsteps, one turned and went down, obviously Edwards going back below stairs, and the other continued, stopping only when Amethyst became aware of Maker coming into the study.

Keeping her unseeing eyes on the contract, Amethyst tried to calm her thumping heart and burning cheeks.

"Forester?"

That was new. Distant and rather unpleasant. Maker must be annoyed with her and she couldn't blame him. Swallowing the lump in her throat, she answered in kind. "Maker."

The seconds till he spoke again ran like sandpaper over her skin.

"Document?"

The muscles across her shoulders tightened. His tone had been more curious than imperious, but she found she was no longer comfortable in his presence.

"Contract." She pushed the word out, forcing her teeth not to clench.

"Sanderson's?"

Not trusting her voice, she just nodded. She couldn't look up at him, though she knew he was walking towards the desk.

"May I?"

"No." She closed the contract and slipped it into the desk drawer. She put her hands together on the desk, kept her eyes on them, although she could see Maker, or at least part of him as he stood before her desk.

"Am-"

"Lord Fotheringham, I believe you and I should dissociate ourselves as much as possible, for the time being at least."

"Why?"

She swallowed and blinked back threatening tears. She had few enough friends, she really couldn't afford to lose any. When she had lost the Professor, having

Maker as a friend had helped fill the gap. To lose him too, even after so short an acquaintance, would hurt. But if she was going to protect his reputation at all, it had to be done. She had grown fond of him. Too fond.

"Reputations take a lifetime to build and a moment to shatter."

"I don't give a damn what people think of me."

The declaration surprised her, by its word count as well as its vehemence. Perhaps he could afford not to care for people's opinions. Suddenly angry, she found the spine to face him. "Well I care what they think of - me." Her voice trailed off as she realised what she was saying. She slumped back in her chair. Closed her eyes and covered her face with her hands. "Oh dear God. I actually *do* care what people think of me. I didn't think I was that worried, but it seems I am."

"Naturally."

"Naturally!" Hardly able to believe he'd said that, her hand dropped to her lap and she stared up at him. "What's natural about caring more for other people's opinion than your own?"

For a moment, she thought he wasn't going to respond, the cold, impassive, expressionless face of marble was in place. Then he blinked and for a moment she thought perhaps he did feel something.

"Everyone needs someone."

She sighed. He was right and it hurt. Who did she have? Only herself. "You have your wife, but Society seems to think you have me too."

His lips momentarily compressed. Was he angry with her? Had she insulted him? Again?

Closing her eyes again, she bowed her head. She didn't deserve anyone, that was the problem.

"Socialise."

She was beginning to understand most of his one-word efforts, but she wasn't sure about this one. She looked up at him. "Socialise?"

Now Maker turned and moved to the mantel. There were a number of stiff invitation cards sitting waiting for her. He picked them up and held them out.

"Socialise."

"But I don't know any of these people."

His eyes remained on her but she got the distinct impression of an eye roll all the same. Drawing the cards back, he looked through, selected one and held it back out to her. This time she took it, read it over.

"You picked this because it's tonight?"

"No."

She glared at him. The carved stone mask was in place again. "Lady Garrington-Smythe." She read aloud. "Is Lady Garrington-Smythe important?"

"Yes."

For a moment, she glared at him. He wasn't helping. "Why?"

"Key."

Amethyst blinked up at him. "Pardon?"

"She's key."

"To what?" Amethyst was confused. "Oh! You mean, if she accepts me, they all will?"

Maker nodded.

Then the Lady really was important. Unfortunately, there was a problem.

"It's a little late in the day to be accepting an invitation now, don't you think?"

"Go."

For a moment more she studied the card. If Lady

Garrington-Smythe was so influential, it was a make or break deal. So she might as well get it over with. She looked back up at Maker.

"Alright, bossy, I'll go. But you should go too. Away from me, that is." She added the last at the raise of his brow. "You know what people are saying, don't give them fuel for the fire."

"Contract?"

Now Amethyst rolled her eyes. Just as she heard Edwards' fast footsteps in the hall.

"Favourable." She stood. "And with any luck that should be Mr Sanderson now." She went to the hall only to find Edwards opening the door to a thickset man with a very red face.

"Where is she?" the man demanded, pushing Edwards out of the way and stomping in.

Amethyst stood level with the foot of the stair. Anger thrummed through this stranger, but it was echoing in her. How dare he barge into her home this way? "I don't know who you're looking for and I don't really care. Get out of this house."

That stopped the man short. His lip had been curled into a snarl, but now he looked her up and down with undisguised distaste. Well aware that she looked normal to the point of dull in her grey gown, Amethyst nonetheless met his scathing gaze. Only more irritated when his eyes fell on the brooch even she was beginning to loathe.

"Where is Miss Forester? My business is with her, not some servant."

This time her shoulders went down, her back ramrod straight. "I am Miss Forester and whatever business you might think we have, you are now very mistaken. Get out of my house, and do not come back."

He looked rather more shocked than angry now. "You're Miss Forester?"

"Yes. Now-"

"You!"

She could feel her own anger starting to boil. She'd been chafing for days at being called Maker's whore, and she'd had no opportunity to vent that anger. This man was giving her the perfect excuse. "Yes. Get out."

"Explain this!"

He waved a letter in front of her face, one she had no chance to read, but she'd only sent one letter that could cause this kind of reaction.

"Ah, you must be one of the Gibson brothers. That's the letter I sent, telling you our negotiations are over and your behaviour at this moment is a perfect demonstration of how correct I was in making that decision. Now, get out."

He wasn't about to move, he pulled himself up to his full height, which really wasn't all that impressive. "You can't pull out of the agreement."

"I can. I have. There was no agreement. Both patents for the glass and the shades are in my name and when you refused to respond to my letters, my unsuccessful attempts to make appointments to see you and your clerk's abrupt manner when I visited your office made it clear to me that you would be impossible to work with. Now the matter is settled. Our association is terminated and you are not welcome in this house."

The letter was crumpling in his fist and his face grew redder. "The Prof and I had a gentleman's agreement."

"Prove it!" Amethyst demanded. "Oh you can't?

Well then? Professor Richards may have been in negotiation with Gibson Glassware, but no clear agreement was reached, no contracts were signed. Now the 'Prof' as you so disrespectfully call him, was a gentleman. I am clearly not and you most certainly are not, so get out of my house!"

Gibson stepped closer. "I will have that glass."

"Never."

Amethyst was surprised the voice wasn't hers. Suddenly she felt Maker standing at her shoulder. Gibson looked up at the taller man and sneered, growling down at Amethyst, who was paying more attention to the younger man now at the door.

"Think your lover will save you?"

Maker's move wasn't big, but it was big enough. Gibson flinched, but recovered. He wasn't in the mood to give up easily. His focus was solely on Amethyst and she looked at him and saw nothing but spite and hate in his eyes.

"Sign my contract!"

Amethyst saw Sanderson's reaction, noted a certain fury in his features.

"You'll never get a better offer!" he bellowed.

"She already has."

Sanderson was closer now; he spoke with calm certainty. Gibson swung round, faced the younger man. Releasing a guttural sound of hate, Gibson swung a fist. Sanderson easily dodged and Maker caught hold of Gibson's arm, twisting it halfway up his back. Sanderson caught the man's other arm as he tried to round on the lord and together Maker and Sanderson manoeuvred the snarling man down the hallway towards the door.

"You haven't heard the last of this!" Gibson shouted over his shoulder. "I'll get what I want and I'll ruin yer! I swear, I'll ruin yer all!"

The three men were now out of the house, but Maker and Sanderson weren't stopping. Amethyst could still hear Gibson shouting, it was distant now and she didn't care to strain to hear.

"I'm sorry, Miss," Edwards said as she sagged against the newel.

"What on earth for?"

"Allowing that man to come in here and attack you."

She hadn't thought of it as an attack on her. And now she did, she suddenly felt quite weak. The one time when Great-Aunt Flora - but no, Flora would have defended and that man might actually have struck a lady. No, it was better Flora was away doing what needed to be done.

But what would she have done had Maker not been here? Sanderson too, of course. Still, that was no reason to make Edwards feel bad. She looked at him. He was thin as a rake; she didn't doubt his capacity to fulfil his duties, but that was the point. "Edwards, you're my butler, not my bodyguard. The situation has been dealt with. Though I could use a drink and I suspect Maker and Sanderson will need one too when they return. For medicinal purposes only, of course."

"Of course, Miss."

Amethyst headed into the drawing room where she sank onto the couch. She found herself rather more shaken than she would like. As Edwards passed her a tumbler she realised that this wasn't from the encounter, but from the implications. She never dreamt that Mr Gibson would visit her home, let alone threaten her.

She put the empty tumbler to one side as she heard the front door close. Sanderson appeared a moment later in the door. He came directly to her side, concern clear in his eyes.

"Miss Forester, are you well?"

She found her smile. "Of course I am. He only shouted at me."

Edwards offered the man a tumbler of whiskey; Sanderson took it, downed it in one.

"He threatened you."

Reaching out, she patted his hand. "Just words."

Glancing up, she saw Maker at the door. She had hoped to see some reaction in him, but his face was its usual stony self, though she was aware of his mute refusal of the proffered drink. She turned back to Sanderson. "You're the one he tried to hit. Are you all right?"

"Perfectly well." He smiled. "I ducked."

But his eyes slid to the side. He wouldn't be able to see Maker, but she was sure Sanderson knew Maker was there behind him. Which just made her all the more curious as to what had happened outside. Either she didn't want to know or she could ask Maker later. It wasn't what she wanted to discuss now.

"Well," she said, concentrating on Sanderson. "Now that that horrible incident is over, shall we get to business?"

*   *   *

"Are you sure you should have signed that?" Maker asked after Sanderson left. He was concerned at the apparent ease with which Amethyst seemed to have signed her rights away. Sanderson was a fair young man, but he was a businessman, Amethyst was still younger, she didn't know much about business, or the world, there were so many pitfalls that could be hidden in the small print. What if she had unwittingly given away more than she realised?

She looked up at him from the Professor's - from her - desk.

"Show me your hands."

"Why?" He didn't need to ask, but a delay might lead to a back down.

"Show me your hands."

Her tone was more demanding as she rose and came to stand before him.

It was pointless to argue, determination was written across her face. He should have known better than to think she'd be so easily diverted. He raised his hands, palms up. Her huff and hard glare berated him, left him feeling like a misbehaving schoolboy. He turned his hands over.

"Ben!"

He was more surprised by the use of his name than the exclamation. He knew from the throbbing that the knuckles of his right hand would be red and swollen. He hadn't realised that the skin over his middle knuckle had actually broken.

Surprisingly cold hands took his right hand in hers and pulled him with her to the laboratory. The sunny day made this part of the house noticeably warmer. It couldn't possibly just be her touch that was raising his temperature. She opened a small wall cabinet above a jug and bowl. Removing the dust cover from the jug, she poured a little water into the bowl.

"Put your hand in there."

He did.

A brown glass bottle and a jar of cotton wool were pulled from the cupboard. He suspected the brown bottle was iodine. Gently, she lifted his hand from the bowl and wrapped it in a pristine white towel, before she tipped iodine onto cotton wool, all the time concentrating on his hand, not looking at him.

"This is going to sting," she warned as she eased the soaked pad over the split skin.

Maker forced himself not to move, but he couldn't avoid the intake of breath. She was right, it did sting.

"Sorry."

Not that she had anything to apologise for.

"You didn't have to hit Gibson."

"Did."

"Oh no." She looked up at him. "You can't start the one word thing when you opened this conversation with a full sentence. Once Gibson was out of the house, he was dealt with. Why would you of all people attack him?"

"He attacked Sanderson."

Her brows raised. "Sanderson couldn't defend himself?"

Maker couldn't remember the last time a woman had made him squirm this way. Violet tended only to make his skin crawl these days. "I had the better shot and I took it."

She looked directly at him, not a ladylike habit, but neither was the anger burning in her eyes. Though as he watched, the flames died away.

"I hate the idea of anyone fighting on my behalf. But thank you."

"Gibson threatened you."

She shrugged. "Angry words. Besides, what can he really do?"

Possessed of a vivid imagination, Maker could foresee any number of unpleasant situations, but there was little point in worrying a lady with uncertain potentials.

"Would you mind if I stayed here tonight?"

"Of course not. It will be nice to have additional company for dinner. I love Great-Aunt Flora, but her conversation can get a little one-sided." The smile spread across her face. "In the completely opposite way to conversation with you; you may even up the balance some."

"Flora?"

"Hmm?"

"Where?"

"Oh." Amethyst looked away, fussing to tidy. "It's a private matter. I'll explain when she's ready to let me. In answer to your original question, yes, I'm sure."

"A lawyer should look through the contract."

The headshake was small but there.

"I'm happy to look through it."

This time she smiled up at him. "You're not a lawyer."

He'd intended to be. "I have a law degree."

Her brows raised and she smiled. "I'm impressed." She looked at his hand. It was still in hers. "You'll live." She threw the used cotton pad into the bowl and headed for the desk. "Here." She picked up the contract and held it out to him. "If you're really so concerned, feel free to read it, but I'm happy with the contract."

When he reached out to take it, she left him alone in the study. An hour later, he could see why she was happy with the agreement. Sanderson had been very fair, generous even. He'd always liked Sanderson. Young, handsome, intelligent. Sanderson was everything a young man ought to be, and Maker had chosen to do all in his power to aid the younger man into Society and in business. But now Sanderson was clearly forming an attachment to Amethyst and she wasn't pushing him away. Maker found his teeth were clenched. Amethyst and Sanderson made an attractive pairing, they suited each other, complimented one another. He should be happy for them. It made little sense not to be.

Makes perfect sense if you -
Shut up!

He pushed the voice away and folded the contract.

Chapter 17

Passing her cloak to the butler, Amethyst took a moment to check herself in the conveniently hung hall mirror. She'd considered wearing the black gown Maker had unnecessarily brought for her, but that had felt wrong for a social event. After all, she wasn't related to the Professor and continuing to wear black now might be misinterpreted. Suddenly she wished she'd made the case to bring Great-Aunt Flora, only Flora hadn't seemed overly keen on the idea once she'd found out who the host was. It was odd, but Flora would not be drawn. Now she was here and the girl in the mirror looked utterly uncertain.

She'd selected the lilac gown her father had bought her for her eighteenth birthday. Fashion, which had been steady for so many years, had moved on a lot in those three years. Bustles replacing crinolines. With the rise of airships and all the wonderful new technology, it wasn't overly unusual to see women in trousers for such modern pursuits. But not at social events, social events were still very much about the niceties of social mores. Trousers were something Amethyst had never worn and suspected she never would, they were a rather bold choice. She brushed up the dense lace that fell from the top of the gown to ensure that everything that needed to be covered was.

The butler coughed. She turned, smiled and followed as he led the way to the first floor. The room to which she was led had a bigger footprint than the Belgravia mansion - excluding the lab, she amended. Opulently appointed, impressive and welcoming, the room was only to be admired, and perhaps a little envied. The same could be said of the occupants, though given their expressions, 'welcoming' might be stretching the definition somewhat.

Having made the decision to attend quite late, Amethyst was unfashionably late in arriving. The room was full of people chattering, all looking very elegant in their fashionable clothes, jewels sparkling. Hair perfect. Those closest to her paused their conversations to look at her. Whoever they had been expecting or hoping to see, she was clearly a disappointment. Nothing new there. They turned away.

Amethyst was suddenly aware that she could feel the pins in her hair slipping. She wasn't wearing any jewellery, just small gold studs in her ears. Her gown was the only crinoline in the room. *Should have worn the black dress.* She looked like a country bumpkin. *Should have stayed at home.* She stepped ba-

"You can't run away now."

Jumping at the voice, Amethyst turned to the speaker. She saw a young man with slicked back dark hair and an immaculately tailored dinner jacket. The high starched collar reached to a perfectly smooth chin and headlined a carefully crafted cravat.

Amethyst knew her etiquette wasn't the best, but she didn't think it was the done thing for a young man to talk to a young woman without a formal introduction. Though in all honesty, she felt such a fish out of water, she couldn't afford to ignore a lifeline when one was thrown.

"Good evening." She bobbed a small curtsey and got a bow in response. "I'm Amethyst Forester."

"Bobbie." Her companion smiled. "Well Roberta,

but everyone calls me Bobbie."

Roberta? Trying not to be too obvious, Amethyst looked over the person again. The body gave nothing away, but there was a gentility about the lips and eyes that suggested femininity. What was clear was that those cheeks had never seen a razor.

Bobbie's smile broadened. "You're surprised."

Now Amethyst felt her cheeks burn. "I'm sorry."

"Don't be. I like surprising people. I understand you're not averse to giving Society a shock or two yourself."

A frown bobbed onto Amethyst's forehead. "Whatever do you mean?"

"Well, studying engineering, inheriting from an unrelated benefactor and setting up home with a married man right under the wife's nos-"

"I have not!"

The ripple of silence radiated out. Amethyst bowed her head and looked behind Bobbie to the door. Could she make it out?

Bobbie was laughing gently again. "Oh you are a treasure."

Bobbie reached out and took her arm, and Amethyst felt she had no choice but to go where she was led; she'd already made more of a spectacle of herself than she wanted.

As they moved through the crowd, Bobbie snagged two champagne flutes from a passing footman and passed one to Amethyst. Though it might relax her, it might also lead to some foolish behaviour, and she'd already indulged in that by simply coming here. *Serves you right for listening to Maker.* Only listening to Maker *had* served her right, in so many other ways. The investments he had suggested were already paying dividends.

"You look rather like a frightened hare."

Bobbie had manoeuvred them to a quiet area of the room near an alcove displaying an alabaster statue of some Greek god. For one seductive and terrible moment, Amethyst saw Maker in that carved likeness, which, in fact, was far too soft and effeminate to be a statue of Maker. She had to get her mind on other things. Things that she needed to set right. She turned to Bobbie.

"I am not setting up home with Lord Fotheringham," she grated under her breath. "We jointly inherited the house and I got everything in it."

Bobbie's smile broadened, showing even white teeth. "Including the Professor's best friend?"

Amethyst opened her mouth to snap at Bobbie, but she recognised the look; it was the same one she'd seen on her brother so many times - while enjoying vexing her to get a reaction. She snapped her jaw closed, and breathed in deeply.

"Did you introduce yourself with the sole intention of deriding me?" She tried for an even tone, but she didn't quite manage it, even though her voice was low.

"No. I introduced myself because our mutual friend has sent word he will be unable to attend this evening and no one else is in a position to introduce us. Besides, from all I've heard, you seem above the ordinary interesting."

"Well clearly you shouldn't believe all you hear."

"Clearly? Should I consider you boring?"

Her back was already straight, but she felt herself rear.

Bobbie was offering that mocking smile. "Are you always so easily offended?"

That felt like a slap. Normally, Amethyst wasn't quick to take offence. Her family had been good training ground for not taking offence. But tonight she was snapping at a stranger for suggesting a connection to a man she held in high regard and too constant thought. Maker. *This is all his fault.*

She sighed, met Bobbie's direct gaze. "Not usually, no. But there again, I don't usually attend social events where I don't know anyone either. Not even the hostess. It makes me nervous."

"Then why did you come?"

"I was told that Lady Garrington-Smythe can make or break a person's social acceptability. And if what you've said is anything to go by, it sounds as if I need all the help I can get."

"That's true. The fact that Lady Garrington-Smythe can make or break societal standing, I mean - not that you need the help," Bobbie quickly explained when Amethyst raised her brows at the insulting implication.

"But you do. Lady Garrington-Smythe is busy with a couple I consider perfectly odious, but I'm happy to introduce you afterwards, if you'd like."

Forcing a smile, Amethyst said she would. "Thank you. Since you know so much about me, tell me about you."

"Oh." Bobbie looked away. "I'm just one of the idle rich."

Amethyst didn't hold back the small laugh. "Now that I don't believe. You've the courage to self-introduce-"

"Some would call that arrogance."

"Some might, but I think it demonstrates a lively curiosity, self-assurance, and in this case some consideration for a person you know to be an outsider. And speaking of curiosities, a woman dressed as a man in High Society also demonstrates not only individualism, but actually a hint of the arrogance you mentioned, that you can live so differently from the rest of us. Not that I think that's a bad thing, but I can see why the sheep would."

"Sheep?" Bobbie was smiling as she looked around the room. "I like that."

"All in all, you seem much more interesting than me, so there must be more to tell, please do."

"I'm a dabbler," Bobbie said after a few minutes. "I can afford to be. I was married at sixteen, and rather relieved to be widowed before I was seventeen. My husband left me independently wealthy and without dependants. So, you see, I can indulge where I want without the fear of interference. I like my unusual life, I get to try many new things. That's how I met your Professor Richards. I don't believe he approved of me much. My interest in engineering was rather more cursory than yours." Bobbie smiled at her. "What do you think of the assembly?"

Under instruction, Amethyst looked around the room. "They look like..." She wondered how to express her thought. "Like the fashionable set."

"While you care nothing for such fripperies."

"I care about fashion. A little. I'm just not very good at it."

"Clearly."

This time Amethyst took no offence and simply smiled. "Says the woman in trousers."

Bobbie's brows rose, her jaw loosened. Amethyst turned to her and as they shared a smile, a small chuckle, something seemed to shift. Amethyst realised a stranger had just become a friend. Relief eased the tension and loosened all the muscles in her spine. It felt sublime.

"After my husband died, I was working in the attics one day and my skirt got caught on a nail. I went down to change and worried that another skirt might get ruined, so I looked at his wardrobe and thought what would it matter if I wore a pair of his trousers instead. It was a magical experience, surprisingly liberating. So much more comfortable than a tight corset. Thankfully, he and I were of similar sizes."

Amethyst looked her up and down. "Those don't look like borrowed clothes to me."

"No." Bobbie smiled. "These I had specially made. My seamstress was much scandalised at the idea, but as is so often the case, she assuaged her guilt by overcharging."

"Ah, I would have asked for the seamstress' name, but for that last comment."

"I'll introduce you all the same. She's really very good. Do you mind me asking, what is that under the lace?"

For a moment Amethyst had no idea what Bobbie was talking about, then she looked down and remembered, automatically covering the lump with her free hand. She'd almost left the brooch off, but a promise was a promise. She'd rather not explain at all, but the hope of getting away with it had been too much.

"Promise you won't laugh."

"Now I'm really curious. I promise."

"It's a brooch."

Now Bobbie was frowning. "Why hide a brooch?"

Amethyst licked her lips, stuck between loyalty and honesty. "Because it's incredibly ugly."

Bobbie laughed.

"You promised not to do that."

"Sorry." She was still smirking. "Why wear something you think is ugly?"

"Because I keep my promises."

"Oh I see," Bobbie said, "it's going to be like that, is it? Well, perhaps you could explain the promise."

"I will, but this time you really have to promise not to laugh."

"Cross my heart," said Bobbie, miming a cross over her heart to solemnise the promise.

"Given what you know of me, I presume you already know I inherited everything from Professor Richards?"

"Almost everything."

"Everything I have," Amethyst clarified. "Before he died, Professor Richards gave me this brooch and made me promise to wear it at all times, regardless of location, company or occasion, until such time as I didn't need to wear it any longer."

"Now why would I laugh at that?"

Amethyst tried not to squirm at the answer. "Because I don't know how I'll know I don't need to wear it any longer."

"Didn't the Professor tell you?"

Shaking her head, Amethyst felt like such a fool. "He was emphatic that I would know when, but gave no direction as to why."

"So you could be stuck wearing a hideous brooch

for the rest of your life?"

"Into the grave, potentially."

"Hmm." Bobbie frowned. "That's really not very funny, is it?"

The thought had robbed the moment of its amusement. "No."

Bobbie's eyes flickered around the room. Something caught her eye. "Ah." It was a small triumph. "The odious couple have moved on." She was already walking, so Amethyst automatically followed. "Come along, I'll introduce you to Lady Garrington-Smythe."

As they moved through the crowd, Amethyst returned her drink to a half empty tray carried by a servant. Her palms were suddenly damp and she didn't want to drop her drink all over herself or, worse, over her hostess.

Bobbie was approaching an older woman. Amethyst didn't have a clear view of the woman herself, but she could see plenty of esteem and a chair raised on a small dais. It wasn't quite a throne, but it was the most throne-like chair Amethyst had ever been in a room with. She saw deference and a little fear in the surrounding crowd. She knew how they felt. A heavily bejewelled hand waved away some of the sycophants. As they moved away, casting curious and sometimes imperious glances at Amethyst, she stepped up to Bobbie's side. The queen bee was not as old as Amethyst had been expecting. A few greys were visible in her otherwise brown hair. The wrinkles were laughter lines, but there was intelligence in those observant eyes. The way the woman looked her up and down wasn't exactly censure, but it reserved friendship all the same. Clearly her apparel wasn't quite acceptable.

Should've worn the black gown.

"Lady Garrington-Smythe." Bobbie offered a smile. "May I present Miss Amethyst Forester. Miss Forester, Lady Garrington-Smythe."

Lowering her head, Amethyst offered a careful curtsey and tried to ignore the elephants trampling her innards. "Pleasure to meet you, Lady Garrington-Smythe."

"So," Lady Garrington-Smythe said, pinning Amethyst with a direst gaze, "you're the young lady everyone's talking about."

Amethyst swallowed. "I hope not, none of them know me well enough to know what they're talking about."

"Including Lord Fotheringham?"

Amethyst clenched her fists behind her back. "Yes. Not that I imagine he's said that much."

"Probably not." Lady Garrington-Smythe smiled. "Yet knowledge is rarely requisite when Society pontificates."

"Pontificates?" Amethyst tried to resist in her annoyance but it wasn't working well. "As in 'acts in a pompous or dramatic manner'?"

The older lady's smile broadened, and she nodded slightly. "That certainly sounds like Society. So, how are you enjoying the society of my daughter?"

For a moment, Amethyst felt floored, unsure what to say. Then she noticed Bobbie grinning at her side. That grin was all but a smirk.

"To be absolutely honest, a touch irritating. The only thing worse than being the subject of gossip is being the subject of a joke you weren't in on."

"Did she hide her family or her femininity?"

"It wasn't so much hidden as not displayed."

"Another metaphor for Society."

"Indeed." Despite her initial expectations, Amethyst found herself liking the imperious lady as much as her daughter, there was an undercurrent of mischievous realism to the pair of them. As she agreed, Amethyst heard a commotion behind her. She gave an involuntary yelp as she was rudely pushed aside.

"Lord Haversham!" Bobbie exclaimed as she helped steady Amethyst.

"Oh shut up, you unfettered harpy."

"Haversham!" Lady Garrington-Smythe exclaimed as Amethyst regained her footing.

"You wanted to see me, you old hag?"

"Are you drunk?" Amethyst couldn't believe her own ears. For any lord to speak so to a lady of worth was a huge breech of etiquette. That she'd spoken out against him only made things worse, and while she hated being the centre of attention, she couldn't back down now. Her stomach sank as Haversham turned to her.

"Well, well. Maker's bit on the side."

Her hands clenched, but she kept her fists at her sides. "I am not!"

"Nah," Haversham sneered. "You're too ugly."

A gasp and a snigger ran the room hand in hand.

"Well you're no oil painting," she threw back. Apparently, she was on an unstoppable trajectory to insult the high born and openly demonstrate her own lack of worth. Still, there was no point in hiding that now. "Except perhaps the *Ugly Duchess*."

The titter of amusement was more obvious this time.

"But this," she said, "is hardly the time or place to discuss the matter, we should both know better than to provide such sport as this for Society."

"Like you'd know. You're no lady."

"I never claimed to be."

"Just as well."

She decided to ignore the snort and the rippling sniggers. "You however, are supposed to be a lord, and-"

"Like Maker," he interrupted. "You know I can't decide if he's a saint or a fool for not taking what's so clearly available."

Her jaw tightened as did her anger. "Maker is a gentleman. He has breeding, taste and good manners. You may have the breeding, but you'll never be a gentlema-"

Her words cut out as anger overflowed like a palpable force. Suddenly the two of them were locked nose to nose, the fist Haversham had swung caught surprisingly swiftly and strongly in Amethyst's palm. The slap of the contact had caught the watching crowd in a bated breath now universally held in frightful anticipation.

"You," Lady Garrington-Smythe's voice cut through the frozen atmosphere with equal chilling force, "Lord Haversham will leave now, and you will not return."

Amethyst could see conflict and combat in Lord Haversham's eyes, and a little confusion, as if he had no understanding of his words or actions, yet was reluctant to back down. Only when hands landed on

Haversham's shoulders did Amethyst see the two burly men who had come to escort him from the house. Their uniforms marked them as Lady Garrington-Smythe's staff. On feeling the pressure ease from Haversham's fist, Amethyst released her own grip. She stood tall as the crowd parted like the Red Sea and the misshapen man was escorted out. Only when he was gone did Amethyst turn back to her hostess.

"My most sincere ap-"

"No, Miss Forester, it is I who should apologise. I had heard that Lord Haversham's behaviour had degenerated somewhat of late, but it never occurred to me he might strike out at a lady in public. I am quite shocked. As no doubt are you. Come." She patted the chair set to the right of hers. "Come sit by me, that we may recover ourselves together."

Even Amethyst was aware of the social honour she was being afforded. Besides, her knees were feeling rather weak. She thanked the lady and sat as directed.

Chapter 18

Maker was impatient to get home. Gossip at the Lords didn't usually interest him. Unusually, the gossip today had been of matters he was keenly intrigued by, yet he had forced himself to feign disinterest not to give himself away. He spent another hour studying papers he wasn't reading. When the words started swimming before his eyes, he finally put the papers down.

"Is everything quite alright, sir?"

Nothing had been right since Orwell, the man now asking the question, had told him about Haversham's behaviour last night. Orwell was a compact little man, clever and capable, efficient and discrete; everything a clerk really ought to be. Generally, he wasn't a gossip either, but he had reported yesterday evening's events to illustrate the change that had overtaken Lord Haversham, a change that included switching from nos to ayes regarding the Aetheric Concession Bill, the real reason that Orwell had mentioned the incident. It seemed resistance to the bill was failing fast. Maker wasn't sure if Orwell knew of his own connection to Amethyst, the man never mentioned it, but it was such common knowledge, Orwell being oblivious was unlikely.

Nothing was right. He had too much to think about. "Defection."

"Lord Haversham?"

Well it was one thing on his mind, it just wasn't his greatest concern. Maker nodded.

"It is a very sudden about face," Orwell agreed, "but it may not be a complete disaster."

"How?"

Orwell, used to Marker's manner, didn't react to the single word.

"He may not be back in time for the actual vote. I heard that he has gone to his estate, plans to stay there for 'some time,' apparently."

Maker frowned. That wasn't like Haversham either. The hunchback would visit his estate regularly, but never for more than a day or two. He and Haversham had been friends for years, and this change of personality made no sense. Maker wished he understood. He wished he had witnessed firsthand what had happened. He should have been there. Only at the last minute, Violet had decided to - no. Decided was unfair, she didn't choose to be of a nervous disposition, it was just her way. She hadn't been in any condition to go out, and nor had he by the time he'd calmed her and the household down. There were few times when he appreciated the presence of Lady Timpson, but her absence last evening had been keenly felt on all fronts.

Maker looked over his desk. All tidy and papers away. He locked the drawers and stood. "Let me know if anything urgent crops up, I'll be at home."

Even as he said it and left, he knew the likelihood of any part of the statement occurring was low. Few things were that urgent, and he was heading to number seven.

What he found when he got there was somewhat short of the haven of calm he'd been hoping for.

"How dare you insult my husband's good name?"

Violet's voice was shrill and carried too far.

"Lady Violet-"

Amethyst's voice was low and controlled. She had clearly taken on board his request, his plea, for her to not argue with Violet. He decided not to comment about the way Edwards rolled his eyes, the man probably didn't appreciate Maker's range of peripheral vision. Instead, Maker strode straight to the drawing room.

Amethyst was sitting on the couch, her hands clasped tightly in her lap. Violet was standing over her, a red-faced tower of rage.

"Don't you 'Lady Violet' me, you little-"

"Violet."

On hearing his voice, Violet straightened and look to her husband. "You have no idea how appallingly this-" She paused to emphasise the word she sneered, "*thing* has behaved. Any association we had should be cut off immediately. How incensed poor Lady Garrington-Smythe must be."

"Lady Garrington-Smythe was incensed," Amethyst said. "By Lord Haversham's behaviour."

"Indeed."

Violet scowled at her husband. "Like you'd know. You weren't there."

"Neither were you," Amethyst pointed out. "But I was. It may not be the most ladylike thing to do, but I did stop Lord Haversham punching me. Something Eugenie, as she was at pains to have me call her-"

Maker groaned inwardly. Amethyst couldn't be expected to know that Violet had once had very short shrift for calling Eugenie, Eugenie.

"-was very grateful for. In fact, she has invited me to a private luncheon tomorrow. Bobbie delivered the invitation personally when she called earlier."

Everything about Violet tensed.

"Violet."

Only when his wife turned eyes full of hate and rage upon him did he speak again. "Timpson."

After so long a marriage, Violet had learned to interpret his single words, and he had made sure to collect Lady Timpson and install her at home before he came across here.

"Well," Violet said, her voice calmer, if overly superior, "of course. I have a guest due."

"Arrived."

"I must hurry." She was already sweeping past.

Surprisingly as she passed, she caught his arm.

"Don't come home tonight."

He inclined his head in agreement. He'd had absolutely no intention of going 'home' tonight. He wasn't about to share the fact that in many respects he felt he was already home. A feeling that intensified with the closing of the front door and the knowledge that Violet was gone.

"Apologies," he said when he looked at Amethyst.

She was flexing out her fingers. He guessed she'd been clenching her fists. "You've nothing to apologise for. Unless you came here to berate me for my appalling public performance as well."

"No." From what he understood, her performance has been far from appalling. He moved across to take his preferred seat by the hearth. His intention to ensure she was in good health after her ordeal was satisfied; she was clearly fighting fit. "Thanks."

For a moment she frowned at him. "For not shouting at your wife? Who by the way very much deserved to be shouted at."

There wasn't much he could say to that, so he simply nodded. She stood and he questioned the action with a look.

"I'll let Mrs Shaw know you'll be staying for dinner. You are staying, aren't you?"

Not trusting his voice, he nodded. In Amethyst's absence, he noticed that there was a book on the couch; Violet had disturbed her mid-read. Even at home she had a habit of doing that to him. He looked more closely at the book; it was the collection of short gothic romances he'd sent her. He smiled to himself, he thought she'd appreciate it and this was greater proof than the thank you note she'd sent. To his right was a small occasional table, slightly recessed from the chair, pushed back out of the way while not in use. The book he'd been reading the last time he was here remained at hand. He picked it up, opened it at the bookmark. He'd read another chapter in the copy he had across the Square. He was flicking through the pages to catch up when Amethyst returned.

"Dinner will be at seven. Just you and I, I'm afraid. Great-Aunt Flora is dining with friends this evening. And I can't offer anything special I'm afraid, we'd not expected company."

"Fine." He only really wanted the tranquillity of the house now he knew Amethyst was well.

She froze in reaching for her book. "Fine as in any offering is acceptable? Fine as in you'll put up with the scraps I'm offering? Is that fine good or fine bad?"

His bookmark went into the book. "Good."

She nodded and sat, the book coming open as she did so. For a moment he just watched her. It didn't take long for her eyeline to rise above the edge of the book, and a beat or two later she looked directly at him.

"Was there something you wanted to know,

Maker?"

Everything about her. He just didn't know how to ask.

"Bobbie?"

"Lovely woman." Saying nothing more, Amethyst kept eye contact, and she was the first to break into a half-smile. "She's different."

"True." But Maker was fond of her too. He liked different. That was doubtless part of why he liked Amethyst.

"We found a lot of common ground. We're interested in a number of the same things, with sufficient differences in experience and knowledge to make it interesting."

"Like?"

She didn't respond immediately, but her smile and expression hinted at a sauciness he found refreshing. "Engineering."

The look hadn't come from so prosaic a subject.

"Amme?" It was part question, part warning; he felt an unaccustomed smile tugging at the corners of his mouth.

Her smile broadened. "I think I'll go and dress for dinner."

He stood as she rose, and suddenly they were face to face. She was so close. An easy reach. He stepped back, offered her a tight bow and watched her leave. He wanted to follow her, to ask her a million and one questions to reassure himself, only he didn't have the right.

They met in the dining, room where dinner was promptly served at seven. The starter, a rather pleasant homemade pate, they ate in silence. When Edwards removed the plates, Amethyst took up her wine glass. Her look to Maker as she drank was considering. Only after Edwards had placed the main course before them and left the room did she speak.

"You know you're only the second person to ever call me Amme."

He raised his brow. "Who?"

"My twin brother."

He nodded, put down his own glass and moved to eat.

"Amme?" he said a few mouthfuls later.

"Ben?"

He liked when she called him Ben. No one else did. Except perhaps his mother. Looking at Amethyst now, alone with him, he felt comfortable, happy. He didn't feel he had to be anything in particular for her, just him. Being him was enough. Together they were everything a couple should be. Only they couldn't be. He couldn't.

"Don't," he warned her.

"You prefer Maker then?"

Not trusting his voice, or the cold edge he'd heard come into hers, he just nodded.

"Alright, Maker. Luckily for you I have no objection to being called Amme, but perhaps we should keep that as our little secret."

There were other big secrets he'd rather share only with her, but such ideas left him in an uncomfortable position. He needed to think of other things.

"Haversham?"

Maker noticed that she was very careful in how she answered, giving a very clinical description of what had actually happened. In conclusion, she looked at him and shrugged.

"I don't know Lord Haversham very well, but it didn't seem like the same man I met when I was with you. Quite the reverse, in fact."

It seemed equally odd to Maker. The Haversham Amethyst had seen at the Lords was the same one that Maker had known for many years. A Haversham who would insult one lady and try to punch another was not a man Maker recognised. He'd last seen Haversham three days ago. The man had been jolly and amusing, taking his usual wry twist on life. He'd been looking forward to some exhibition or other, talking in greater than necessary detail of his latest conquest, full of life and exuberance. He couldn't understand what had happened. What did it mean for the upcoming vote?

"But on to more interesting topics." Amethyst's positive tone pulled Maker from his thoughts. "I understand you and Roberta Davenport are good friends."

Maker couldn't, didn't want to hold back the smile. He wouldn't have phrased it quite that way.

"My God, an actual smile." Amethyst's eyes were twinkling as she looked at him. "Does that mean I'll get more than a single word response?"

Carefully, he controlled his features. "Perhaps."

She rolled her eyes. "You really are hopeless!" After a sip of wine, she spoke again. "Bobbie says you've known one another for some time. Fourteen or fifteen years?"

Maker nodded.

"She was rather cagey about how she met you. The exact circumstances were kept hidden. She became strangely evasive when directly asked. Why is that?"

Maker considered the truth, only it didn't reflect

well on either him or Bobbie. He didn't doubt Amethyst's ability to understand, it was more that he had a feeling that she held him in rather high regard, and he didn't want that to change, he wouldn't risk her seeing the worst of him. He shrugged.

"But the two of you are friends?"

"Yes."

"I got the impression she doesn't get on well with your wife."

Sometimes he wondered if anyone did. There again, Lady Timpson was keeping Violet happy and out of his hair, so he shouldn't be too harsh.

"No."

"Then can I ask something of you that I couldn't ask her?"

It was dangerous ground, but he had to give some way. A small movement of his head indicated his permission.

"Would I be wrong in believing that Bobbie thinks more like a man than a woman?"

There were so many ways in which that were true, but there were other factors to consider. In many respects, Amme's own analytical mind would classify her as thinking more like a man than a woman.

"Thinking?"

"In terms of, well..." Amethyst was physically squirming. "I mean... I know this isn't a socially acceptable topic. Especially given..." Her hand gestured vaguely between them.

"Given?"

She swallowed. "That you are married and I am not."

The significance of that was not lost on him, and he

suspected he knew where this was going. He wasn't sure he wanted to go there with her.

"Sex," she said.

Breath halted in his lungs. He swallowed a rising panic at the images he had to push away.

"I mean talking about it," she added quietly. "We shouldn't." Suddenly her chair scraped back, and she rushed out.

For a moment, he continued to stare at the empty doorway. Was she too soft to finish the discussion, or too delicate?

"Miss Forester won't be having dessert, sir?"

Maker turned to Edwards. "Nor I."

He placed his napkin on the table and stood.

"Thank Shaw."

Edwards nodded, as Maker walked from the dining room. The empty drawing room wasn't much of a surprise, and neither was finding Amethyst pacing in the study. There were papers in her hand, but she wasn't attending to them. He stepped over to her. She stopped, allowed him to take the papers and return them to the desk. She hadn't moved when he shifted to stand straight in front of her. They were closer than his usual personal space would allow, but not as close as he would really like. *Stop it.* He could see confusion in her eyes. The curiosity, perhaps seduction. Perhaps he was just transferring his own wants onto her. No question he needed to think about something else.

"Ask." If she asked him to kiss her, he doubted he'd have the strength to refuse.

"Is Bobbie a erm... is Bobbie a lesbian?"

He was surprised she was so forthright about it. Surprised and pleased. So many couldn't even face acknowledging the existence of such women. "Yes."

She nodded. "Thought so."

"Implication?" Was that cold tone his? He watched as she drew back; clearly his tone and the single word had somehow insulted her.

"None. Not to me. What she does in the privacy of her of her own bedchamber is her business. I'm not that way inclined, and I won't condemn her making her own choice."

"Good." But that left another question.

"Whatever the law says."

"It doesn't."

She frowned up at him. "Homosexuality is definitely against the law."

"For men."

For a moment she looked up, her jaw slightly loose. "Oh. Thought it covered all."

"Technicalities."

Now she was frowning. "In the writing of the law."

He nodded, but there were still questions. "Why ask?"

"Just to be sure. I don't want to accidently offend her by making an assumption either way."

"Worried?"

"What about?"

She looked truly confused, as if she couldn't fathom a reason why she should be worried.

"Advances."

She still looked confused. Then she blinked, her brows raised, she obviously realised his meaning. Then she laughed.

"Oh Maker - you are funny. Why would I expect a woman to make advances towards me? Men don't. You should know that better than most." Still laughing, she turned away to take up her papers and sit behind her desk. He and her question were clearly forgotten.

He couldn't forget. Leaving her, he went to the drawing room to pace in peace. Did she really not see that she was attractive? He could easily see Bobbie making advances - he'd have to have words, make sure she didn't. Perhaps Amethyst didn't realise that other men might consider her and her keen intellect unduly masculine, think she was too like Bobbie. Maker decided he wouldn't mention that to Amethyst; he suspected that she would be upset that people didn't see her for what she was. He saw, and he liked what he saw. Clearly Sanderson did too. The man practically drooled in her presence. He himself wasn't much better. There again if Amethyst could laugh so openly in his face, she was obviously oblivious to his attraction. Which was just as well. Unless she wasn't, and was just putting a socially acceptable spin on an impossible situation. Perhaps she simply didn't return the attraction. Or did and wanted to deny it.

Urgh!

Unable to stand this circuitous thinking any more, Maker turned on his heels, and marched out without a word.

Chapter 19

Amethyst sat in the study and looked at the pile of post in front of her. Various social invitations. Maker had been right. Now Lady Garrington-Smythe had accepted her, it seemed they all had. She didn't know what to do. She wasn't comfortable socialising, she didn't really know who she should accept and who she could refuse.

Maker would know.

She drove the thought from her mind with a definite shake of the head. Maker hadn't been near in two days.

But she knew someone else who would know just who she should see. She gathered the invitations into a pile and went to her room to fetch a bag. After collecting a coat and gathering the invitations, she went to see Bobbie.

Thankfully, Bobbie was home and accepted her call. Lady Garrington-Smythe was herself out calling on others, something Amethyst was surprisingly pleased about. As much as Eugenie had proved to be extremely friendly and a very gracious host, Amethyst didn't feel entirely comfortable, as if she wasn't in the least bit worthy of being in the presence of a true lady. But she kept that thought to herself, not wishing to insult Bobbie. Bobbie was much more understandable to Amethyst, she knew where she was with Bobbie, even if every moment she suspected sarcasm. All the same, she was comfortable explaining the dilemma she was facing to Bobbie.

"Well just accept the ones from people you liked when you met them here."

"That's part of the problem," Amethyst explained as

the two shared tea and conversation in Bobbie's private sitting room, "I can't remember half of them."

The other girl laughed.

"Oh don't," Amethyst begged, feeling quite foolish, "there were so many names and faces, your dear mother introduced me to so many that they all merged and confused. And I'd been drinking."

"You had a sip or two of champagne to start the evening and a small glass of watered wine later. You had hardly been drinking." Bobbie was looking through the stiff invitation cards. "Oh."

That sounded disappointed. "What was that for?"

Bobbie glanced up. "There's no invitation from Lord Montgomery."

"Lord Montgomery?" Amethyst frowned. "Who was he and why should there be an invitation?"

Bobbie's lips widened into a genuine smile. "Oh you'll remember Lord Montgomery. He's very tall, broad-shouldered, really rather a dashing gentleman. He's the one who couldn't take his eyes off you all evening, and your eyes tended often in his direction too."

Amethyst felt her face burn. "You mean the gentleman with the auburn hair and clear blue eyes?"

Bobbie laughed. "That's the one. He doesn't come to town often but I understood that he was going to be opening up the Montgomery estate for a summer party this year, I expected that you would be first among the guests. Still, here's one you should accept. Lady Matilda…"

As Bobbie went on, she gave a potted history and a general standing of each of the potential hosts, often in such a humorous way that Amethyst found the tension she hadn't realised she was carrying flow from her.

Eventually, after she had taken Bobbie's advice, Bobbie moved the conversation onto her relationship with Sanderson.

"Is business the only association you seek there?"

It was a point worth considering. "Mr Sanderson is a very nice man, but he's made no indication of interest." She laughed. "In fact the only man who has is, of all people, Lord Haversham."

Bobbie laughed with her and told her about Miss Brightmoor. After a very pleasant two hours, Amethyst walked home. She had to admit that Maker's absence was weighing on her mind. As was the lack of information from the police over the Professor's death. Inspector Jenson had promised that he would keep her informed, but had that been nothing more than a platitude?

She was just writing the last of her acceptances at the second desk, which she had come to think of as her social desk, when she heard the front door open. Edwards' ability to get to the door before a visitor knocked really was quite impressive. Curious, she stepped out into the hall, and found herself facing Maker.

"Oh." She wasn't quite sure why she was disappointed. His defection for the last few days had been a disappointment too. Apparently she wasn't about to be satisfied with anything. "I wasn't expecting to see you today." She looked at the briefcase in his hand. "Is there a problem?"

"No," Maker said.

Edwards had closed the door and disappeared back downstairs so they were alone again. And again his word economy scraped her nerves.

"Well if you want to use the study feel free, I won't disturb you."

Heading into the drawing room, she decided not to notice what he did. But it brought back her other questions about the man, his potential questions over her. Which reminded her. Going back to the study, she picked up the responses she had made. She couldn't avoid looking at Maker as she pored over the papers he'd spread out on the working desk. There was something very strained about his expression and his posture.

"Maker?"

He looked up at her, his face typically expressionless.

"I know I said that I wouldn't disturb you," she said as she picked up her letters, "but is everything well with you?"

He took a moment to consider her. For a second she wondered if he might actually tell her what was wrong.

"Yes."

So maybe not. Of course, she had no reason to expect him to confide in her, and she shouldn't encourage it. "Well, you know where I am if you have an aberration and want to talk to me."

Striding out of the study, she headed down to the butler's pantry where she asked Edwards to see to the delivery of her letters, then went to the kitchen to discuss provisions and servings with Shaw.

Over dinner, she told Maker and Great-Aunt Flora of her visit to Bobbie. Neither had much to say. From Maker that was usual, and Flora being subdued was to be expected tonight, as the old lady had received bad news during the day, its personal nature was too close to home for the old lady. Amethyst had to respect that. So Amethyst prattled on in order that they didn't all sit in extreme silence. Prattled and wondered. She couldn't tell what was going on in Maker's head. His face was for the most part neutral and inexpressive. But every time he moved, there was a tightness about his features that suggested he was in pain. It was a tightness that gathered whenever he took a deep breath. She'd seen that kind of injury on her brothers, and what it followed was never good. She remembered the ease with which he had punched Gibson. Was Maker some kind of private pugilist?

Whatever he was, he wasn't talking about it and she was really rather relieved when he excused himself early and headed for bed. Great-Aunt Flora was similarly inclined. Given the cause of her silence was a strain on her physically as well, Amethyst was relieved Maker offered to help the old lady upstairs, admiring the fact that he helped despite not knowing what was going on. In the wake of their departure, Amethyst slumped in her chair and stared into the fire. She really didn't understand Maker. Why did he come to her home if he didn't want to talk to her? Why stay here? She suspected that must cause his wife consternation. She knew it caused rumours she'd rather not face. Which in turn begged the question of why she allowed it? That was simple; she couldn't refuse him. She wanted to see him, talk to him, be his friend. Friend? If she was honest with herself, what she wanted was more than friendship, but that was impossible and he would offer nothing more. She was a fool in a trap of her own making.

Finding she could no longer focus on the words of her book, she put it aside, but her hand lingered lovingly over the leather cover. Why would Maker make her a present of such a thing? She was thoroughly enjoying each of the short horror stories, but it was an odd gift and she wasn't at all sure what it said about her, or his impression of her. Still, it had easily become her favourite possession, and one she again cradled to her breast as she retired to her own room.

* * *

Not as ready for sleep as she'd thought, Amethyst sat at her dressing table and brushed out her hair. Not that it made that much difference, it still curled all over the place. Amethyst realised she was getting too jumpy, and it wasn't because of the horror stories. It had to do with knowing Maker was in the house. His presence shouldn't bother her, but it did. She refused to acknowledge why, she couldn't make that too real.

There again, not having him around bothered her more than she wanted to admit. So much for independent living being such a great move, she was hardly sleeping for fear of what the night might bring while she was alone. It was foolish and she knew it, but coming from such a large family, being alone was both a cherished possibility and a dread she didn't know how to deal with. Perhaps her father had been right, perhaps she should move back home.

She sighed and pushed that idea away. If he was right, and that was a big if, her father was right for all the wrong reasons. He hadn't exactly told her she was no longer considered a member of the family, but none of her letters home had been answered, so she had to make the assumption. Of course, she could actually go home and find out, but then she might find out for certain something she didn't want to know.

Slamming down her hairbrush, Amethyst got up to pace. She hadn't even undressed yet, only taken off her shoes and let her hair down because the pins were beginning to dig.

Mid-stride, she stopped. That sound hadn't been her footsteps. Not daring to breathe, she strained to hear. There it was again. Someone was walking about downstairs. Probably it was just Edwards, but she glanced at the clock. Quarter to one in the morning. Edwards was probably in bed by now. Perhaps Maker had got up. That 'perhaps' was too big and she needed to be sure. Her hand was on the cricket bat before she even thought about it. It had originally been Jade's, but now she kept it. It was probably a stupid idea, and if it was Maker moving about on the landing, she was going to look a fool. Her grip tightened, and she carefully opened the door. Better a fool with a weapon then a vulnerable victim if it wasn't Maker.

Creeping down the shadowed hallway, she raised the bat to her shoulder, best to be ready. Then she saw it, the man's shadow. It was tall and menacing, broad and solid.

Amethyst swallowed. Whoever that was, it wasn't Maker and it certainly wasn't Edwards. Heart pounding, she rounded the corner and there he was. He loomed over her. Every feature ominous in the shadows. He stepped towards her. She swung the bat. He yelled out, fell back and to the side, and she stepped forward to try again. Her bat caught on something. She yanked, but suddenly there was an arm around her waist, pulling her from her feet, while her captor tried to pull the bat from her resisting hands. Two of them. She couldn't help it. She screamed as she started to kick back.

At least she had the satisfaction of connecting with his shin and hearing a grunt of pain.

"Amethyst!"

That was Maker's voice in her ear.

"Stop!"

Stunned into stillness, she looked over her shoulder to see that it was Maker who had hold of her.

"Explain."

He was calm, she wasn't.

"He's breaking in!"

"No."

How dare he be so calm when she was near breaking point? "Well someone has been."

He took a breath. It sounded shaky. "Evidence?"

"I am not imagining it." Though even she realised it was starting to look that way.

"Yeah, well I'm not breaking in, that's why I'm not running to avoid gettin' caught."

She looked across at the man's sarcasm, at the fact that he was simply standing there watching the two of them. "Yes, I admit, that is odd." She looked back over her shoulder. "You know him?"

The thump-shuffle was the last thing Amethyst wanted to hear, especially when she felt Maker flinch at the noise too. He put her back on her feet, but when she tried to move away, he wouldn't let go of the bat, so she had to, she couldn't allow Great-Aunt Flora to see her being that close with Maker.

"What are you youngsters up to at this hour?"

"It's nothing, Great-Aunt Flora." Amethyst tried for a normal tone, but wasn't sure that she achieved it.

"Nothing?"

"Yes."

"With a cricket bat?"

"Well…" she floundered and turned to Maker; he fell back on his usual silence. She needed his support, but she couldn't ask easily. She'd been trying to ignore how she has felt when he held her and the fact that he was clearly wearing nothing but a long nightshirt. Thankfully it *was* long. Though she kept her eyes up, she was surprisingly aware of how lean and shapely Maker's lower legs were. And hairy, but not unpleasantly so. The purple bruise on his shin was worrying though. Surely she couldn't have caused that? She really shouldn't be thinking about his legs. Or any part of his body. Or undressing him. Or the way he was looked at her. Or…

"Amethyst?"

She turned to face Flora, not sure what she was supposed to say.

"The cricket bat?"

"It was Jade's."

Flora's features pinched at the name.

"Who's Jade?"

She swung on the man. "Who are you?"

"Blanchard." The tone was too haughty for a man in his position. "His Lordship's valet."

She looked at the big man. He looked more like a heavy, a bodyguard perhaps. "I didn't know he had one." There again, he was a lord. "Well, I hadn't actually thought about it." Now she really felt like a fool. She also felt she had to defend herself. "That doesn't explain why you're creeping about my house in the middle of the night."

"It's my job to see to my lord's dress and undress."

Don't think about it.

"I needed to confirm his outfit for tomorrow."

She noticed his accent became much more refined as he spoke. Clearly he was used to covering his origins. She wasn't sure she could trust this Blanchard. "Wonderful. Does that mean you'll be creeping around in the morning as well, then?"

"I won't creep, Miss, if you won't be armed."

"Blanchard," Maker admonished.

"Cricket bat?"

They all turned to Flora.

"I… err… was going to hit him with it."

The old lady's far too seeing eyes crinkled and she glanced at Maker. "You'd be better off hitting his cricket bat."

Frowning Amethyst glanced at Maker, at the bat still in his hand. Then back to Flora.

"It's definitely Jade's bat."

Flora smiled came closer and lovingly patted Amethyst's cheek. "Such innocence." With just a swivel of her eyes, she pinned Maker with a look. "Innocence you will not corrupt."

"Flora!" Amethyst found the idea irksome. "I am not some ignorant child."

"You didn't get the point," then Flora was laughing. "Thankfully."

"It's Jade's cricket ba-Oh my God!" Her hands covered her burning face and her eyes wide as she realised what Flora was talking about. "Oh lord."

Unable to publically bear the thought, she rushed away from the others and hid in her room. She closed the door firmly and declared she was never going out again.

Chapter 20

"What would I do with a lady's maid?"

Uncertain what to say, Maker stepped to the hallway, looking towards the laboratory and listening for sounds upstairs. He knew what Violet did with her lady's maid but suggesting that to Amethyst was out of the question, she just was not the same kind of woman. There was little point in appealing to her on grounds of ostentation or easing her own personal burden, she simply wouldn't worry about such things. There was one thing that seemed to concern her though. They had finished breakfast, a strained affair not least because the bruising of his ribs and shin felt worse today. Violet's rages were becoming uncontrollable. Still, he wouldn't think of that now, he had another lady to be concerned with.

"Are you looking for Great-Aunt Flora?"

At Amethyst's question, he returned his attention to her, moved back into the room.

"While I don't doubt she would positively agree with you, she's not here."

"Why?"

He was surprised by the way Amethyst looked away, had to steel herself to look back and answer. "I didn't want to tell you without her permission, but she said I could last night. Great-Aunt Flora came to London to visit her son, Malachi. He's 63 and gravely ill. She would have been with him the whole time, only my mother discovered Flora was in town and asked her to stay here instead. Seems my mother is as concerned for my reputation as my father, but sought to protect it in rather a different manner." She sighed. "Since the doctors suggest that Malachi might not have long, Flora has decided to stay with him as much as possible, so we may not see her for a few days. But that's why she's been so out of sorts lately."

Maker's felt his surprise manifest with a brow lift.

"Oh, trust me, were Flora her normal self, you and I would have felt the wrath of that cane far more than we have." The indulgent smile didn't last, turning instead to a small frown. "But you were telling me of lady's maids. Why should I?"

"Conform."

She frowned at him. "Conform to what? Societal rule?"

"Yes."

The idea clearly didn't please her.

"Are you telling me that just because I'm an heiress now, I have to be something I'm not? That I have to adhere to some stupid set of ridiculously strict rules just because Society says so?"

"Yes."

"Rules made by the same Society that tells me I can't go to university or study engineering just because I'm a girl."

He couldn't fault the truth of her statement or blame her for her disdain. And there was no way to respond with a single word. Thankfully, with Amethyst he didn't feel he had to. She had been very complimentary about his arguments in Parliament. "Your position now is very different to what it was when you lived in Kew. If you want to be considered and accepted as a young lady of worth, and move freely in Society, you will need the help of a lady's maid. Preferably one who can help you select more suitable attire."

She reared; he'd clearly affronted her. She glanced at the gown, another plain offering, brown this time. "You know I think I like you better when you're monosyllabic."

"Many of the words I use have multiple syllables."

For a moment, her lips compressed and her eyes narrowed. "Mono-" she couldn't think of the word at that point, but then he wasn't sure there was one. "Mono-word-ic then."

Whatever the word might or might not have been, that was not it, and apparently he'd upset her enough that she shifted in her seat and opened her book, distinctly ignoring him. He could see her book was upside down, but he wouldn't mention it. He took up his own book, and returned to the passage he was reading. He was largely lost in the pages when he heard her mutter.

"I wouldn't know how, anyway."

He put his book aside and looked at Amethyst. She looked like she was still reading, but he knew she was not.

"Sorry?"

She threw a glare across the room. It wasn't nearly as pointed as Violet could get, and was softened by the small smile she was unsuccessfully trying to hide. "I said I wouldn't know how."

"Expand."

Her lips pursed again, and the fact that she had to hold them there a few seconds suggested she was trying not to smile. He had to fight the urge himself.

"I wouldn't know how to go about getting a lady's maid."

There were a number of ways, but if she preferred single words, she could have them. "Advertise."

"Where? How?" Her book went to the occasional table and she stood and started to pace. "I wouldn't know what to say in the advertisement, or what to look for in any responses, in any applicant." She had completed a circuit of the room and now stood before him, her pale fingers entwined and her brow furrowed in vexation. "I suppose you'd know all these things."

He looked up at her; there was something of the little girl lost about her that was really quite sweet. Though he suspected she would hate for him to say so. "Largely."

"Then will you help me?"

"Naturally."

Her hands unclasped and for a second looked as though they would reach for him, but she pulled herself back.

"Thank you."

It wasn't fair that she had to pull herself back. If there was a woman in the world he wanted to reach for him, it was this woman. Instead, he was trapped with the unfeeling Violet, her infernal selfishness and unavoidable nerves. That thought brought up another. Violet had had a number of lady's maids over the last couple of years, one who had been summarily dismissed,' rather unfairly in Maker's view. She'd been a capable and intelligent young woman, who had shown signs of good breeding and manners that would easily support Amethyst. Maker knew what had happened to make her leave, and what Violet had said and done to cost the woman her prospects. Amethyst wasn't Violet.

Chapter 21

Maker had spent a lot of the afternoon and most of the evening trying to rally support against the Aetheric Concessions Bill, but it had been a frustrating experience. Even those who had been tentatively inclined to support his cause were starting to dismiss his arguments without reason, consideration or explanation. While he still firmly believed that his objections were valid and right, he was starting to wonder if he was fighting a losing battle.

Looking at number 30, he realised that that was definitely a losing, if not lost, battle. Instead, he turned. It was at times like this he needed Professor Richards to talk to. The calming presence of a hand on the shoulder; the listening his father never did; the feeling that he wasn't on his own; those were the things he missed.

Edwards had the door open before Maker could use his key.

"Sorry to disturb you so late." Maker kept his voice down.

"I was just locking up, sir," Edwards said as he locked the front door.

"Miss Forester?"

"Retired a couple hours ago, sir."

That was early. Maker frowned. "Is she unwell?"

"Just tired, I believe sir. I understand she's had some trouble sleeping. She probably isn't used to the sounds this house makes at night yet, sir. It's quite a change for her."

"Indeed."

"And is there any word of Lady Gordon?"

"Only that she won't be returning tonight. Can I get you anything, milord? A nightcap?"

"No." Maker offered no expression in response to the other man's consideration. "I'll go straight to my room." He moved to do so, but stopped on the first step. "Edwards?"

The man looked up at him. "Sir?"

"Have you evidence of any break-ins?"

The man looked uncomfortable.

"Edwards?"

"No evidence, sir, but…"

He waited.

"Sometimes I'm sure that things have been moved. I check the doors and windows every night, I'm sure Miss Forester does too, and they are always locked. Yet there have been several mornings where I have found windows unlocked."

Not exactly evidence, but unnerving all the same. Maker thanked the man and moved up.

Upstairs and alone, Maker found this bedroom a much more comfortable refuge than the club. It was more personal, his. One of the few places that *was* his. He knew that his room across the street was subject to Violet's frequent snooping. Not that he had anything to hide, but he valued the idea of actually having some privacy.

He laughed at himself as he removed his jacket. What would he do with privacy if he actually had it? His marriage was a sham, but he wouldn't break his vows. Society had many rules, so many he felt chained by them. Yet the keeping of a mistress by a married man was often knowingly ignored, if not openly tolerated. The image of Amethyst by his side had to be pushed away. Society might tolerate it, but Violet, hypocrite that she was, never would. He owed her and her delicate nerves some measure of care.

He wasn't sure why.

A promise made-

In frustration he threw his cravat pointlessly across the room.

He heard a rattle, turned in time to see that the cravat had caught the top of the oil lamp, a lamp he had absentmindedly placed partly off the top of a tallboy. He was helpless, moving too slowly as the inevitable fall came. The lamp tipped off the edge, his hands were still rising and his step half taken as the glass shade shattered across the floor and oil began to leak.

With the shatter, time returned to normal and he swept up the brass body, stamping out the small fire that had started.

This time he was more careful in his placement of the lamp. Looking down, he saw broken glass and a small oil spill that would stain the floorboards. It wasn't enough to worry about now. Perhaps it would serve as a reminder that whenever he released any emotion, bad things happened.

He moved to the bed and sat, pulling up one shoe, from which he pulled a small sliver of glass that had caught when he'd stamped out the fire. For a moment he turned it around, watching the edges catch the light. Then he flicked it to join the rest of the scatter on the floor.

Removing his cufflinks, he told himself that he should at least go warn Mrs Shaw of the danger, but he was dog tired and just wanted to sleep. Taking hold of his shirt, he pulled it from his trousers – he froze.

Straining his ears, holding his breath, he listened.

A floorboard creaked.

Moving as quietly as he could to the door, avoiding the glass, he took hold of the handle. Twisting suddenly, he pulled the door towards him.

"Argh!"

The sudden scream was cut off. Amethyst was now leaning against the far wall of the hall, her right hand holding a trembling candle and the left covering her mouth. Her eyes were wide and frightened. She was wrapped in that ageing dressing gown, he could see several of the large lace layers were adrift at the seams. More than before or had he just not noticed how bad it was?

Now her brows drew down and she scowled at him when her hand dropped away.

"Maker! You scared me."

He could say the same thing, though his heart was rapidly recovering.

"I thought I heard someone downstairs."

Quite why she was whispering, he wasn't sure.

"Me."

She rolled her eyes. "It sounded like glass breaking."

Maker looked across to the shattered glass on his floor. "Me."

For a moment she frowned, then moved to the doorway, leaning in to look where he had indicated. It was impossible to ignore the sensation of her hair, freed from its binding and falling in glorious disarray across his exposed chest. It tickled and seduced. He swallowed and closed his eyes, his hands rising to re-button the fabric of his long shirt; he didn't want her noticing his shame.

"You broke a lamp? You didn't hurt yourself, did you?"

Opening his eyes, he found her standing straight and looking at him. Was that actual concern in her eyes? Something tightened in his gut.

"No."

"Good. Why were you at the door, anyway? Did you hear something too?"

Schooling his emotions, he kept his face as blank as possible. "You."

Surprise flicked across her face, then she smiled. "So you disturb me and I disturb you."

She had no idea how much she disturbed him. Though if he disturbed her in any way, she didn't show it. Would she seem so comfortable with him as they were, in such a state of undress, if she were actually in any way affected by him?

Now she checked the corridor before turning back to him. "Since we are both awake, may I ask a favour?"

With no idea what she might ask, he nodded. His breath caught when she walked into his room and placed her candle on the side.

"I have a bit of a knotty problem."

There wasn't enough oxygen in the world when she undid the tie of her nightgown and let it slide from her shoulders to her wrists. He stared at her turned back. She still wore her corset and petticoats. It had been some time since he'd seen a woman in her underwear and he had to school his body not to react. It was clear why she hadn't removed the garments, the ties that bound them had become hopelessly entangled.

Stepping up behind her and reaching for the knot

was an unavoidable mistake. He could smell her lavender scent. Wild curls tickled his face, his eyes were fixed on the creamy whiteness of her shoulder. He leaned forward, his height and her innocence providing a rare and precious view. Dear God in Heaven, the temptation of flesh.

"Maker?"

Her voice was soft and warm. "Hmm?"

"You're not undoing the knot."

Indeed he wasn't. It was in his hand and he was pulling it towards him, keeping her close. "No."

Some strange paralysis had overtaken his mind and body. She was here, close.

"Ben?"

The word whispered to him, drugging him. Finally able to move his eyes, he looked into hers. She'd twisted her neck up so she could look at him. He could feel the warmth of her breath on his face. Only an inch-

A crash resounded from the ground floor.

They both jumped, heads turned to the door.

"Well that wasn't either of us."

Her ability to function surprised him as she stepped away, pulling her dressing gown back on. The spell she had cast over him broke, and he reached out, pulling her back when she headed for the door.

"Stay."

She seemed to comply as he strode from the room, away from temptation. The light was only that filtering into the house from outside, which wasn't much. Each step of the stairs was taken carefully.

Now his heart was thumping for a new reason. The cold ate at the knots in his stomach. Amethyst had said she'd thought she'd heard someone in the house. It seemed he should have trusted her judgement.

At the foot of the stairs he paused, straining to hear. Something seemed to be moving in the back of the house. He crept to the end of the hallway trying to make out if the noise came from the laboratory or was echoing up from the kitchen and servants area below.

A table scraped across a floor.

Moving back from the entrance to below stairs, he turned to the study door, but something caught the corner of his eye.

Amethyst.

Standing in the hall by the front door. The candle was in her hand and her dressing gown firmly and demurely tied. She looked pale and a little frightened.

"I know you told me to stay upstairs," she whispered, "but I'm not good at taking orders."

He was rapidly learning that, and held himself back from rolling his eyes. Turning back to the study door, the slight rustling of Amethyst's petticoats told him she had moved closer. Carefully, he twisted the handle of the study door. He glanced back to Amethyst.

"Stay." This time he waited to see her nod.

Switching his attention back to the door, he thrust it open and stepped inside. It was dark, but his keen eyes scanned the scanned the study, hoping to make out a shape that didn't fit, that wasn't right in the room.

Something hit a wall. Amethyst yelped.

Maker turned to see her crumpling to the floor. Force hit him square in the chest. He staggered back. He managed to catch himself against a bookcase, past pains echoing against the new. By the time he had recovered sufficiently to go after the intruder, there was no sight of the man.

"Sir?"

Maker moved to the door and saw Edwards at the head of the stairs up from the kitchen. Although the servants' quarters were at the top of the house, the butler kept his room downstairs. The older man wore only his nightcap and gown and looked rather ghostlike. But Maker's greater concern was that Amethyst was still on the floor and not moving.

Within a step, he was at her side, kneeling and helping her to sit up. Thankfully she hadn't lost consciousness, but she was still leaning heavily against the wall and she looked especially pale. The candle was at her side, but had gone out in the fall. The light shifted as Edwards moved towards them with an aetheric lamp. The rainbow light cast odd colours, but at least it was light.

Maker reached out, turned her head to him. "Amme?"

"I'm alright."

The weakness of her voice suggested otherwise. As did the self-deprecating little smile.

"A little dazed, perhaps," she admitted.

His hand dropped as she turned away, leaning against the wall as she moved to stand. "Do you think we should-oh!"

Instinctively, Maker caught her as she tried to stand without support and started to fall. Since for once it wasn't beyond the realms of the permissible, he held her close.

"Apparently, I'm more dazed than I thought."

The words were muffled against his shirt.

"Shall I dress and go for the doctor, Your Lordship?"

"I don't need a doctor."

Maker looked down at her looking up at him. "Really?"

There was a moment of rebellion in her eyes, but it disappeared when she failed to stand without his aid. Maker turned to Edwards.

"Go."

As the man went back downstairs, Maker shifted Amethyst's weight and swept her up. Her exclamation was surprise, she grabbed his shoulders, and he ignored the pain in his left arm. As he straightened, she put her arms around his neck.

"What are you doing?"

He thought that was fairly obvious as he started up the stairs. Her breath tickled his chin as they moved. It had been too long since he had physically been this close to a woman. Possibly not since the disappointment of his wedding night. He'd expected a bashful virgin, and got a demanding whore. It had been fun, instructive, and oft repeated, until the night seven months later when he realised just why she had been so keen to secure him.

Carrying Amethyst, it was clear to him that while she was heavier, she was much less burdensome.

"We should have called the Inspector, not a doctor."

"Tomorrow." The man was long gone, and it was unlikely he'd be back now he knew the house was awake.

"But we've had an intruder, we've got an open house where he broke in."

A valid point, but he wasn't used to women being so considerate of things outside themselves. He had reached her bedroom. It wasn't somewhere he should set foot. Amethyst shifted to reach down and open the door. It swung open like a nightmare invitation.

"Shouldn't."

She turned back to him, her hand returning to his shoulder. "You're going to have to. I've still got a knotty problem, remember? If I try to cut the ribbons myself, at this point, I'll probably cut my hands instead."

Why did she have to be so practical? How could he refuse a lady in need, especially an injured lady? Why did she have to lay her head on his shoulder like that? As though she trusted him, when all he wanted to do was throw her on that bed and -

"Maker if you don't move soon, you'll take root."

I am going to Hell for this.

He stepped forward. At her bedside, he moved to let her stand. For a moment she clung to him. She needed to steady herself and he didn't want to let go.

"There's a knife on the dresser there."

Not entirely letting her go unsupported, Maker stretched towards the dresser and reached the folding knife. He wondered why she had it, but there again, it had been the Professor's and the room still contained a number of boxes tied with string to be broken into. Closer to her again, he wasn't sure how he felt about the fact that her hands were on his waist, clutching at the now fading bruises as she steadied herself. The pain, though slight, was enough to remind him why he couldn't follow his basest instincts. With just the light from the unfettered windows, everything was shadow, though the shadow that concerned him was the one rapidly developing on Amethyst's forehead. The skin had swollen and had taken on a shiny quality that did not bode well.

"Head?" he asked.

"Painful." She tipped her chin to look up at him. "Which is why I'd like to lie down, preferably out of this corset." Her head bowed again. "Preferably with you at my side."

He froze and studied the back of her head. *No, she didn't say that. I just imagined it.*

Now he imagined pulling her into his arms. What would it feel like to pull her against him, to feel her whole length pressed against his? To feel her arms wound around his neck, her fingers moving into his hair. What would it be, to cut away that damned corset and every other item of her clothing and feel her naked beneath him?

"Turn."

He closed his eyes as her petticoats rustled her obedience. This woman was a true threat to his equilibrium and he had never been in as much danger as he felt in that moment.

Remember your wedding vows.

Just because Violet didn't keep them, didn't mean they meant nothing to him.

Dragging in a breath, he opened his eyes and took hold of the hopelessly entangled cloth and cord. This was what was stopping her getting naked. If he cut this he could have her free of clothes in a trice.

"Ben?" The soft call seemed so siren and so far away. He would crash on her shores.

"Hmm?"

"Is this why you think I need a lady's maid?"

The sharp blade cut quickly through the knot and he walked away as fast as his long legs would allow him.

Chapter 22

Amethyst felt sick. She was certainly sick of lying in bed, so she'd sat up, but even that simple act had her head spinning. The corset and the petticoats she'd left crumpled on the floor had been cleared away. She wasn't sure how she felt about knowing someone had been in the room while she'd been sleeping. Given that they'd had an intruder last night, it finally dawned on her how dangerous such solid sleep could be.

There was no way she was going to be able to manage a corset today. Suddenly the idea of a lady's maid seemed quite tempting.

It was nearly an hour later when she finally reached the bottom of the stairs. She'd felt a little dizzy as she had gone down. But a few deep breaths took care of that.

There was a mass of work still to be done in the lab, but she wasn't up to that yet. A quiet day was all she could contend with today. Her book sat on the side table. She'd nearly finished it. Perhaps she'd read for a while. She headed into the drawing room. There she sat. While she didn't quite feel exhausted, her head was unsteady, as were her knees. Her concentration was gone. She put the book back down, unable to get into this new tale.

Nothing wrong with her hearing though. She heard Edwards come up, then she heard the knock at the door as Edwards rushed past the open drawing room door. The visitor must be unexpected and Edwards must have been looking the other way; Edwards prided himself on always being at the door when anyone knocked. It was an impossible task to Amethyst's mind, but Edwards was his own man and she wouldn't dream of trying to change him.

"I'd like to see Miss Forester."

She recognised the voice as belonging to Inspector Jenson.

"I'm sorry, sir. Miss Forester is unavailable today."

She smiled at Edwards' solemn return.

"On the contrary," she called through, "I'm available for the Inspector."

It was only a few heartbeats later that the Inspector appeared at the open door. He was hatless, his grey hair kinked where the brim of his bowler usually sat. She could tell by the way he looked her over that he was wondering about the loose clothing, the already fraying plait over her shoulder where she should be more formally attired at this visiting hour. A real lady would never be seen without being properly dressed, hair done. Thankfully, Amethyst knew she was no real lady.

"Thank you for coming so swiftly."

He stopped almost mid-step. "Swiftly?"

She checked the mantel clock. Just gone noon. Eleven hours since the incident. "Yes, Maker promised he'd call on you today. I'm surprised to see you here though. I'm not sure I can add anything to what you will already have been told."

"Told?"

She blinked up at him. "Inspector, are you quite all right? It would rather appear you've been hit on the head instead of me." Looking up, she saw Edwards hovering by the door. "Edwards, would you have Mrs Shaw put together a light lunch for the Inspector and I? A little soup and bread. Cold cuts perhaps?"

"That won't be necessary."

"Yes it is," Amethyst laughed the response. "I'm hungry, and I insist. I don't get much opportunity to entertain. Oddly, after living all these years in a large family when I longed for solitude, I am surprised to find I miss company, and Great-Aunt Flora being away for only a single night has left me surprisingly in need of company. Besides, we have details to discuss, and you look like you need a bit of a feed. I'm sure a light lunch will do us both the power of good. Now, please do sit down. I'm feeling positively disadvantaged and I don't have the stamina for too much standing today."

There was a small moment of struggle in his expression before the Inspector sank into the chair opposite her, on the other side of the fire.

"I had thought you moved in alone. I'm glad you have the protection now of your great-aunt chaperoning you."

She smiled. "Then you and Maker agree on something. Now, should I surmise by the confusion you displayed when I thanked you for coming so swiftly that you were, in fact, entirely self-motivated in coming here today?"

For the first time, Amethyst noted how straight and dark his eyebrows were. The only hair he had that wasn't showing signs of greying.

"I came to tell you that I spoke with the pathologist about Professor Richards' death."

Every nerve was suddenly on edge as she listened intently. "And?"

"And he found a massive amount of opiate in the Professor's blood."

"Opiate?" Amethyst didn't believe it. "But he didn't

use drugs of any kind. He wouldn't even take an infusion of willow bark to ease a headache. Hallucinogens were not his thing."

The Inspector gave no indication of reaction. "The doctor found a needle mark in the Professor's forearm. There was no sign of bruising to suggest he'd been held down."

Amethyst frowned. "But if he'd injected himself, why was there no syringe near the body? Nor indeed anywhere in the room - the whole house, even?"

Now the Inspector was frowning at her. "You're absolutely sure?"

"Absolutely."

She would have gone on, but Edwards appeared at the door.

"Luncheon is served, Miss."

Uncomfortable as she was with the form of address, Amethyst thanked the man and stood, pausing a moment to calm her swirling head.

"Miss Forester?"

She raised a hand to stop the Inspector and quickly gathered her wits. "It's fine, Inspector, just a little dizzy. Must have stood too quickly."

"Or you have a concussion. What did the doctor say?" he asked as he offered his arm.

For a moment, Amethyst's instinct to brush him off was strong, but thankfully, her sense was stronger and she took the offered support.

"You have seen a doctor, haven't you?"

"Yes," she assured him, guiding him from the room. "Maker was insistent, sent Edwards in the middle of the night to collect Doctor Brady. He said that I should rest for the next few days but that I'll be fine."

They had reached the dining room and she read momentary surprise on the Inspector's face.

"The formal dining room's upstairs," Amethyst said as she invited her guest to sit with a gesture. "The Professor had it shut up, not being a great lover of too much company, and I haven't got to the point of opening it up yet. Though I suppose I must."

The Inspector queried her with a look.

Do they teach boys to do that in school? It was an oddly Maker-esque expression.

"I've received a number of invitations since becoming an heiress. If I am to accept them, I must also reciprocate them."

As the man murmured agreement, she looked at what had been set for them. Two bowls of hot vegetable soup with bread, butter and cold cuts to hand as required.

"Are you sure you shouldn't be resting abed?" the Inspector asked as they started to eat.

"Tried that. I got bored. To go back to where we were though, I am absolutely sure there were no syringes in the house. Between us, Mrs Shaw and I have tidied and cleaned every ground floor room and the main bedrooms. Plus a couple of other rooms. If the Professor used needles, I didn't find any, but if you need confirmation, feel free to ask Edwards and Mrs Shaw. If the Professor was indulging a habit, I might be unaware, but it's unlikely they would be."

Jenson nodded. "If you don't mind, I will speak with them. It's not that I don't believe you, but I need to be thorough."

"Of course."

"Now, do you want to tell me why you have such a

bruise on your forehead?"

The Inspector sat quiet and attentive as Amethyst told him about the previous night's intruder.

"Did you actually see the man at all?"

She gave the slightest shake of her head. "He hit me from behind, so no. However, Maker might have seen him. There again, it was dark so I can't say he'll have got a good look."

Jenson considered all she'd told him. "What you do think they were after?"

"I'm not sure," Amethyst said, moving the now empty bowl to one side. "The first time I thought someone broke in, they made enough noise that my coming to investigate disturbed them. I think there have been two, possibly three other intrusions. They're clearly looking for something specific because nothing is missing."

"And you have no idea what they could be looking for?"

"No." She tried to shake her head more emphatically, but it was too painful. "Well, not really."

The Inspector's brows rose. "That's a little ambiguous, Miss Forester."

She sighed. "I know. Sorry. There are a couple of things that it is possible they are after, but I can't imagine anyone killing the Professor for them."

"Why assume the death and the break-ins are related?"

"Occam's razor."

"The simplest answer is usually the correct one?"

"In competing theories, select the one with the fewest assumptions," Amethyst corrected.

"But you're assuming Professor Richards was

murdered."

"And you're assuming he was an opiate addict, which I know he wasn't. If we look at the evidence, there are problems from the moment the body was discovered."

"The lamp being too far from the desk?"

"The Professor being dead at all. Then there's the opiates and the needle mark. The lack of a syringe in the house tells me someone else was involved."

"Edwards and Mrs Shaw were both in the house. Perhaps one of them removed it so as not to disgrace the Professor's memory."

She considered it, but not even for a full second. "Something I'm sure you'll ask them about."

"Maybe they didn't want to implicate themselves."

Her jaw slackened as she took in the implications of that. Snapping her jaw shut, she pushed away the insult and remembered it was his job to consider all possibilities. "Something else you can ask them, and while asking, ask them what possible reason they could have for murdering their employer. If I hadn't inherited, they could both have been out of work on his demise. In fact, even if they had known I'd inherit, they couldn't be sure I'd continue to employ them. I didn't even know I would until I did."

Jenson was nodding, so she was reassured that he was, at least, following her logic. "So what do you think might have motivated murder?"

"Greed. Or professional envy. You see, when I was going through the Professor's belongings, I discovered a number of his experiments were missing. It seems they were missing from the moment of or before the Professor's death, but they can't have been stolen, or why keep coming back?"

"Do you know what these experiments were?"

"Not really. All I've found is a reference in his financial accounts. There were various purchases, including aetheric material, which suggest that the AE prefix of the references stands for Aetheric Experiment."

"What makes you think these would be the target?"

"The fact that they're missing and pretty much the only thing that the Professor hasn't published a paper on. With information in the public domain there's nothing else to learn from the Professor's other experiments."

"Is it possible that the Professor stored them anywhere else? At the University or-" He took a moment to consider. "-a deposit box?"

"I've got access to his deposit box and the only things in there are some family jewels and a valuable Shakespeare folio." She sighed. "You could try the University but they already sent all his personal items to me and any data he might have had would be their property. I'm not aware of anyone trying to break in there."

"I'll look into it, just in case. In the meantime I can ask the local constables to increase their patrols around the Square."

"That's good of you, but I'm not sure how much use a constable out the front would be."

"Why not?"

She smiled at the affronted tone. "Sorry, Inspector, I didn't mean to be insulting. It's simply that all the break-ins have happened from the rear of the house. By the time I've fetched a constable from the front, the intruder will be well away through the back."

"Always the back?"

She nodded, but carefully. "Seems to be a weak spot. I'll have to get a carpenter in to look at the windows and doors. Hopefully there's some way of improving security."

"Or you could get a big dog." The Inspector smiled.

"There is that, except for one small hitch."

"You don't like dogs?"

"I don't dislike dogs, however a big dog needs a lot of room to run around in and there isn't sufficient garden here to give it enough run space. I fear it would be unfair to the dog."

"Talking of the garden, how easy is it to access?"

"Not easy at all, actually. It's surrounded on all sides by neighbouring gardens and houses.

"Have any of your neighbours reported any intruders?"

"I have no idea. My neighbours tend not to speak with me."

The Inspector's dark brows shot up again. "Why ever not?"

Amethyst shrugged. "As far as I can tell, people think I've traded being Professor Richards' mistress for being Lord Fotheringham's."

Jenson swallowed and looked away, as if uncomfortable.

"Ahh, you'd assumed roughly the same thing. Poor form for an investigator. But then I've found Society, well people, can be very judgemental on matters of which they are entirely ignorant."

"My apologies, Miss Forester. I made a poor assumption which I didn't think to verify or repeat as I didn't consider it significant to the case at hand. How you choose to live your life, as long as it's legal, is no concern of mine."

"Extra-marital affairs break morality codes."

"That's not for me to judge. I'm employed to uphold the law of the land, not the laws of God." He seemed to consider something. "Mind, if there ever is a law against sleeping with anyone but your spouse, half the population will be behind bars."

"If there were ever a law against judging a person in the absence of facts, we'd all be behind bars. You look more lively for having eaten."

"As do you," he returned with his thanks. "Now, can you tell me if there were any new people in the Professor's life who might have an interest in something that may be in this house?"

Amethyst found the return to business a relief. She looked at the dark red wall and thought about the question.

"The only one I know of is a Mr Brown. Unfortunately, I don't have any more details than that about him. Edwards or Lord Fotheringham may know more, but I believe His Lordship only met Mr Brown once and that was when I was here, three days before the Professor's death."

Jenson nodded. "Do you mind if I take a look at the back of the house?"

"Of course not, I'd welcome any suggestions for increasing security - except the dog." She smiled as she stood. Then she had to stop, supporting herself lightly against the table. "Would you consider it terribly rude of me if I left you to look alone? I'm feeling oddly woozy again."

Chapter 23

Edwards was at the door with it open as Maker and his young companion approached number seven. Stepping inside, Maker removed his own hat but paused instead of putting it aside. There was already a bowler on the hat stand.

Black, not brown.

Amethyst, not Violet.

Only once the door was closed and his black-dressed companion was standing inside, looking rather nervous while Edwards did his best to show no curiosity at all, did Maker make the introductions.

"Edwards, this is Miss Dickens. She's Miss Forester's new lady's maid. Would you find her a room and show her the house? When you're finished, I'll take her to Miss Forester. How is she today?"

"Neither dead nor deaf!"

The fact that the voice came from the drawing room was more of a surprise than the tone or the words. He had hoped to break the news more gently to her. Preferably when she was in no condition to argue, and Miss Dickens was out of earshot if she did.

"So hadn't you best introduce me to my new maid?"

It was clear to Maker that both Edwards and particularly Dickens were tense, uncertain. He understood how they felt. If he'd done this to Violet, there'd be hell to pay. Still, they were looking to him for direction and Amethyst wasn't Violet. Moreover, Dickens was a capable individual; if she couldn't handle Amethyst now, she probably didn't deserve the job.

"Leave your bag here and come with me." He passed his hat to Edwards, smoothing his hair as he led Dickens to the drawing room.

Amethyst was sitting in the chair by the fire, the one that faced the door. That was his usual seat and a momentary affront had to be swiftly tamped. He didn't have the right to be proprietorial about anything in this house. Worse was the feeling of possessiveness he had to quell for the woman herself. She looked pale beneath the dark bruise on her forehead. Much of the damage was covered by the way she had left her hair in a loose plait. Her usual tight corset and plain gown had been replaced with a looser day outfit, a black skirt and white blouse. She seemed surprisingly delicate, yet still her eyes blazed. He realised that a little additional formality might be required. A momentary glance said there was no man in the room. So who owned the bowler? Was it another of Amethyst's unusual choices?

"Lord Fotheringham."

The tone was cold. Her eyes slid to the woman at his side. She took a breath.

"You're Dickens, are you?"

Maker was grateful her tone was gentler on the redhead.

"I am, Miss." Dickens gave a small curtsey.

Amethyst seemed impressed as she looked the maid over. "How old are you?"

"Twenty-two, Miss."

"And you have experience of being a lady's maid?"

"I do."

"How long?"

Dickens paused this time. "A few months, Miss."

Time seemed suspended as Amethyst said nothing. Maker knew this feeling of uncertain discomfort. He felt this way virtually every time he was with Violet. He'd hoped never to feel this way with Amethyst, but, he supposed, he was still getting to know her and her moods.

"I'm less convinced than Lord Fotheringham," Amethyst said carefully, "that I actually need a lady's maid. If you're to stay, you'll have to take on duties not generally considered within a lady's maid's remit. Cleaning, helping in the kitchen. Anything else that might crop up."

Dickens nodded. "Yes Miss, I understand this is a small household and I'm not afraid of hard work."

"Good. Well, assuming that Lord Fotheringham has undertaken sufficient checks to consider employing you on my behalf, I'm willing to give this a try, temporarily at least."

The tone suggested that she wasn't entirely happy with this turn of events.

"Go and see Edwards, he'll find you a room and show you the house. I suspect you'll need some time to make your bed up. I won't need anything for a while and if I do, I'll ring."

Dickens bobbed a small curtsey and left.

"Close the door, please," Amethyst asked as Dickens was stepping across the threshold.

Maker schooled himself not to react. It was a good sign that she'd agreed to give Dickens a chance, but if she was asking for a closed door, he was probably in trouble. Internally, he braced for a tirade.

"Lord Fotheringham."

Oh dear. The less happy she was, the more formal

she got. Going straight for his title was a bad sign. He also had to allow that given her experiences last night, she was unlikely to be in the best of moods.

"Do you understand the meaning of the phrase 'high handed'?"

"Yes." There was no point trying to deny it. If he'd done this to Violet, she'd be breaking things by now, throwing them at his head.

"And you do realise that I am not your wife, your daughter, your sister or even your bloody mistress?"

Maker kept still as Amethyst closed her eyes after the last escalation. Her hands gripped the arms of the chair. He'd clearly upset her greatly. She sucked in a breath and carefully released it. Finally, she looked back at him. Her eyes were still blazing so she was still angry with him, but she seemed to have calmed a little.

"I appreciate that you're trying to be helpful. I know I asked for your help, but that was what I was asking for - help. I wanted you to *help* me, not take the whole damn thing out of my hands. I won't immediately overturn your decision this time; that would be unfair on Dickens, but if I ever ask for your help again, check with me first."

Quite how a woman twelve years his junior could make him feel like a naughty schoolboy, he wasn't sure. He wasn't entirely sure how to react, either. Unreasonable women were a breeze compared to this.

"Oh for God's sake man, unclench. Looking at you so up-tight is making me feel tense."

Unclench? He could barely remember a time when he'd been able to relax in a woman's presence. Except Bobbie, but she was a very different case. Knowing he needed to make an effort, he stepped towards the chair opposite Amethyst. Before he could sit, he had to ask about what bothered him.

"Bowler?"

For a second she frowned at him. "Are you asking who owns the bowler hat in the hall?"

He nodded as he sat.

"Inspector Jenson."

"Here?"

Amethyst gave a single nod. "He's taking a look at the windows in the lab."

Interesting. "Would you mind…" He pointed at the door.

"Go. Go. You're giving me a headache anyway."

As she said it, she buried her head in her hands. Hesitating, he considered going to her, but the wound of her statement still stung. She wasn't his wife, daughter, sister or mistress. Unfortunately. Steering his body where his heart didn't want him to go, Maker stepped into the hallway just in time to meet Inspector Jenson as he came from the study.

The two men greeted one another with cool civility.

"Findings?"

Jenson straightened slightly. Maker was used to such reactions. He didn't intend to cause offence, but until people knew his manner, he tended to.

"Apologies," he sighed. "Did you find anything?"

"Not a lot. But I can tell you your intruder isn't a professional burglar," Jenson said. "The way the shutters and windows have been broken, that's brute force and pointless when you've a lock on the back door that can be picked in seconds."

"How do you know?"

"I just picked it."

Maker offered a small nod of acknowledgement. "There were two men last night," he said. "And the back door was wide open when I checked."

"Miss Forester only reported one."

"Miss Forester would only have seen one."

Now Jenson was frowning. "What's your version of last night's events?"

"We heard something. I came down to investigate; Miss Forester was a few steps behind me. I told her to wait by the stairs, she stopped about..." He took one step forward and looked around to check his position. "Here, and I walked to the study door where you are. When I opened that door, I disturbed a figure in the lab. I was about to go after him when I heard a crash and Miss Forester cried out. I turned and another man hit me square in the chest." The blow upon previous blows was what had winded him. "I didn't have a solid footing, so I fell, but I saw the second man running out through the back door. After that I was more concerned about the fact that Miss Forester couldn't stand unaided."

Jenson was attentive and nodded his understanding through the explanation.

"Why return?"

Jenson shrugged. "They haven't found what they're looking for, probably. Which fits with the non-professional."

Maker didn't understand. "Sorry?"

"A professional burglar would have cleaned this house out by now. You and Miss Forester have a lot of resalable items on display. That someone is breaking in that badly and not taking the valuables means they're looking for something specific and clearly, it's something they haven't found yet."

Meaning they'd be back until it was found.

Jenson pointed to the wall under the stairs. "What happened to that?"

Maker turned to the wall. The wood panel, against which Amethyst had been pushed, was sitting recessed from the other panels. Moving over, Maker saw wood behind the panelling. Unexpected.

"Is that where Miss Forester was pushed?" the Inspector asked, stepping closer. "Where she hit her head?"

"Yes." Maker reached out and touched the panel with his fingertips. The slim panel clattered down behind the rest of the panelling. The square, roughly twelve by eighteen inches, showed that behind the panelling was a door.

"What are you doing?"

Maker turned his head right; Amethyst was standing at the drawing room door. She looked both exhausted and curious.

"Door."

She frowned; he moved back to give her a better view. "There's a door behind the panelling?" she asked as she stepped closer. "Wonder what's behind it."

"And why was it boarded up?"

"Uh." Amethyst rolled her eyes. "Trust a police officer to suspect something bad."

"Who says I suspect something bad?"

"Your tone."

Maker was surprised that he and Amethyst had spoken in perfect unison. Surprised and a little pleased, or perturbed. To quell any further disturbance from the woman, he tested the solidity of the stiles and rails around the missing panel.

"Hey, before you start tearing the whole wall down, do you remember what the Professor used to say? For real scientific discovery one must always-"

"Push right through," Maker finished. The Professor had always said it and Maker had always assumed that the Professor had meant you had to go to the right to get through the study and into the laboratory that was originally designed to be a conservatory.

"Push what right?" Jenson asked.

"Good question."

For a moment they stood back and looked at the wall. The panelling was completely unadorned, nothing to suggest a mechanism. Maker reached out and tested a couple of the stiles, but nothing moved. Amethyst tried a couple lower down, pushing in as well as to the right.

"Do you think I might have broken something when I hit it?" she asked. "Aside from the obvious panel."

"Technically, you didn't hit it," Jenson pointed out.

"So why am I the one with the headache?"

"He means this is not your fault."

A small strangled noise escaped from Amethyst's throat. Looking down at her, Maker saw her eyes were sparkling and her smile only controlled by the fact that she was obviously biting down on her own lips. He realised she wanted to tease him about something but didn't dare while in company. For that at least, he was grateful. Dignity wasn't much, but it was one of the few things he still had.

"Of course it's not your fault," the Inspector agreed. "We don't even know for sure that there is any fault. That door may not open, it may not go anywhere."

"Unlikely," Maker considered. Why hide a door if it

goes nowhere?

"Perhaps we should ask Edwards," Amethyst suggested. "He knows the house better than the rest of us."

"Not necessarily." Having known the Professor for fourteen years, Maker knew Edwards had only been with Richards for six years. Mrs Shaw for eight. He was also aware that this house was supposed to be the same design as his own, and yet the room the Professor used as an informal dining room was much smaller than the corresponding room in his house. He reached out and knocked the door; a hollow sound retuned.

"Void."

"Pardon?" Amethyst asked.

"He means," said Jenson, "that there's a void behind the door. Which would indicate a room or cupboard behind the panelling." Jenson raised himself onto his toes, pushed his head closer to the panelling, then reached inside. With a little manoeuvring and a sharp intake of breath, he managed to pull the fallen panel from the narrow gap. As he withdrew the thin sheet of wood, Maker noticed a little blood on the Inspector's knuckle. Once the panel was out of the way, Jenson looked in again.

"I can see a doorknob. It looks like it's been cut down to accommodate the narrow gap. I can't guarantee it'll move." As he spoke, he reached in again. The expression on his face suggested that the tight squeeze and odd angling was uncomfortable, if not downright painful. He shifted to the balls of his feet, nearly overbalancing. To steady himself, he grabbed the small gaslight fixed to the wall.

Jenson's small gasp was nearly lost under a click as

the lamp twisted to the right and a section of the wall panelling swung out, clearly hinged. Near to where Amethyst was standing, there was now a gap of about three inches next to Jenson. Carefully removing his hand, the Inspector moved back. The three of them looked at the hinged section. It was about seven feet tall and four feet wide. Maker reached out and it swung easily open. He moved to the left and Amethyst moved around him to better see what the entrance revealed. Another door. This one, as Jenson had said, had a cut back doorknob. Maker frowned. This door hinged the opposite way from the concealing section of panelling. Without a word, he reached out and tried the door. It was an uncomfortable hold with the thinner grip, but it gave easily enough, and it also swung out towards them. No way for this door to be opened without first opening the other.

There was a little jostling so they could all see the gap behind the door.

The two open doors formed an enclosed space, keeping the three of them rather closer than Maker was entirely comfortable with. He looked up and saw the thick cord to the top of the outer door; he suspected that was the closing mechanism once inside.

Leading the way in, Maker stepped into a short corridor that led under the stairs to an empty doorway. What lay behind that doorway was impossible to tell, there was insufficient light.

"I suppose the Professor knew to bring a lamp with him every time," Amethyst said.

As he turned to look at her, Maker found his eyes were adjusting to the gloom and noticed the small switch just inside the inner doorframe. "Not necessarily." He reached out, flicked the switch, and a lamp behind the door cast a momentary rainbow before it settled to white light. The switch controlled an aetheric lamp inside the blank doorway. It was sitting on a fixed bench and topped with a round shade of prismatic glass.

"I wondered what had happened to that one!"

Quite why Amethyst's remark amused him, Maker didn't know, but he stepped forward to cover the smile he couldn't quite hold back.

"To what?" the Inspector asked.

"That lampshade," Amethyst said, "it's one of my attempts to see how best to make the shades, I knew it was missing, but I assumed it had been broken. That's the thing with prismatic glass, makes aetheric light white and useful, but is fragile as a butterfly wing."

Maker had stepped into a windowless room. Clearly this was the Professor's secret lab. He wondered why the older man hadn't mentioned it anything but obliquely. He turned to the side as Amethyst preceded Jenson into the room. Such workspaces were much more her area of expertise than his. This area was much smaller than the other laboratory, but just as much of a mass of odd gadgetry and weird construction, though the bench on the opposite side of the room looked like it was missing something.

"What is all this stuff?" Jenson asked.

Amethyst was already inspecting the various instruments and notes, the small machines and parts. She was picking up papers that Maker could see were covered in the Professor's handwriting, but it wasn't written in English.

"Experiments," Maker supplied, seeing Amethyst

absorbed by her reading.

"The missing ones, I take it?"

"Looks like," Amethyst said without looking up. She was frowning as she scanned the pages. "Not that this makes any sense."

She moved on, doing a circuit of the benches that lined the perimeter of the room, picking up more scraps of paper. Maker watched as she gathered all the papers and came to stand beside him before she laid the papers out on the bench. He turned, looking over her shoulder as the Inspector came to stand at her other side.

"That's not English," Jenson said. "And I know I'm no expert, but it doesn't even look like mathematical notation."

"Code," Maker supplied.

"Well, *some* code," Amethyst said, "some mathematical equations and some aetheric notation of the Professor's own devising. He was, after all, one of the leading researchers in the early days."

Jenson was frowning at Amethyst. "You can read that?"

"Most of it."

Amethyst seemed surprisingly coy. Maker frowned; that wasn't like her.

"Only what I'm reading, either I'm misinterpreting or the Professor was going into an area of research I never even considered."

"Area?"

The way she looked up at him was an eloquent rebuke for using just a single word again.

"Well - if I'm reading this right - mind control."

Maker froze, didn't even blink. Mind control? The idea was ludicrous. Maker knew his own mind clearly enough to know he was the one in control of it. He might moderate his actions in consideration of his wife's sensibilities, but the only thing she couldn't control was his mind. His thoughts were his own and he could imagine it no other way.

"Mind control?"

Judging by the tone, Maker presumed Jenson had much the same reaction as he.

"Yes, I know, I understand the reservation, gentlemen. I am, perhaps, misreading this code, or perhaps the Professor was just heading for Bedlam. I don't know. What I do know is that all this you see around is just AE59-1 and -2. Three and four are missing."

"Sure?"

Of course she was sure, and her look was pointed enough to tell Maker that more clearly than any words could have.

Jenson was looking around. "Miss Forester, if you're right about these being what your intruder is looking for, then it's clear why they haven't been found."

"True, but it's only half the problem. A third, really."

Maker frowned at her. "Third?"

When she turned her head to look up at him directly, he could almost see the intelligence working behind her eyes.

"Half the experiments are still missing and we've managed to expose the room, so three problems. Only one third solved."

"Covering the entrance again should be simple enough, with the door open, fixing that panel back into place is only a few minutes' work."

Amethyst was nodding. "I'll arrange a carpenter."

"I'll fix it before I go," Jenson offered, forestalling Amethyst when she tried to object.

Chapter 24

Another evening, another argument. Maker was finding such times harder to bear. After all these years, he should be used to it, but cracks were starting to show. After all the recent evenings sitting in companionable silence or more welcome conversation with Amethyst, he was realising just what he'd been missing all these years. A wife he could share his life with was what he'd always wanted, just not what he'd got.

As much as he wanted to run over to number seven, it really wasn't the best idea, so instead he headed for the club.

Signing in, he was rather surprised to see that Haversham was there before him. He was aware that Haversham was a member, but he couldn't remember the last time he'd seen him in the place. The other lord was notorious for claiming that membership was a social must, but felt that personal attendance was more of a personal must-not.

After what Haversham had done at Lady Garrington-Smythe's, Maker was torn about seeing the man. Part of him would relish the inevitable conflict, but then *escaping* conflict was why he was here. He wasn't sure he had the energy for another fight.

Instead, he headed for the library.

The history texts he was most interested to lose himself in tonight were on the mezzanine. He was browsing when he heard a familiar voice below him.

"Of course I just adore abstract art."

Unable to believe the combination of statement and voice, Maker was quite precipitously halted in his reading. Haversham, he could quote, hated abstract art, thinking 'some idiot dropped a pallet then slipped over it with absolutely no idea of artistry or art.' The book open and unread in his hands, Maker turned quietly around and looked down.

That was indeed Haversham. The man with him, Maker didn't recognise. He was probably a guest for the evening, yet there was something familiar about him. The man had a quieter voice than Haversham and his words did not travel to Maker's ears; it was odd that in a club that contained several rooms where speaking was not allowed, the library wasn't one of them.

Despite straining to hear, Maker couldn't make out the conversation. He must have been watching too closely, for Haversham looked up at him and scowled. Instantly, the other man looked up. Mr Brown. Maker was for once thankful for years of marriage having taught him how not to react.

"Well look, it's Mr Nosey."

Haversham's snide remark was surprisingly cutting. Maker did not stick his nose where it wasn't wanted. He didn't want anyone else sticking their noses into his business, so he wasn't about to do it to anyone else. Again, years of acting impervious came to his rescue. He said nothing. This was less about Haversham's reaction than the fact that Mr Brown was here. All he needed to do now was get a message to Inspector Jenson.

Taking the book with him, he moved down the spiral staircase and across to one of the study desks. He nodded to Haversham and Brown. "Gentlemen."

Sitting down, he reached for a scrap of note paper and while trying to look as though he were writing notes from the text, he penned a message to the Inspector.

"Scribbling notes?"

Maker refused to react to the way Haversham sneered. This was so unlike the man, but right now Mr Brown was more of an issue. Jenson had to be called.

"Shouldn't you go home and and do that young slut of yours?"

The pen stopped mid-word. His jaw clenched. To speak that way about Amethyst was a step too far. He - No.

Dragging in a breath, he finished his note, returned the pen to its groove and folded the paper.

"What is it with you, Maker? You want to live like a monk? Or it is true that you just can't get it up?"

Moving carefully, Maker stood. Popping the note into his pocket, he stepped forward to leave the room. Haversham got in his way.

"You a coward as well as a cuckold?"

I'm a man who knows to rise above stupidity. Stepping around the shorter man, he tried to leave, only to be snapped back. A grunt of pain escaped him as the punch to the kidney forced the air from his lungs.

All the pain of the evening, the tension of his marriage, the hate he berated himself for, the desires he could do nothing about. The physical pain that he couldn't avoid. He spun on the ball of his left foot, his fist cracked Haversham's nose as his right leg swept the hunchback's legs out for under him. Maker completed the turn and stalked from the room as Brown scrambled to help Haversham up and the lord cursed and promised to have Maker banned from the club.

At that point, his fist throbbing, Maker didn't

especially care. The club was often his sanctuary, but there were other clubs. Other places he could go. In the lobby, he had a quiet word with one of the staff, one who looked lean enough to run like a hare. The note and the boy were gone before Haversham and Brown appeared. Haversham was bleeding profusely from the nose and calling for the bursar.

The feeling that he should just leave was strong, but if he stayed he should be able to keep an eye on Brown. Only as staff and members began to gather at the unprecedented sound of shouting and ranting, Brown started to back away. As Haversham shouted, despite the bursar's attempts to have him quieten down, Maker tried to follow, but was prevented. Using his height and stretching his neck, he was able to watch what Brown was doing. Very carefully, surreptitiously moving back, allowing new arrivals to move in front of him, almost as if he wasn't moving at all, just letting the crowd flow around him.

Maker's attention was drawn back to Haversham just in time to dodge so the punch to his chest glanced off his arm instead. Suddenly he was crushed in the crowd, Haversham was being dragged off, and he stood, looked around.

As Jenson arrived, Brown was nowhere to be seen.

Chapter 25

"On the desk." Amethyst struggled to speak under the effort of taking the weight of one end of the large mahogany box. She was trying to ignore the pounding in her head, the strain was bothering her bruising.

Both she and Dickens were glowing profusely by the time they managed to get the heavy thing on the desk. Thankfully, Amethyst knew the bottom was covered in thick baize or she'd have been horrified by the way they had to slide the contraption across the polished wood.

Once she was satisfied that it was secure, she undid the ten clasps attaching the cover to the bottom of the carry case. She knew the Professor had been unable to carry this on his own, she couldn't imagine who might be able to. Carefully lifting the top straight up revealed a gleaming machine, glorious in polished brass, resplendent on the green baize of the carrier bottom. It was clear the thing could have been taken off the bottom wood but at this point Amethyst was happy to leave it where it was, she and Dickens had lifted enough for one day. She reached over, unhooked a metal tablet from the side, pushed it into a waiting slot and switched the machine on. The aetheric engine whirled into life as Dickens took the top part of the box to the other desk and Amethyst sat in front of the machine.

"Excuse me, ma'am,"

Amethyst looked up, craning her neck to see over the mechanism. Dickens was looking over the cogs and wheels of the machine. "Yes? Sorry, I didn't mean to just slip away into my own world and be rude."

"You weren't, ma'am, I'm sorry, I didn't mean to imply…"

Amethyst waved the objection away.

"I was just going to say that it's Mrs Shaw's evening off. I was wondering if you wanted me to cook for you?"

For a moment, Amethyst wasn't sure what to say. "I, er, hadn't given it much thought. If you don't mind cooking, I would appreciate it. It would save me the time. It doesn't have to be much. Mrs Shaw is an excellent cook, but, and I mean no insult by this, I don't expect you to be. I'm happy with something simple."

Dickens smiled. "Good, if your expectations aren't too high I'm not likely to disappoint you, ma'am." Then she was frowning. "May I ask?" She gestured to the machine. "What *is* this?"

"Aside from very heavy?"

Dickens nodded.

Amethyst wondered if the serious woman would ever understand her humour. With a small sigh, she looked down at the machine before her. It was about four feet wide, two thirds the width of the desk, about twenty inches deep, and twenty-four inches high. It almost looked like a miniature church organ from Amethyst's point of view. Brass towers of cogs and number wheels formed the backbone of the piece; the two extreme towers were linked by a chain that was guided around the slightly curved machine by the other tower spindles. At the front was a keyboard; each key was round and sat perched on levers which were hit to give the desired result. The central front of the keyboard was normal letters, while around the edges other keys were etched with mathematical symbols, some of which were the Professor's own notations while a number were still blank. It was these keys that Amethyst was going to work on. Above the keys, in front on the cogs, a screen had been perched. Edged in filigree-decorated brass, an oblong of thin white cotton was stretched tight. The fabric had been treated with various solutions, one of which must have been ammonia-based - Amethyst remembered the smell when the Professor had first shown her how to use the thing. Thankfully that smell was gone. The screen still did what it needed to do, which was glow with coloured images of whatever she typed. There was a thin barrel on each side of the machine set horizontally in front of the number towers. The one on the right was the barrel from a typewriter, another roll of paper sat above it and the mechanism between the barrel and the number towers could print upon the paper. The barrel on the left allowed the small card-like metal strips to be slid in. They went in blank and came out scored and sometimes pierced. When reinserted, whatever information had been stored on them could be either viewed on the screen or printed out. There were a box of such cards stored beside the machine in the cupboard, and room for the special one to be hooked and secured above the left barrel. This was the card that had to be inserted every time the machine was switched on - without it, the machine simply didn't work.

"This is CAMM," Amethyst explained, "the Professor's Calculation and Memory Machine."

"And what does it do?"

"It runs calculations and remembers things." Amethyst smiled up at Dickens. Only when she knew that the other woman was seeing the funny side did she continue. "I'm going to make it understand what the symbols in the Professor's notes mean, so that I can type them up and instantly translate them. That should be easier and quicker than me trying to do it all by hand."

"Oh. Sounds…" Dickens struggled to find the word. "Complicated."

"I think building it was, but using it is relatively simply once you understand the logic. I'll show you another day."

As Dickens bobbed a curtsey and left, Amethyst doubted Dickens would be interested. Dickens would be capable with application, but such things weren't why she'd agreed to hire the girl and Dickens had already proved her usefulness in many other avenues where Amethyst found herself lacking.

Alone again, she turned to the softly glowing screen - she had to wait a moment for the mechanism to indicate that she could start. Then she removed the start-up card and inserted a blank one as she opened the Professor's notes and started teaching the machine what the unique codes meant.

It was some hours later when she remembered the letter Dickens had actually come in to deliver.

Chapter 26

Unable to sleep, Amethyst stared at the unseen ceiling and wondered what was wrong with her? She had received a letter from Mr Sanderson that morning, inviting her to visit his home in Swansea and inspect the preparations for making prismatic glass. There was a clear overtone to his letter that had nothing to do with business. It was in fact the kind of invitation that a woman in her position should relish to receive. Of course she'd visit, but she would have to insist on staying in a hotel, not his home. Now more than ever, she needed to be careful of her reputation.

Yet it was not her reputation that had her worried. Sanderson, Craig, she now knew, was a perfectly good man. Just the sort of friendly, intelligent, handsome but not too handsome, kind and generous man she would normally have been attracted to. Yet now she was attracted to a stand-offish, intelligent, stoic man who, in all fairness, did display many a sign of generosity, even though his frugality with words was legendary.

There was something wrong with her, obviously. When it came to men, she always made the wrong choice. Her parents had been telling her that for years. She'd had her chances. Two proposals, no less. But all she'd felt was a sense of obligation, duty-bound. She couldn't see herself being happy with either of them. So she'd said no.

Why would she now feel so much for a man who could never even ask?

"You're a contrary mare."

Her mother's unaffectionate tone in saying those

words was both unusual and cutting. It had marked the beginning of the deterioration of her relationship with her parents. She just didn't fit in with their view of how she should be.

Every muscle contracted.

Her heart hammered.

The sound of movement downstairs was too obvious to be ignored.

Blanchard?

Unlikely. Maker had retired earlier than she had, coming in and going straight up. She hadn't seen much of him, but she'd seen his knuckles on the banister. Somehow the idea of him 'fighting again' just didn't sit comfortably with the rest of the image he presented. She pushed the memory out of her head and strained to stay still, to hear anything else.

Something scraped below.

"That's in the lab."

Throwing off the covers, she swung her feet to the floor. Thankfully she had a thick rug placed there so she knew she'd make no sound as she stood and shook down her nightshirt. Her mother was appalled at the masculine choice, said she should use proper feminine nightgowns. She had those too. But they always seemed to wrap too tightly around her, she'd feel uncomfortable and get hobbled for getting out of bed. A shirt was much easier. Though knowing that Maker wore an identical shirt didn't make the choice any easier.

On her feet, she strained to listen. Yes, there were noises downstairs.

Stepping carefully, she headed for the door. She had yet to get the cricket bat back, but she had a rather sturdy umbrella she often used as a walking stick.

Hefting it, she carefully opened her bedroom door. The noises were clearer as she moved silently down the hall. She was past Maker's door before it opened.

"Shush!"

She turned with the whisper.

She wasn't sure if his compliance was the result of her whisper or the warning in her look, but in truth it didn't matter, only the action did. He was quiet as he knotted the belt of his, well she was pretty sure it was actually a smoking jacket but since he never *wore* a smoking jacket, she couldn't be sure.

Turning back to the source of the sound, she led the way down the stairs. As they reached the bottom, she suddenly felt the weight of his hand on her shoulder.

She turned her head to look at him. He had a finger to his lips. Holding her in place, he walked around her, taking the lead.

The sounds were clearly coming from the laboratory at the back of the house. Swallowing the lump in her throat, Amethyst walked slower than Maker. She didn't *want* to confront an intruder. The idea of being knocked down to her shame again was not appealing. But she didn't want to leave Maker to deal with it alone either.

The study was closed. Maker moved in close, she saw the pale length of his fingers curl carefully around the handle. His torso shifted as he took a breath.

Her head was throbbing from the memory of the last attack. Her heart was pounding, fear constricted her throat. Knowing how she'd been caught out last time, Amethyst kept an eye on the drawing room door, the sharp end of the umbrella pointed that way.

Maker opened the door, bursting through.

Amethyst immediately heard a scuffle. One last glance at the drawing room door assured her it wasn't about to open. She stepped into the study. Maker was wrestling with a shorter, stockier man in black, his face covered with a neckerchief. Maker threw a punch, tight and controlled. The intruder's head snapped back and he stumbled to the hearth. Iron clattered against iron as the man grabbed the poker from the companion set. Maker reared back as the wrought iron swung. The intruder stepped forward. Amethyst reacted, the umbrella slip forward, inverting as she swung. The curved handle caught his arm. She yanked back, and the poker the intruder had skittered across the floor. She jumped to avoid it landing on her feet. The intruder was off balance, so Maker grabbed his shoulder, spun him round and hit him with a right hook. Amethyst hoped the sickening crunch of bone was the intruder's nose breaking, not Maker's knuckles. The man fell back against the wall.

Blanchard appeared at the door.

"Fetch the police," Amethyst told him.

Maker punched the would-be thief in the gut.

Blanchard looked to the fight, assessed it then turned away.

Clearly his assessment that Maker had won matched hers as the intruder fell to his knees. Maker delivered one last double-handed blow to the man's nape and the hapless housebreaker went down, sprawled, and gave a groan as he tried to push himself up. He flopped back down, still and silent.

*   *   *

The bed was cold when Amethyst returned to it. Once the intruder was out for the count, Maker knelt beside him and pulled away the kerchief tied around his face.

Gibson.

To think the man she had nearly done business with would attack her so blatantly. What kind of a man had she so nearly chained herself to? How lucky an escape had she had there? Raising her hand to her forehead, she felt the tenderness of the fading bruise, though the lump had disappeared. Professor Richards couldn't have known what kind of man Gibson was.

She worried too about Maker. He was in every respect a true gentleman, he had demonstrated that again in the way he had suggested that she retire before the police arrived. Yet he had punched Gibson with the vigour and accuracy of a professional boxer. This wasn't the first fight he'd been in, possibly not even today. Clearly, there was a great deal she didn't know about the man.

The knock at the door was soft, but distinct.

"Come in."

For a moment the candlelight dazzled her, but it was easy to see Maker beyond the door. It was just as easy, for one small moment, to see that he was struggling with something. Or perhaps she was just imagining it.

"It's alright," she said. "You didn't wake me." She pushed herself up to sit. "But if you're coming in, come in. Leaving the door open like that creates a draft." As if to prove her point, a stray gust blew a skein of her loose hair into her eyes. She tucked it back behind her ear.

Closing the door with a gentle click, Maker moved over to the bed. There was a moment of hesitation before he put the candle on the bedside table and sat on the bed, facing her.

"Thank you."

That didn't make sense. "Whatever for?"

"Saving me."

She snorted. "Don't see how, I didn't do anything."

He gave her one of those looks. She glanced away. She didn't think she'd done that much, but she was glad she'd helped, glad Maker hadn't been hit with an iron bar. Still, what could have been wasn't something she wanted to dwell on.

"Blanchard found a policeman quickly, then?" There hadn't been enough time for him to have had any problems finding assistance.

Maker nodded.

"One that Inspector Jenson set around the Square?"

Again he nodded.

"Did he take Gibson away?"

"Handcuffed," Maker confirmed.

"Did Gibson say anything about what he was up to?"

This time, Maker shook his head. So many questions ran around Amethyst's head that she couldn't form a single one to ask. Instead, she just looked at him. With his hair slightly mussed from sleeping and the shadow of beard on his jaw, he looked more rugged than she had ever seen him. More ruggedly handsome. Her stomach knotted, and she automatically clenched her thighs. He wasn't hers to want. For a moment, she glanced at his hand. His right knuckles were red, but not as swollen as she might expect. She suspected ice and some antiseptic had already been applied.

Moving her eyes back up to his, she found he was

watching her closely. The gaze was hypnotic. She leaned towards him. Was he leaning towards her too? Even reflecting the candle flame, his eyes looked darker, ever more inviting.

A cold void filled the space where Maker had been, the door closed a little too sharply.

Left not knowing if she should curse or thank him, Amethyst turned to the candle, the brightness of its flame now an affront to her. She blew it out with a savage breath.

Chapter 27

As Dickens helped her to dress, the lady's maid told Amethyst that Lord Fotheringham had left the house early that morning.

"In truth, I'm not even sure he returned to bed after all that commotion last night."

All that commotion wasn't what had kept Amethyst awake all night. That had been down to thoughts of Maker. Finally she had slept, but fitfully. Today she knew she had to get out of the house for a few hours at least. A walk in Regent's Park was bound to clear her head.

After three hours of walking her head was clear, but her feet were sore. They shouldn't be this sore this quickly. That bothered her. It suggested that her new found wealth and comfort had made her soft. She could go straight home, but there was nothing to do and no one there, so she could go anywhere, do anything.

There were plenty of benches provided and when an old man stood and left one empty, Amethyst sat for a moment.

What am I going to do?

It wasn't just an idle question related to now. She had to work out what she wanted to do with her life. The Professor's generosity meant she never had to work and she was comfortable enough not to need a man to marry to secure her future. She was very fortunate in that. On the other hand, she didn't want to be alone or idle. A few weeks of not walking had made her feet soft, what would a few years of not working do to her brain?

Finding how to make prismatic glass had been a thoroughly enjoyable project. But it was just a project, one problem to solve. She needed something to focus on. All the Professor's work was still available to her and she would continue to study it. There was every chance she would find something in there to follow, but there again, that was his work, not hers, more idle curiosity than any burning need. She had found the aetheric light issue on her own, solved it largely on her own, for all the Professor was happy to help where he could. Most of that help was his lab, his reference books, allowing her to use him as a sounding board, listening to his advice, but it really was her own idea, her solution.

She sighed and leant back. Overhead, she watched an airship pass almost silently. Having never taken a trip in an airship, she longed to do so. Thus far, she'd never had a good enough reason to go anywhere to justify the expense, not to her father, whose resources were understandably stretched, and not to herself either. Now she had the money, she could travel if she wanted to. Go to a different country for the first time in her life. The idea spread a smile across her face, a rare wide smile. All she had to do was decide where she wanted to go. *Everywhere.* That seemed somewhat excessive. There again, plenty of young men did the Grand Tour, she'd be willing to bet that Maker had; why shouldn't she? Could she afford it? There was only one way to find out.

Steadier now she had an idea of what the future could hold, Amethyst stood. The immediate future was still to be planned, but the immediate future had its roots in the immediate past. She had to visit Inspector

Jenson.

*   *   *

"Sorry, Miss, he's not available," the uniformed officer under the impressive handlebar moustache said.

"Oh." Life was full of little disappointments. "Do you have any idea when you expect him back?"

"Oh, he's here Miss, but he's interviewing a prisoner. Sometimes these things are over quickly, sometimes they take hours. But he said he was eager to complete this one, and didn't want to be interrupted unless absolutely necessary."

Her wanting an update wasn't an absolute necessity. "If he's here," Amethyst said, "I'll wait a while at least, if that's acceptable?"

Now the man looked uncomfortable. As he dissembled he looked to the door, his eyes widening. Amethyst looked across too. Another, younger-looking officer was dragging in a woman who wasn't as young as she was painting herself to be. There were grey hairs appearing from beneath the scraggy black wig. The ragged red dress just about covered everything. The woman's language was spicy enough to make a sailor blush. Amethyst was quietly scandalised, she felt her cheeks burn at the vocabulary, let alone the rich and vivid descriptions of acts she'd never even contemplated, let alone tried. Nor did she particularly want to. The woman and the officer came to the same reception desk where Amethyst stood. She stepped back to give them room, though with the pair of them in her way, she didn't have the opportunity to get away from them.

"Wot's your problem, Lady Muck?"

The woman's breath was as foul as her yellow and broken teeth. Amethyst blinked, but tried not to react.

"No problem, it's just that your language was rather more... colourful that I expected."

The torrent of abuse had the uniformed officer turning the woman to face him.

"Hold your tongue, woman. You've no right to speak to a fine lady that way."

"Constable," Amethyst said evenly, "Miss..." she looked at the woman who had half turned back.

"Godby."

Amethyst focused back on the constable. "Miss Godby has as much right to speak to me as anyone else does. I was surprised by her language, not offended."

Not knowing what to say, the constable turned away to book Miss Godby, for soliciting apparently. Amethyst took the moment to turn and look at the noticeboard behind her. The various 'Wanted' posters. She wondered how accurate the pictures were. Each face looked disreputable, but was that because the real faces were, or was it just the way they were drawn?

Behind her, Amethyst could hear plenty of movement. She was aware of Miss Godby being moved out, to a cell she supposed. Amethyst stepped aside, further from the desk so she didn't get blocked in again. The inner door had barely closed when the front door opened. She heard steps, a pause, then the steps moved in her direction. Instinctively, she knew who was at her side.

"Maker."

"Forester."

The greeting felt odd. He didn't usually use her

surname. There again, he didn't usually greet her in public. Turning towards him, she had to look up to face him.

"Why are you here?"

"Jenson."

"Oh." Of course, she should have known.

"You?"

"Same. Apparently, Inspector Jenson is occupied, could be some time. I said I'd wait."

"Duration?"

She shrugged. "Five minutes so far."

He turned his head to look about. "Shall we?"

Amethyst looked where he indicated; there was a bench against one wall. She headed that way.

She felt surprisingly uncomfortable as she lifted the back of her dress a little to allow her to sit and he parted his coat tails for the same purpose. Side by side, his arm was touching hers, they were closer than they had been last night, but she felt they were further apart than ever. There were things they should talk about, but she knew they wouldn't. The thought of taking an airship and leaving the city - the country - looked ever more appealing.

"Did you do the Grand Tour?" The question was blurted out just because for the first time ever, the silence was too heavy between them.

"No."

Well that both surprised her and cut the conversation dead.

"Why?"

She shrugged. "I was thinking of doing some travelling. Wondered if there was anywhere you could recommend."

Watching as the desk sergeant turned, she heard him speak to someone inside the room behind the counter that she couldn't see.

"There's a young lady to see you, sir."

Inspector Jenson, then.

"And a gentleman who arrived after."

Jenson appeared behind the counter. "Miss Forester. Lord Fotheringham."

They stood, Amethyst offered a small curtsey and Maker a simple nod of acknowledgement.

Jenson lifted a panel in the counter and came out into the front. "Since you'll both be here about the same thing, you'd both best come with me."

Maker indicated that she was to follow first, then with Jenson leading the way they moved the short distance into his office. It seemed the wall they had been sitting against was the wall to that office. Inside, Jenson invited them to sit as he took up his place behind his desk.

"Well, thank you for saving me a trip to Belgravia. We've had a rash of trouble this morning and I don't know when I would have had the time."

"Serious?"

Jenson looked to Maker. "As a local magistrate, I'm sure you'll find out when the time's right."

Amethyst hid her surprise. She hadn't known that Maker was a magistrate, nor that Jenson knew it. Did that mean the two had known one another before the Professor had died? She pushed the thought from her mind. It didn't matter one way or the other.

"Now, your break-in."

Amethyst sat in rigid silence as Jenson told her about Gibson. Apparently, he'd broken in a number of times, which explained all the sleepless nights. Since he hadn't been able to find anything in the lab, he'd branched out to the drawing room, which was when he'd knocked the pair of them out of the way, and then he'd been going to check other rooms when Maker had disturbed him the previous evening. He was looking for the formula for the aetheric glass, feeling it was the way for his ailing business to secure its future. He was angry that Sanderson had, as he saw it, stolen the contract from him.

"It was Gibson's own ignorance in not dealing with me that lost him the contract," Amethyst said.

"Yes, well, whatever it was, it's over now."

Amethyst was aware that Jenson sent her what was meant to be a reassuring smile. Only she didn't feel reassured.

"But how did he get into the garden to get in through the back of the house? It's totally enclosed."

"One on the houses that backs onto your garden actually rents out rooms to businessmen looking to spend a few nights in the capital. It seems Gibson had taken up residence there so he could cross the wall between the two properties with relative ease."

That made frightening sense, and opened up a new set of worries. If Gibson could do that, who couldn't? "What of his accomplice?"

"Gibson claims he doesn't have an accomplice." Jenson sat straight in his chair, his hands rested on the desk top. "He also says he broke in only four times. Yet you two have reported nine possible incidents."

"Theory?"

"The one already postulated. You have two burglars, but they are not working together. Perhaps each is looking for something different. Something specific. Gibson after the glass, the other probably after something of the Professor's," Jenson said.

"Brown?"

Jenson shook his head. "The University says he and his grant money have disappeared, but I'll keep looking."

So it's not over.

"Miss Forester, are you quite well?"

She offered what she knew would be a weak smile, and nodded.

"You're uncommonly quiet."

That brought out a more genuine smile. "Apparently, we take that in turns." She indicated Maker and the smile fell away like a dream she couldn't keep hold of.

"You must find these troubles quite trying."

Not really. Maker on the other hand...

"Perhaps you could stay with friends until we find the culprit?"

"No." The word was sharper than she had intended, but the truth was simple. She wasn't sure she had anywhere to go. Taking a deep breath, she tried again. "Thank you for your concern, but I won't be frightened out of my own home. And thank you for the care you've taken over this incident. If you need a statement from me, just ask, but if you gentlemen will excuse me, I find I need some air."

The chair scraped back a little as she stood suddenly, and she had her back to the two men when she stopped. She might feel sick, but there were more important things in life. One hand went to her stomach, the other to the wall; she hated that that hand was shaking.

"Miss Forester?"

Her knees felt like aspic, not quite solid enough. A chair moved, she felt a presence at her side. She only turned her head when she realised that it was Inspector Jenson at her side.

"You're very pale, Miss Forester, perhaps you should sit down."

She appreciated that his voice was low, gentle. It was good to realise that he cared. She offered another weak smile.

"I've been thinking. If the Professor's notes are correct, if he needed the AE59 machines, that implies someone has worked out how to control minds. What are they going to do with that?"

She saw the man's jaw drop slightly; it moved like he was trying to say something.

"No, I don't want to think about it either."

Unable to face that thought, she rushed from the room. On the pavement outside, she put one hand on the railing to steady herself. Her breath shuddered as she filled her lungs as much as her corset would allow. Fresh air wasn't helping. Not that it felt overly fresh; the stench of passing horses clogged in her throat, fighting with the rising bile.

The intrusions weren't over. She wanted them over. Gibson was stopped, but what of the other intruder? How could she stop him? Home was supposed to be a haven, how could she live in a house where she was afraid to get up in the night?

Chapter 28

Even when she got home, Amethyst still felt like she needed air. So as Edwards stood with the front door open, Amethyst hesitated, unable to take another step towards him. She tried to say something, but couldn't find the words. Finally, she turned around and headed into the Square, finding the nearest bench to sink down on.

The idea of her congenial Professor having enemies was pushing at her head. Maker had told her about what Brookmyre had said, and he had told Jenson too, but it had led to a dead end - Brookmyre didn't have any contact details for Mr Brown. Her deciphering of the sheets was going well enough, but there was still a way to go. She felt like everything was crowding in on her all of a sudden, her head seemed to want to explode. She put her elbows on her knees and her head in her hands.

"Ma'am?"

She didn't want to respond to the voice, she didn't want to contemplate what it represented. But then Dickens spoke again, more urgently, the sound from a closer and lower angle. She had to open her eyes and found Dickens kneeling next to her, looking worried.

"Miss Amethyst, what's wrong?"

Her eyesight was a little blurred, she blinked and sat straighter. "Nothing. I'm alright." She wasn't at all, she actually felt rather sick and feared an attack of 'the vapours' - something she had never suffered before and wasn't about to start now. She reached out and patted the seat beside her. "Don't crouch like that, it's unladylike."

"I'm not a lady," Dickens said, moving to sit as instructed.

"Neither am I," Amethyst pointed out.

"Closer."

That really didn't help.

"What do you think you're doing?!"

That screech didn't help either. Amethyst turned to see Lady Violet, resplendent in sky blue silk, bearing down on them. She might not feel as well as she should, but even she could tell there was extra tension in Dickens.

"Lady Violet," Amethyst acknowledged. "Lovely afternoon, isn't it?"

"What are you doing with *that*?"

Amethyst had to think for a moment, wondering what the other woman meant, then she realised she was talking about *Dickens*.

"Dickens is my maid."

"You employed a liar?" Lady Violet spat. "I should have expected no better."

Having given her word to Maker that she'd do her best not to upset his wife, Amethyst was prepared to let a lot slide, but today she had had enough of the Makers and she was not going to roll over and play dead.

"Dickens is not a liar."

"Did she tell you she was my lady's maid, briefly. I had to dispense with her services when she lied to my husband."

Amethyst stood - looking up at someone to scold them was never easy. Even standing, she still had to look up a little, but it was much less. She did her best to channel Great-Aunt Flora. "Lady Violet, I know how high your standards are, and I take the fact that you employed Dickens, however briefly, as a recommendation."

Lady Violet seemed torn on how to take that, as if unsure whether she'd been insulted or complimented. Without recognising the implication, Amethyst heard hooves and wheels clattering along the road around the Square. She was more focused on the rising ire of the lady before her.

"You should get rid of her directly."

"If she does anything wrong, perhaps I will, but not without reason."

Moving to turn, Amethyst was surprised to find a tight grip on her arm pulling her back. Lady Violet's eyes were full of anger and hate.

"You listen to me, you... *nothing*, you will do what you're told or I will ruin you-"

"Violet."

Both women jumped at the cold tone. Lady Violet's grip grew impossibly, painfully tight as Amethyst looked up to see Maker striding towards them.

"She won't listen to me." Lady Violet's voice was whiny and arrogant all at the same time.

Maker said nothing, simply kept his eyes on his wife and reached for the wrist connected to Amethyst. Watching as his hand curled around Lady Violet's wrist, Amethyst could see the power of his grip, could feel the quaking of their power struggle through her arm. She was bound to bruise, but she couldn't cry out at the pain, she wouldn't give Lady Violet that satisfaction. Finally, the grip fell from her arm and Maker turned his wife, forcing her back towards their home.

As she turned to her maid, Amethyst spotted Mrs Silvestri watching with interest from the other side of the Square. The old woman disappeared as soon as she realised she had been spotted.

Completing her turn, Amethyst looked at Dickens. She wasn't entirely sure what the high colour in the maid's cheeks meant. "Let's go home." The maid seemed to relax as she nodded. "Then you can tell me all about it."

*　　*　　*

Despite his desperation to know what was happening with Amethyst and Dickens, Maker didn't dare go over to find out. Violet had vented and quieted, and now he sat ensconced in his own library and tried to work out if there was anything more he could do with the investigation into the Professor's death. He knew there wasn't, Jenson had already moved that further than he could have.

Opposition to the Aetheric Concession Bill seemed to be slipping *en masse* and he didn't know what he could do to stop the leak.

He threw down his book in frustration and paced across to the window. Nothing was working. The knock at the door suggested anyone but Violet.

"Come."

He turned to find Blanchard entering and closing the door carefully behind him.

"I spoke to my contact."

Maker had long ago decided not to ask the details of who Blanchard's contact was.

"There are a lot of Mr Browns. Some of them even

match the description we have, but none seem to have any links with the University or any aetheric connections."

"Unusual for your contact to come up with nothing."

"Yes, sir, but enquiries will continue."

Maker nodded. "I suppose that the lack of results is indicative of Mr Brown being a pseudonym."

"That's my contact's thinking."

Thanking the man, Maker moved back towards his desk.

"There's something else you might like to know, sir."

Focusing his attention on Blanchard, Maker enquired without words.

"On my way back, I visited number seven. Miss Forester has retained Miss Dickens' services. Apparently Dickens was compelled to give full details of her employment in this house, and though surprised, Miss Forester assured her that Dickens would not face the same issues under her employ, but if Dickens should lie to her again, even by omission, her employment will be terminated."

Maker almost gave into the temptation of a smile. How like Amethyst to be both forgiving and utterly clear. There was, however, one question left.

"How did you know that I was worried about Dickens?"

He had to admire the man's composure, only blinking twice before-

"Ah," Maker surmised, "you just went to see Dickens because you had the opportunity?"

There was a tiny shrug. "I hope you don't object,

sir."

"Of course not, one of us should have a life."

Chapter 29

Two days later, Amethyst was pacing. Jenson had visited yesterday to say that Gibson had been refused bail by the magistrate, (not Maker, but it was bound to be one of his cronies), and would remain in jail until his trial, when there was little doubt of a guilty plea and verdict. She'd had a locksmith in to change the locks on the rear doors. She felt more secure, but not safe.

While Gibson and his motives were now understood, the other intruder wasn't. This had to be about the Professor's experiments. She'd been working her way through the notes but she still couldn't understand quite what the Professor was getting at. The machine had translated most of it, and she didn't think there was anything wrong with the translation, but the science was at the limit of her understanding. She had to make sense of it all, but couldn't stand to sit before that machine any longer. She knew things had yet to fall into place, and they would, she had all the right pieces, they would fit together, but the pattern was eluding her. She had the puzzle, but not the picture to construct.

The light tap at the study door surprised her. She turned to find Edwards in the doorway.

"Lady -" he paused in surprise as her visitor stormed in. "Fotheringham."

"Where is he?"

Amethyst frowned. "Whom?"

"My husband."

Amethyst shrugged. "I don't know. I haven't seen him for a couple of days."

"Is that so?"

Violet's look made Amethyst feel about two inches tall.

"Are you seriously going to claim he didn't sleep here last night? Will you add lying to your other accomplishments?"

Pushing down her rising fury, Amethyst reached for calm and tried not to crumple the invitation card in her hand. "I wouldn't be lying to say Maker wasn't here last night, because he wasn't. Was he, Edwards?"

The man looked uncomfortable. Now she felt worse than a worm.

"Actually, ma'am, he was. He arrived after you retired for the evening and was away before you rose this morning."

"Oh." She looked at the superior Lady Violet. "My apologies, apparently he did spend the night in this house, I just didn't know it."

Violet's look was less than trusting. Amethyst turned again to her butler. "Edwards, did Lord Fotheringham give any indication as to where he was going and if he'd be returning here?"

"I'm sorry ma'am, but no."

Amethyst glanced at the printed card in her hand, then around the room. It was neat and tidy now, only CAMM and the books she was using were out. None of it was overly urgent, but nor did it give her a clue as to how to handle her clearly impatient visitor.

"I'm sorry we can't help you more, Lady Fotheringham." She realised she was tapping the card against her skirts so she stilled her hand. "You're welcome to stay and wait, to see if Maker returns here, but I've no expectation of his doing so."

Lady Fotheringham's delicate nose wrinkled as she looked around.

"We'll go into the drawing room," Amethyst suggested, moving towards the lady. "Edwards, would you bring tea to the drawing room and some of those delicious little cakes Mrs Shaw made?"

Lady Violet led the way to the drawing room - after all, this house was the mirror of her own. She paused by the door, obviously surprised to find it open.

"Do go in."

Amethyst had a little satisfaction in seeing the annoyed stiffening of Violet's shoulders. *Did she expect me to bow and scrape and open the door for her? Probably.* Still, Amethyst had promised Maker that she'd be nice to his wife and she always tried to keep her promises.

Violet stepped in and stopped in the middle of the room. Amethyst moved around her to stand by the hearth. Only when she realised this was Maker's usual position did she move to sit in the wingback chair at the fireside, facing the door. Also Maker's preference, but it was too late now.

"You've redecorated," said Lady Violet as she sat.

"Actually no," Amethyst said. *Small talk. Just because you hate it, doesn't mean you can't do it.* "I've tidied up. Much as I loved Professor Richards, he was a terrible clutter bug. I put the books and equipment back where they belong and put away most of the curios. I am thinking of changing the drapes though." She looked behind her at the thick dark velvet curtains. They were brown and dull. "I was thinking a cream damask, maybe. Perhaps green to compliment the walls. I'm not sure yet." She turned back to Lady Violet, who seemed to be considering her suggestion.

"I'd suggest cream."

Green it is then. Be nice.

"Perhaps you could provide me with the details of your decorator?" *So I'll know who to avoid.*

"Monsieur Pierre is always so obliging."

Given the preening, Amethyst assumed Lady Violet liked to be asked favours. Amethyst understood that feeling. She was used to being overlooked and it felt good when someone actually valued her opinion. Was that Violet's problem, that she felt undervalued? *Be nice but don't take it too far.*

The door opened and Edwards delivered the tray of tea and tiny cakes.

"I could recommend a seamstress too."

Uncomfortable under Violet's critical gaze, Amethyst wondered why she bothered. Her grey was serviceable.

"No need."

Amethyst wasn't sure how to take Lady Violet's look. It seemed part pity, part curiosity, as though she were a trapped specimen Lady Violet didn't know how to categorise. She watched the older woman open her mouth to speak, think better of whatever she was going to say and try again.

"Miss Forester, you are an heiress. Of no inconsiderable fortune."

"My fortune is nothing to your own."

"Of course not, but the point is that Society will watch you now. Is already watching you. Do you know what Society is saying?"

"That I'm dowdy?"

"That you're my-" Violet paused, looking as though

there was a bad smell beneath her nose. "-my husband's mistress."

Someone had sucked all the oxygen from the air. It was one thing to hear it from her father, but from Maker's wife! "How could anyone possibly think that he would have any interest in me?"

"You're living in his house."

"It's half mine."

"But you're no-one. Society doesn't know you. You've appeared out of nowhere at my husband's side. It's bad enough to be thought to be passed over for anyone, but for one who's considered a drudge..." She looked down her nose at Amethyst. "Well, it is not to be borne."

Amethyst swallowed. She could believe people would believe such a thing of her, but to besmirch Maker this way was a shame. Especially when his own wife thought the same thing. No wife would willingly tell another woman such a thing if it weren't true. But there was only so much she could take.

"I'm neither a drudge nor anyone's mistress."

"Then you'll need to prove both. Start by dressing and acting like a lady."

The only way to do that was to go out into Society and be seen. She gritted her teeth, but tried to force a pleasant tone. Clearly Lady Violet wasn't aware of the latest developments or her most recent forays into Society; in the last week, quietly and privately, Bobbie had been guiding her through the intricacy and intimacy of having her own seamstress. Amethyst had expected to hate every moment of the process but it had all been surprisingly agreeable.

"Thank you, Lady Fotheringham, but I have

followed Lady Garrington-Smythe's advice in this matter and have secured the services of a very able couture house. I took delivery of the first outfits just this morning. Others are in production."

For once, it seemed Lady Violet had nothing to say on the matter.

They both heard the front door open and since Edwards hadn't passed, there was only one person it could be. The fact that Maker soon appeared in the doorway only confirmed it.

Elegantly suited in charcoal grey, he stepped into the room. For a moment, Amethyst thought she detected an emotion, and it seemed a pleasant one, but it was quashed by his usual blank mask as he saw his wife. He offered each lady a small bow in greeting.

"We were just discussing fashion," Amethyst said, as lightly as she could manage. Anything to fill the suddenly strained silence. "Apparently, Society says I'm a drudge."

A small movement of his brow acknowledged a little surprise before he turned to his wife.

"I didn't say she was a drudge, I said she dressed like one."

Tension contracted every muscle as Amethyst watched the couple. Maker was silent and Lady Violet looked like the one who'd been offended. She bristled.

"Well what word would you use?" the lady demanded.

Glancing at her grey dress, Amethyst wondered what word she'd use. Unfortunately 'drudge' was the one that seemed most appropriate. Maker, however, wasn't bothering to look at her at all.

"Governess," Maker said at last.

Lady Violet's look raked over Amethyst, she felt grazed by the experience. Her only defence was a direct challenging gaze. For a moment she felt the clash of Lady Violet's cold gaze and then the woman shrugged and turned to her husband.

"You said you were going to take me to the Royal Academy this afternoon. To the exhibition."

"The Aetheric Painters?" Amethyst asked.

"Yes."

Maker's single word answers were as illuminating as ever.

"We," said Violet, retrieving something from her bag, "have an invitation to the private gallery." She held up the invitation with pride.

Such invitations were so sought-after they might have been printed on solid gold. While the main gallery was open to all, there was a private gallery to the exhibition, to which only the truly high born and influential had received invitations. That, of course, meant that every other member of Society wanted an invite too.

"Snap."

To Lady Violet's surprise and apparent disgust, Amethyst held up the invitation she'd been absently tapping. It was her own invitation to the private gallery. It had arrived that morning and she was wondering if it would be quite the done thing to attend alone. She suspected not, but she wasn't sure she had a choice.

"Join us."

It was difficult to know who was most surprised by Maker's invitation. For a second, she even thought Maker looked surprised, but the expression didn't last long enough to be certain. For a moment, she could only stare at him. She'd just been accused of being his mistress and a drudge. Was he seriously suggesting that she now be seen in public with him and his wife at one of the most exclusive exhibitions ever held? What would Society say?

I don't care! She had nothing to hide or to be ashamed of. There again, Lady Violet had made one good point. She was very poorly dressed.

"I'd need to change."

For a moment he just looked at her. "Snap."

*   *   *

It might not, Maker acknowledged to himself, have been the best move in the world to drop in on Amethyst before collecting Violet, yet how was he to know that Violet would be there? Why had she been there? He had been clear enough telling her to stay away. Yet the women hadn't been at each other's throats - should he take that as a good sign? It would make his life easier if they could find a way to get along. But he knew Violet better than that. He also knew that while Amethyst would try, her patience wasn't without limits.

Cravat tied, he looked at the tie pins Blanchard held for him. They nestled quietly in the velvet-lined case. Usually he wore the emerald, but he'd been wearing that all week.

"The am-" he cut himself off. No he couldn't wear an amethyst while being seen out with a woman named Amethyst, people would read too much into it. "The opal, I think." Yes, that was safer. Violet, he had noted when he'd seen her, had selected her opal pendant to match the lilac outfit she wore. This way he matched with his wife. As he should. One last check in the mirror. No, nothing for Violet to complain about.

"I'm attending the House this evening, so I shan't be needing you again tonight, Blanchard."

"Yes, sir. Shall I lay out your morning suit here or at number seven?"

He should stay here of course. "Do you know if Lady Fotheringham is expecting company this evening?"

"Not that I'm aware of, sir."

"Here then, Blanchard. Leave the side door unlocked, that way I won't disturb anyone coming in."

"As you wish, milord."

The walk across the Square was refreshing, though the carriage was slowing behind him before he was fully through the front door of number seven. He moved directly to the drawing room.

He was greeted by the sight of his wife inspecting some of Amethyst's knick-knacks. At that moment she was inspecting a particularly finely crafted silver singing bird. To his horror, the bird was heading for her handbag.

"Violet!"

She turned to him. "Why can't I have it?"

There were times when he couldn't believe how stupid his wife could be. "Violet," he hissed.

She slammed the trinket down so hard he feared she might break it, or at least scratch the shelf.

"You care more about Miss Forester than you do me."

He wasn't a good enough liar to gainsay that. He moved closer to his wife, leaned down to speak quietly. He would bend to her will frequently, but not always.

"Exhibition or home?"

Her eyes narrowed. He knew her ways. She'd comply for now, but he'd have to pay for his disloyalty later. Perhaps he'd go to the club tonight, his membership was still intact. He wasn't sure about Haversham's. There again, that would only increase her annoyance and her retribution. Better to accept the inevitable and get it over with.

Footsteps on the stair made Maker straighten and offer his wife a tight smile as he turned in time to see Amethyst appear in the doorway.

The governess was gone and in her place an elegant young lady bedecked in light purple with a darker trim. The jacket bore a wide band of lace in the matching darker purple that emphasised the narrowness of her waist. Maker clenched his hands behind his back to control the urge to reach out and check if he could span that waist. This time her top hat sported not only a matching purple band and bow, but a small veil of the same lace as the waistband.

He assumed this was part of the new wardrobe she had told him about. He heartily approved. The hat and veil very neatly covered the bruise remaining on her forehead. He could feel Violet beside him positively bristling.

"Well at least you're not wearing that awful brooch!" On that imperious note, Violet swept from the room. "Come along," she ordered them both. "We've wasted enough time already."

In her wake, Maker watched Amethyst look up at him. Offering a small conspiratorial smile, she flipped up the collar of the jacket to display said dreaded brooch. He desperately tried to control his answering smile, at least until she turned away. Then he allowed the smile to spread widely, but only long enough for him to cross the room, his features were their usual implacable mask as he joined the ladies.

*   *   *

The Royal Academy was fairly close, and had Amethyst the choice, she would have walked, though perhaps not in this new gown. That would not befit the image Maker and Dickens were trying to get her to project. Though perhaps she could have ordered a cab - one with an Aetheric engine, perhaps. There again, if alone with a cabbie and an engine she might have started asking questions which would have been just as unsuitable.

Still, a standard open hansom in a blizzard could not have been as frosty as this private carriage with Lord and Lady Fotheringham. This carriage was enclosed, and Amethyst absently wondered how many carriages the couple owned, and where they stored them. The urge to ask was crushed by the silence.

Lady Violet sat facing the direction of travel, and despite her own preference, Amethyst sat with her back to the direction of travel, as was expected of a guest of the carriage owner. Maker, the last to enter, sat beside his wife. From the moment he closed the door and the carriage pulled away, he determinedly watched the passing scenery out of the window. Amethyst doubted he was enjoying the view, it couldn't have been anything that he hadn't seen a thousand times before.

The only time he'd turned from the view was when Lady Violet took his arm. His surprise was as clear to

Amethyst as the implied message; Lady Violet wanted her to know that Maker was taken. *As if I don't already know that.*

Instead, she offered Lady Violet a small, approving smile. Then she turned her head to look out of the window. So what if she was acting as Maker's mirror, Lady Violet could hardly object.

Watching the passing roads, Amethyst couldn't but wonder how these two managed to become a couple. With no sign of them ever having become parents, she doubted it was a marriage of choice. These two were so cold, she had an image of two ice-sculptures trying to get into bed together. With a shiver, she pushed that image from her head. Maybe they hadn't always been this way, maybe things had changed over the years.

She turned to lady Violet. "How long have you been married?"

"Coming up to sixteen years."

"Really?" Amethyst felt her brows rise. Sixteen years ago, she'd been only five, these two must have been in their late teens at most. If he was married that young, it was likely that that was the reason he hadn't toured the continent; it wasn't the sort of thing young men did with their young wives. "I'm sorry," she gasped, trying to cover her embarrassment at being rather rude, "but neither of you look old enough to have been married so long. Still-" She had to find a proper compliment. "-you must have been a beautiful bride."

Lady Violet smiled, pleased at the image.

"Glowing."

Now Amethyst frowned at Maker. She didn't understand his dark tone, nor the tight-lipped glare Lady Violet shot him. The look the two ladies passed was glancing and awkward. Each turned to look instead from their nearest window.

On reaching the gallery, Maker offered each of them a hand from the carriage. Even through the kid gloves she wore, Amethyst could feel the warmth of his hand, so different from the chill of his eyes.

Without a word, Maker dropped her hand and offered his wife his arm. Of course, that was how it should be. She had no right to the unexpected stab of jealousy. Amethyst trailed uncomfortably behind them into the impressive Royal Academy building.

Chapter 30

Over a hundred years old, Burlington House was in the Palladian style, which to Amethyst meant breathtaking Georgian elegance. She'd passed the building any number of times and enjoyed just looking up at the columns and windows. Being alone, she'd never dared set foot in the place before though.

You're an heiress now. You've as much right as anyone.

She hurried after the Makers, a few steps behind as they crossed the threshold. Of course, she'd always had as much right as anyone to step inside. The Academy often had public exhibitions.

Inside, Amethyst thought the architecture alone was stunning. She hadn't expected quite such high ceilings. Natural light flooded the gallery, the domed oblong of the glass roof looking incredible in and of itself.

There was a small crowd lining the walls, everyone intent on one picture or another. Many of them seemed to be shifting from side to side, almost like swaying meadow grass. *Or a bunch of Bedlam patients.* Not knowing what the polite thing to do was, Amethyst trailed quietly after Lord and Lady Fotheringham and stopped at the first painting on the left.

The pastoral scene wasn't to her taste, but she could see a certain skill in the execution and an added dimension she had never seen before. Whatever the Aetheric Painters were doing with the pigment, there was a different quality to the paint. The colours seemed more vivid, the water and sky alive with movement, and as she moved, the image shifted as if it had depth and form instead of being a flat painting. She shifted each way, suddenly understanding why people were swaying. She shift- she stopped dead, remembering her first impression.

As they made their way slowly around the room, she heard the others talking quietly. Lady Violet expressed opinions, passed comment, and Maker said nothing. Since her own opinions weren't solicited, she chanced a single remark on how often she disagreed with Lady Violet's interpretations.

"Hello."

Amethyst jumped at the sound of the voice by her shoulder. She had been absorbed by the more abstract piece she was now standing before, she hadn't realised someone had moved up behind her. Her yelp brought too much attention to her, and she felt her cheeks burning under the accusatory gazes of strangers. She mumbled a general apology. Lady Violet's censure was hardly helping, but Amethyst refused to be so put down for long. She lifted her chin and looked at the smiling man who had surprised her.

"Mr Sanderson," she said with quiet censure that didn't quite work with the unavoidable grin, "you really shouldn't creep up on a lady that way."

Both Amethyst and Sanderson ignored Lady Violet's comment about her not being a lady, and Maker's hard look had no effect on his wife.

"My apologies, Miss Forester, I hadn't intended to startle you so." He offered a small bow then turned to Lord and Lady Fotheringham and greeted them formally.

The civility was returned, though coldly, especially from Lady Violet, whose button nose rose as she turned away. The hold Lady Violet had on Maker's arm turned him too.

Amethyst watched Sanderson's brows rise at the apparent snub. Then he turned and offered not only his arm, but a genuinely happy smile that lit up his face.

"I'm pleased I managed to catch up to you," he said as they moved on together and others came to view the abstract.

"I didn't realise I was running away." She returned his smile and while they paused at the next painting, Amethyst realised she was no longer interested in the art. After the initial interest in the new treatment of colour, she had realised that neither the quality of the artistry nor the choice of subject matter was really what she had been expecting or hoping for. She didn't paint herself, but Ruby did, and Ruby produced much better work than this.

"And I hope you never do."

There was something in the warmth of his expression that made her stomach clutch in the most intriguing manner. She did feel some attraction to him. He might not be so perfect looking as a certain peer, but at least Sanderson looked at her as though *she* were perfect. No one had ever done that before. It was a new and seductive experience.

"So why did you have to catch me?"

"I'm taking the train back to Swansea later this afternoon, and I wanted to see you again before I go."

"Did we miss something in the contracts?" They were just meandering now, vaguely keeping up with Lord and Lady Fotheringham, but not paying any particular attention to anyone or anything other than each other.

"No. But I was hoping for an answer to my invitation."

She frowned for a moment. "But I sent one back the next day. Never mind, I'm honoured by the invitation to the factory, which I would love to accept, but I feel I must stay in a hotel. I wouldn't want your reputation sullied by my presence."

"Hardly likely, I live with my parents, and my mother loves to have guests. She's been hosting my father's business contacts for decades, she'd consider me totally lacking in manners, to say nothing of business acumen, if I were to allow you to stay in a hotel and not our home."

"Ah. And you wouldn't mind if I were to bring my maid?"

"Of course not." His smile was broadening.

"Well in that case…"

"Good."

He was grinning at her. All she could do was smile back. She felt rather foolish, but in the best way possible. Unusually, she didn't feel any particular need to fill the silence.

You don't feel the need to talk around Maker either.

No, I usually feel the urge to slap him.

That was different, she decided as she looked forward, the smile slipping somewhat. She didn't talk much to Maker because he wouldn't always talk to her. When he did, it was usually business or a lecture on Society rules. Conform and make money. Besides, he came to her house for peace and quiet. She looked up to the backs of Lord and Lady Fotheringham. Again she wondered what their home life was like if Maker came to her home to relax. She didn't know and probably never would. Whatever Society might say of the arrangement, she could hardly put a stop to it. After all, he was the joint owner of the house. As they walked on, she was watching the floor more than anything else. For a moment the silence was fine, but its weight was becoming unbearable.

"Sir?"

Blinking, Amethyst turned to the young man who had addressed her companion. Only now did she realise that they had followed the peer and his wife all the way to the door of the private exhibition. Maker was looking back over his shoulder at her, as unreadable as ever. Lady Violet was sneering at her. Amethyst suddenly remembered the private exhibition was by invitation only.

"I'll need to see your invitation, sir."

Her eye line slipped back to the lithe young man in uniform barring their way.

"Ah," Mr Sanderson said, "I'm afraid I don't have one."

Amethyst looked up at him as she finally removed her hand from his arm. "I, however, do." She pulled the small bag hanging from its shoulder strap at her side and held it before her. The bag was plain, but the hinged clip was ornately decorated. She snapped the bag open and pulled out the small invitation card, and held it out to the doorman.

After a quick look at the card, the man nodded and smiled. Stepping back, he removed the red rope and held it open, allowing the couple to go through. "Enjoy the exhibition, Miss Forester. And guest."

She didn't particularly like the way he'd said that last, but who was she to be picky?

Clipping the rope back in place, the man opened the last door, the door by which Maker had been standing and through which he had disappeared. The bright wide rooms of the main exhibition area gave way to a much darker space beyond. The walls were painted black, black chiffon curtains separated the artworks and seemed to form a maze for the viewers to follow. The door clicked closed behind them, lowering the light levels even further. Amethyst tried not to think of the click as ominous.

They paused to allow their eyes to adjust to the change of light levels. As they stood there, Amethyst became aware of background music.

"Well that's annoying," she muttered.

Sanderson turned to look at her; she was on his right side. "What is?"

"The music."

Sanderson shrugged and shook his head. "I can't hear it."

Amethyst felt her cheeks burn and hoped under her veil and in this dimmer light that he wouldn't notice. "Of course, I'm sorry, but there again, you're probably better off. It's not exactly helping."

The artworks here were much larger pieces than in the main hall. The only lights were directly onto the canvases. They moved along the line prescribed by the chiffon curtaining. Through those partitions, Amethyst could see Lord and Lady Fotheringham ahead of them. There was something different about the way they were standing together, Maker seemed somehow less rigid, they were closer.

Reaching the first picture, Amethyst and Sanderson stopped before the canvas. At roughly four feet wide and three high, the image was a view of a naked lady lounging on a chaise, the room in the painting was covered in more chiffon-like curtains. They appeared to pulsate and shimmer as if blown by a light breeze. Amethyst assumed they were rendered in the aetheric paint. She began to feel uncomfortable, the moving veils suggested that the viewer was looking through a forbidden window and that at any moment the curtains might part and give them an uninterrupted view of the woman's nakedness.

"That's erm…"

"Voyeuristic?" Amethyst suggested.

"I was thinking risky."

Amethyst frowned for a moment. "Sorry do you mean risky or risqué?"

"Risky," Sanderson affirmed. "To make the first offering of the exhibition a nude, it risks offending certain elements."

"Hmm. Possibly." She contemplated the point. "It does, I suppose, assure that people move on. The prudes from offence, the salacious from the will to see more."

"More than a ripe bottom and a pert nipple? It's a virtual invitation to sexual intercourse as it is."

Amethyst's cheeks burned; she wasn't sure where to look. She couldn't face Sanderson and at that moment wouldn't face the painting. Perhaps she was a prude, but she wasn't at all sure that this was an appropriate conversation for two unmarried people. Or maybe it was just her.

"Shall we move on?"

They were standing in front of the next piece, a seascape, before Sanderson spoke again.

"I'm sorry Miss Forester, I didn't mean to offend

you. My apologies."

"I wasn't offended." Though she still couldn't face him. "A little shocked, yes, but not offended. It's not really a suitable conversation for an unmarried couple." Uncomfortable with even this conversation, Amethyst ploughed on. "Is it me or is that galleon particularly badly painted?"

Sanderson tipped his head first one way and then the other. "It doesn't appear especially proportional." His voice had slowed. "It could be illusory because of the apparent shifting... of the sea... and... err... sky..."

A glance told her that his jaw had slackened slightly. It wasn't his most attractive expression. Perhaps she could enliven that expression with a little humour.

"As disproportional and obscured as a ripe bottom and pert nipple?"

Sanderson had started swaying, staring at the painting almost without blinking. She waited a moment, then pushed his arm. He turned slowly to her.

"I'd like to see your ripe bottom and pert nipples."

Her breath froze in her throat. Her hand fell from his arm. Her eyes widened. Her mind wouldn't function. She couldn't believe he'd said that. The way he was looking at her - leering at her - made her stomach churn.

So different from with Maker, he affects your belly in a very different way. You like that way.

Pushing the voice away and not sure what else she could do, Amethyst turned and stalked to the next exhibit. This one was more abstract, she had no idea how to describe the swirling mass of incoherent colour. It didn't really matter, she wasn't especially looking at it and the music was increasing in volume, reverberating through the floor and in her bones. *Most annoying.* It also seemed to be getting warmer. Breathing was becoming difficult. Her corset felt rather too tight. It seemed to tighten more as she felt Sanderson step up beside her. Suddenly she missed her crinoline, it would have kept him at least a little further way. His hand rested on her back, just above the bustle of her gown. She was sure he wouldn't become over-amorous. Mostly. She looked around to see where Lord and Lady Fotheringham had got to - just in case. Unfortunately, she couldn't see either of them.

When she turned to the picture, she found that Mr Sanderson had leant in even closer. He spoke almost in her ear.

"What do you think of the couple writhing before us?"

Amethyst looked around. As far as she could tell they were alone. She frowned at him. "Do you mean the painting?"

"Exactly."

Now she turned to scrutinise him. His eyes were glued to the canvas, and Amethyst turned to it. It still looked like an incoherent mess to her. It was actually making her eyes ache. Which was the perfect match for the headache she was getting from the terrible music, its heavy unchanging beat feeling like a hammer in her ear. Her chest felt oddly warm. A hand to her heart put her fingers over the edge of the brooch the Professor had left her. Her fingers tingled, it was unusually warm.

Suddenly she spotted a pattern in the swirl, though the second she saw it, it was gone. Logic said she wouldn't have seen what she thought she'd seen but at least it made her think. The letters AE had jumped out at her. Suddenly her mind was full of all the notes and possibilities posed and left by Professor Richards.

If aetheric powers really could be mind-altering, then this was the place to achieve that. The Professor had made her promise to wear the brooch until she no longer needed it – and now she knew why. Amethyst looked around the room, spotting the exit at the back of the room.

"Come on."

Grabbing Sanderson's hand, she slapped the curtains out of the way and dragged him to the door. As she threw the door open, there was a suspended moment as she realised she recognised the shocked man staring back at her. Mr Brown. He turned quickly and left the room as the uniformed guard who had let them into the exhibition moved over to stop them following.

"Miss Forester, Mr Err…"

"You weren't given his name," Amethyst pointed out.

The man looked surprisingly pleased by her rudeness.

"Did you enjoy the show?"

"Oh yes."

Amethyst was surprised by Sanderson's simpering response. This was unlike him.

"It was most innovative."

The man looked happy with that response. "So you see now the value of aetheric works."

Oh, she saw it all too clearly, but the truth wasn't what this man wanted to hear. She instinctively knew that right now the truth would be injurious to her health. "Oh I do." She hoped she reached the right tone of simpering admiration. "I mean how would we live without it? It's clearly meant to enhance our lives in every way."

"We appreciate your support. Be sure to share the good news."

"Oh, don't worry, I can assure you I'll tell everyone I know about what I've learned here today." It felt like her face would split, she was forcing the smile so much. "You're welcome, did you see Lord and Lady Fotheringham? I must make sure that they see things that way too."

The man looked slightly less comfortable now. "Lord and Lady Fotheringham exited the exhibition a few minutes ago. I believe they left."

Feeling Sanderson's hands snaking around her waist again, his inappropriate nearness, she offered another fake smile as she controlled Sanderson's hands. She scowled up at the glassmaker. "Let's get you home." *Before I have to slap you.*

"Such eagerness. Like it."

Amethyst blushed like a volcano. The liveried man's smile was nothing short of salacious.

"If I might suggest, the nearest exit is this way."

Following the man's indication, Amethyst headed for the door. The fresh air was a relief. There was little point going to look for the Fotheringhams or their coach, it would be on the other side of the building if it was even still there, which was unlikely. She walked swiftly to the edge of the road. Lifting her hand, she hailed a taxi. The one that stopped had an aetheric engine. Aetheric power, that was the last thing she wanted to be around, but with Sanderson becoming increasingly inappropriate, it was the only choice she had. She bundled Sanderson in before her and gave the driver the Belgravia address.

Sanderson moved in too close, squeezing her against the side of the cab as it started off.

"Mr Sanderson, please."

She tried pushing him away, but he wouldn't be budged. As she pushed and he leaned in, they reached a stalemate and she realised his eyes were glazed. She also realised that her heart was thumping, she couldn't breathe properly. There were more stars bursting at the edges of her vision. She was afraid there was no reasoning with him and for the first time she realised just how vulnerable she was, a single woman alone.

"Oh come on," Sanderson said as he leaned over her. She had to twist her head away to avoid searching lips. "You know you like me."

She did, but not this way. Right now though, his superior strength was gaining the upper hand.

"Mr Sanderson, stop!"

Her hand slipped off his arm, his hand bashed into her chest, forcing what little air there was from her lungs, and an unavoidable yelp escaped her. The hatch between them and the cabbie opened.

"Ow, mister!" the rough voice thundered down. "Get yer 'ands off 'er."

Even through her shaking, Amethyst could tell Sanderson's manner had changed. The tension had reduced, he wasn't so much leaning in as leaning on. Support, not attack. He was blinking as he looked up at the cabbie. He looked back at Amethyst, his eyes filling with horror when he realised where his hand was - which was almost directly over her breast.

With a surprised if inarticulate cry, Sanderson

pulled his hand away, scooting back off as far as the cab would allow him. The cab was coming to a halt.

"Oh Lord! I'm so sorry," he stumbled the apology. "I don't know what came over me."

Even though Amethyst was reasonably certain she knew exactly what had come over him, that didn't make her any less afraid of the events or, in that moment, of the man. She knew she'd get over it, but not yet.

"I think you should get out now, Mr Sanderson."

"But -"

"Lady said out," the gruff voice came from above. "So you gettin' out or do I 'ave to come down there and get you out?"

Looking confused and horrified, Sanderson looked to Amethyst for direction. She almost felt sorry for him. Almost.

"I will doubtless forgive you, but not instantly, and I don't want to be anywhere near you right now. Please, get out."

Still stumbling through apologies, Sanderson finally moved. He was hardly out of the cab, the door just touching closed when the cabbie pulled away again.

Heart still thumping, emotions jumping like a march hare gone mad, Amethyst sat back. This was only her second ever aetheric cab ride, and she couldn't help but compare it to the first. It was a completely unfair comparison, of course. No woman should compare her experience with one man to another, especially when the second man could reasonably be described as under the influence of, well, outside influences. She couldn't very well hold his actions against him. If she twisted the situation, it was almost complimentary that he was so keen. On the other hand, if the aetheric mind control was making men do things not normally in their character, did that make it the apparent attraction or the *acting* on the attraction that was against Sanderson's character?

Of course all those possibilities made her think about Maker. It wasn't like him to have invited her to join them and then leave without her. Lady Violet, perhaps, but not Maker. And again - mind control? But why? She looked at the engine and the rainbow glow of its power source. It was undoubtable that aetheric power was clean and versatile. And she was now about to make money from the aetheric industry, albeit peripherally, which split her loyalties a little, but she clearly remembered everything Maker had said in his speech. She knew he was right. The Aetheric Concessions Bill was unfair, it should be fought. Maker was fighting it and she was sure that would work. Except that Lord Haversham had been as actively against the bill the first time she'd met him. Then at Lady Garrington-Smythe's, he'd been the exact opposite of the man she'd first met. After attending the Royal Academy, would Maker be so easily diverted? She considered what she'd seen. Maker never showed much inclination towards Violet, yet the last time she'd spotted him, he had definitely been leaning towards his wife. Had he been altered as Sanderson had?

"Miss? Are you quite alright?"

The voice brought her back to the here and now as she blinked to focus. She found the cabbie was on the pavement at her side, rather than behind her. He actually looked concerned. They were in Belgravia Square. They were home.

Her hands were shaking as she found her purse and

the few coins to pay the man, thanking him for his help.

Chapter 31

"Miss, is everything alright?"

Edwards' concern as he closed the door was almost as worrying as the fact that her hands were still shaking as she removed her hat. Now the door was closed, she knew it was only her and Edwards, whose professional discretion she was sure she could trust.

"Actually, no. Thank you for asking. Could you bring me some tea? I'll be in the study."

She didn't exactly collapse into her chair, but it was a close run thing. Unlocking the desk drawer, she pulled out the papers they'd found in the Professor's hidden lab. She'd been making good headway, but now she more fully understood what was possible, some clarity had come with the decoding. She slid the card into the machine and started it up.

Edwards appeared quickly with the tea. "Is there anything else I can get for you, Miss?"

"Some peace of mind would be good."

Edwards' face fell.

"Sorry, my sense of humour is a little twisted." Still, it wasn't such a bad idea. "Actually, you could help with that. It's a lot of ask, so say no if you don't want to do it. Any chance you could go over and speak to Mr Blanchard, find out if he's heard anything from Maker? Maker and Lady Fotheringham left the exhibition without me and that doesn't seem characteristic of either of them. Just don't let on I'm worried. Or that I asked. Sorry to ask you-"

Edwards held up his hand. "I understand your position Miss, and I'm happy to do what I can."

"Thank you."

Edwards left and she returned to her decryption. Once she'd reprogrammed a couple of symbol meanings, she ran the translation again. She printed out the result and sat staring at it. The re-read made frightening sense.

"Miss?"

She looked up at Edwards.

"Sorry to report that Lord and Lady Fotheringham have yet to return home."

She nodded and thanked the man, who turned and left. The Makers' continuing absence didn't seem so out of place with everything else she now knew. She removed the brooch from beneath her lapel. It was still the same awful, ugly thing it had always been, but now she knew it had saved her from some form of disaster, she really rather admired it. She also noted it was cold now. When she'd touched it at the exhibition it had definitely been - warm. Did it matter? She turned back to her paper.

"Ma'am?"

Amethyst looked up. "Yes, Dickens?"

"Did you want to change?"

"Not now, but in case I decide to, please put out something that doesn't require a damned corset. Other than that, I just need some peace and quiet to get on. I'll call you if I need you."

Thankfully, an hour alone was enough to allow her to make clear progress on the Professor's notes, at the end of which, she understood completely. The brooch, which she could now identify as AE59-3, had activated to save her in the presence of the overwhelming force generated by the aetheric paintings, which had worked in combination with the warmth and the heartbeat music. It hadn't worked on Sanderson until he'd touched it because that was the way it was designed. So now she had to get Maker to touch it. The question was how.

After a few moments thought, she reached for her pen.

"You rang, Miss?"

"I did, Dickens." She smiled at the younger woman. "Would you kindly take this across the road?"

* * *

Maker had been carousing. It wasn't his usual choice, but his usual choices were boring and it was long past time he cut himself free. It was something many of the friends he had been drinking with had told him - Haversham excluded, who had gone against type and not drunk with them. The Lords' Parliamentary bar had been busier than usual. Rowdier. Afterwards, they'd gone to the club, but their volume had led to a request to leave. It had been suggested they head to a well-frequented local tavern, and Maker understood why. All the same, he had had the unaccountable desire to go home to his wife. Stumbling from the tavern, he'd hailed a taxi and headed home.

To be greeted by Blanchard and a note. A very appealing note. It was time to teach Violet a lesson to be a better wife, but there were more ways than one to instruct. He batted Blanchard's hands away. He'd already divested himself of the cravat and jacket. His waistcoat could stay, even unbuttoned.

"Am goin' out." The floor shifted as though he were

at sea, but he managed to right himself and ignore Blanchard's counter-suggestion.

The night air was cold, refreshing. It felt like an ice bucket over his head. Half way across the gardens, it occurred to him that a visit at this hour might not be such a good idea. He stumbled over to sit on one of the wrought iron benches.

"Sir, I really think you should return home."

He turned to scowl at his valet.

It was nearly three in the morning. Amethyst would be curled up in her bed, all warm and soft. Inviting. He stood up.

"Oh, get lost!"

*   *   *

Eventually, Amethyst's exhaustion had gotten to her. With grainy eyes, she'd given up deciphering the last of the Professor's papers and decided to await Maker in the drawing room. It hadn't taken long to realise that was pointless, and head for bed. She'd been asleep as soon as her head hit the pillow.

The commotion downstairs woke her. A glance at the mantel clock told it it was ten past three. After all the break-ins, Amethyst feared the worst.

Finally, she heard the unmistakable sound of Maker yelling her name. It was so unlike him she knew he was under the influence. Scrambling from the bed, she grabbed the brooch and flicked the lever she hadn't realised was there until reading about it. She was still struggling with her dressing gown when her door was flung open. Maker stood there, one hand on the doorknob, the other on the jamb. She was fairly sure he was using the position to hold himself upright. He was in his shirtsleeves and his waistcoat unbuttoned. He looked delectable - *wild*. He looked wild. And a little bit frightening. What was more, he was looking at her in a way he had never looked at her before; like he wanted to ravish her.

Her abdomen clenched as her hand around the brooch tightened. His look heated her blood as the metal heated her palm. Maker wild was even more scrumptious than the cold statue Maker. Even fear was just a piquant addition.

Get a grip.

Thankfully, the press of the brooch kept her grounded.

"Have you been drinking?"

He stood up straighter, his eyes roving over her, making her feel things she had never felt before.

"So?"

So he's drunk. This isn't Maker.

"Mmm." The sound shimmered across the air between them as Maker stood properly and looked her up and down. This was far more overt than Sanderson had been but she wasn't afraid this time. Well she was, but in a very different, much more pleasing way.

He stepped towards her, which was just as well - she needed him closer, but seemed to have forgotten how to walk herself.

A clattering in the hallway drew her attention. Behind Maker, Edwards and Blanchard appeared, both looking red-faced. Edwards appeared to have a split lip.

"Stop!" Amethyst held up her hand to halt the two servants in the doorway.

"See?" Maker turned as he approached her. She

suspected he was grinning, which should give the other men enough warning. "She wants me. Her note said so." He brandished the note before he turned unsteadily back to her.

"It says 'I want to see you.'" As he reached for her, she reached out her hand and grabbed his wrist. With the other hand, she slapped the brooch into his palm.

What happened next seemed to fracture time. On the one hand it happened instantly and on the other, so slowly, she watched every beat as though it lasted a lifetime.

The look of surprise on his face. His brows rose. His jaw dropped. His eyes widened. Looked confused. His arm slackened, and she gripped his hand in both of hers to keep the brooch in his grip. Pain replaced confusion. His forward momentum turned into downward force as he collapsed to his knees. Like Sanderson, he seemed to have lost momentary control, but more so. Given the greater influence the aether had had over Maker, she wasn't surprised. He was lurching to fall full face on the floor, so she shifted to support him. His head pressed into her belly. She put one hand on his head as he struggled with the change.

She looked up to see Edwards and Blanchard looking on, totally bemused. Quickly, she explained. "The aetheric painters hypnotised him to make him change his vote. Professor Richards worked out how to counteract it. He put the technology into that hideous brooch I've been wearing."

She looked down, Maker's dark head against her stomach. His left arm hung useless at his side and his right was mostly limp in her hand. She took the brooch and dropped his arm. It thumped to the floor, Maker groaned and his weight shifted like he'd fall, but she grabbed his shoulders and kept him with her.

Carefully, she pushed him slightly back, used both hands to tip his face toward hers.

"Ben?"

He was slack-jawed and unfocused. She couldn't ever have predicted this. Looking up, she saw Edwards and Blanchard, looking uncertain by the door.

"Gentlemen, I believe Lord Fotheringham is in need of your assistance."

Chapter 32

Despite the disturbed night, Amethyst was still up early. After a light breakfast, she moved back to the study. The progress she'd made on the Professor's notes was both gratifying and worrying.

Though she normally ate in the study, today, not wanting to disturb CAMM, she asked to be served in the dining room. Which was where she was sitting when Maker appeared carefully around the door. He was dressed and clean shaven, looking as smart as ever. She assumed that was more to do with Blanchard than Maker. He maintained his usual rigidly erect posture, but he was walking more carefully than normal.

"Afternoon," she said as he came into the room.

He moved to his usual seat, but unusually, he didn't immediately sit. Looking up, she saw the same carved features as ever, though his eyes were perhaps a little more bloodshot. He didn't say a word.

"Society," she said as softly as could, "would suggest that you owe me an apology. Luckily for you, since you seem to have a problem with the one obvious word you could be uttering at this point, Society doesn't know what you did so won't censure you, and I wouldn't let Society bother me if it did. I'm also in the unusual position of totally understanding that you really were not in control of yourself last night. So no apology needed, just sit down and eat something if you can stomach it."

Maker was sitting as Edwards arrived with an odd-looking drink on a silver tray. He placed the tall glass before Maker.

"Mrs Shaw assures me that if you drink this in one and then eat the meal she's preparing, you should be right as rain in an hour."

Maker said nothing.

"Do me the kindness," Amethyst said, "of looking at my butler."

She watched as Maker moved carefully. She saw the shoulders slump as the lord saw the split lip and bruised jaw. She understood and forgave Maker for what he had done to her, well, what he'd wanted to do. Edwards knew what had happened too, the headlines anyway, but the availability of his forgiveness was more questionable.

Maker stood. "Edwards, my most sincere apologies. I don't know what came over me."

The butler met the lord's look squarely. "May I speak freely, sir?"

Maker went to nod, but clearly it was too painful. "Please do."

"You had clearly had too much to drink last night. Perhaps you would find comfort in the Methodist way of thinking."

"Thank you, Edwards." The two men offered slight bows, Edwards left and Maker sat slowly down. He looked at the drink. Amethyst didn't think it looked at all appetising. To be fair, Maker picked it up and Amethyst watched in half horror as he drank every drop and returned the glass to the table. He looked vaguely disgusted.

"That was probably Shaw's revenge," she said before continuing with her own meal.

"I really must apologise for my behaviour last night."

She looked up, almost glared at him. "You should, but I've already told you, you don't need to. I know that wasn't you. You wouldn't normally act that way. What was it like, though? Being... well... changed like that?"

He hung his head. "Shameful."

"I meant," she asked when he didn't elaborate, "what did it feel like when you were in the gallery, when they were, well, changing you?"

"Odd."

She raised her brows in his direction.

"Uncontrolled."

Again he didn't expand.

"Bet you hated that."

Maker closed his eyes and hung his head. "Disgraceful. I hate to think what others will say of my behaviour."

"Your behaviour?"

A small groan seemed like agreement.

"How much do you remember?"

"Everything."

"But you didn't mind doing it."

His head shook. "I knew it wasn't what I would normally do, but I didn't care enough to stop."

"Was any of it worse than what you did when you got here?"

"God, no!"

She shrugged and tried not to be insulted. "Well, there you are. You've got over the worst of it already."

He was shaking his head. "I doubt my friends will be so forgiving."

"You doubt-" She stopped when she saw the meal Edwards was bringing in. Maker thanked the man as Amethyst looked on in disbelief at the piled high fried everything with which Shaw had filled the plate. Edwards set the plate down and left.

"Now this is *definitely* Shaw's revenge."

Amethyst smiled, nearly laughed. "Probably. But as I was saying, if you doubt your friends will forgive you, then you need new friends. You are well liked, well thought of in Society. Your friends will consider it a momentary aberration. Possibly even as proof that you are human after all. And you're not elected to the Lords, so who cares what your enemies think?"

She could tell from his look that he cared all the same.

"What exactly did you do?"

"Shameful, drunken behaviour."

Amethyst shrugged. "It happens. What do you remember after you got to my room?"

This time he couldn't look at her and his cheeks reddened. She watched him swallow. "I remember going home. I was thinking of some terrible things I could do. Then I got your note. I remember coming over here, what I did... I remember reaching for you, there was heat in my hand and then, I don't remember much after that. I've also noticed you aren't wearing that brooch anymore."

"And I've noticed that you're talking more than normal. It's unnerving, can we get back to your usual taciturn nature."

"Probably not until after this conversation."

"Fair comment. My brooch is in the study, it's also the warmth you felt in your hand, and it's AE59-3." She recounted all she'd discovered, including that AE59-4 was designed to overcome the effects of the control on a larger scale.

"We know that at an absolute minimum, you and Haversham have been affected by this control. We know that it's been achieved through the use of aetheric technology. We also know that you and Haversham were two of the strongest voices against the Aetheric Concession Bill. Didn't you also say some of the MPs had been behaving oddly for the last few weeks?"

Maker nodded. "You think there's been some long term plan here?"

"Oh yes. It probably started with coercion, lobbying, perhaps even bribery, to get the initial white paper put together at least. But this apparent mind control must have come in at some point. They have to have tried it out on people first, before this exhibition."

Maker was nodding again, clearly considering the point.

"When's the next vote?"

"Tomorrow."

Amethyst sat back, feeling suddenly defeated.

"Amme?"

"We can't do it."

"What?"

"Release all of them from the control."

"Why?"

"Even if we start with Haversham, we won't be able to get to every voting Lord to ensure that those affected are freed from the control."

"You said AE59-4 was a mass antidote."

"That's the way it was designed, yes."

"Then-"

"I don't *have* AE59-4."

"Then how do you know?"

"It's in the Professor's notes. And I found some

other things in the hidden lab, including the design specifications and what I'd need to do to build it."

"Then-"

"It would take more than a day and that's all I've got."

"What if you had more resources? Someone who could help you build it?"

"Like who?"

"Bobbie."

Amethyst considered it. Bobbie was obviously a clever woman, though she had said herself that she was more of a dabbler.

"It could work," she mused. "*If* Bobbie would do it."

"I'll send her -"

He stopped as Amethyst speared an untouched rasher of bacon from his plate, folded it up and popped it in her mouth.

"You really don't follow Society's rules, do you?"

She grinned at him. "Not when bacon's going to waste, no. If you send word to Bobbie, I'll get started as soon as we've dealt with the other immediate problem."

He frowned. "Which is?"

"Well, you weren't alone at the exhibition. You were affected; don't you think Lady Violet might have been too?"

Chapter 34

Head banging, Maker sat at Amethyst's desk to compose a note to Bobbie. He hadn't had a hangover this bad since the night he'd realised just what kind of a woman he had tied himself to. It had felt as if he'd been trying to drink the world dry that night. But wallowing in self-pity now would do no good.

He glanced over at the lab. Amethyst was working. She'd pulled on sleeve protectors and put a brown apron over her grey dress to get on with building AE59-4. And she hadn't condemned him for his appalling behaviour last night. Thank God she was too innocent to understand what he'd been planning to do. Thank God she'd stopped him. Please God he could stop wanting to -

He turned back to the note, completed it and stood to ring the bell. He was a little surprised that Blanchard responded, though it was just as well - given the task at hand.

As he was completing his instructions, Maker was more surprised when Edwards entered and announced the arrival of Violet, who only entered on permission. *Unusual.* Immediately, Maker felt himself tense. He'd told Violet never to come here, and he wasn't sure he could cope with a fight between his wife and his... friend.

Violet swept in, perfect as a picture as always, but for once smiling broadly, and exuding an air of real happiness, an edge to be careful of. Just like the girl he'd fallen for. It was a lie back then and it was a lie now. His awareness focused on the brooch to his left.

He picked it up and switched it on.

"Good afternoon, my dear Maker." She offered him an elegant curtsey. She hadn't done that since their introduction.

"Violet." He was on uncertain ground now and he didn't want to risk tripping down a mineshaft.

"I'm sorry to bother you but I was wondering, will you be home tonight?"

Her hands were behind her back and she was twisting back and forth. He'd seen little girls do that. It wasn't so appealing on a 34 year-old woman.

He hadn't made any plans either way, and he suspected she wouldn't want him home. "Perhaps."

She looked disappointed. "Oh please, I have something for you."

What she normally had for him wasn't something to rush home for.

"Maker, I need-" Amethyst came in from the lab, her voice cutting out as she registered Lady Violet's presence.

"Miss Forester, how wonderful to see you."

Maker was uncertain who was more shocked when Violet stepped over and greeted Amethyst, him, Amethyst, Blanchard or Edwards. The greeting hug and air kiss was something she normally reserved for the greatest and mightiest.

Amethyst looked stunned as Violet started talking to her. Properly talking.

The contrast was so, so sharp. For all the muted colours she wore, Amethyst was much more vivid, somehow more real, solid. This was not the Violet he was used to. Apparently, from their slightly slack-jawed expressions and the fact they they hadn't done the usual thing of moving quietly away, Edwards and Blanchard felt the same way.

"Blanchard."

"Yes, sir?"

Why they both felt the necessity of keeping their voices down he wasn't sure, but it probably wasn't a bad idea.

"Delivery."

"Yes, sir. May I have the note?"

The question drew Maker's attention back from the ladies. The letter for Bobbie was still on the desk before him. He picked it up and reached over the CAMM to hold it out to his valet. Blanchard took the fold of paper and left. Edwards took the opportunity to disappear too, leaving the three together.

Maker looked back to the two ladies. They were actually smiling at one another, acting like they were real friends. How would it be if they were? Would it make his life easier or harder? His life with Violet was bound to be more pleasant, it might even take his mind off other distractions. His look moved to Amethyst. Distraction. Not necessarily one he wanted to get rid of. But it was the right thing to do. Sadly, he picked up the brooch. It was warm now.

He remembered last night when touching it had torn down the walls splitting his mind. The truth was that yesterday he'd been enjoying himself. All the restraints, the inhibitions that held him back had been released. It was the first time he'd relaxed and kicked back since his - no wait, it was pretty much the *only* time in his life he'd been able to do that. Even in university he had been a married man, duty-bound to go home to his wife. The way Amethyst had looked at him last night though.

There'd been desire in her eyes, he'd read her temptation to let events unfold, to let him - then her eyes had gone steely and she'd slapped this thing into his hand and torn him into pieces. Still, he should be grateful. Amethyst didn't know what he could have done to her and he would never have forgiven himself for shattering that innocence.

Looking up, he seemed to catch Amethyst's eye. She glanced at him, at the brooch in his hand, then back to his eyes. She didn't look any happier about what was to come than he was.

"Lady Violet, why don't we go into the drawing room? You'll be more comfortable..."

Violet turned and left as Maker stood to take the brooch with him.

"When you collapse on touching that," Amethyst added under her breath as she turned to him. "Do we really have to do this? This version's fair nicer."

Maker took a breath. "Would you want someone to make that decision for you?"

Her silent response demonstrated both her understanding and regret. As she preceded him, he knew exactly how she felt. Again he paused as Amethyst and Violet sat and looked like friends. How he'd like them to be.

Violet sat in the centre of the couch, her bag on her lap, Amethyst to her side. The side nearest the door, with her back to Maker. As they spoke, Violet patted the bag, then her eyes switched up to him. The way she smiled made his heart catch. Then Amethyst turned too, and the way she lost her smile twisted his heart.

Slowly he paced over to sit on the other side of Violet.

"Why not give it to him now?"

Maker frowned at Amethyst's odd comment.

"You think I should?"

Violet sounding eager to please almost sent shivers down his spine.

"I doubt there'll ever be another moment more appropriate."

"You're right."

Maker guessed Violet didn't have the vaguest idea of how right as she agreed and pulled something from her bag. She handed over a box roughly two inches square and one deep. The deep green leather was closed with a golden bow.

Putting the brooch in his lap, Maker took the box and thanked his wife. For a moment, he just looked at it.

"Well, it's not some snake. It won't bite you."

"Open it," Amethyst encouraged.

There wasn't any other option, so he pulled on the gold bow, allowed it to fall as he pulled the box top clear of the base. Inside on deep green velvet was a beautiful fob watch. Tiny cogs sat along the front in an artistic representation of the solar system. He'd loved to look at the stars when he was younger, but his studies of the law had taken over - those and Violet's demands on his time. He picked it out. A quick pressure on the side button and the front opened to show a perfect clear face. The maker's name made him still. One of the best watchmakers in England. Engraved on the inside of the cover were the words 'You are my world.' It was beautiful. The most thoughtful gift he'd ever received and at any other time, he'd have been overjoyed to receive it. But now, at a time when he knew Violet was acting against her own nature, it simply underlined the cruelty of the joke that was his marriage.

"I saw it and thought of you. I thought you'd like it. You do like it, don't you?"

"Yes." He closed it carefully and placed it back in the box.

"And you'll be proud to wear it too," Amethyst said with forced jollity, "won't you, Maker?"

He looked up at her. When she had his eye she tipped her head towards Violet.

"Yes," he said, turning to Violet, who for once looked eager for his approval. He smiled. The expression felt strained and unnatural.

"What's that?"

His smile slipped away as he realised she meant the thing in his lap, AE59-3. "Brooch."

"It's ugly."

"It's mine." Amethyst said. "Maker was mending the clasp for me."

"Oh well, you'd better have it back."

Before Maker could even think of stopping Violet, she'd reached out and grabbed the brooch.

She stilled, her eyes went wide, then she slumped. Maker caught her. Her body jerked, spasmed and then she went limp.

"Is she alright?"

Moving from under her, Maker lowered his wife to the couch, heedless of the brooch falling away. As he laid her head carefully on the cushions he saw the thin throb of the pulse in her neck.

"Fainted."

"Probably best if we let her sleep to recover," Amethyst said as she stood and eased Violet's feet up on the couch.

Brushing the hair back from his wife's face, it was impossible to miss the perfection of her countenance.

"She really is angelically beautiful, isn't she?"

Amethyst had put his precise thought into words.

"Shame she's usually such a bitch."

The deeper gripe mirrored but enhanced his thoughts again.

"Still, I've got work to do."

As Amethyst left, Maker stayed on his knees. Caring for his wife.

Chapter 35

Edwards had the door open before Amethyst was fully up the steps. She stormed over the threshold, slammed her bag on the side and turned to Edwards as he closed the door.

"I wish you wouldn't always do that," she virtually growled.

"Miss Amethyst?"

"There are times, like now," she snarled, her voice starting out reasonable but rapidly reaching a crescendo, "when I would really like to slam the bloody door!"

Edwards looked scandalised. "That really wouldn't be very ladylike, ma'am."

"Nor," Dickens said quietly from further into the house, "is the swearing."

Drawing in a breath, Amethyst apologised to Edwards before she turned to her maid. "This is my house and if I want to swear like a navvy, I will. Is that clear?"

Dickens paled. "Sorry, ma'am, but I didn't want you to offend your visitor."

Amethyst rolled her eyes. The last thing she needed was to have to deal with the harpy right now. "Oh God, is Lady Violet still here?"

"If she were," a new voice called from the study, "I wouldn't be."

Amethyst felt some of the annoyance drain from her as she pulled the hat pin and hat from her head.

"Bobbie!" She passed the hat and pin to Dickens and went through to the study and her guest. "I'm sorry

I wasn't here to greet you," Amethyst said as they met.

"Not a problem. Maker was here. As was Lady Violet. Excuse me for being presumptuous but I decided to hide in here rather than deal with Lady Violet when she came to. Maker took her home about..." Bobbie checked the clock. "...twenty minutes ago."

"I take it Maker explained why he asked you here?"

"He did. I was just looking over the schematics." They drifted towards the desk, where the plans were laid out. CAMM had been put back away. "This is sheer genius."

The thought made Amethyst smile. "That's Professor Richards for you. We have a problem though. I checked through the component stores and the other contraptions that the Professor left and we're missing three vital components; a Rynold capacitor, a compensator and an aetheric power source of the right voltage. The power source I can, at a pinch-"

"Which is where we seem to be."

"Exactly, but that I can cobble that from a lamp. The capacitor and compensator, however, I can't. And I can't seem to buy them either."

Bobbie was frowning at her. "Did you try Sergeants in Sloane Street?"

Amethyst nodded. "Twice, I went there first and last. I also tried Williams and Havers, Danvers, Steampower, Wilsons and finally the University, who were the most condescending bunch of-" She stopped herself. She could feel her blood pressure rising. "They all but told me it wasn't a woman's place to be concerned about such things. Well actually, that's exactly what they told me, but they were even more patronising and insulting about Professor Richards."

"No wonder you're in a foul mood."

"It's not just that." To use up some of the nervous energy building inside her, Amethyst started pacing, bringing the papers from the desk to the laboratory bench. "It's how important this is. I'm all for aetheric innovations, but not unfair concessions. I know less about electrical power, but it seems as useful. Steam's good but rather messy, and heavy. This country needs a cleaner power source before we're all choking in the streets."

Amethyst turned to find Bobbie watching her. The older woman was leaning with her shoulder on the wall between the study and the lab. There was a smile on her face.

"Am I ranting pointlessly?"

"More preaching to the converted," Bobbie said. "It's a shame you aren't in politics, that was quite a speech. But trust me, I know how it feels to be discriminated against for no better reason than being female."

Given that she was again wearing men's clothes, Amethyst wasn't the least bit surprised.

"On the other hand," Bobbie said, "it's good to see you passionate about something. It's like seeing Maker get worked up for the first time."

Amethyst couldn't stop herself laughing. The idea of Maker getting worked up seemed ridiculous - until she remembered the intensity of his look last night. An aberration - an act against his natural inclination, that was what the mind control did.

She sighed. "If we're to complete this, we'd better get started."

"Is there any point without the capacitor and compensator?"

Air rushed from her lungs as her shoulders slumped and her head hung. "Not really, but I can try."

"I-" Bobbie stood more erect. She considered her words as Amethyst turned to her. "That is, appearances can be judged on, but some can break past that judgement. I have some contacts, they may be able to secure the pieces you need. Would that help?"

"Just how illegal a contact are we talking about here?"

Bobbie's smile became both self-deprecating and slightly impressed.

"I really don't want to know the answer to that question, do I?"

"Don't worry," Bobbie assured her, "it's more a case of shady contacts than shady deals. I'll be back as soon as I can."

*   *   *

Amethyst's eyes were grainy and her sight was starting to swim by the time Bobbie returned three hours later. She wasn't looking happy either.

Switching off the blowtorch, Amethyst set it and her mask aside to greet her guest. "No luck?"

Bobbie was shaking her head as they both sat by the fireplace in the study. "Some. It's very odd and altogether disappointing. I finally got to the bottom of it though. Sort of."

"Sort of?"

"Well, a couple told me their stock was due in tomorrow, which is fair enough, but one of them couldn't meet my eye when he said it. In the end I had to threaten physical violence and financial ruin to find out that several, possibly all potential suppliers had already received such threats. The instruction being not to supply any woman with aetheric parts until after the 24th."

"The 24th?" Amethyst sat back. "The day after tomorrow."

"I don't see the significance."

"The day *after* the voting on the Aetheric Concession Bill. The thing someone is trying to control, and the control that I am trying to break." Amethyst focused on Bobbie. "Did you find out who issued this edict?"

The woman shook her head. "Someone scarier than me was all I found out."

"And there's no way I can make the Professor's machine work without those parts. I can cobble a power source from something else, might even be able to build the compensator now I've found more of the Professor's notes on how to do it, but there's no way I can rig a Rynold capacitor." Feeling totally deflated, she looked out to the lab. Just because she was the wrong gender... What if... She stood and looked at Bobbie. "What if I send Edwards?"

Bobbie shook her head. "You've made enough of an impact on society that he'd be known and refused."

"Hmm." She bit her bottom lip. Then smiled. "What if I asked Jenson or one of his men?"

Bobbie shrugged. "Might work, if he'd be agreeable to deception, and if we can get hold of him, Detectives are notoriously busy and we don't have any other contacts. Besides, when I was in the last two suppliers, they were refusing to sell to men too. I think we have, as they say, kicked a hornet's nest."

Drumming her fingers against her crossed arms, Amethyst paced towards the lab. All the parts she had were neatly set out. Useless. The evening sun was still streaming through the skylights. Just the kind of evening that was perfect for a walk.

"Hyde Park," Amethyst called as she strode towards the door.

"What about it?" Bobbie looked confused.

"I'll explain as we go. Come on."

*   *   *

Heart thumping, Amethyst sat high in the horse-drawn cab they had hailed. The demonstrator she had seen that day when she'd ridden with Maker, the day they'd found the Professor dead, wasn't at his usual spot. She'd come this way irregularly over the weeks since and he'd always been in the same place, but not today.

"Typical," Amethyst grumped, but she couldn't give up just yet, the man might simply have moved. "Once around the park, please Cabbie," she called.

They had reached the far corner of the park and Amethyst was about to give up hope when she spotted a likely crowd. She directed the cabbie over. Once he'd stopped, Amethyst jumped out, asking Bobbie to wait with the vehicle.

The salesman was in full flow, talking about his revolutionary relaxation machine. From what Amethyst could see, it was a leather chair that seemed to have rotating blocks under the leather to act as some kind of massager. At the front of the arms, two rests, which reminded Amethyst greatly of rollocks, awaited the user. Apparently these exuded aetheric power, the health benefits of which were expounded beyond anything Amethyst was prepared to believe. The important thing however was that the salesman was selling not only that chair, but a box of spares - for easy, cost-effective home maintenance. Amethyst studied the large hand-painted sign that declared the contents of the spares box. It included a Rynold capacitor and a compensator.

The crowd was now talking to the member of the public who had been trying the chair. From her various walks past, Amethyst was reasonably certain the randomly selected member of the public was actually the same woman she'd seen trying the machine on at least three occasions. Either she was overly keen or a plant. Amethyst thought the later, then berated herself for her cynicism. As the crowd flocked to the woman, Amethyst moved in on the salesman.

Five minutes of wrangling and paying over the odds, and Amethyst had secured the box of spares.

"You got them, then?" Bobbie said as Amethyst passed her the box and got back into the cab. With a small jolt, they started back towards Belgravia.

"Yes. I'm afraid I used both Maker and your mother quite ill, suggesting that Lord Fotheringham would only buy if he knew the parts were of the highest quality and if Lord Fotheringham bought, he'd recommend it to Lady Garrington-Smythe, and if she purchased, why the whole of London Society would be wanting his wares."

Bobbie laughed. "You naughty girl. I heartily approve. Are they quality parts?"

"From the glance I had, I hope so. But I pulled the

whole 'what-would-I-know-I'm-just-a-girl' routine to get away from him. Mind you-" She patted the box now sitting between them. "-any issue with these and I'll be sure that he and his customers know all about it."

By the time they returned to number seven, Shaw had a light dinner awaiting them. Having missed or ruined so many of Shaw's meals lately, Amethyst announced they should have plenty of time to complete the construction by tomorrow, even taking an hour out for dinner.

It proved to be a very pleasant and restorative fifty minutes as they enjoyed fine food and pleasant conversation. For once, Amethyst felt at ease, much of the pressure she had felt earlier in the day having evaporated.

Going into the laboratory, she felt refreshed and ready for the challenge ahead. Taking the necessary parts from the box of spares, Amethyst laid them out in sequence on the bench, and with constant reference to the Professor's build notes, the two women made swift progress.

* * *

When Amethyst caught Bobbie yawning for the second time, she looked at the clock, surprised to find it was already twenty to three in the morning.

"Why don't you go up to bed?" Amethyst suggested. Over dinner, Edwards had informed them that Mrs Shaw had made up a spare room and Bobbie had used it to change from her pristine suit shirt into an older one Amethyst lent her to work in.

"I've not been much use, have I?"

"On the contrary. You've been the second pair of hands I needed and you've kept me sane when the Professor's notes would have driven me to Bedlam. So you have been of use, but you won't be for much longer if you fall asleep."

"True." Bobbie yawned as she stood. "What about you?"

Amethyst smiled. "Utterly exhausted, but I want to complete this section before I stop. You go on up, I won't be far behind you."

Once Bobbie was gone, Amethyst leant against the bench and released a heartfelt sigh. She hadn't been overplaying the exhaustion. Her grainy eyes felt scratched with every blink. Still, there wasn't much of this section left to do. She'd do that, then call it a night. First, she'd refresh her eyes. She closed them for a moment, or two, but when she felt herself starting to doze, she struggled to open them. Water. Yes, she'd fetch a glass of water. As she turned, she got the distinct impression of a figure before she found herself falling and the world went blank.

Chapter 36

Maker decided he would call on Amethyst early. He'd had an extremely difficult evening and night with Violet and felt the early hours were best for this visit so he could be back home before Violet awoke. It was a surprise to have Dickens open the door; she looked all eyes, as if she'd been crying. Her face was pale, her expression worried and oddly disappointed to see him.

"Lord Fotheringham," she said as she stepped back to let him in. As he moved inside, she immediately returned to the door, looking out.

"Dr Brady!" she called out as a cab drew up outside. Maker watched dumbfounded as Dickens welcomed the distinguished doctor.

"What's going on?" Maker asked.

"She's this way," Dickens said as she led the doctor through.

Throat dry and stomach in knots, Maker allowed the doctor to precede him, and every fast-paced step to follow the others made him feel more sick. Inside the study, he remained by the door. The stout and hardy Mrs Shaw was to one side, her grey uniform and white cap neat as always, while the woman looked stricken, her usually red cheeks pale. Dickens was by the hearth now, concern clearly on her face. Bobbie, wearing the nightshirt and dressing gown he knew Amethyst left in the guest room, sat on the arm of the chair applying a cold compress to the back of Amethyst's head. The doctor knelt to attend his patient, and in the chair Amethyst was pale. She wore yesterday's clothes, which looked particularly dusty.

"I really don't need a doctor."

"I'll be the judge of that, young lady."

As Bobbie removed the white flannel, Maker saw blood on the pad. He glanced around the room. There was some mess by the lab, but he couldn't see what was what. He looked to the worried lady's maid.

"Dickens?"

The young woman looked up, almost surprised to see him there. He questioned her with a look. Dickens moved closer and explained in a low voice.

"When I went up to light Miss Forester's fire in her room, Mrs Shaw came to do the downstairs fires. I was just registering that Miss Forester wasn't in her bed when I heard a scream. By the time I got here, Mr Edwards and Mrs Shaw were helping Miss Forester into the chair there and Mrs Davenport was soon down behind me."

Which explained the lady's attire.

"Edwards?"

"He was sent to get the doctor and then Inspector Jenson."

"Lady Gordon?"

"She stayed the night at her son's, the last night most likely. We aren't allowed to call her."

"Amethyst?"

Dickens nodded. "And she insists she doesn't need a doctor."

"Not to mention," Amethyst added, "I'm sitting right here, and can hear every word you say, so don't talk about me as if I'm dead or not in the room. I'm fine."

"Not quite," Doctor Brady amended. "You've got a nasty bump to the head that I need to stitch. And after that, you'll need to rest."

"I'll rest when I *am* dead."

"Many more cracks on the head and you will be, young lady."

She smiled unpleasantly at the doctor. "Well, thank you for that cheery prognosis."

When she turned to Maker, her expression turned from pain to sadness. "I'm really sorry."

Maker felt his heart twist for the sorrow in her eyes, but he didn't understand it. "Why?"

"Whoever did this," Bobbie said as she stood, "also did *this*."

Maker followed as Bobbie led to the opening to the lab. She pointed and all he could do was stare. As impossibly untidy as the Professor had been, this was much worse. Maker had never seen a place in such a mess. He soon understood. Whoever had broken in and attacked Amethyst had also taken what she'd been making. What they couldn't take, they had smashed.

"We're sunk."

There was no way such destruction could be recouped in the little time they had before that evening. There was no hope of salvaging the vote. There was only one thing that mattered now. He turned to see Doctor Brady standing. He moved over.

"Sor-"

"Don't." He stopped Amethyst and looked to Brady. "Well?"

Maker had known Brady for seventeen years, so the man had grown used to his single word habit as he had out of necessity developed it.

"She'll be fine, headaches, possibly some nausea. Make sure she rests."

As Maker escorted the doctor from the house, he wondered if anyone could make Amethyst do anything she didn't want to do. He thanked Brady all the same. They were two steps into the hallway when Edwards and Inspector Jenson came through the front door.

"Don't worry," Brady was saying, "the hour will be reflected in my bill. Good day to you, sir."

Edwards offered Brady his hat as Maker and Jenson nodded in greeting.

"Is Miss Forester well?"

"Come through." Maker led the way.

"Were you here?"

"No."

Once inside the study, Jenson started asking questions, but before she answered, Amethyst shooed the other ladies out of the room.

"Thank goodness for that," Amethyst half laughed once the door was closed. "I appreciate the concern, but so much attention gets cloying."

Taking the offered seat opposite Amethyst, Inspector Jenson quietly and efficiently drew out the details of the previous night's attack, which turned out to be this morning's attack.

Maker was filled with undirectable anger that yet again someone had hurt his Amme. He clenched his hands behind his back and stood by the desk, watching the pair. Keeping his reactions in was his habit, but it wasn't easy.

When the Inspector ran out of questions, he stood and moved over to the lab. Amethyst sat back and looked up at him.

"I was thinking you might be able to do some good, if you take that brooch, you could still visit Haversham and a couple of the others. Turn them back, maybe?"

It was a worthy idea, but there was a simple truth he couldn't avoid. Even if he could reach one or two, five or six even-

"Insufficient."

"Sorry, but I can't rebuild the machine before your debate. Not even if I had all the parts, which I don't."

He kept his hands behind his back and shrugged. There were a million and one things he wanted to say to her, mostly that he didn't give a damn as long as she was all right. Though that wasn't entirely honest. He did give a damn about the Aetheric Concessions Bill going through unopposed, but he wouldn't stop that at the cost of Amethyst's life.

"And you have no idea who'd be coming for this?"

"Only," Amethyst grouched, "the amorphous Mr Brown. Though I have got slightly more news on that front."

As she told the Inspector about seeing Mr Brown at the Aetheric Painters exhibition, and the effects that had had on Maker and Lady Violet, Bobbie returned to the room, dressed again in her habitual suit.

"Unfortunately I doubt Brown is his real name, and I have no idea how you can find him."

"Where did you last see him?"

"At the exhibition," Amethyst said, rising as Edwards entered the room carrying the silver tray he always used for correspondence.

Maker saw her wobble a little, but she wasn't going to give in to that.

"This came for you, ma'am."

When Amethyst took the letter it put her closer to the door than Maker.

"Anywhere else?"

Maker turned away from Jenson, towards the door; he wanted to be ready if Amethyst got giddy. "Here," he told Jenson.

A surprised noise escaped Amethyst and Maker focused on her.

"News?" he asked, nodding to the letter, but she was staring at him wide-eyed, her lips slightly parted. Then she blinked and looked at him a moment more before understanding the question.

"Oh, this?" She lifted the letter. "It's a very sweet apology from Sanderson."

"What does he have to apologise for?"

For a moment Amethyst focused on Jenson. "Nothing, really." Her gaze turned back to Maker. "What did you just say?"

"Here." It wasn't much of a word, why was it important?

"Why?" she asked.

"Because," said Jenson, moving to stand beside Maker, "I asked where else you had met or seen Mr Brown."

For a moment, she looked between the two of them, then realisation became a visible thing. "Oh! Idiot!" Amethyst palm-slapped her forehead, instantly groaning and groping for the support of the chair, which she missed. Maker reached for her, supported her.

"That was a mistake."

He hoped she meant the self-slap, not his hold. Maker shifted his weight, pulling and guiding her to sit down in the other chair.

"Edwards, fetch a weak tea for Miss Forester," Bobbie said.

"No!" Amethyst halted the butler's retreat. "No, Edwards, go to my room and fetch the brown leather bag the Professor gave me. It's by the window, on top of some tea chests, you won't be able to miss it."

"Amethyst, you need sustenance, not baggage," Bobbie scolded.

"Fine." The hand Amethyst had been holding to her head finally dropped and she shot a momentarily poisonous look at Bobbie. "Edwards fetch tea for all, but send Dickens for the bag."

"Amme?"

At last she turned to him and for the first time, Maker got the impression she was actually seeing him. She offered a glimpse of a smile. "Don't worry." She patted his hand. "I haven't gone completely doolally. Think about it, we've had multiple intrusions, people looking for things they can't find, but nothing stolen. When we caught Gibson, it became obvious that he was looking for the glass, but we knew that didn't explain everything that had happened." She looked up at Jenson. "You yourself said you thought there were two intruders. The professional and the amateur. Gibson was an amateur, the one who attacked me this morning was the professional. What if they're the ones Mr Brown hired to find the Professor's aetheric experiments? Clearly anyone powerful enough to create the whole Aetheric Painter movement to affect mind control isn't going to let someone create a machine that could stop them without trying to... stop them..." Her voice faded off. She frowned up at Maker. "Did that make sense?"

He nearly offered a smile in return. "Perfectly."

"The Professor was one of the leading academics on

aetheric power, but he'd published a number of articles speaking against the overuse of it."

She stopped as Dickens entered, carrying the heavy bag. "You wanted this bag, ma'am?"

"Indeed I do," Amethyst said. "Bring it here."

Dickens brought the bag around the chair and placed it in front of Amethyst, then left. Now Maker recognised the bag.

"The Professor obviously hid most of his more precious experiments in the secret room, but even secret rooms can be found. We found it. So he, the Professor, gave me AE59-3, the brooch to protect me. But he also needed to protect AE59-4 and the best way he could do that was to get it out of the house. So I think-" She reached forward and unclasped the bag. "-he also gave that to me."

As she spoke, she opened the bag that Maker had almost forgotten about. Inside the battered leather was a large boxlike thing in bright copper and brass.

Amethyst reached to pick it out, but quickly looked to Maker for help. As he bent and pulled the contraption up, Maker was surprised how heavy it was. He remembered the moment when she had hit him in the thigh with it: little wonder it had left a bruise. All in all he was lucky it was his thigh she'd hit.

Looking at it now, he saw a pipe curled around the box-body of the machine leading up to an open end, some kind of exhaust, Maker presumed. There was a small square cut out in the copper, about a third of the way up. He raised the machine to look inside. He could see all manner of works and cogs that made no sense to him, but there was a switch and a gap just big enough for a finger to go through and flick the switch.

He could see the Inspector looking from the machine to the piece of paper he had come back from the laboratory with.

"That's the last page of the build document," Bobbie said as she looked over his shoulder at the paper. "I thought all those were gone, where did you find that?"

"It was loose outside by the conservatory door," he explained. "Must have been dropped when the man made his getaway."

"And that," Bobbie marvelled, pointing to the machine Maker was now placing on the desk, "is the finished machine."

Relief flooded Maker. Amethyst was well and they had the machine they needed. Sometimes the world really did provide.

"Where is he?!"

The piercing screech was instantly recognisable. He should have known the moment of joy couldn't last. He should also have known he'd been here too long, he hadn't been watching the clock, but clearly Violet had woken and dressed and stormed across the Square. He moved to the door, stepping back just in time to miss it being flung open in his face.

Violet was obviously in a rage. He would rather not have this confrontation in front of people, but there wasn't a person in the room he didn't trust. Oddly, he realised, that included Jenson.

As Violet began to berate him, he tuned out. He had learned the best way to deal with her was to maintain eye contact, seeming to listen to her while actually not. What he was aware of was how quiet the others were. Something he was grateful for as Violet accused him of caring more about Amethyst than her, which was true, and that Amethyst was a harpy and whore, which was not. He could slap-

"How dare you!"

Amethyst was incandescent with rage, even if she did have to reach for the wing of the chair to steady herself after her sudden rise to her feet.

"How dare you barge into my home and insult me?"

She was snarling at Violet and for all he knew he would pay for this once they were in private, Maker wasn't going to stop Amethyst; she had more right to shout at anyone in this house than Violet did.

"The only harpy here is you, but if you don't get the hell out of my house this instant I will show you all manner of hellish retribution!"

Maker felt frozen to the spot, he shouldn't let this continue, but even he could see that Jenson was as immobilised as he and as for Bobbie, well she wasn't exactly smiling, but Maker guessed she would be enjoying the show.

Violet pulled herself up to her full height. "You've no way of hurting me."

"No?" Amethyst's eyes were flashing.

"Amethyst, please."

But his soft request went unnoticed; Amethyst was entirely focused on Violet. "How do you think Society would react if they knew what you and Lady Timpson really get up to?"

There was a sharp intake of breath. How had Amethyst worked that one out?

"What about what you and Mrs Davenport get up to?"

"Engineering! Thinking. Maybe you should try it

sometime!"

Maker saw Violet's hands curl into tight little fists. "Maybe you should stop whoring with my husband!"

"Unlike you, Maker knows how to keep his wedding vows. The only whore here is you. Is there a man or woman in Christendom you wouldn't have congress with?"

Violet's mouth moved into a sharp O, her knuckles were white and she was trembling with rage. Maker had seen this before. Quickly he stepped forward, but too late!

There was a slap of skin on skin. Amethyst blocked Violet's right fist with her left forearm. There was no way to stop Amethyst's right hand prescribing the perfect arc to slap Violet loudly across the face.

Cheering would be inappropriate, not least because Violet had stumbled back and the room had become preternaturally silent.

Maker stared at Amethyst, who was staring at Violet, but looked as completely shocked by what had happened as Violet did. He had no choice now. Grabbing up his thankfully silent wife, he picked her off her feet, forcibly removing her from the room.

The only one suffering any hellish retribution tonight was going to be him.

Chapter 37

"Are you sure this will work?" Bobbie asked late that afternoon.

After Violet's intrusion which, being British, none of them referred to, Amethyst had felt completely drained and had follow the doctor's orders to take an hour or two in bed. Not that she'd had much choice, Jenson had threatened to stay and protect her if she didn't put at least one floor of safety between her and any potential intruder. Logical reasoning that the deed and damage had already been done did not dissuade the Inspector. The fact that Blanchard arrived didn't go unnoticed and although, again, nothing was said, Amethyst was reasonably certain that Maker had sent him over to be her protector. At least, she thought, climbing the stairs, it freed Inspector Jenson up to go and investigate, which was what they needed him to do.

In truth, the extra sleep had done her a power of good. A light lunch had helped too. She felt she'd slept much better for taking the machine up with her. So far, no intruder had been seen upstairs. At least, not today: her going for Blanchard with a cricket bat didn't count. He wasn't an intruder. She really must get that bat back.

But there was one thing she couldn't ignore.

Taking the machine with her, she went down to the lab, then she went in search of Bobbie, finding her asleep in the guest bedroom.

"Well hello," Bobbie smiled as she blinked awake and sat up.

"Hello, can I ask you something?"

Bobbie reached up and stroked Amethyst's face.

"You can ask me anything."

Too distracted to think about reacting to the action, Amethyst ploughed on. "How large is, erm?"

As Bobbie's fingers curled around her ear and into her hairline, Amethyst tried to ignore the odd sensations shivering through her body. Each breath seemed suddenly harder to take. She had to concentrate.

"The Lords. Ha - oh - how big?"

"You like that?" Bobbie asked.

Her eyelids felt unaccountably heavy, and she saw little reason to keep them open in the half light of the room. "Hmm." She did like it, but she wasn't sure why. The bed shifted, Bobbie was moving. It seemed so natural to lean into the caress. Bobbie's other hand was gentle on the other side of her face, she felt the woman shifting towards her. Just like when Maker -

Eyes springing open, Amethyst shifted her head.

Bobbie's hands stilled, and for a moment the two of them sat just inches apart, staring at one another.

"You were enjoying that."

"I was," Amethyst agreed. She wasn't sorry she'd stopped, but she wasn't sorry they were still so close, either. She swallowed. "Excuse the presumption, but were you actually going to kiss me then?"

"I was." Bobbie smiled. "I still might. Would you object?"

Amethyst gave a small amused huff, for a moment looking down. "Apparently." One of Bobbie's hands moved away, but Amethyst caught it in her own and brought the knuckles to her lips and kissed them. "Forgive me, you are becoming my dearest friend, but…"

"But your attraction lies in a different direction?"

As she said it, Bobbie's other hand moved away and they both sat up, their four hands in a knot between them.

"Well, yes." Amethyst felt there was little point denying the truth. "But also, no one's ever actually kissed me before. I'm not sure that I'd be any good at it."

Bobbie's laugh was gentle and her hand squeeze encouraging. "I could teach you."

Amethyst smiled. "I'm sure you could. I'm fairly sure there's no man who wants to. Still," she mused, sitting up and forcing a smile, "a life of spinsterhood is tomorrow's problem. Right now I need to know how big the Lords Chamber is in Parliament."

"About forty by one hundred feet, I think."

"Shame." Amethyst patted Bobbie's hand and stood. "Why?"

The question only registered through the whirling in her mind as Amethyst was part way down the stairs, but it was too late to go back and explain by then. She had calculations to make.

"Why does the size of the chamber matter?" Bobbie asked as she came into the lab a few minutes later, perfectly dressed. Apparently there were other advantages to dressing like a man.

Standing up, Amethyst looked at Bobbie over the open mechanism of the AE59-4 machine. She pointed at the machine. "If my reading of the Professor's notes is right, this is a scaled-up version of AE59-3, my brooch. That only worked on me though Sanderson was at my side the whole time. That's less than two feet. This is about ten times bigger, but unlike most power sources, there's no increase output to volume ratio with aetheric power."

"I vaguely remember the Professor saying something about that. Didn't understand it then or now."

"It's an oddity of aetheric power. A nice steady output for a long time, but it's a steady output, hard to magnify too much. That doesn't matter right now anyway." Amethyst shrugged. "What it means matters, and that is that ten times the size is about ten times the power."

"So a maximum radius of twenty feet. That will still cover the majority of the room."

Amethyst was shaking her head. "Only if we were in the middle of the room, but in the viewing gallery, we'll be on the very edge. I need to boost that range by two to five times."

Bobbie came closer and looked at the machine. "Can you do that?"

"Possibly." Amethyst looked at the machine, explaining as she worked. First she doubled up the power source. Then increased the rotation on the capacitor and the torque on the compensator. Then she started squeezing the open ends on the two pipes that had been external to the casing.

"Why are you doing that? Aren't those the exhaust ports?"

"Actually, no, this," she pointed to a brass tube near the bottom of the machine, "is the exhaust. These are the emitters. I'm hoping that by restricting the aperture that the force of the emission will lead to a higher expulsion rate and that that will force the effect into a wider range."

"Sounds good. What happens if you turn it on?"

Amethyst shrugged. "If it's anything like the brooch, it'll warm up, but until people are affected by it, I won't know for certain if it's even working."

Bobbie nodded and reached for the gap in the metal. "How-"

"No." Amethyst caught the other woman's hand to stop her. "At this stage either it will work or it won't. Really, you know as much as I do now, so please stop with the questions I can't answer."

Bobbie looked at her, deadpan. "I was going to ask how you plan to get it into the Houses of Parliament tonight?"

"Oh." She grinned ruefully. "Well. As it happens, that's another question I can't answer."

"Shall I call in our carriage at seven, we can travel together. Getting into the public gallery shouldn't be a problem; it's a public gallery after all, getting into it is part of the point."

"There might be one problem." She hated to be the bearer of bad news, but she had to be honest. "When I went in with Maker I wasn't carrying so much as a clutch purse, but I saw those that were, were asked to open their bags for inspection. Do you think a bag with this in is going to go unnoticed?"

"Hmm." Bobbie considered it. "We'll just have to improvise. Besides, I am Baroness Davenport, I can still pull a few strings."

"I suppose we could arrange to meet Maker somewhere out of the Square." She thought about the first time she had met Lady Violet in the Square. She hadn't exactly been friendly then. Today she'd been an embarrassment. "If he can get away from home."

"Hmm."

There was obvious knowledge behind that wordless agreement. While Amethyst was eager to know what Bobbie might know, she also knew it was none of her business, so she didn't ask.

"Amethyst?"

From the tone, she knew Bobbie had something difficult to tell her.

"Yes?"

"There's something you should know."

Amethyst felt the blood running from her face. "Should I be worried?"

Bobbie shook her head. "It's just something you should know about Maker."

"Alright." Amethyst braced herself.

"He is absolutely a man of his word."

Amethyst frowned. "Yes."

"Absolutely a man of his word."

Amethyst still didn't understand. "I never doubted that."

Bobbie was also frowning, as if Amethyst was being a particularly dense child. "My point is that when Maker makes a vow, he will honour it. Whatever the cost. And nothing will dissuade him from that, not even his own abhorrence of the vow."

*   *   *

Dickens had assured Amethyst that she looked like a fine lady in the new black pin-stripe dress and jacket. She felt like a fraud. Who was she to think she could do something so important? It was as ridiculous as thinking she could steer Maker from his course of vow-keeping.

The debate was due to start at eight. She wanted to be in the gallery by seven-thirty to give the machine time to warm up and work.

So when she heard Edwards' steps in the hall, relief washed through her. A glance to the mantel showed her it was twelve minutes to seven. So she was somewhat surprised when she saw her visitor.

"Inspector!"

He offered a small, neat bow, and looked surprise when she rushed to him and grasped his hand tight.

"I am so pleased to see you."

Now he was frowning. "Miss Forester is everything all right?" He studied her face a little closer. "Have you been crying?"

This time her hands went to her cheeks and smoothed under her eyes. "Not for a while."

"What's happened?"

"My Great-Aunt Flora returned home an hour ago. Her son, Malachi, died this afternoon. Sorry, for not following societal rules, I suddenly felt the need for a little human contact."

This time he took her hand. "Understandable. You were close?"

"To Great-Aunt Flora yes, so her pain pains me, but in truth I hardly knew Malachi. We are related only by blood, and he was older than my father, so Malachi and I were aware of one another only distantly." She took a deep steadying breath, enjoying the support she felt, just having her hand in his. It had been a while since she had felt such friendship. "But to more immediate matters - did you find Mr Brown?" She didn't like the pause that answered that eager question. "You didn't find him?"

"Not exactly. What I found suggests that Mr Brown doesn't even exist." He raised his hand to cut off her objection. "I'm not questioning your veracity, please let me explain."

She invited him to sit and though they broke contact and took opposite ends of the couch, she still felt the support he had offered and it strengthened her to face the rest of the evening. Jenson explained that he had gone directly to the Royal Academy, but the exhibition was gone.

"Gone? How can it be gone? It's supposed to be there another three weeks yet."

"The public exhibition yes, but the private exhibition that you were invited to, that's gone, and it had nothing to do with the Aetheric Painters group. The Royal Academy were very helpful, they allowed me to go through their paperwork."

He reported the evidence trail proving that the two exhibitions were separate. He explained how he'd followed the paper trail to an empty rented office. He'd spoken to the occupiers of the neighbouring units and the landlords. They'd given a very similar description of a man who could be Mr Brown, but who called himself Mr Quinn. Following that identity hadn't helped resolve anything.

Amethyst couldn't believe what she was hearing and shot to her feet. She paced slightly and when she swung back to Inspector Jenson, she was surprised to find him on his feet too.

"Are you saying that there's nothing more to do? That he's going to get away with murdering the Professor and trying to rig a political vote completely scot free?"

Jenson sighed. "I'm not giving up yet, but I've been doing my job a long time, I know cases like this, men like Mr Brown. They take time to crack. I will find him, but it won't be soon. Right now there are more important matters at hand."

"Like what?"

"Well, if you're going to go through with the plan to take the machine to Parliament, I reasoned it was best if there was a policeman on hand."

She frowned, knots tying her stomach. "In case you need to arrest me for treason?"

He offered a small laugh. "Possibly, but more to avoid you becoming the target of another attack."

The knots suddenly felt like a noose. Finding her knees jelly-like, she sank to the couch. "I thought that danger was over. They must think they have what they wanted."

The worst of the pain in her head was gone but the area was still tender, Dickens had had to be extra careful with her hair tonight.

"I'm sorry to worry you, but the danger won't be over until the final problem is solved."

"Of course. I should have thought. Of course, they'll fight on till the end. Thank you." She stood up and looked at him more squarely. "You must think me a terrible fool for not seeing the danger."

He shook his head. "I think a young lady like you shouldn't need to think of such things. I'm glad you can not only survive all you've been through these last couple of months, but retain a belief in the general goodness of people. It quite restores my faith in human nature."

As the Inspector spoke, Amethyst heard Edwards in

the hall so she wasn't overly surprised to see Bobbie enter, though the white face was a surprise.

"Oh my God, what's happened?" Bobbie demanded.

Amethyst's heart rate jumped as she and the Inspector turned to Bobbie.

"What do you mean?"

Bobbie looked between the two of them. "There's a police vehicle outside. I thought you might have been attacked again."

"No, I'm fine."

"Thank God!"

"It's mine," Jenson explained. "I have an idea."

Chapter 38

Maker felt torn. The state Violet had worried herself into was fearful, and eventually he had had to give Blanchard the nod to add a sleeping draft to her drink. He hated himself for doing it, but there were times when he really didn't have a choice. Drugs were a better option than the alternatives.

With having to send Blanchard over to protect Amethyst, he had left Violet slightly vulnerable. Perhaps he should have stayed home. On another night he would have, but the importance of tonight's vote was just too great. A fact rammed home by the lengths some aetheric inventors were prepared to go to to ensure the bill was passed.

The clock gave the simple half hour strike and Maker headed for the chamber. The young lady in her black pin-stripe was elegant and beautiful, though for a moment he'd mistaken her suited companion for a man.

"Lord Fotheringham!"

He couldn't afford to let himself be distracted. Facing resolutely forward, his long stride drove him quickly out of the public area.

*　　*　　*

"How rude!"

"He's got things to do, Bobbie," Amethyst forced herself to be reasonable against her instant inclination. "He doesn't have time to waste. And nor do we. Come on."

However stung she felt at being ignored by Maker,

there was a job to do here and they had to do it. Without Maker at her side she had been subject to a search, opening her purse for a visual inspection. The guard apologised for the intrusion but claimed threats had been made and they couldn't be too careful. For all she'd smiled and moved on, Amethyst had itched to point out if they really wanted to be careful, they wouldn't have allowed the public in at all. It all left her wondering how the Inspector had got on. Now she was anxious to get to their agreed meeting place in the gallery above the Lords. *Please God let Jenson and the machine have made it in.*

Thankfully, she had a good memory for directions and found her way easily up to the gallery above the Lords. There were more observers than she'd expected, including one particular knot of men in suits, none of whom looked particularly happy. Something in their air suggested to Amethyst that they were from the various electrical companies. There were other viewers, but the man in the bowler hat caught her attention and she headed straight for the Inspector. Amethyst stood close, closer than she would normally to a man, but she wanted to help hide the brown bag behind her skirt.

"I'm so glad to see you." She kept her voice low and leaned in to speak to him.

He smiled. "It's been a long time since a lovely young lady said something like that to me."

Amethyst looked at Bobbie for the odd sound she made. She didn't understand what Bobbie was grinning about, so she turned back to Jenson.

"You didn't have any trouble getting in?"

He shook his head and she got the feeling that there was something he wasn't telling her.

"Good."

They were at the front of the viewing gallery, roughly central to the chamber.

Turning to the chamber, Amethyst was surprised and disappointed to see how empty the red benches appeared.

"Where are they?"

"Who?" asked Jenson at her side.

"All the lords," she said. "There are hundreds of them and yet barely a tenth are here."

"Be fair," Bobbie countered, "it's about a third."

"Most of them only turn up for the important things. State opening, bills they feel passionate about," Jenson explained.

"This bill is important."

"To us yes," Jenson agreed, "but not particularly so in the run of things for Parliament. Besides, it's as well for those who would push the yes vote to persuade the no voters to stay away as to change their votes."

Mutely agreeing with him, Amethyst looked into the Lords. Maker was already in his place. The same place as before. If that had any significance she neither knew nor cared. What she did care about was his slighting her in the hall and now, though he glanced at her, he was utterly devoid of emotion or even any sign of recognition. He turned away, his attention going to the current speaker.

*   *   *

Maker forced himself to focus on the lord speaking. Another voice that couldn't hold his attention. His peripheral vision showed him Lord Haversham. He'd tried talking to the man earlier and been met with a torrent of abuse; there had been no hope of getting Haversham to touch the brooch and free himself from aetheric interference. Even now, he was talking to the ultra-conservative Lord Shellford.

The oddity was that Shellford despised Haversham for his misshapenness, claiming that imperfections to such a degree should be eradicated at birth. Explaining that the humped growth of his spine had been just that - a matter of growth - hadn't worked, Shellford wouldn't listen. Haversham hated him for the obvious reason. But now they were acting like the best of friends.

Maker felt like the only friend he had left was Bobbie, though with what was going to happen, he wasn't sure how much longer that friendship would last.

At least he had seen Jenson coming in with that bag. Being able to wave him through and know that the machine was in the chamber was a relief. They were one step closer anyway. All they had to do now was switch the machine on and hope it was effective.

He didn't dare look up at the gallery. As ever his eye was drawn immediately to Amethyst. While he had every faith in Inspector Jenson's intelligence and integrity, he didn't like the way the two of them stood so close or the smiles they'd shared as they'd met. He had no right to be jealous and he had to accept that his life was the result of the choices he had made. He also had to find a way to overcome the absolute jealousy he did feel. To think that the night before last he'd been to her room, she'd looked at him like she could have -

No!

He must not allow such thoughts to distract him. He

had a job to do. Amethyst and Jenson had a job to do to. All he could do now was hope they could do it.

Now would be good.

* * *

"What time is it?"

At Amethyst's question, Jenson checked his pocket watch. "Ten to eight."

"The debate starts in ten minutes, then." She calculated the time the brooch had taken to warm and work to reflect the larger mechanism. "Time to start, I think."

The three of them were in a tight knot as Jenson crouched to open the bag. Bobbie reached in and lifted the machine, Amethyst flicked the switch then Bobbie swiftly placed it on the floor near the front banister.

"There. Him!"

Amethyst turned and saw two uniformed officers were being pointed towards Inspector Jenson. The man doing the pointing she instantly recognised.

"Mr Brown!"

That statement stopped one of the constables in his tracks, but the other was much closer. Instinctively, Amethyst lifted her hooped petticoat and covered the machine, moving as close to it as she could. She had to, this was no crinoline and there was much less room. For a moment she was focused solely on Mr Brown. His ordinary brown eyes were suddenly, uniquely filled with hatred. All of it shrewd and focused on her.

"The bomb's in the bag!"

The word 'bomb' caused uproar. Others in the viewing gallery were suddenly calling out and rushing for exits even as Jenson attempted to calmly assure them there was no bomb. He opened the bag, proved it was empty as Bobbie ran after the rapidly disappearing Mr Brown.

Amethyst didn't dare move with the machine in place and working under her skirt, however hot it was getting under there. Revealing the machine would make the temperature out here that much hotter. So all she could do was watch as Jenson declared his rank, shoved the bag at the one officer and rushed after Bobbie, only to be blocked by the second officer.

"For God's sake man, the real criminal is getting away!"

"Sir, we can't let -"

"Got away."

Like Jenson, Amethyst looked up at Bobbie, as she stated the fact.

"Sorry," she continued, "I lost him in the crowd."

The Inspector's shoulders slumped at the news. Amethyst's heart sank. Brown clean away was not the best possible outcome, but there were other outcomes they needed more. While the Inspector spoke quietly to the police officers, including showing his warrant card and calming the situation, Bobbie came back to stand beside Amethyst.

"I'm sorry, he just seemed to melt into the crowd."

Amethyst nodded. "He was dressed in a black suit, how many men in here weren't? Besides, try describing him. He's average." She shrugged and sighed. "Average people are always much harder to keep track of. You can't miss Maker on the other hand, because he's too tall and distinctive-looking." She sighed again. "Hopefully Inspector Jenson will find some other way of catching up with him. Right now, we have other problems." She nodded behind her, where a voice she didn't recognise was extolling the virtues of aetheric power, and puffed out another breath.

"Are you feeling all right?" Bobbie continued in an undertone.

"Fine."

"Really? You're huffing and puffing a bit and you're rather red-faced."

"Not surprised." The smile she turned on Bobbie was fixed so she could better control her lips as she spoke. "The machine is heating up and I feel like I might actually start melting any second."

Bobbie turned away to lean on the banister and watch the debate, but Amethyst saw her shoulders quaking and knew it was disguised laughter. She turned back to focus on the Inspector; his more relaxed posture and the slightly cowed expression of the two uniformed officers suggested their issues had been resolved.

"Are you feeling quite well, Miss?"

Amethyst refocused on the young man in the deep blue uniform. She smiled. "I'm fine."

"You're very red."

And she could feel herself getting hotter and redder by the second. "I'm fine. Just worried." She held out her hand to Jenson. "About you attacking my friend." Thankfully, Jenson reached out and took her hand. As their fingers curled around each other, she pulled him towards her, since she could not move to him.

Jenson offered a sweet smile as he moved to her side, tucking her hand into the crook of his arm. If they looked like a couple right now, so much the better.

At long last, the officers seemed ready to leave. As

they turned away, a cry was heard from the floor of the chamber. One officer and Jenson looked down over the banister. Amethyst turned as much as she could.

One of the lords had passed out; a couple of others looked unwell. The machine was working. Jenson looked at the officers.

"Whatever you were told, the real problem seems to be down there."

When the two uniformed men left, Amethyst realised only she, Bobbie and Jenson were left. Moving quickly, she gathered up her skirts and stepped away from the machine.

"Oh, that's better!" The relief was instant, and as unladylike as it was, she kept her skirt partly raised to cool the air beneath.

"Seems to be working," Bobbie said as Amethyst and Jenson joined her at the rail.

Haversham was on his feet, the unconscious lord was being carried out. The speech was pro-aetheric concession. The pale-looking Lords had increased in number. Haversham grabbed the back of the bench in front of him, bowed his head, his words trailing off.

"Lord Haversham?" the Speaker asked. "Are you unwell?"

Haversham shook his head and looked up. "I'm sorry… for a moment there I… I just felt a little ill."

"It seems the kitchens have surpassed themselves today."

A titter ran around the chamber.

"Indeed, Mr Speaker. Now, where was I? Erm…"

"You were saying how aetheric power is already in every household," the Speaker supplied.

"Ahh, yes."

*   *   *

At the first realisation that affected individuals were being released from their thrall, Maker's heart lifted. There were fifty minutes of debate left. He had no idea what the commotion on the viewing gallery had been, but it seemed Jenson had smoothed it over. Now the gallery was empty of all but Bobbie, Amethyst and Jenson. The Inspector was far too close to Amme.

"Ah yes," Haversham was saying. "We all have aetheric power in our homes already. And look how many accidents there have been with it. Why only last week, a family of five died in Lewisham when their cottage burned to the ground, an aetheric lamp having been left on and burnt a curtain, then the whole house."

The crowd roared in anger and support. Maker stayed seated and silent as his insides cheered. He privately thanked God, Professor Richards, Amme and Jenson for getting everything resolved. He risked a glance up. Amethyst was being squashed in the middle of a three-way hug, but her broad smile said it all.

Still tight in the embrace, Amethyst looked straight at him. The urge to smile back threatened, but the memory of what he had promised Violet was more menacing. He turned away.

*   *   *

Squeezed in celebration, Amethyst looked down at Maker, at his complete lack of expression. Then he just looked away. Not a single indication of gratitude. Every ounce of jubilation rushed away from her.

Dragging in a sad breath, she pulled away from the others. They were busy agreeing they'd done a good job.

Swallowing hard, she fiddled with the machine then turned to the Inspector. "The machine is off now, but too hot to bag up. Would you mind tidying up here?"

Jenson looked worried.

"I'm sorry to put this burden on you," she said. "I have to go."

"Are you unwell?"

She forced a smile. "I just need some air."

"I'll-" said Bobbie.

"Stay and help the Inspector," Amethyst insisted. "I'm fine, I just need to cool down. I'll walk home. It's not a problem."

She turned, but Jenson's hand curled around her upper arm. "Don't go."

He moved in close. She looked up at very earnest eyes.

"I understand how you feel, but we don't know where Mr Brown went. I wouldn't want you going out there and into his clutches. Besides, whatever anyone else might fail to see, the result here is as much by your efforts as anyone. You deserve to see this."

Seeing sympathy rise in Jenson's eyes, Amethyst swallowed, blinked to keep the tears inside. She nodded and moved back to the banister with him.

* * *

The vote had been called and counted, and as the Speaker rose to give the result, Amethyst found she was holding her breath. She had a grip on Jenson's hand, was aware of his holding her just as tight. She wasn't the only one interested in the outcome. She glanced at Maker, but as his eyes were fixed on the Speaker, her attention moved that way too.

As the man stood, all pomp and circumstance, Amethyst felt Bobbie take her other hand. They were all desperate to know that this bill had been defeated.

She was so anxious she could not register the numbers, couldn't work out which side had won. She knew others were reacting, but she didn't know which side. Had they won or lost?

The Speaker was speaking again. "The Not-Contents have it."

Something pulled on her arm; Bobbie was jumping up and down. Amethyst found the jubilation infectious, her grin split across her face and she found herself swept up, hugging Bobbie, accepting a kiss on the lips. Her hand was still locked in Jenson's and as Bobbie moved to hug him and laugh, he hugged her in turn. His kiss was more of a surprise, apparently to both of them.

He coughed and she stepped back, each looking away uncertain.

Knowing the bill had been defeated, Amethyst felt that she could breathe easier, but what of Maker? She'd done this mostly for him, was he happy about it?

She moved to the rail. Maker's face was towards them, but his eyes were tight closed. A prayer of thanks? His expression wasn't thankful, it was... His expression was bitter.

Amethyst heard a metal scrape; the machine was cool enough to put back in the bag. Jenson was beside her. His hand was next to hers on the rail, the other around her waist.

"Time to go."

Maker didn't open his eyes as he turned his head away, stood and left.

"Time to go," she repeated.

Chapter 39

"Miss Forester!"

Amethyst really didn't want to linger, not here, not in the lobby to the Lords. Bobbie had already left, Jenson insisting on taking Amethyst and the machine home since Bobbie lived in the opposite direction, and he would pass Belgravia to get home. All Amethyst wanted to do was go home and lick her wounds. Not that Maker's apparent defection should wound her, but logic and emotion had so little in common and –

That was Lord Haversham calling her. Putting a hand on Jenson's arm to halt him, Amethyst stopped and looked at the man approaching her. His awkward gait made his progress slow but she waited, wondering who the tall, dour man shadowing Haversham was.

"Miss Forester, I really must apologise to you."

"For not introducing me to your companion?" She saw his frown, his imminent interruption. "You have naught else to apologise to me for, sir."

Haversham looked at her. "We both know that's not true. I really don't know what came over me."

All Amethyst could do was stare, then she realised that Haversham simply wouldn't know. So she explained. The man went white. "So you see, you've no need to apologise to me, I know you weren't yourselves."

"I do remember finding the whole exhibition experience odd, but I don't remember the exhibition itself," Haversham said. "I have sort of wondered why I was behaving differently, but then I've never been anything but self-indulgent."

Amethyst smiled. "Now I know that isn't true. I've heard you address Parliament, and there was nothing self-indulgent about the way you defended the nay vote tonight. Moreover, I have it on very good authority that you like to play the blackheart, though in truth you're not."

Haversham looked around, nervous of being overheard. "Maker dissembles."

"No he doesn't, and it wasn't Maker's comment. Still, we've done what we could."

"May I ask something?" said the gaunt gentleman, whom Haversham still hadn't introduced. "You say that the changes in Lord Haversham -"

"And you," Haversham added.

"- and I." The man did not look happy at the reminder. "You say they were the result of attending the Aetheric Painting Exhibition."

Amethyst nodded. "The by-invitation-only exhibition, yes."

The man was nodding. "So what about those who weren't here tonight?"

Amethyst swallowed. "I'm not entirely sure. Hopefully the effects will wear off, but I can't guarantee when. I do have ways of releasing individuals, but it's difficult to get a lot of the affected in a room at one time."

The ring on his left hand caught the light as he clenched and unclenched his fist. "If you believe your wife is affected, I'll be happy to attend to her personally."

"Yes, that might be advisable, but I was more concerned about the Prime Minister."

Amethyst frowned. "You believe he has been

affected?"

"Indeed I do." The man was emphatically nodding. "I considered his behaviour odd when I saw him this morning and I know he visited the exhibition a week or so ago."

"Then perhaps tomorrow-"

"That might be too late."

Feeling her heart hammer, Amethyst struggled to find the words. "What's happening tonight that tomorrow would be too late?"

"The Tsar!" Haversham whispered.

Suddenly, he took hold of Amethyst's arm. His sense of urgency infected her.

"We have to get to their meeting, the effect of any control must be countered."

"By all means, but how can we get there?"

"It's in the Magdalena State Rooms," the tall man said. "I can get us in there."

They had all started towards the exit. Amethyst looked to Inspector Jenson, who was still carrying the machine in that brown bag.

"I still don't understand what the urgency is," Amethyst said as she allowed herself to be guided, Jenson close on her heels.

"The Tsar and his advisers are here to meet the Prime Minister and some cabinet ministers to agree a trade deal on airship routes and security at either end. But more importantly-" They were at a carriage Amethyst didn't recognise now, though the crest painted on the door suggested that it belonged to an aristocrat. They all got in. "- there is growing unrest in Russia, many of the people want to depose the ruling family."

"I suppose that deposing a Tsar would be easier when he's out of the country," Amethyst mused.

"And killing him in some other country would be cleaner."

She turned to Jenson at his dark comment. "But there's a big difference between deposing and disposing of."

Jenson offered a small smile. It reminded her of his 'naïve' comment earlier. Was she being a fool?

"It's cleaner from a progression point of view if you kill the figurehead," Jenson explained. "That way, there is less likelihood of the old monarch coming back to challenge the new rule."

"Like when Cromwell was set aside again for the monarchy?"

"Exactly," he agreed.

"But in this case there's even more of a reason."

Jenson looked to Haversham at his comment. "You mean if Tsar Nicholas dies as the hands of a capitalist, democratic monarchy, the very system that the Communists most despise, it would be all the better for them."

"Aye," agreed Haversham with some political zeal. "All that 'look at the Capitalist dogs tearing themselves apart' codswallop. 'You have nothing to lose but your wossnames.'"

"Exactly."

Amethyst slouched back in the carriage as they bounded along the cobbled streets. Well, she slouched as much as the tight corset would allow. The implications were staggering.

"Do you think they could do it though?" she asked, looking to Haversham for an answer. "Do you really think that they could make an honest citizen into a murderer?"

He nodded carefully. "I look back now and see how very differently I've been acting these last few weeks, doing things I would never in my right mind do - so yes. Yes, I think they could do it."

Sitting forward, Amethyst was suddenly very interested in the process. "What do you remember of what they did to you?"

Haversham looked away. "Nothing."

"There's no need to be ashamed, it wasn't your fault."

"I remember," the other lord said. "I remember being confused and dizzy. I felt rather sick. Towards the end of the exhibition room, or possibly they took me elsewhere, but it was a very dark room. There was a chair." For a moment he stared into the middle distance, shuddered at the memory. "It's all rather hazy, but I remember the voice, over and over. Vote for the Aetheric Concessions Bill. Vote for the Aetheric Concessions Bill. Again and again."

Now Haversham was nodding. "I think I had something similar. Could have been the same words. It felt like everything I think, everything I believed in was being turned on its head."

"Maker said it felt uncontrolled," Amethyst added. "That he remembered everything he did, knew he shouldn't, but couldn't not do it."

"Exactly."

The two gentlemen agreed in unison.

"In which case, turning a man into a murderer wouldn't be beyond belief."

That thought left them all rather deflated. For a

moment they indulged the dread. It was Jenson, ever practical, who brought them back to the moment and the necessity to make plans.

Chapter 40

The Magdalena State Rooms turned out to be the third floor of the much larger than expected Crompton Buildings. The cream stone edifice had given way to a marble and stone lobby. Liveried footmen and uniformed guards were clearly in place to greet them, though at first it seemed to Amethyst they might as easily repel them instead.

She wanted to scream at them to get out of the way, that it could be too late for the Tsar already, but she couldn't. The almost overpowering urge to push on past these obstructions was ill-advised. Nor was it likely to result in success. Whatever else they tried, they couldn't just blurt out that the Prime Minister was under the control of a mind-altering hypnosis and about to kill a foreign leader. They would all four be rushed to a secure room, and Amethyst feared they'd be offered jackets with over-long arms and too many buckles.

So she stayed quiet and allowed the men to do the talking, every moment praying that they would be allowed through. Haversham moved constantly, little shifts of muscles that betrayed his nerves. Amethyst could see the keen-eyed officer talking to the gaunt gentleman, glancing at the movement and wondering. However, the gentleman, who had said he was Lord Carmarthen, commanded attention, and even though she didn't know him well, she thought she detected a higher stress to his voice. He caught the eye of one of the footmen, who moved over to whisper something to the guard getting in their way. Even Jenson looked tight. His moustache was hanging differently, as if he were holding his top lip between his teeth to keep from blurting out their knowledge. She could see the tension in his back muscles, in how white his knuckles were around the handle of her bag. Jenson proving he was a police officer was a surprising grease to the wheels, freeing up the agreement of the guard much more readily than the presence of two Lords of the Realm.

"Everyone's guilty of something, and no one wants their life disrupted by an investigation," Jenson said when she whispered the observation to him while they headed for the back of the building. "But more likely it was the revelation that Lord Carmarthen owns the building that did it."

That also explained how Lord Carmarthen knew the building well enough to swear that he would keep the small group out of sight of the honoured guests. Another footman greeted the peer as they stepped into the servants' area.

There seemed to be people rushing everywhere, organised chaos as a vast array of food and drink was carried up and down by more uniformed men; the kitchen staff, mostly women, were red-faced in their efforts to prepare the feast with precise timing and singular spectacle.

"Wait a moment."

Amethyst's words pulled Carmarthen to the edge of the narrow stair they had just come down.

"Young lady, we don't have time to waste."

"This won't be a waste," Amethyst said as she pulled Jenson, with the machine, to the unoccupied area under the stairs. The two lords followed.

At her indication, Jenson took the machine from the bag and held it while she switched it on, and then she turned to Haversham.

"Sorry to do this, but I think you should stay here. Servants' corridors are usually tight and you won't be able to keep the pace that they have to." She turned to Jenson. "I'll stay too; fewer bodies will make this easier."

"No, you'll come with us." Jenson was clear. "I'll carry this, it's heavy, but if something goes wrong with it, you're the only one who can fix it."

"He's right," Haversham said, taking the now empty case from her hands. "You're needed, but I'm not. The three of you go."

Thanking Haversham with a squeeze of his arm, Amethyst rushed after the two long-legged men, doing her best to stay in their wake and not get in the way of the servants.

Given the number of stairs and the narrowness of some, Amethyst was amazed food reached the table good and hot. Then they reached an antechamber where she saw hot fires and warming plates and understood that some of that temperature was modified before the food reached the tables.

Carmarthen moved them too one side, his voice low as he spoke. "There's a small area where the servers leave this space to go through into the dining room. It's screened from the rest of the room, but open enough to let that thing work as it did in the Lords."

Seeing Jenson trying to shift the weight of the machine, Amethyst reached out and touched it carefully. "It's warming well, we should get it in place before it gets too hot to hold."

The three of them crowded into the restricted space behind the screen.

"There." The word was mouthed more than said as Carmarthen pointed to the narrow side table where various wines and decanters were stacked. He shifted a few to give Jenson the space the machine needed. Amethyst tried to disappear inside the wall, overly aware of the disapproving looks she was getting from the servants. Those who served the rich and powerful always seemed to think they were better than the rest, even though they were still just servants.

She reached around Jenson and tested the heat of the machine. It was very warm, so if they were to see any affect, they should see it soon.

The high pitched whine started quietly, but soon people were looking for its source. Amethyst looked into the working area, half expecting to see a kettle on the hot plate, but as she looked she turned her head and realised that the noise was coming from her side. Terrified of what she was going to see, she looked towards AE59-4. Others were starting to look now, the whistling growing every second. An older footman appeared around the screen.

"Whatever that is, stop it now."

They couldn't stop it. It had to work.

"The pair of you, get out, you're in the way." The words were hissed, and the man, a healthier version of Edwards, glared at Amethyst in a way that split her in two. Half of her wanted to run away crying, the other half wanted to punch him.

"No." She just about kept her voice low. "Lord Carmarthen said we could be here."

"Lord Carmarthen isn't he-"

"I am."

The man's eyes widened as he heard the voice.

Only then did he turn to Lord Carmarthen. "Sir, this really isn't appropriate."

"Swinton, it really isn't appropriate for you to question my choices."

Swinton was obviously wise enough to know what his choices really were. He glanced towards the hall. "Sir, I'm just concerned. These things aren't usually so... rowdy."

"I appreciate that, but you'll just have to put up."

Swinton looked back at the machine, at Amethyst as she bent over it. "That whining is irritating, can't you shut it off?"

"I can't." She held up a hand against his objection.

Moving her head around, she saw that the exhaust pipe was starting to come adrift from the body of the piece. The hole it was creating was acting like the mouthpiece of a flute, and now it was starting to play like one. "Just keep them happy a few more minutes."

Swinton stepped closer, standing over Amethyst as if to intimidate her. "Stop that thing before it really sets them off, I can't keep pushing food in front of any man who looks about to argue, they all do."

As the man tried to reach for the machine, Jenson moved between the two, holding him back.

"I understand sir, but you don't know -"

"I know I have a Tsar and a Prime Minister, not to mention the cabinets of both. I don't want war breaking out in my dining room."

"Keep it going." Carmarthen's voice was stronger. "Whatever the cost."

"If you let me sort this out," Amethyst said quietly to the man, "there won't be a fight. I need something to mend this hole."

Resplendent in his livery, Swinton tutted and strode into the antechamber. Amethyst stood and watched him rattle through a drawer, seemingly looking for a tool. She needed a solution. And the multi-tier cake being brought it was it.

Much to the horror of all the footmen, she stepped straight in front of where they and the white-jacketed pastry chef were stacking the cake, which clearly couldn't have been stacked in the kitchen and still moved up three sets of stairs.

"Wait, wait, wait, wait, wait!" she said as she moved up to the cake, which was currently only two tiers. She took a deep breath and pushed her fingers into the very middle of the cake, broke through the icing, grabbed a handful of the marzipan covering beneath, and worked out a small circle about a thumb length in diameter. The pastry chef yelled in horror. Amethyst was aware that now Carmarthen was the one protecting her as Jenson kept Swinton from stopping the machine. "You can cover that with the next tier," she told the chef as she turned back. It was a crime against Royal Icing. *Icing Treason!* She tried not to giggle at the stupid thought, but there was more to worry about.

Rushing back to the machine, she wrapped the white covered sweet paste around the joint. The heat was prickling at her fingers, but she had to make sure that this layer stayed in place. The heat would at first melt the marzipan, but then bake it as hard as pastry.

"Will that work?" Jenson asked.

"Uncooked pastry would be better, but this is what I've got. Besides, it's working for now." But she was already gritting her teeth against the heat in her hand, and her fingertips were starting to burn. "Get a bowl of cold water," she told Jenson. "And you -" She turned to Swinton. "- you do whatever you have to to keep that lot as calm as they can be." She was struggling against the pain, fighting to control her breathing; her fear was growing, gnawing at her innards, destroying her confidence, she had to hold on while she still could. "In a few minutes, everything is going to change. Please." Only as she said that word did the burning in her eyes make sense. The tears were hot and heavy and felt like molten lava as they poured from her eyes. Maker had defected. Her work was in jeopardy. She was in physical pain. "Please, help me."

Swinton looked at her. She had no idea what he was thinking but heartbeats pounded her into the ground as he just stood there. Suddenly he turned, pointed at others under his command, drawing them into the main room.

Voices were being raised, some in a language she presumed was Russian. Carmarthen had moved back to the edge of the screen, there was a small grille in the panel there, one that would allow the servants to look out and see for timing of service, she presumed.

"What's happening?"

"Swinton's good. He is getting between the worst of the annoyed-looking men."

Amethyst shifted and noticed there was another grille in the panel by her. If she stood on tiptoe, she could just about see while keeping hold of the marzipan. There was a large man sitting beside Swinton, who pushed unsteadily to his feet.

"Who is that?"

"The Chancellor," Carmarthen spoke quietly.

Amethyst watched the rotund man sway. "Is he

drunk?"

"Err, unlikely." Carmarthen did not sound convinced.

Amethyst frowned and turned to the lord. "Why?"

"The Chancellor's a Methodist."

For a moment, Amethyst couldn't see the point - then she remembered that Methodists didn't drink alcohol. "Affected then." As she stretched to observe the scene, she remembered that being unsteady on their feet was one of the first signs the men in the Lords chamber had shown of being freed of the mind control. The AE59-4 machine must be working. She tried releasing her grip, but could feel the paste moving from the pipe too and she didn't want that whistling to start again. So she gripped as she watched.

The Chancellor raised an unsteady hand towards the Tsar, words were slurred and largely muted by the noise in the banqueting hall and the sound of Amethyst's own blood pumping through her ears. Now the Prime Minister was on his feet.

The paste wasn't hardening, but her skin was heating to levels that-

Don't even think of letting go.

She had to do this. But all she could think about was the way Maker had looked at her. Like she was nothing.

I am nothing if I can't do this.

The Chancellor was talking, slurring whatever it was he was trying to say. She couldn't make it out.

Tears of pain rolled down her face as Jenson appeared with a bowl of water.

"Is it working?"

"The machine is working, but the patch isn't." She sniffed.

"The Chancellor has collapsed!"

Amethyst went on tiptoe to see, but she had a more immediate problem. "This marzipan's not thick enough to stick. So I have to keep hold to stop the whistling."

"But that thing gets very hot."

"Yes, and it's my fingers it's burning!" she hissed. "Sorry, I shouldn't snap."

Jenson looked at the water in his bowl, at her hand. He pulled the kerchief from his top pocket, soaked it in the water and held the dripping fabric over her hand. He wouldn't be able to get to her fingers as they were lost in the mechanism, but as she tipped her hand, the excess of water ran down and around her fingers, a soothing, cooling respite.

"Thank you." She was still looking out at the hall. The Prime Minister was now shoulder to shoulder with the Chancellor and they were glowering over at the Tsar, who looked as red and angry as her fingers were getting. Without Jenson helping her, her skin would be burning by now. He was applying the water, and as drops fell on certain areas, they spat slightly and steamed, but it was helping.

"Try these." The pastry chef moved from his icing and held a platter towards her.

"Fruit isn't going to help, it'll just burn."

"They're all made out of marzipan."

Amethyst could hardly credit how real it all looked, but now wasn't the time to admire artistry. Risking letting go, she plunged one hand gratefully into the water bowl Jenson still held, the other selected a plump cherry, which she squeezed into a convex.

"Good God," Carmarthen exclaimed, "the Prime Minister has taken up a knife!"

The whistling was starting again, but that wasn't the pressing problem. She looked up at Jenson as she grabbed the bowl, careless of slopping water. "You have to get out there and do something." The bowl went to the table as with her wet right hand, she pushed the cherry in place of the disintegrated paste. With her left, she plucked a frond from the top of the pineapple, and wrapped it like a bandage over the marzipan and pipe, before plunging her hand into the cold water again for a moment of blessed relief.

"Can you make that work any faster?" Carmarthen asked.

She shook her head. Jenson rushed into the hall, the uproar of which couldn't be held back by the screen. The pastry chef turned and virtually threw the platter on a side table and rushed after the Inspector. Amethyst got to the screen just in time to see the pastry chef rugby tackle a big, bearded man in a three-quarter length coat of the Russian style as he moved to throw a metal serving plate at the Prime Minister. The Prime Minister was already being pulled back by Swinton and Carmarthen. And the man Amethyst recognised from reports in the papers as the Trade Secretary was in a fist fight with Jenson, who was trying to stop him reaching for the Tsar to strangle him.

Men she couldn't identify were fighting, Russians and British distinguished only by the cut of their coats. A small knot separated near the top of the table. Three men, the one in the middle wearing a sash and huge jewelled broach-crest thing that Amethyst was sure there was a name for. She ran towards him.

"Tsar Alexander, please!" She had his attention at least, though the men at his side clearly considered her a threat. She held her hands up and open, showing she carried no weapon, though one hand was dripping wet and still bore traces of white icing. "Please tell your men to stop fighting, this will finish very soon."

Around her, men were dropping, passing out as the machine released them from their thrall, and some from the impact of Russian fists.

"I'll explain it all later. Please, just stop your men."

In a booming voice that quite surprised Amethyst, and in words she didn't understand, the Tsar commanded his men, standing tall and strong. Several looked surprised and defiant, but that didn't last and the Russians moved back, away from the Brits who were all looking rather the worse for wear. She heard a utensil drop, clattering onto plates and skittering across the table, which was a wreck of its former self.

"Carmarthen!" The Prime Minister blinked up at the man still pinning him back across the table. "What are you doing here?"

Seeing that the PM was back to himself, Carmarthen moved back and helped him to stand up straight. "I can explain. Well, she can."

Carmarthen's indication and everyone's attention focused on Amethyst. She looked around the room. The British on one side, the Russians on the other. None of them were going to come out of this looking good.

"Why can I smell burned almonds?"

Amethyst looked from the confused face of the Tsar who had spoken so clearly, to the screen, behind which she knew the machine was busy cooking marzipan.

"I'll sort that," Jenson said, moving away, but he was still looking at Amethyst. "You explain."

She took a deep breath and decided she couldn't

possibly make this situation any worse. "Gentlemen, what happened was…"

Chapter 41

Edwards closed the door and disappeared on confirmation of nothing further being needed. Jenson put the bag with AE59-4 in to the side of the hall.

"I'll never be able to smell almonds again without thinking of tonight."

Even now the scent lingered, the marzipan having baked onto the brass.

"I'm not sure I'll ever stop thinking about tonight anyway." Amethyst smiled. "So much happened! And you haven't stopped grinning since we left the state rooms. Happy with your Parliamentary Commission, Inspector? All the resources the Government can give you, to investigate what Brown or Quinn or whatever-his-name-was was up to."

Jenson smiled. "That's true. If it wasn't just said to placate the Tsar in a difficult position, but that's not why I'm smiling. The thing is, I can't stop thinking about what you did. You just saved a Tsar, a trade deal and Britain's blushes - with marzipan."

They both laughed at that.

"And that tops the day off beautifully."

Amethyst looked curiously at him. "What does?"

"Hearing you laugh. After we left the Lords chamber, I feared that dark mood would never lift."

She looked down and away. "I'm sorry."

"Don't be sorry, Miss Forester... Amethyst? May I call you Amethyst?"

"I think after tonight, you should, but in return, you will have to tell me your name."

He smiled. "It's Dean."

"Hello Dean."

"Amethyst, you did a great deal of good tonight."

She shrugged. "Maker, and more specifically, Haversham won the vote."

"They couldn't have done that without you."

"And that didn't even warrant a look from Lord Fotheringham. He won, he should have been jubilant."

"Today's battle," Jenson acknowledged. "He won today. Well, yesterday now to be exact. He won the battle but he lost the war. He lost that war years ago."

"Why do you men do that?"

Jenson looked at her, clearly baffled.

"You talk of battles and war, but what you really mean is honour and duty. You, I believe, are as much a man of honour and duty as Lord Fotheringham. The two of you have differing sensibilities, but the same underlying core. So, why do men talk to women of such things as if we have no knowledge of them?"

Jenson looked uncomfortable; he clearly knew the answer paid neither gender any compliment.

"We know, better than men, the cost of honour. A woman loses her honour and it is our expected duty to slink away from Society even when the dishonour is not truly ours. Society is saying some terrible things about me, and I finally do something that Society might actually consider honourable, and every man there agreed that it would never be spoken of. So my one moment is lost, but I can live with that. Just as well, given that I have no choice."

She looked away. She could say that she could live with it. But she wasn't so sure. Inside she wanted to scream that she'd done something that no man could. But that wasn't an option. At least Jenson knew the truth, she would probably need him to acknowledge that occasionally. But there was another truth he should know.

"Do you know, I actually consider myself very fortunate. Thanks to the Professor, and in fact to Maker, I have a very secure future. Financially, at least. I am what they call a woman of substance, but isn't it ridiculous that the only substance that matters for a woman is the money she has? So I shall allow this bruise to fade." She indicated the bruise on her forehead as she removed her hat and put it to the side. "Then I will go to Swansea and help Sanderson set up the production line for the prismatic glass, and then I am free to do anything I want. I thought I might travel. Do my duty and leave." Finally she looked at Jenson properly. "Inspector, I may say nothing, but that does not mean I am unaware of the difficulties of Maker's situation."

Jenson nodded, offered what she thought was something of a sad smile. "You are a rare and special woman, Miss Forester. I do not believe there is or should be any shade upon your honour."

"Then you and I have very different social circles."

"Well I'm not an heiress, but I am tired and I'm sure you are too. I should leave."

Amethyst moved with him to the door, but as he stepped through, he stopped, swallowed and drew what she supposed was a fortifying breath.

"Might I take the liberty of calling on you in the next few days? I should very much like to consider you a friend?"

Amethyst smiled as she reached out and shook his hand. "Now that, I would consider an honour."

Gail B Williams

Author Acknowledgements

I just want to say thank you. There are a lot of people who stand shoulder to shoulder with an author – other authors usually, family and friends – it all helps. Thank you to my husband and children for not only putting up with but whole heartedly joining in with the weird conversations.

Thank you to Tony Fyler of Jefferson Franklin Editing for being an even tougher critic. Tony – you don't let me get away with anything, and you make be better so it. Some of this would never have happened without you slapping me upside the head and forcing me to be a better writer.

Thank you to Penny Freeman. You inspired me to find Flora, and she's a wonder who I can't wait to get to know better.

Thank you to Lisa Jenkins for the publishing advise, and to Kim and Darja of Deranged Doctor Designs for producing such fabulous artwork for the cover and marketing.

And thank you, of course – thank you reader.

Thank you for reading, because that really is the whole point of writing after all.

If you like this book and you want to see more of what I'm up to, check out my website and social networks:

Website: www.gailbwilliams.com
Twitter: @ShadesOfAether
Blog: thewriteroute.wordpress.com

Gail B Williams

About the Author

Gail Williams lives in her own private dungeon populated with all the weird and the wonderful she can imagine. Some of it's very weird, and the odd bits and pieces are a bit wonderful. Well okay, she lives in Swansea with her husband and daughter. And the world's most demanding cat.

Well okay, the truth is I was born and bred in Kent, I moved to South Wales as a supposedly first step on a year around the world.

Then I met this guy. Kept the guy, kissed the travel goodbye.

Since then, I've worked, married, had two great kids, you know, the usual. The one job I'm most proud of is being a fiction editor - have met some wonderful people that way.

But here's the thing, I have always written. I don't remember a time when I didn't and I can't foresee a time when I won't - I tried that - made my brain itch. So I figured it was time to share. If you want to know more about me or my work, check out my website, gailbwilliams.com.

Oh but I do actually live with the world's most imperious and demanding cat.

Gail B Williams

Excerpt from Echoes of Aether

Chapter 1

It was hard to breath in the crush. It felt like the whole of London was attempting to get into Hyde Park - possibly through this one gate. Being of no more than average height, Amethyst Forester couldn't see over the shoulders of the crowd around her.

Above, the Park was circled at height by a ring of commercial airships all here to hail the unveiling of the latest design for transatlantic airship travel. With no choice but to move with the crowd, Amethyst found herself pushed forward. The eagerness of such a large number of people knocked her favourite modified top hat from her head. She caught it, but not in time to save it from being crushed between her and the crowd.

A young man near the edge of the flow cried out as he tripped, being pushed into the boarder plants as others sought to gain ground. Amethyst feared what would happen to him, but if she fell, here in the middle of the crowd, she would be trampled, so she dare not keep up.

An additional sourness of sweat seasoned the scent of humanity and as they moved with a single minded determination to see what was hidden in the centre of the park. Suddenly the crush lessened, there was air to breath. They were through the gate and into the park.

Unburdened by friend or family, Amethyst was free to move alone and flow through the throng without hindrance. Finally she could see it, the point of convergence, a large sheet of material covered a heap of what must be the massive airship to be unveiled.

She could see a horseshoe of white painted viewing stands for those who could afford the luxury, and who had had the sense to book in advance. The Royal Standard flew above one. As she made her way forward, Amethyst could hear distant fairground sounds; music, voices laughing and squealing, the call of street vendors.

She was within the horseshoe now. The white painted wooden structures were at least ten feet high, no problem seeing over the crowd from them. No crowds taking advantage of the construction either, the sides were solid and sheer, no possibility of climbing. Steps at the side were guarded by big burly men in smart suits who deterred anyone attempting to gain an advantage they hadn't paid for.

Moving forward, Amethyst found herself struggling to get much of a view. The crowd was much lighter here than near the gates but it wasn't easy to spot any vantage point from which she'd be able to see much when that sheet fell. Then she stopped looking. They were here to see an airship. All she had to do was look up.

A hand landed on her shoulder. She jumped, turning to strike out but the deep call of her name, stopped her. She didn't recognise the man she now faced. She did however recognise the livery.

"Miss Forester, Lady Garrington-Smythe wishes to extend her invitation for you to join her party on her viewing platform."

Since the man indicated the relevant platform, Amethyst looked up to see Lady Garrington-Smythe and her gathering. At the great lady's side was Lady Roberta Davenport, though Bobbie was wearing a morning suit and had chosen a short masculine haircut, so recognising her as a lady would be difficult unless you were in the know. Smiling broadly at her friend, Amethyst told the man to lead on, all the time trying not to react to who else was there.

Lord and Lady Fotheringham. The two were bane and balm in her life, or more accurately balm and bane. In the five weeks she'd been away, she had hoped she would overcome this weakness about Lord Fotheringham, but no. She had spent far too many hours thinking of him and his emerald eyes. Thinking of how he had helped her when she had unexpectedly become an heiress. He had even helped her establish the business relationship which had kept her away. And he had done it all without expectation of repayment. His only reward seemed to be his wife's scorn.

Even as Amethyst held up the front hem of her dress to take the thin steps of the platform, she was aware of Lady Fotheringham's disdain pouring over her.

As she moved up, the stifling heat of the crowd eased, and breathing grew easier in spite of her tight corset. She hadn't expected to be 'seen' today, but thankfully as she'd picked a lightweight summer dress, new and fashionable though a little informal, she wasn't ashamed to been seen wearing it.

When she reached the platform, she saw a party of ten with two livered footmen, three including her escort. She recognised all of the gathering that she could see, though several had their backs to her. She joined her host, standing by the front rail, the best viewing position, and offered a small curtsey.

"Good afternoon, Lady Garrington-Smythe. Thank you so much for including me in your party."

"Had I known you would be back I would have sent a formal invitation."

"Not that we need too much formality."

Amethyst refocused on the woman between her and Lady Garrington-Smythe. Bobbie offered her a smile.

"We may not need too much formality, but a little rarely hurts." She turned back to Bobbie's mother, Lady Garrington-Smythe. "I appreciate the thought. In all honesty I wasn't sure when I'd be back. My train got in an hour ago and when I heard the launch was today, I just had to come see it."

Even Lady Garrington-Smythe had what Amethyst would call a girlish smile. "It's very exciting, isn't it?"

Behind Lady Garrington-Smythe, Amethyst was aware she was under scrutiny by Lord and Lady Fotheringham. Her eyes flicked back to her hostess, her smile not dimming one watt. "I couldn't agree more, Eugenie."

Lord Fotheringham's carved emotionless features flinched for a beat and Lady Fotheringham's face pinched.

"And I am fortunate indeed to be able to enjoy it among so many friends." This time Amethyst deliberately looked over the duchess's shoulder directly. "Good day Maker, Lady Fotheringham."

Maker's small nod shifted his top hat. Amethyst preferred it at the slight angle. The tiny imperfection humanised a man at great risk of being too perfect.

His wife, however, was always picture perfect. Not very happy right now, but perfect all the same. Beautiful. Blonde, slim, the best clothes, always elegant, never a hair out of place. Everything, of course, Amethyst wasn't.

"Lady Garrington-Smythe," Lady Fotheringham said quietly, "do you think we are quite safe with this... woman in the area."

The older woman looked directly at her immaculate guest. "Most of us."

Amethyst controlled her smirk as Lady Fotheringham's lips pursed.

"Perhaps you are not aware Lady Garrington-Smythe, that Miss Forester has a history of physically attacking me!"

Amethyst drew breath but Bobbie's hand on her arm stopped her.

"I am fully aware, Lady Fotheringham, that when you went into Miss Forester's home and abused her, Amethyst ably blocked your attack and returned a slap."

Amethyst was glad for the low volume, only the five of them could hear.

"Now, you have a choice, Lady Fotheringham, you can act to your title in public as you clearly do not in private, or you can leave."

Amethyst watched Lady Fotheringham's cold eyes send ice shards at her. She offered Lady Garrington-Smythe a small curtsey and moved a step away, pulling her husband with her.

Lady Garrington-Smythe turned to face the waiting spectacle.

"So how was the wild west?" Bobbie asked as they stood side by side.

Amethyst laughed at the description. "I was in Swansea, not the Americas. It wasn't terribly wild, just terribly busy. Still, we arranged to scale up the prismatic process successfully, so the production is set up, and all is well."

"I saw the launch invitation."

The smile seemed to spread without her intention. "I saw your RSVP. So glad you are able to come."

"I'm not sure-"

Amethyst clenched her teeth at Lady Violet's tone.

"-that a lady should involve herself in common trade."

A number of responses galloped through Amethyst's head, but she decided discretion was the better option and held her tongue.

"Commerce is certainly not for everyone," Lady Garrington-Smythe mused. "Nor is every woman capable of commerce."

Deciding to ignore the waves of hostility threatening to drown her, Amethyst faced forward to study the crowd and the waving sheets at the centre of the park. While she tried to appreciate the size and grandeur of the new airship, to anticipate its potential appearance, all she was really aware of was that she stood at the end of a line that started with Lady Fotheringham, Lady Garrington-Smythe, Lady Davenport - then her - plain old Miss Forester. More worryingly, she was aware that just behind Lady Fotheringham stood her husband.

Maker.

Her stomach really should not clench just to think his name. Yet it did. He stood facing forward. That beautifully proportioned face as perfect as carved marble showed no emotion. Most painfully, he'd barely shown any recognition of her. They had, she thought, been friends once. But apparently no more.

"Once the product is launched, what will you do?"

Lady Garrington-Smythe's question surprised Amethyst.

"Erm, I'm not sure. I…" She shrugged. "I suppose I don't have anything more to do."

"Perhaps you should go to the Redland Academy."

Amethyst frowned and turned to look at Violet. Who was smiling at her. A bad sign. Amethyst looked to Bobbie, asking in an undertone, "Is that an insult?"

Bobbie was frowning as she turned from Violet to Amethyst. "I think it was meant to be, but actually it was rather complimentary."

"Oh well, in that case," Amethyst leaned forward slightly to smile at the woman at the end of the line. "Thank you for the suggestion, Lady Fotheringham, I'll look more into that. Though in all honesty I've been considering travelling. If there are still tickets for the Sunriser's maiden voyage I may-"

"There aren't," Bobbie quickly assured her. Too quickly.

"Whatever you decide to do, I hope you won't go too soon," Lady Garrington-Smythe said quietly, gaining all attention. "You should join us at Lord Montgomery's house party next month."

Amethyst had only met the man once, but she had been quite impressed. She remembered Lord Montgomery; tall, broad-shouldered, dashing, blue eyes and auburn hair. A vision of perfect manhood. "I am sure I should enjoy that," she spoke mostly from a sense of duty - having no idea what a house party was like meant she had no idea whether or not she would enjoy it. "If Lord Montgomery were happy to include me in the party." Which was unlikely at such a short notice.

"I'd be more than happy to."

Amethyst swung around the find the dashing Lord Montgomery behind her. Her breath caught, he was even more handsome than she remembered. She was surprised she hadn't singled him out in the group when she'd entered the platform. Maker had held her attention at that point. She grabbed the rail in case her jellied knees got too weak to hold her. His eyes really were the clearest blue. The way he looked at her made it feel like she was the only one there. And she wasn't going to acknowledge the weight of certain green eyes boring into her back either.

Gail B Williams

OTHER WORKS
BY THE SAME AUTHOR

STEAMPUNK

The Steel Inside - part of the Steel & Bone anthology

CONTEMPORARY CRIME
(as GB Williams)

Locked Up
Last Cut Casebook

Gail B Williams